Susan Stephens was a ⟨...⟩ meeting her husband o⟨...⟩ of Malta. In true Mills ⟨...⟩ Monday, became engaged on Friday ⟨...⟩ three months later. Susan enjoys entertaining, travel and going to the theatre. To relax she reads, cooks and plays the piano, and when she's had enough of relaxing she throws herself off mountains on skis or gallops through the countryside singing loudly.

Chantelle Shaw lives on the Kent coast and thinks up her stories while walking on the beach. She has been married for over thirty years and has six children. Her love affair with reading and writing Mills & Boon stories began as a teenager, and her first book was published in 2006. She likes strong-willed, slightly unusual characters. Chantelle also loves gardening, walking and wine!

PREGNANT BY THE DESERT KING

SUSAN STEPHENS

THE VIRGIN'S SICILIAN PROTECTOR

CHANTELLE SHAW

MILLS & BOON

First Published in Great Britain 2018
by Mills & Boon, an imprint of HarperCollins*Publishers*
1 London Bridge Street, London, SE1 9GF

Pregnant by the Desert King © 2018 by Susan Stephens

The Virgin's Sicilian Protector © 2018 by Chantelle Shaw

ISBN: 978-0-263-93559-2

MIX
Paper from
responsible sources
FSC C007454

This book is produced from independently certified FSC™ paper
to ensure responsible forest management.
For more information visit www.harpercollins.co.uk/green.

Printed and bound in Spain
by CPI, Barcelona

PREGNANT BY THE DESERT KING

SUSAN STEPHENS

For my wonderful ever-expanding,
ever-supportive family.

PROLOGUE

Present day...

TADJ'S WORLD TILTED on its axis as a woman in a red dress stepped out of the kitchen.

'Excuse me, Your Excellency,' he said, startling his ambassador to London. 'Something extraordinary has just happened.'

'Of course, Your Majesty...' Raising his portly form as quickly as he could the ambassador bowed to his ruler and employer, the Emir of Qalala, as Tadj, an exceptionally striking-looking man, left the table where they'd been dining incognito, to stride across the floor.

Sensing his approach, the young woman turned and stared, paling, as if she'd seen a ghost.

CHAPTER ONE

Three months earlier...

A CASUAL COFFEE in the steamy café next door in her lunch break from work at the laundry had never involved plugging Lucy's body into a power source before. Lined up at the counter behind a red-hot Goliath with shoulders wide enough to hoist an ox, she reasoned it was only natural to be distracted, as her heart beat nineteen to the dozen. He was deeply tanned, with thick, inky-black hair that curled possessively over his neck in a way that made her fantasise about making it even more unruly; his short, rugged jacket might have been designed for no better purpose than to display his iron-hard butt, and long, lean legs. He was so big he achieved the impossible by making her feel dainty for the first time in her life. She was the woman targeted by slimming magazines who always planned to lose weight. And she would, just as soon as chocolate was written out of history.

'Would you like to go ahead of me?'

She almost fainted when he swung around.

'Are you speaking to me?' popped out of her mouth before her brain was in gear. Silly question, when the most devastating black stare was directed straight into her eyes. It was the most arousal-inducing stare she'd ever been subjected to. There were eyes of all description, some of them very beautiful, but these were astonishingly beautiful eyes.

'Can you move along, please? People are waiting to be served.'

Jerking alert as the lady behind the counter bellowed the instruction, Lucy shuffled along in line, and in doing so managed to stumble into Goliath.

'Perhaps you should sit down before you cause a pile-up,' he advised with amusement. His deep, husky voice with the intriguing accent, combined with his big, firm hands steadying her, blew her mind. 'Now?' he suggested as she stared at him transfixed. 'I'll get the drinks while you find the table.'

Finally, she came to. 'Do I know you?'

'I don't believe so,' he said, staring down from his great height. 'Coffee? Tea? Hot chocolate? Something to eat, perhaps?'

By now, people had turned to stare. One or two, having recognised Lucy, nodded and gave her a thumbs-up expression. She didn't want to make a fuss. This was her local greasy spoon. Nor did she want to bolt, giving the man the impression he intimidated her. Who was he? she wondered. There was only one way to find out. 'Coffee would be nice…thank you. Skimmed milk, two shots, please.'

As he turned to place their order she became aware of the buzz of interest in the café; most of it directed her way. Should she know him? Was he a celebrity? If only she paid more attention to the press. Maybe he had called in at the laundry while she was working in the back; no one could forget a face like that. He could pass for a sailor with his deep tan and super-fit appearance, but, with his commanding manner and expensive casual look, he didn't strike her as crew.

'When you're ready,' he prompted as he waited for their coffee to be prepared. 'The table,' he reminded her. 'There aren't many free. Better get moving.'

'Yes, sir,' she said, saluting ironically, but not before she'd absorbed his clean, spicy scent.

She did go to find a table, even though she wasn't a fan of domineering men. This man had redeemed himself with that curving, dark-eyed smile. She guessed he used it a lot, but this was a packed café, and not much could go wrong over a coffee. It wouldn't hurt to give him five minutes to see how he turned out. Her chums at the laundry were always complaining that nothing exciting ever happened, so at the least she'd be able to tell them about this when she got back to work.

She'd hidden herself away long enough.

As the unwanted thought shot into her mind, she shivered involuntarily, and recollections of her cruel, abusive stepfather came flooding back. Her mother's second husband headed up a criminal empire peopled by ruthless thugs. Thank goodness he was in prison where he belonged. Lucy had left home at her mother's insistence, to escape the increasingly unpleasant attention of her stepfather's henchmen. She'd been lucky enough to find genuine friends on King's Dock.

Having paused to acknowledge a couple of friends, she glanced at the man, only to see that he had not only paid for their drinks, but for an elderly couple's pot of tea. He'd be up a tree, saving a cat next, Lucy thought with a smile as he crossed the café towards her. She had to stop being so suspicious of men. They weren't all bad.

'Something wrong?' her new friend asked, frowning attractively as he drew near.

'Nothing,' she said, noticing how much attention he was getting. Both he and her stepfather were big, powerful men, but that was where the similarity ended. Her stepfather was a ruthless bully, and she could see nothing of the snake in this man. If eyes mirrored the soul she was safe; there was no evil in them.

Just heat, Lucy reflected with a bubble of excitement and amusement as he indicated that she should sit down. 'Or are you going to stand here all day, blocking the aisle?'

When he lifted one sweeping ebony brow like that, and smiled into her eyes, it was impossible not to respond. Her stepfather hadn't crushed her spirit yet.

'Are you going to join me?' she invited once she was settled.

She had to move the table to let him in. He was what might be referred to as a big unit, and she was hardly petite. And though he might be a player, and she his latest target, one cup of coffee did not a drama make. People knew her here, and she could leave any time she liked.

Today was turning out better than anticipated, Tadj concluded as he studied the lush-figured woman sitting opposite him. She had magnificent breasts, which even her bulky winter clothes couldn't hide. But it wasn't his automatic male assessment that struck him most, but her natural poise and unaffected manner. It was such a welcome change from the women who usually flocked around him, hoping for the position of wife, or mistress at the very least.

He'd been walking the dock, filling in time before a

party that evening on board his friend Sheikh Khalid's yacht, the *Sapphire*. Leaving behind the razzmatazz that went with the title Emir of Qalala, to mix with the crowds on the dock like any other visitor to the high-end marina, was a welcome release from the pressure of celebrity. Spending time with a woman who didn't appear to recognise him was a novelty. The fact that this woman probably wouldn't have cared less if she had known who he was was an unexpected bonus. He planned to stay on the *Sapphire* tonight, and a strange bed was always warmer with an agreeable companion at his side.

Or underneath him.

'Are you sure this is okay for you?' she asked, glancing around. 'You seem to be creating some interest. Should I know you?'

'You do now. And in answer to your question, this is perfect.'

'You didn't answer *my* question,' she pointed out.

'No. I didn't,' he agreed.

A tense, electric silence sprang between them. He'd sensed her before he'd spotted her in the café. His senses were always fine-tuned where women were concerned, but she had intrigued him from the first moment, with her elfin looks, and full, voluptuous figure. She wasn't remotely in awe of him, which only added to her allure. Half his size, she was quite a bit younger, though her character made up for any lack of experience.

'Good coffee?' she said, breaking the silence.

'Excellent,' he murmured, maintaining eye contact until she blushed.

In the course of his duties as ruler of one of the fabulously wealthy Sapphire States, he met many women, but never remembered them for long. None held such instant appeal. He weighed up her clothes and the body underneath. The cheap, unbuttoned coat was open over a clinging cotton sweater that spurred an urge to introduce her to fabrics that would caress her body. Kissing that challenging look off her face was another must, before bringing her to the heights of pleasure.

'You really didn't need to do this,' she said as he asked the waitress for a top-up.

'But I *really* want to,' he said, holding her stare.

'Do you always get what you want?'

'Most times,' he admitted.

He only had to raise a brow for her to read him easily. 'Lucy,' she said. 'Lucy Gillingham.'

The name meant nothing to him, but he made a mental note to ask his security team to check her out.

'Careful,' he said as she dipped her head to take a sip of the refreshed coffee. 'It's hot.'

'I'm always careful,' she said with a look that left him in no doubt she would never be a pushover.

The most astonishing jade-green eyes pierced his, tilted up at the outer corners. Lucy's expressive gaze was enhanced by a thick fringe of black lashes that added a feline touch to what was already a highly attractive package.

'Sorry,' she said, pulling back, and blushed attractively when their knees brushed.

'No problem,' he said, sliding his long legs between hers without touching her, but her blush deepened as if she was deeply conscious of the intimacy forced upon them by the narrow table. Colour tinted her Slavic cheekbones an attractive shade of rose. 'You have beautiful hair,' he said to distract her.

'And you have big feet,' she said, shuffling around to remove all chance of them touching.

Lucy wore her hair in a no-nonsense short, urchin-cut style. It suited her strong personality. In a rich shade of auburn, it reminded him of autumn on his English country estate when the leaves had turned from vibrant green to take on the tint of fire. She was fiery. She'd be amazing in bed.

'Oh, that's better,' she said, having drained the mug. 'I'm good for nothing before a coffee. How about you?'

'I'm good for some things,' he said.

Her cheeks burned red. He hadn't enjoyed himself so much in a long time.

How could talking about coffee be so dangerous? Lucy spent a lot of time daydreaming, but none of them turned out like this. If only she'd paid more attention to the press and laundry gossip, she might have a clue who the intriguing man was. 'You're new in port,' she prompted, waiting on more information.

'Another coffee?'

'Yes, please.' As he turned to speak to the waitress, her mind strayed to lazy days on a sugar-sand beach, with blocks of chilled chocolate at her side, and a bucket of lemon sorbet Bellinis to share with the mystery man as a prelude to very good sex, the details of which escaped her for now.

'Something wrong?' he queried as she frowned.

'Yes. As a matter of fact, there is. I told you my name. Or, do you have something to hide?'

He laughed and his entire face lit up. Attractive didn't even begin to describe the creases around his eyes and the flash of those strong white teeth. Raunchy? Her nipples were prickling without him even looking at them.

Close enough for her to detect his minty breath, and to register the fact that he didn't like shaving, he was an incredible lure with those incredible black eyes burning into hers.

'My name is Tadj.'

'Ah—like the Taj Mahal,' she said, relaxing.

'Tadj with a D,' he explained.

'Oh.' Her cheeks flamed up again. 'I suppose you hear that dozens of times.'

'Some,' he agreed.

The killer smile had returned to his face, but she settled for regarding him coolly. With his thick black hair curling wildly around cheekbones that would have sent Michelangelo crazy for his chisel, she guessed he must be used to admiration, and was determined not to add to it, though couldn't help herself wondering what that sharp black stubble would feel like if he rasped it very gently against her skin. Imagining her rounded curves accommodating his impressive hard-muscled frame led her to shift position on the bench seat.

'Tadj,' she repeated to distract herself fast. 'Nice.'

He was still staring at her with that faintly amused expression on his face, which led to one quick thought... melted chocolate, heated gently before being spread liberally over her naked body, for him to lick off. 'Okay, Tadj with a D, so now I know your name, but not your occupation.'

'That's right. You don't,' he said.

'Cagey,' she observed, narrowing her eyes. 'I'm genuinely curious.'

'And I'm genuinely cagey,' he countered with a scorching look.

They both laughed and the atmosphere lightened.

'So?' she prompted, coffee mug hovering in front of her lips.

'So, what? What do you want to know?'

'Let's start with everything?' she said.

'We don't have time.'

'Should I be worried that you're being so evasive?'

'Here?' He glanced around. 'Probably not.'

But later, she thought. She killed the thought as soon as it sprang into her head. There'd be no later. She'd try another tack to dig for information. 'So, what brings you to King's Dock?'

'Old friends and business,' he said.

'Intriguing.'

'Not really,' he admitted, sitting back. 'King's Dock is a convenient place to meet, that's all.' He raised a brow, as if challenging her to ask more questions.

'I must be keeping you from your friends,' she stated, reaching for her bag.

'You're not,' he said, still relaxed, still surveying her as a soft-pawed predator might observe his next meal.

As they stared at each other, a quiver of arousal tracked down her spine. He was enjoying this, she thought. And so was she. A lot more than was wise. Why had this extraordinary-looking man landed in the middle of an ordinary day? Time to take a tougher line. 'You sat me down, force-fed me coffee, so now you have to pay for the pleasure of my company with information.'

'You think?' Few women had ever made him laugh as Lucy did. Being so irreverent and funny was part of her charm. 'You won't get round me,' he warned when she pulled a mock-disappointed face.

'Why not?' she complained in the same style. 'Is what you do for a living classified information? Maybe you're a secret agent,' she speculated with a lift of her finely drawn brow.

'And maybe I'm a man drinking coffee in a café and minding his own business as best he can...'

'How boring. I prefer my version.'

'I'm in security,' he admitted finally. This was the truth. One of his many companies was responsible for the safety of some of the most prominent people on the planet. As the ruler of a country it was in his interest to hire the best.

'Aha.' Sitting back, Lucy appeared to relax. 'Now it makes sense.'

'What does?'

'Your evasiveness,' she explained. 'I'm guessing you handle security for one of the those big fat potentates on their big fat superyachts.' She angled her chin towards the window, beyond which a line of imposing vessels loomed like huge white ghosts against the steel-grey sky. 'What's it like working for the super-rich, mystery man?'

Her naivety was irresistible, but her innocence compelled him to tell the truth. 'Actually, I'm one of them.'

'A big, fat potentate?' she exclaimed, frowning in a way that made him laugh.

'I thought it was the yachts you thought big and fat.'

'You're being serious, aren't you?' she said in a very different tone.

'Your expression does my ego no good at all,' he admitted.

'Well, this changes things,' she said, 'and I can't help the way I look.'

'Having money changes your opinion of me?'

She hummed and frowned again. 'I don't have an opinion about you yet,' she admitted honestly. 'I don't know you well enough.'

He would be the first to admit he was touchy about money. His late uncle had plundered the Qalalan treasury, leaving it empty when Tadj inherited the throne. Tadj had built up a bankrupt country brick by brick. Even then, when everything was back on an even keel, a family to whose daughter he'd been engaged since his birth turned up to demand he marry the girl right away. It had cost him a king's ransom to sort that out. The experience had left him with a horror of state marriages, together with the distinct impression that a mistress was far preferable to a wife. He had to marry one day to provide Qalala with an heir as the constitution demanded, but not yet, and his thoughts regarding taking a mistress in the interim had just taken on a new and vigorous lease of life.

CHAPTER TWO

'IF YOU'VE MADE so much money out of the security business...' What was coming next, he wondered as Lucy gave him one of her wide-eyed cheeky, teasing looks. 'Can I ask you for a loan?'

He knew this was a joke, but bridled anyway at the possibility that she might be like all the rest. 'Ten pounds until pay day?' she pressed blithely, but she couldn't hold back the laughter, and, sitting back, she said, 'You should see your face.'

He adopted a stern look. 'You'll get away with that this time.'

'You mean there'll be a next time?' Quick as a whip, he thought as she added, 'That's assuming rather a lot, isn't it? How do you know I'll want to see you again?'

His groin tightened as he told her, 'Educated guess.'

Resting her chin on her hand, she stared at him in a way that made him wish he were clothed in flowing robes rather that snug-fitting jeans.

'Surely, you can run to a miserly ten pounds?' she pressed.

He reached for his wallet.

'Don't you dare,' she said.

'Can't I pay the bill for the extra coffee?'

'Touché,' she said. 'Just bear this in mind, Mr Security Man. I don't want your money. I don't want anyone's money. I'm doing fine as I am. Here—let me contribute. Save your money for your next coffee-shop adventure.'

'I doubt there'll be one.'

'Too much of a security risk for you to keep taking up with strangers?' she suggested.

'Something like that.' He stared at her intently, but there was no sign that she'd recognised him.

'I guess you have to be careful in the security business.'

'My involvement is in the security of a country,' he explained.

'Big stuff,' she said.

'You could say that.' He grinned.

'You must be pretty powerful. And yet you look so normal.'

He tried hard not to laugh. 'Why thank you.'

'Well, this has all been very nice.' She sighed as she gathered up her things. 'But now it's time for me to go. Some of us have to work,' she added.

'Let me walk you back—where do you work?' He wasn't ready to let her go.

'At Miss Francine's laundry,' she said with a touch of defiance.

He got it. Some of the rich yachties could be real snobs. If he turned out to be one of them, she'd rather know now. 'The laundry on the marina?' he prompted, having noticed the bustling establishment on his walk.

'Yes.' She pulled another of her comic faces. 'We've moved on from banging out dirt with stones at the stream.'

'Uh-huh. So, what's your job at the laundry?'

'Ironing and finishing.'

'You any good?'

'You bet I am.'

His lips twitched and then she laughed. It must have dawned on them both at the same moment that two strangers could share a table and chat over coffee, without things getting heavy.

'I'm sorry,' she said with a graceful flutter of her slender hands. 'I didn't mean to bite your head off. It's just that some visitors to King's Dock are snobby idiots and I wanted to be sure you weren't one of them.'

'I'd never have guessed,' he said dryly.

'So long as you're not a trust-fund yachtie with nothing better to do than spend your inherited money, I guess I'm okay with that.'

'Touchy about money?' he probed as they navigated their way out through the crowded café.

'Every sensible person cares about money,' she said.

'Well, I can reassure you on that score. Everything I've got I've earned. All I inherited was debt.'

'There must be something else wrong with you,' she said as they reached the door. 'No one's perfect.'

'Feel free to examine my faults,' he invited.

'Not likely! So, who left the debt?' she asked with her hand on the door. 'A close relative?'

'My uncle.' As he spoke and took over opening the door, he realised that he hadn't been this frank with anyone ever, let alone on such short acquaintance.

'So you repaid your uncle's debt as a matter of honour,' she guessed as they stepped out into icy air from the steaming warmth of the busy café.

He shrugged as he thought back to when Qalala's future had depended on a financial rescue package, and how lucky he was to have already made a fortune in tech. This had allowed him to vastly improve the lot of his people, and save the sapphire mines his uncle had been plundering for years.

'Let's just say my uncle almost ruined the family business,' he told her as they walked along.

'And you saved it,' she said confidently.

'You've got a lot of faith in a man you've only just met,' he commented.

Her extraordinary green eyes shot him a penetrating glance. 'I don't feel like this about everyone.'

For some strange reason, he felt the same, and wanted to tell her more about the history of his country, and how deeply he felt for Qalala. Meeting Lucy had turned out to be a real wake-up call. The type of wife his royal council was urging him to take would be a matter of business for both parties, whereas a mistress like Lucy would give as good as she got. 'So now you've got me all worked out, what's next for you?' he probed.

'I'd like to hear more about you,' she said.

'Some other time,' he proposed as they reached the marina.

'There you go again,' she said with an amused sideways look. 'That would mean seeing each other again,' she explained. 'So, where do you come from? You don't have an office pallor, so I'm guessing somewhere hot...'

'Somewhere far away,' he said.

'Come on, Mr Security Man. I need specifics.'

'So you can tell your friends?'

'Can't I be interested?'

Was he going to talk about the billions he'd made in tech? She'd run a mile. Lucy just wasn't the type to be impressed by money. And he wanted to keep her around a little longer. Should he tell her that he used to be known as the Playboy Prince, and his people, who had been downtrodden for years by his profligate uncle, hadn't expected anything of him? They couldn't have guessed that he'd been waiting for this chance to serve his country, and would seize the opportunity with both hands. Putting his business acumen to its most demanding test yet, he had transformed Qalala, and would continue to put the country before himself.

'And you accuse me of daydreaming,' Lucy accused.

He linked arms with her as they crossed the road. It was a gesture that came as naturally as breathing.

Tadj was gorgeous. And yes, she was smitten. She'd have to be a block of wood not to be affected by his firm touch on her arm, or those amazing eyes, scanning the street to make sure they were safe before he crossed. He was so rugged and tall and tanned, it felt amazing to be linking arms with him.

'Watch out,' he exclaimed as, distracted, she almost tripped over the kerb.

As his grip tightened and their faces came dangerously close, she determined to discover Tadj's true identity when she returned to the laundry. Someone was bound to know. Gossip was rife on King's Dock, and spread like wildfire. A man like Tadj would hardly go unnoticed. Her workmates would have all the juice, which would almost certainly include the fact that she'd been seen drinking coffee with him.

'I'm afraid this is where we part,' she said as they approached her workplace.

'Afraid? You?' he queried with a wry look. 'Those two things don't fit.'

'I'm not a thing,' she said, warming under his gaze. 'And I'm not afraid of you,' she added.

'I'm very pleased to hear it,' he said, making her a mock bow.

Everything about this encounter was new to her. She'd never had so much fun with a man. She'd never had fun at all. It was such a shame they would probably never meet again.

He frowned deeply. 'Do you have to go straight back to work?'

Her pulse raced. So he felt the connection too. 'Yes,' she said, instinct telling her not to make things too easy for him. 'Some other time, perhaps…'

'When?'

She hadn't expected him to be quite so direct. 'Soon,' she said airily as her heart tried to pound its way out of her chest. 'I'd like that,' she added honestly, feeling she'd been a bit harsh. 'And you don't have to walk me to the door.'

'But I insist,' he said.

'Do you always get your own way?'

'Always,' he said in a way that made a quiver of excitement tremble low in her belly and her nipples tighten to the point of pain.

'Thanks for the coffee,' she said when they reached the laundry.

'Just tell me one thing before you go,' he insisted.

She looked at his hand on her arm. He let her go. 'Okay,' she agreed.

'What would you do if you had all the money in the world?'

She didn't even have to think about it. 'I'd buy new machinery for Miss Francine's laundry and make sure she took a proper holiday. Did I say something funny?' She frowned.

'Only what I expected of you, I suppose.'

Lucy's heart pounded even faster as Tadj's magnificent shoulders eased in a casual shrug. 'Your wish is highly commendable,' he added, staring down at her with warmth and laughter in his eyes.

'But you're not the genie in the bottle,' she observed sensibly.

'I could be…'

'Not this time,' she said, warning him off with a mock-stern look.

As she was speaking, she was digging around in her shopper to find her purse.

'What are you doing?' he asked, frowning as she brought it out.

'Paying for my coffee,' she said. 'I don't like to be in debt to anyone—and you've had enough trouble, from what you've told me. I would have paid at the café, but you got in fast. Here. Take it,' she insisted, thrusting some cash towards him.

'I'll leave it as a tip for the wait staff when I walk past,' he agreed.

'Brownie points to you,' she said approvingly. 'Well, I can't be late for work.'

'Don't forget tonight—'

'Tonight?' she interrupted.

'When I see you again.'

'Oh, I don't know about that. I've got studying to do when I finish work.'

'Studying what?' he pressed, frowning.

'History of art. My dream is to be a curator, or a conservator one day,' she explained.

'Working in a museum or an art gallery?' he proposed.

'Exactly.'

Tadj stared at her long and hard. 'Anything else?' he said at last.

'I'll let you know if I think of something,' she promised cheekily with a glance inside the laundry.

'Don't let me keep you,' Tadj said dryly.

'I won't.'

'Just one thing,' he said.

'Which is?' she pressed.

'You'll need a party dress for tonight.'

'I've already told you, I'm not coming out tonight.'

'But you've got a party to go to.'

'No, I don't,' she argued, enjoying the game. How could she not, when Tadj's wicked black eyes were full of amusement?

'Yes, you do,' he insisted, acting stern.

'With you? Not likely!' she countered, wanting to prolong the moment of parting.

'On board the *Sapphire* tonight,' he tempted.

'You're kidding me! You know I can't resist an invitation like that.'

'Good.' His lips pressed down attractively, making her wonder what it would feel like if he kissed her. So much so, she almost missed his next statement. 'My friend Sheikh Khalid is having a party tonight, and you're invited as my guest.'

'That's news to me,' she said, heart pounding as she lifted her chin to confront those dangerous eyes.

'I can't think of anyone I'd rather take as my plus one. At least we'll have a laugh. What do you say?'

'Can't you find someone else to have a laugh with? Someone more suitable?' Lucy suggested, as the enormity of what she could be agreeing to struck home. A glamorous party on board a yacht that could slip its moorings at any point? However attractive she might find Tadj, or maybe because of it, her sensible self advised caution.

'I'm right out of amusing women at the moment,' he said with a somewhat cynical look that suggested this might actually be the case. 'And I don't relish being bored to tears by people trying to find out if the person they're talking to is as important as they are.'

'Good plan. But why me, when there must be dozens of better qualified companions?'

'Qualified in what way?' he demanded, pretending to be shocked.

'There must be dozens of people who'd love to go to that party.' *With you*, she left out, deciding that with his good looks Tadj probably didn't need his ego massaging.

'No one with your unique qualities,' he assured her, straight-faced.

She hummed and frowned. 'I'd love to know what they are.'

'That will become apparent as the evening goes on,' he promised.

'But as I'm not coming to the party…'

'Those unique qualities will force you to,' he insisted. 'You won't be able to resist.'

He might be right, Lucy concluded. 'Go on.'

'You work a real job, and meet real people on a daily basis. You're interested in everything and everyone, and you have your own quirky take on what you see.'

'You've gathered a lot about me in a very short time.'

He certainly had, Tadj thought. 'My point is you're real and I like that. You have no idea how rare that is.'

She thought about this for a moment. 'You make a very persuasive case,' she said at last.

And he wasn't about to give up. 'You'll be my honoured guest tonight.'

'Better that than dishonoured—and you can put *that* away,' she flashed when he pulled out his wallet.

'For the dress you'll be wearing tonight,' he explained.

She tightened her lips. Now he'd offended her. 'I'm not entirely penniless. I'm sure I can rustle something up.'

'Then, you agree?'

She looked at him and heaved a theatrical sigh. 'You got me,' she admitted.

'Just one thing. Don't keep me waiting when I pick you up tonight.'

'Making conditions now? I can always change my mind.'

'You won't,' he said confidently.

'And you can keep the killer smile for someone who will appreciate it,' she added with a mock-stern frown.

'Someone like you?' he suggested, staring deep into her eyes.

'I've changed my mind. I'd be right out of my depth—and crazy to agree.'

'Too late. The deal is done.'

'No, it isn't,' Lucy argued, 'and now you're making me late for work.'

'You're making yourself late for work by taking so long to confirm the details of our date tonight.'

'Please take your hand off the door and let me go in.'

'No sense of adventure?' he said, going nowhere. 'I thought a lot more of you than that.'

'I've got plenty of sense of adventure,' Lucy assured him, 'and plenty of common sense too.'

'Prove it,' he said.

'I will, by refusing an invitation from someone I hardly know.'

'Every relationship has to start somewhere...'

Tadj looked so sexy, leaning against the door. Say yes to this ridiculous proposal and she could at least satisfy her workmates' curiosity about the *Sapphire*, as well as her own about Tadj. Say no, and she might regret it for the rest of her life.

'I'm not sure about risking my virtue on board that ship tonight,' she said, voicing her thoughts out loud.

'Your virtue?' Tadj commented with amusement. 'I didn't know that was on offer.'

'It isn't,' she said with a steely look.

'Shame,' he murmured, but with humour tugging at his mouth.

'Okay,' she said, decision made. She trusted herself to act sensibly if she accepted his invitation, and it was the opportunity of a lifetime. 'I have decided to come to the party tonight.'

'Excellent.'

Tadj's wolfish smile sent tremors to all her erogenous zones, to the point where she almost missed him adding, 'No tiaras. It's just a casual get-together.'

'Between billionaires?' she suggested.

'Between you and me,' he corrected her.

All she had to do was laugh it off and walk through that door. She need never see him again. Life would return to normal. But normal could be boring, and Tadj was right about adventure beckoning, but only if the adventure was on her terms.

'Don't *you* be late,' she warned. 'It's cold at night, standing in this doorway.'

CHAPTER THREE

WHAT HAD SHE DONE? *What had she done?* How had she allowed herself to be talked into this? Wicked eyes blazing into hers hadn't helped, Lucy reflected later as she got ready in her small bedsit above the laundry. Nor had feeling as if Tadj and she had known each other longer than it took to drink a couple of cups of coffee. But now was not the time to reflect on why it was possible to feel like that about someone, and not about others. Her decision to go to the party had been made, and she had no intention of skulking in her room, or asking her friends to send Tadj away when he arrived. It would be fascinating to discover how the other half lived, and she could report back to her friends at the laundry.

The only remaining problem was what to wear. She had one decent dress; a cheap sale-rail spectacular she still wasn't entirely sure was her colour. Red hair and freckles didn't always blend well with bright red, especially when the weather turned her skin blue with cold. She'd only worn it once, to the Christmas party when everyone made an effort for the sake of the elderly owner of the laundry. Miss Francine went to so much trouble for them, it was the least they could do.

So... Tadj was older than she was, and obviously more

sophisticated, and much richer, suggesting he'd be used to women in designer clothes. Too bad, she thought as she plucked the dress from its hanger. He'd pressed her to accompany him tonight, so he'd have to put up with her dress being a bit too short and too tight. The sale rail didn't offer custom made.

Tadj must be around early thirties, she thought. She was twenty-three, and definitely not glamorous, or sophisticated. Or successful...not yet. But she could keep a roof over her head, which was something to be proud about, and she had the best of friends, which was more important than anything else. And she had no intention of putting out for the price of a gourmet meal, let alone a date on board the flashiest vessel in the harbour, Lucy determined, firming her jaw. A polite thank-you note would have to be enough, she concluded as a noisy group of excited friends, having spied on her from inside the laundry while she was negotiating with Tadj, burst into the room.

'So?' they chorused, nearly deafening her as they gathered around. 'You've been seen.'

'Really?' She acted daft.

'With the best-looking man on King's Dock,' one of them confided with a jerk of her head to her friends.

'Hmm.' Staring heavenwards, Lucy pretended to think about this. If she'd had more experience of men, maybe she could have joked along with her girlfriends, but somehow Tadj was special—unique in her experience—and she didn't want to exchange banter concerning him while the tender green shoot of a first meeting was still so fragile. 'I did meet someone who works in security,' she admitted frankly. 'He bought me coffee, and that's all there is to it.'

'So you won't be seeing him again?' her friends pressed, exchanging knowing glances with each other.

'I didn't say that. What?' she demanded when her girl-friends started to laugh.

'It's not what you're telling us, but what you're not telling us,' one of them insisted. 'Unless, of course, you really don't know?'

'Don't know what?' She'd been warm and safe here, and surrounded by friends since the day she'd arrived. Had she thrown all that away for the sake of a wicked smile and mocking eyes?

'Didn't the guy tell you his name?' one of her closest friends prompted.

'His name is Tadj. He doesn't have to hide anything,' Lucy insisted.

But did he? she wondered. The spear of anxiety had returned, and with it thoughts of her vicious gangland thug of a stepfather, who was currently serving a lengthy term in prison for his crimes. He had plenty to hide, and could still charm the pants off anyone who didn't know his reputation, and who met him for the first time.

'Tadj,' another friend prompted, breaking into Lucy's troubled thoughts. 'Did this Tadj have a surname?'

It was a relief when Tadj's stunningly attractive face swam into Lucy's mind, completely eclipsing the evil mask of her stepfather. 'I don't think so,' she murmured as she racked her brains. 'First names are enough at a first encounter over coffee.'

'Did he tell you about his job?' another friend pressed.

'Yes—security. I already told you.'

Her stepfather had eyes like a shark, black, dead and cold, she remembered, without a flicker of expression in them. There was no evil in Tadj's eyes. He could look a bit fierce at times—all right, most of the time—but there was also good humour and warmth. And, of course, the sexual heat that flared off him. Better not to think about that now.

More friends had joined them, and her tiny room was overcrowded. Miss Francine was known locally as the Old Woman Who Lived in a Shoe, because of her generosity towards the women she hired. The bedsits she let out for a peppercorn rent might be cramped and old-fashioned, but, for women seeking sanctuary, not even the finest five-star hotel could compare.

'So, I've been seen with a man,' Lucy accepted with a good-humoured shrug, making a joke of it as she stared around.

'With the Emir of Qalala, no less,' her best friend informed the rest.

Lucy froze like a child playing statues. 'What did you say?'

She had heard perfectly well, but…*the Emir of Qalala*? *Tadj was the Emir of Qalala*?

She tried and failed to process the information. And what was she supposed to say now? *I'm a dope—I didn't recognise him? I didn't read the papers today? I don't watch local TV?* All true, unfortunately.

'Oh, come on—potential Emira,' her friends coaxed. 'Tell us what the Emir is really like…'

'I'm afraid I don't know,' Lucy admitted. 'He seems nice enough.'

'And as hot as hell,' one of her friends put in to an agreeing chorus of raunchy suggestions.

'Might have been,' Lucy conceded.

'His photograph is all over the news,' another friend

insisted, in a tone that said she should have known. 'And nice doesn't begin to describe him.'

'Sex on two hard-muscled legs,' someone else shouted out.

'With a body made for sin,' another drooled as she thrust a magazine cover in front of Lucy's nose.

Lucy inhaled sharply at the sight of Tadj, tanned and buff, wearing a pair of figure-hugging swim shorts.

'Either he's a prize-winning swimmer, or he likes to show that thing off.'

'Stop,' Lucy implored her friends. 'I had a coffee with him, nothing more.'

'He'd definitely need security if I shared a hot drink with him,' a friend exclaimed as she read the article over Lucy's shoulder. 'And he's one of the infamous Sapphire Sheikhs—so-called because they are as rich as Croesus, and as insatiable as a pack of ravening wolves.'

Lucy's pulse raced off the scale. So Tadj was not only ridiculously wealthy, but all-powerful and royal too. It was too late to refuse his invitation without appearing to be a coward. She didn't have a number to call him, and she could hardly breach security to ask one of his men to deliver a message. Out of her depth and out of her mind didn't even begin to cover this mess! Adventure was one thing, but not on this scale.

'The Emir of Qalala,' she murmured, biting her lip, turning away as she tried to reconcile the little she knew about a hot guy in a café who had turned out to be one of the world-renowned Sapphire Sheikhs. 'I had no idea,' she murmured.

And if she had, would she have accepted Tadj's invitation?

He was an extraordinary man, and, yes, she probably

would have taken the chance. Did his title make a difference? He'd asked if money could change her opinion.
She'd never considered a royal title, but she understood
that great privilege came with restrictions and complications. Her usual good humour kicked in at this point.
No half measures. If she was going to dip her toe in the
dating pool, why not go for full-body immersion? She
wouldn't simply be out of her depth at the Sheikh's party,
she'd be like Orphan Annie at the feast, but that chance
to peep inside a very different world proved irresistible.
Spinning around, she faced her friends. 'Could you help
me get ready for tonight?'

When they chorused, 'Yes!' she knew there was no
turning back.

Security expert indeed, Lucy thought as her friends
jostled around. Just wait until she saw Tadj again! 'I own
one dress, and no high-heeled shoes,' she explained. 'My
dress is sleeveless and it will be freezing out tonight. If
I could also borrow an evening bag, big enough for a lip
gloss and my bus fare home?'

Drowned out by laughter and offers of help, she made
a silent promise that she would be safely tucked up in her
own bed by midnight.

He'd never been uncertain of a woman. He should have
brought Lucy back with him to make sure he'd see her
again, Tadj concluded as he strode on board his friend's
superyacht. Lucy was unique and unpredictable. There
were no guarantees she'd show up tonight. For once, that
really mattered to him.

'All women are unique, my friend,' his friend Sheikh
Khalid insisted when they met on his arrival in the grand

salon. 'You seem preoccupied,' the Sheikh added when Tadj grimaced.

'Unfinished business,' he supplied economically. Usually, he would welcome both Khalid's company and his interest, but not this time, because all he wanted to think about was Lucy.

Walking out on deck, he scanned the dock as if she might suddenly appear. Was her head buried in one of her college books, or was she getting ready for the party? There was no way to tell.

'What do you do with a woman you can't read?' he asked Khalid as his friend joined him out on deck.

'Bed her?'

'That's not helpful.'

'It's always a good start,' Khalid argued with an ironic smile.

Everything on board the *Sapphire* was geared towards seduction tonight, Tadj thought as they both pulled away from the rail. An army of talented florists was currently adding last-minute touches to the container-loads of exotic blooms.

'You'll be staying in the Golden Suite,' Khalid informed him, 'if that suits you. Make the most of it while you can.'

They shared a wry laugh. 'That temple to all things gold,' Tadj commented. 'It's enough to put anyone off their stride with the addition of those outrageous erotic hangings.'

'Not you, my friend,' Khalid assured him. 'I would have thought you found those hangings rather tame.'

'If I didn't know you better, I'd think you were trying to set me up with this woman,' Tadj responded.

'How could that be true?' Khalid queried. 'I've only

just learned about her. But, good hunting—you'd be surprised how many women are delighted to be seduced in the Golden Suite.'

'No doubt spurred on by the inspiration provided by the artwork,' Tadj commented dryly. 'But this one's different.'

'Different how? She's a woman, isn't she?'

Seeing his expression, Khalid shrugged. 'You've got it bad, my friend.'

Bad? Tadj ground his jaw as he sprang out of the *Sapphire*'s lap pool. Bad was putting it mildly. Grabbing a towel, he dried his exercise-pumped body with impatience. Warnings should be issued with Lucy, that she could change the direction of his thoughts within ten minutes of meeting her. Even exercise hadn't helped him today. He'd never known anything like this. Women didn't get to him; he got to them. Lucy was so young and unsophisticated, she couldn't know the tricks that others played. Funny, blunt and challenging, she was absolutely irresistible, and irresistible was the one thing he didn't need. His usual type knew the score, and were sophisticated enough to use him for what they wanted, without complication. The feeling was mutual, but he couldn't be that way with Lucy. Innocence came at a price, and, though he was no saint, the thought of waking her to physical pleasure was driving him crazy.

Having dressed and checked every timepiece and lump of tech on board in order to convince himself that minutes really could tick by so slowly, he parked the shave and transferred his pacing from ship to shore. He hadn't experienced this level of anticipation since he'd been an overeager youth. When he spotted Lucy standing in the doorway of the laundry, it was as if an atomic reaction went off in his brain. They locked eyes, and he walked towards her. It was the challenge on her face that aroused him. Her body language said she knew who he was, and intended to make him pay for withholding the information.

'You have a lot of explaining to do,' she said.

All he was aware of now was her intoxicating wild-flower scent.

'Am I late?' he said, glancing at his wristwatch and frowning, as if he didn't know what she meant.

'Don't try that on me,' she warned him, narrowing her astonishing jade-green eyes in the very best type of threat.

'Good evening to you too,' he murmured mildly, main-taining eye contact.

'Good evening, Your *Majesty*.'

'My name is Tadj,' he reminded her quietly.

'The Emir of Qalala, I believe.'

He wanted to kiss her as her expressive mouth twisted in a wry smile.

'What are you doing?' she protested as he dragged her close.

'What does a title change about me?'

'Everything,' she said as he brushed her lips teasingly with his. 'Are you going to let me go now?'

'No.'

The first kiss was extraordinary in that it fired every part of him, and made it vital there were more. 'Let's start over,' he said, releasing her before she was quite ready. 'Good evening,' he murmured.

'Good evening, Your Majesty,' she teased him, still trying to catch her breath. They stared at each other with a mixture of acceptance and humour. 'You've got a long way to go to recover your credibility,' she warned, testing her kiss-bruised lips with the tip of her tongue.

'More tolerance required,' he suggested.

'On my part?' she queried.

'Yes, on your part,' he confirmed. 'Shall we?' He glanced in the direction of the super yacht.

The *Sapphire* was a fabulous vessel. Even he was impressed from here, where he could appreciate every inch of it, blazing with light from bow to stern. Party planners had been working tirelessly all day to create a fairyland for the guests, and, though she might still be reeling from the unexpected start to their evening, even Lucy couldn't hide her excitement.

'No more deception, and no more surprises,' she warned as they approached the security gates. 'Promise—or I'm not going any further.'

'When you look at me like that…'

'What?' she murmured, her eyes darkening.

He would promise her almost anything, he thought, but sensibly confined himself to a wry smile and a shrug.

'So you're really the Emir of Qalala?' she said as the security guards waved them through.

'I really am,' he confirmed.

'I'm impressed.'

'No, you're not,' he argued with amusement. 'Not by my title, anyway.'

'Are you always so confident?'

'Always.' Except for tonight, he thought, because Lucy was a whole new experience.

'You're one of the infamous Sapphire Sheikhs,' she observed. 'That alone is supposed to impress me, isn't it?'

'Legendary, rather than infamous, I'd hope.'

She shrugged and halted. 'You should have told me you're one of the world's richest men.'

'Told you, why?' he asked. They were approaching the gangplank where a queue of guests was forming.

'Because it makes us very different,' she said.

'If we're so ill matched, why are you here? For a glimpse into the life of the super-rich?'

'That's part of it,' she admitted frankly.

If he'd been looking for a smooth-tongued casual date, a woman who would do and say everything she could to impress him, he'd got it badly wrong—and thank goodness for that!

CHAPTER FOUR

'SIR...'

One of the security guards, having recognised Tadj, escorted them to a second boarding point a bit further along than the first.

'What's that the other guests are holding?' Lucy asked him as she gazed at those queuing patiently to have their identities checked before being allowed on board.

This was her first taste of life on the other side of the Sapphire Sheikh divide, he reminded himself as he explained, 'Sheikh Khalid's invitations have been issued in silver boxes, studded with sapphires.'

'Recyclable, I hope,' she teased him with a cheeky smile.

'Yes,' he confirmed, matching her mood. 'The box has to be large enough to hold a passport and other documentation, such as a visa.'

'You need passports to get on board?' Lucy exclaimed, staring up at him with an engaging mix of indignation and surprise.

'Only when certain guests disembark in certain countries,' he explained with a shrug. 'The party doesn't last for one night,' he added when she looked at him in bemusement. 'It lasts at least a week.'

'Not for me, it doesn't,' she assured him. 'And, anyway, I don't have my passport with me.'

'None needed,' he confirmed. 'The umbrella of diplomatic immunity covers both of us.'

'I beg your pardon?' she said, turning serious and concerned. 'I haven't signed up for a cruise. A couple of hours with you will be enough.'

'For me too,' he assured her dryly.

They laughed so easily now, but then she flashed him a look to warn that her next statement must be taken seriously. 'I have to be back by midnight,' she said, 'or alarms will ring at the laundry, and the police will come looking for me. I made sure everyone knows where I am tonight,' she explained.

'Nice to know you trust me,' he mocked lightly, 'but sensible.'

'I thought so,' she agreed. 'I don't take chances.'

'Nor should you,' he confirmed as a uniformed officer stepped forward to escort them on deck. He liked Lucy more and more, and couldn't help comparing her to all the other women who wound around him like clinging vines in the hope that things might progress. Not Lucy. She slapped her cards down on the table face up, no nonsense.

'So, Your Importance,' she murmured as they walked ahead of the other guests, 'privilege all the way for you. What am I supposed to call you in front of people?'

'Nothing rude.'

'Then, be nice to me.'

'I intend to be,' he assured her. 'Call me Tadj—or Lord and Master, if you prefer.'

'Tadj will do nicely,' she said.

'Sir...'

'Yes?' He glanced sideways at the officer detailed to escort them.

'Sheikh Khalid is waiting to greet you.'

He glanced up and saw his striking friend watching their embarkation with amusement. 'Of course,' he murmured, acknowledging the officer with a brief dip of his head. 'Come on,' he added to Lucy. 'There's a lot I want you to see before you meet our host.' He didn't feel like sharing her. 'I don't want you to miss a single moment on board the *Sapphire* tonight.'

His determination intensified as Lucy's eyes sparkled with excitement; whether that was for him, or for this fabulous event, for once, he didn't know.

This was partying on a scale Lucy could never have imagined, even in her wildest fantasy. Jewel-studded boxes to hold the invitations…guests in diamonds, exuding clouds of exclusive scent…limos lined up on the dock as more guests arrived, and then those guests being made to stand in line while Lucy walked past on the arm of the Emir of Qalala. That was just crazy. Accepting that a vessel as huge as the *Sapphire* was privately owned took another immense leap of faith. There were so many decks, so many bands playing, so many guests milling about, and floral installations beyond magnificent that gave Kew Gardens at the height of summer a run for its money. The scent of blossom was intoxicating, as was the tang of ozone, but, above everything else, it was the smell of money, of outrageous wealth, that really threatened to choke her.

'Feeling nauseous?' Tadj commented when she made a noise down deep in her throat. 'And we're not even moving yet.'

'Nor will we, I hope,' she said, recovering fast. 'At least, not while I'm on board. I'm just feeling a bit out of place,' she admitted, 'amongst all these diamonds and pin-thin figures dressed in designer clothes.'

'Nonsense,' Tadj insisted with a dismissive wave of his hand. 'You're the most beautiful woman here. And the most intelligent.'

'Did you give everyone an IQ test?' she queried, with the reminder not to take herself so seriously. 'Okay, so you know most of the women here,' she remarked with a grin, as Tadj looked at her in a certain way. 'I should have known.'

'Most of them aren't renowned for their academic qualifications,' he admitted, 'but they have other qualities.'

'Spare me,' she begged. 'I don't need a rundown of the sordid details.'

'Relax. Enjoy yourself,' he advised.

Why not? This was incredible. 'Thank you for inviting me,' she said. It was just unfortunate that her gaze slipped to his mouth as she added, 'I've never seen anything like this before.'

He laughed softly down deep in his chest. 'Feast your eyes,' he invited.

She would. This was the Emir of Qalala, and the Emir of Qalala had kissed her. She had no idea if he would ever do so again, but she would remember that kiss for the rest of her life. He was one hot guy, so why not enjoy this as Tadj suggested? It wasn't every day that fantasy turned into the best type of reality. She liked him more and more. He was courteous and fun to be with, and as hot as hell.

'Drink?' he suggested.

'Sparkling water, please.' Must keep a level head, she

warned herself, and something told her that wouldn't be easy tonight.

'Sparkling water, *mademoiselle*?' a steward invited, handing Lucy a crystal glass.

'Are you hungry?' Tadj enquired when the steward had left them.

'Shouldn't we go and meet our host?' she asked, wishing her body wouldn't respond quite so willingly to the amused heat in Tadj's eyes.

'No hurry. The other guests will keep him busy for a while.'

'I'm okay with water for now, thank you.' How could she eat while her senses were being subjected to an overload of testosterone? Tadj made her long for all things forbidden, and she had to remind herself that she was nothing more than a dockside novelty for him.

Several wine fountains had been installed on board the *Sapphire*, and it was here that couples seemed to be congregating. She couldn't stop staring at them—arms entwined, bodies touching, laughing intimately into each other's faces.

'Would you like me to fill your glass?' Tadj prompted with a curving smile as he glanced at the glittering stream.

For a moment she was lost for words, and then came to with a jolt. 'No, thank you. I'm steering clear of the hard stuff tonight, and only drinking water.'

He laughed. 'Sensible.'

'Always,' she confirmed.

They stared at each other for a few potent moments, during which time Tadj looked like a mythical hero, while she tried to stop her cheeks flaming red. But if there was a cure for blushing, she hadn't found it yet, something to do with her pale Celtic skin that showed every emotion whether she wanted it to or not.

'Why did you invite me tonight?'

'Fireworks,' he said.

She blinked and then realised what he meant as plumes of light began to explode all around the ship. 'I really want to know,' she pressed.

This was dangerous. She was always so cool where men were concerned, and with good reason, having the experience of her stepfather behind her, but with Tadj cool was becoming increasingly impossible.

'Look!'

His touch on her arm made her jump, and it took her a moment to follow his stare to the circus performers in glittering green costumes, swinging high over their heads. She gasped, and not just because of the risks the acrobats were taking, but because Tadj had swung an arm possessively around her shoulders, which was a risk right here.

'And down there,' he said as she was about to wriggle free.

And breathe, Lucy instructed herself firmly, making herself relax as Tadj turned her to see the fire-eaters and jugglers performing.

'We've got a lot more to see,' he said as he moved and took her with him across the deck.

He wasn't joking. The next place they stopped had been transformed into a souk, complete with flower stalls and food outlets, as well as flashy gifts of every type. The attendants behind the stalls were exotically and colourfully robed, and played a good part as they shouted their wares to the passing guests. No money changed hands, and there was quite a crowd competing for the hats, shawls, beads and ornaments, with which to adorn their designer clothes.

'This isn't a party, it's a theatrical production,' Lucy commented as she glanced up at Tadj.

'One man's ludicrous is another man's normal,' he remarked. 'And you look sensational, by the way,' he added as they walked on. 'No need for strings of beads, or even a hat to hide your face.'

'Watch it, mister,' she said, smiling as she faked a punch, and Tadj ducked. 'Actually, you don't look bad yourself, now I take a proper look...' Massive understatement. Tadj looked sensational in nothing more than a pair of well-cut jeans and an open-neck shirt, with a casual jacket left open to reveal his powerful chest. He could have worn a boiler suit, and still looked fabulous. Better still naked, she thought.

And here she was in borrowed clothes, carrying the flag for her friends. Tipping up her chin, she met his teasing stare head-on, and was rewarded by the warmth in Tadj's eyes. Make that heat, she thought as her body responded with enthusiasm.

'Champagne?' Tadj proposed as he selected two crystal flutes from a tray a passing waiter was carrying.

'No, thanks. I'm a cheap drunk, so I'll stick to water, if you don't mind. And even if you do,' she added good-humouredly. Tonight was going better than expected—far better than she'd dared to hope.

'To us,' he said as they raised their glasses.

'To a wonderful evening,' Lucy replied, calling on her natural caution. She might be having the time of her life—might have kissed the hottest man at the party, but she had no intention of completely losing her head.

Tadj achieved the impossible, by finding them a quiet

and sheltered spot on the *Sapphire*'s crowded deck. Taking her glass out of her hand, he put it down next to his. *Was he going to kiss her again?* Every part of her body tingled at the thought. She could feel him in every fibre of her being, as if he were the virtuoso who had temporarily laid aside his violin. Her strings were certainly twanging at the memory of his touch, Lucy thought, carefully concealing her amusement at a body running riot while the sensible head supposedly guiding it was temporarily unavailable.

'It's so beautiful here,' she said, looking around. The floral decorations were incredible, though the blossom was in a more restrained colour palette than the rest of the *Sapphire*, as if this area had been designed for lovers. It was like standing in the middle of a fragrant ocean of palest pink and white. Drawing on the heady scent, she closed her eyes, only for the unwelcome thought that she should be leaving soon to pop into her head. 'Tadj, I...'

'Tadj what?' he murmured.

He'd dipped his head to stare into her eyes, and their mouths were almost touching.

'Don't,' she begged.

'Why not?' he teased.

Her lips were tingling. His warm, clean, spicy scent was drugging her senses. She wanted another kiss and was in no hurry to move. Sighing raggedly as he began to tease her lips with his, she wondered if anything that felt this good could be bad for her. The touch of Tadj's hands on her arms was so light and yet so dangerous. She didn't want to break away. She wanted more of his skilful touches. He was so gentle, and yet so firm in a way she had never experienced before. He promised more pleasure than she could imagine.

'Something amusing you?' he asked, frowning as he stared down.

True, her mood had changed and no wonder. 'This *is* a film set,' she said, as a cloud of pink smoke drifted up from a lower deck, threatening to envelop them in its scented embrace.

'Where you are, anything's possible,' Tadj said dryly as he wafted it away. 'Look down there, and you'll see an oasis complete with sandy beach and palm trees.'

'And all for the amusement of the Sheikh's guests,' Lucy commented with a wry smile. 'And what about up here?' she queried softly, holding Tadj's burning stare.

He gave her a considering look. 'Up here you will find two people, namely you and me, who have more sense than to be taken in by a fantasy.'

If only, she thought as he smiled faintly. Tadj might have his sensible head screwed on tightly, but she'd lost hers when he'd kissed her.

'You're beautiful,' he whispered just as she was reflecting that there would never be another night like this.

'No, I'm not,' she said. 'I'm just okay, but you're beautiful.' When he frowned at this, she added, 'All right, then, you're not just beautiful, you're rugged and tough too.'

'That's better,' he agreed with a grin. 'But it's only your opinion.'

'And I'm always right,' she said.

He laughed and, cupping her chin in one hand, he kissed her again. By the time he'd finished kissing her, she was ready to agree to anything he suggested. Deep down, she knew she should move away, slow things down, but she couldn't—she didn't want to. She wanted more breath-stealing kisses, and more caresses from those knowing hands. More than ready to accept that one night couldn't last for ever, she knew that memories like these would stand the test of time.

The cloud of pink smoke added to the sense of unreality, making things seem possible that she would never have considered on a regular first date. Being close to Tadj and touching him like this was as far from Lucy's normal as it was possible to get. This was definitely the most romantic night of her life, she thought as she stared into his dark, compelling stare, and she was in no hurry to put the brakes on.

Everything about Lucy enchanted him. She felt perfect beneath his hands, and was full of surprises. Passion of all types fired off her, and she wasn't afraid to stand up to him. Quirky and inexperienced, as he had thought her, she had responded to his kisses, not on his terms, but on hers, and he liked that about Lucy best of all. He admired her openness. What you saw was what you got, and the night was just beginning.

'Nice dress,' he remarked as she straightened the folds of fabric, smoothing it over her thighs, as he would like to do.

'I have my friends to thank for helping me put this outfit together,' she admitted. 'Oh, I see,' she said, reading him with her usual ease. 'You like the dress because it leaves my back bare.'

'That's part of it,' he admitted. The tasteful knee-length dress was Lucy's choice, he guessed. The glittering shoulder bag encrusted with diamanté, together with its matching high-heeled shoes, didn't strike him as Lucy's taste. She was all about understatement, and the shoes were too big, which kind of gave it away. The sensible, if dated poncho she'd handed over to an attendant at the entrance to the *Sapphire* would certainly keep her warm, but he couldn't imagine Lucy spending her hard-earned cash on such a bulky and unflattering item. 'You've got some good friends,' he commented.

'The best,' she agreed.

The fact so many people had wanted to contribute to Lucy enjoying herself tonight told him a lot about her character, as well as her resourcefulness, not to mention good judgement when it came to choosing her friends.

'Let's make a move,' he suggested as a fresh wave of pink mist made its way towards them from the lower deck. Taking hold of her hand, he linked their fingers as he led her towards the infamous Golden Suite on board the *Sapphire*.

'Shouldn't we meet the Sheikh first?' she asked, glancing over her shoulder as impatience to have her truly alone led him to increase his pace.

'He's not going anywhere.'

But they were, Lucy thought. And where was Tadj taking her? Her sensible mind caused her to worry her bottom lip, but her wayward body thrilled as she considered the possibilities.

CHAPTER FIVE

TADJ HAD EXPLAINED that the stateroom he was about to show Lucy was unique. Not only was it full of treasures beyond compare in the historical sense, but also it was stuffed to the gunnels with golden ornaments and furniture, as well as the fabulous, famous sapphires.

'Do I get to see your etchings too?' she asked lightly.

'No etchings. Erotic hangings,' Tadj informed her. 'No joke,' he assured Lucy when she looked at him in surprise. 'So, I hope you're not easily shocked.'

'Me? No,' she said on a throat turned suddenly dry.

'Extremely erotic hangings,' Tadj teased, seeing her discomfort.

'I'm not entirely unaware of the workings of the human body.'

He laughed. 'These aren't so much workings, as the most outlandish contortions.'

Lucy gave him one of her 'so you think I'm dumb' looks. 'Well, it sounds like a very special room.'

'Sarcastic,' he commented, smiling faintly.

'Curious,' she said honestly. And then she frowned. 'But it doesn't sound much like a room for lingering in.'

'You might change your mind.'

'I doubt it.'

This was a deck reserved for *very* special guests, Lucy thought as a security guard, having recognised Tadj, stood back to let them through. The corridor was as luxurious as everywhere else on the ship, with plush carpets, pristine ivory walls, decorated with fascinating *objets d'art*, all shown to best advantage by discreet lighting. Plump upholstered seating invited a pause at convenient intervals—goodness knew what went on there, Lucy thought, but Tadj wasn't interested in lagging behind to explain, and curiosity propelled her forward. For some crazy reason, she trusted him. With no real foundation, that was reckless maybe, but she had a good feeling about him that she couldn't explain.

Even so, it was better not to take any chances, she thought as he stopped outside the most stunning golden door. 'Five minutes and I'm out of here,' she warned in a teasing tone to soften the information.

Seemingly unconcerned, he shrugged.

'I'm impressed,' Lucy admitted as she stood back to admire the door's intricate ornamentation.

'Wait until you see inside,' Tadj advised. Opening the door, he invited her to enter the Golden Chamber.

Having overdosed on luxury for the past hour or so, Lucy was complacent, thinking she was ready for anything, but her first sight of the unique room stunned her into silence. It was so bling, she wasn't sure if she liked it or not. But, 'Wow,' she exclaimed as she stared around. Her feet sank into a carpet that was deep, sapphire-blue, while every surface, wall, ceiling, and piece of furniture was composed of solid gold. She guessed the ornaments would be the same, and these were studded with glowing blue sapphires, and were quite obviously precious artefacts from some ancient time.

'I'm not sure about the elevator music,' she teased Tadj, turning to face him and raise a brow at the strings playing softly in the background.

He laughed. 'Me neither. I guess it's supposed to improve the ambience.'

'It smells good, anyway,' Lucy conceded. Incense was burning in golden salvers, and, closing her eyes, she drew deep on the exotic scent.

'Time to look at the shocking hangings,' she said matter-of-factly, opening her eyes. She stared around, but her gaze always returned to Tadj. He was more interesting than the erotic hangings, though she did have a few questions for him.

'Is that pose even possible?' she asked, tipping her head to one side. 'I had no idea human bodies were even capable of doing that.' She wasn't easily shocked, just perplexed.

Smiling his unreadable smile, Tadj made no answer. Opening a second, heavily ornamented door, he revealed another glittering golden stateroom, one so large it easily accommodated several glittering crystal chandeliers.

To swing from? Lucy wondered.

'You're laughing,' Tadj commented with interest. 'Don't you like it?'

'Sensory overload,' Lucy explained. 'Otherwise, I actually feel quite humble to be invited here to see what must be one of the hidden wonders of the world.'

'I'm glad you think so,' he said with a touch of humour in his tone.

She wasn't only thinking about that, but fantasising about Tadj lowering her slowly down on top of the thick, soft wool rug they were currently standing on.

'This is my topic,' she reminded him. 'The display

of important historical works of art falls well within my field of interest.'

'Then, I'm glad I brought you here,' he said.

Propping a hip against a console table that appeared to be made of solid gold, Tadj folded his arms and stared at her. 'You're hard to read,' he said. 'Tell me more about yourself...'

'Am I?' she said, ignoring the question. The connection between them was stronger than ever, and more than ever she wanted to stay and chat, but the atmosphere inside this room was just too seductive. 'I can't stay too long at the party,' she said in a reminder to them both, 'and I want to make the most of it,' she added, moving towards the door. 'I have responsibilities.'

'As do I,' Tadj assured her.

Stalemate. Several tense seconds ticked by, while Lucy gazed out at the brilliantly lit marina, where the bustle of ordinary life carried on in what seemed like a million miles from where they were standing. She'd be back there soon enough. She certainly wouldn't remain on board when *Sapphire* slipped its moorings.

'Penny for them?' Tadj prompted.

Turning, she lifted her chin so she could stare him in the eyes. 'I'm just taking everything in—you...me...this,' she admitted, glancing around. 'Very soon the *Sapphire* will sail, and you'll sail with it.'

'Will you miss me?' he teased.

'No,' she lied. The time had come to examine her feelings, and decide whether to stay, or go.

He sensed the change in Lucy. From pure enjoyment and wonder, she had paused to consider her feelings, and where she fitted into this scenario. Her decision was typical Lucy, in that it both pleased and surprised him.

'I want you,' she whispered with a shrug of her slender shoulders.

Her candour fired his hunger as nothing else could. Slowly drawing her towards him, he kissed her neck, before brushing her lips teasingly with his. Turning in his arms, she rested back against his chest, so he kissed her again and felt her tremble. Innocence demanded a measured response, and for once in his life he wasn't sure he was in full command of his control.

'Isn't this beautiful?' she murmured, staring out of the floor-to-ceiling balcony window, to where the soft pop of gunpowder heralded the sight of fireworks bursting into vivid flame.

His answer was to rasp his stubble very lightly across her neck. The rush of light across the night sky seemed appropriate, somehow. Was there more to this than sex? Lucy was exceptional. And impatient, he concluded with amusement, as she moved restlessly in his arms. But she wasn't done surprising him just yet. Turning to face him, she reached up and laced her fingers through his hair, bringing him down to kiss her, as a far more experienced woman might have done. Instantly hard when she rubbed her lush, warm body against his, he mapped her breasts appreciatively and was rewarded by her nipples turning pebble-hard against his palm.

'Don't tease me,' she begged. 'By the way,' she added with one of her comic looks that only revealed how vulnerable she was feeling, 'you don't think I'm fat, do you?'

He smiled to reassure her, with what must surely be a perplexed expression on his face. 'Fat? You're perfect.'

She relaxed and smiled mischievously up at him. 'Then…?'

'Delay is the servant of pleasure.'

'Don't give me that,' she warned him teasingly. 'Give me you…'

'Your wish is my command.' Swinging her into his arms, he carried her into the bedroom. As he laid her down on crisply dressed sheets, it felt more like taking a lover of long standing to bed than a woman he'd just met. He had no explanation for this, other than to say being with Lucy felt right. Her freshness and inexperience had won him over, and introducing her to pleasure was the only thing on his mind.

'Tadj…'

As she reached for him, he stared into eyes that had turned black, apart from a small rim of jade green around her pupils. 'Soon,' he promised, and, dipping down so he could kiss her, he smiled against her softly yielding mouth.

'Now,' she argued hotly, digging her fingers into him.

Lifting his head, he stared down with amusement. 'You'll regret it, if you rush.'

'I'm prepared to risk it.' Then her mind switched up a gear. 'I'm tired of being steady and prudent,' she admitted. 'I want tonight to be different. You're different. And I trust you—sort of,' she added with a rueful smile.

'That's quite a responsibility you've given me,' he said, grinning down.

Running her small hands appreciatively over his shoulders, she commented, 'I think you can take it.'

Shrugging off his jacket, he dropped it on a chair. Lucy was already pulling at her dress. He helped her. In just a bra and thong, she was the Venus de Milo made flesh, unbelievably beautiful and lush—and wild with impatience. Yanking at the buttons on his shirt, she managed to pull a couple off. As they flew across the floor, he freed his sapphire cufflinks and put them safely out of reach. They didn't lose eye contact for a second while all this was going on, and by the time he'd kicked off his shoes, she was working on his belt. Snapping it out of its loops, she gave a sound of triumph and fell back.

'Hussy,' he accused as she greedily sucked in air.

'You bet,' she said. 'You don't know how long I've waited for this.'

'From the first moment you saw me in the café?'

She laughed. 'Something like that.'

'Still, savour the moment—make it last…'

'Not a chance,' she assured him.

He sucked in air between his teeth as she boldly brushed her hand over his body. Her hand was tiny and he was big. Lucy wasn't the only one being seduced here.

'You're loving this,' she gasped, her pupils huge and black with excitement. 'The chase, I mean. Have I spoiled it for you, by becoming the aggressor?'

'Not at all—and that might change soon,' he warned.

She shrugged, but for a moment he thought she seemed uncertain. He loved sex, and did nothing to stop her as she explored him with exquisite skill. Sex had never been so much fun before, he thought as she slipped her hand into his boxers. It was just a hunger like anything else, to be satisfied on demand. With Lucy, sex had become an open-ended possibility. Her lack of experience was no deterrent to enthusiasm. When she stared into his eyes, there was fire in the depth of the black, as if she was claiming her mate.

'Do you trust me?' she demanded.

In the moment it took to answer, he hooked a thumb into the neck of his shirt, ready to pull it over his head.

'Trust works both ways,' she insisted, stilling as she stared at him, waiting for his answer.

'Trust has to be earned,' he countered as he tossed his shirt aside.

The most plausible liars could arrive in the most pleasing of packages, he had discovered in his youth. Lucy had gone some way to wipe out his recollection of an older woman who had found it all too easy to convince a gullible young prince, whose brain had been firmly lodged below his belt at the time, that fate intended them to be together. To help fate along, a loan from Tadj would really help her to build her business, she'd said. The jewels she'd plundered from the Emir's palace were to form part of an important exhibition, she had explained in court, after walking out on him in the middle of the night. His heart had turned to stone when her duplicity had been uncovered, and he had focused his mind solely on Qalala, vowing never to be duped again. So yes, trust was an issue for him. It was as vital as the air he breathed, and he was always waiting to be disappointed. But he'd put all that aside for this one night.

'When you surrender to pleasure there are no barriers left,' he told Lucy as she undressed him.

'And none required,' she promised as her nimble fingers flew over his remaining clothes.

Placing her hands palms flat against Tadj's chest, Lucy indicated that she would set the pace. He could have thrown her back and done anything he wanted, but that was what she meant by trust. One night to remember for all the right reasons, she thought, though her inner self warned that one night wouldn't be nearly enough. It would have to be, she thought.

Beneath Tadj's control, she sensed a fire raging. She

had never felt like this...so excited and lustful, which was hardly surprising when he stood before her naked and magnificent, like a bronze cast by Michelangelo. Fear of sex with such a big man had quickly been replaced by a hunger to know him inside her. Tadj would put her needs first, of that she was sure. He was such a compelling presence, he had pushed all the horrors she'd witnessed at home behind her with no effort at all. If he hadn't been the Emir of Qalala, and she no one in particular, she could easily have fallen in love with him.

'My turn now,' he said.

There'd be no argument there, she thought as he deftly removed her bra, maintaining eye contact while he did so.

'Good?' he murmured, surely knowing that everything he did was so much better than good.

Lucy couldn't help her shiver of delight. Burying her face in Tadj's hard, warm chest, she listened to the steady beat of his heart. It calmed her, and seemed to promise that whatever happened next, she would know pleasure as never before. Stretching out his length alongside her, he proved to be even bigger than she'd imagined. Against him, she was like a slender twig with breasts— breasts he seemed to admire—and she gasped with pleasure when he gave them his attention. She craved him, ached for him, and only one thing could ease that, but Tadj appeared to be in no hurry to relieve her frustration. Moving down the bed, he began by massaging her feet and kissing them. Sensation overload, she thought as the pleasure transferred to her core. Turning her, he dropped kisses on the back of her knees. More sensation...more gasping for sufficient breath—she'd had no idea she was so sensitive.

She was naked apart from her tiny lace thong, and

shivering with arousal in his arms. Writhing against the sheets, she craved firmer contact and yearned for release. Tadj answered this with firm-handed strokes down the length of her back, as if he were taming a spirited pony. Shaking uncontrollably, she finally settled again, and had to wait to see what he'd do next.

'You're very sensitive,' he commented, as if this pleased him.

She could do no more than hum contentedly, though she cried out with excitement when Tadj transferred his skill to her thighs. Almost without knowing she was doing so, she parted her legs in a blatant invitation for him to explore. She had never ached with need like this before, and was almost begging by the time he allowed his fingertips to brush against her. Grabbing a pillow, she clutched it to her chest as if that could imbue her with the strength to wait.

'Turn onto your back,' he instructed.

His tone aroused her beyond bearing, and she hurried to do as he said.

Scraping his stubble across the very sensitive skin at the nape of her neck, he made her cry out with need. If this was being instructed in the art of pleasure, she was the most willing student there could ever be.

Resting her legs over his shoulders, Tadj concentrated his attention on that area that had waited so patiently, while she moaned softly and rhythmically as he attended to her needs with his tongue.

'Now,' he prompted in a low, yet commanding tone, and, lifting his head, he watched her reaction as he replaced the touch of his tongue with his hand.

She couldn't hold on—impossible. The thought that she was exposing herself, body and soul, flashed briefly across her mind, but carnal hunger had soon extinguished the last of her doubts, and she fell greedily, screaming repeatedly with pleasure as the most powerful release took her over.

'Good,' Tadj praised, soothing her with kisses as he slowly brought her down.

Good didn't even begin to describe what she had experienced. Clinging to him, she silently begged for more... and not so silently, which made him laugh, just a low chuckle down deep in his chest, but it was the feeling of closeness she valued most of all. She couldn't allow herself to believe that this must end. Tadj was so right for her in every way. There was only one thing wrong with that thought, which was that reality had to intrude at some point.

'Beautiful,' he whispered, pulling back.

She wasn't beautiful, but he made her feel beautiful. Somehow, her hang-ups deserted her with Tadj. Which was strange when the contrast between them was so stark. He was beautiful. Built like a gladiator, swarthy and tanned, he was tough, yet careful with her, and exceptionally easy on the eye. No other man could compare, which almost certainly meant she'd never have another lover. Fate was a cruel mistress. Tadj was the Emir of Qalala and out of reach, but that couldn't stop them enjoying each other's bodies.

'What's amusing you now?' he asked with one of his dark smiles.

'Just one of my fantasies,' she admitted.

'Forget fantasies,' he advised, moving over her. 'Reality is much more fun. And don't tense up when there's no need.'

Was he joking? It would take both her hands to encompass him, and then only just.

'I won't hurt you,' he promised. 'Greedy must wait,' he warned, teasing her with kisses as she thrashed her head about on the pillows.

'But not for long,' she argued fiercely.

Finding her needy place, he gave it his close attention, which brought her to the edge in moments. But just as she was about to tip over into pleasure, he withdrew his coaxing hand, leaving her panting and unsatisfied.

'Part your legs wider,' he commanded softly. 'That's better,' he approved. 'Now…' Reaching for a pillow, he slipped it beneath her buttocks, raising her even higher for his attention. She was completely exposed, completely vulnerable, which allowed Tadj to stimulate the area all around her sensitive core, without allowing her the release she so badly needed.

'I can't hold on,' she heard herself wail.

'You must,' Tadj insisted, 'or I'll stop.'

With a noisy gust of frustration, she raged, 'But I can't—I need it now!'

'You need *me* to teach *you* the benefit of restraint,' he argued softly.

'Just a bit more,' she begged in what she hoped was her most appealing voice.

'And have you lose control?' Tadj asked. He gave her one of his looks.

'Why shouldn't I lose control? Isn't that what this is about?'

'As I said, you have a lot to learn,' he told her. 'You will lose control, not once, but many times, if you listen to my instruction. Hold your legs open for me,' he commanded.

He only had to brush his fingertips across that painfully sensitive place to send her screaming off the edge. Arcing her body towards him, she thrust mindlessly in a rhythmical pattern that was an age-old hunt for union with her mate.

Tadj coolly denied her his hand. 'Wider,' he insisted.

By this point she was glad to do anything he suggested. 'More,' she managed on a shaking breath.

He brought her to the edge again, easing into her fractionally. When he withdrew, the agony of frustration was indescribable. Reaching out, she clamped her hands around his buttocks.

'Not yet,' he warned.

'I'm done with waiting,' she said fiercely, and as she spoke she claimed him. Tadj could have held her off with ease, but a line had been crossed, and they both knew it, and with a growl of triumph he pressed her into the bed, and took over.

However much he wanted this, wanted Lucy, he was determined to go slowly, so she would remember this for all the right reasons. However eager she might be, he would hold back. His body cried out for immediate satisfaction, but he ruled it ruthlessly. Pinning Lucy's hands above her head on the soft bank of pillows, he took her slowly and deeply, taking his time to make sure she savoured every moment of pleasure. His reward was that she lost control immediately, and as she bucked wildly beneath him he held her in position to ensure she explored what was possible.

Making love to Lucy was as natural as breathing. They each responded without the need for words, and grew closer, in amusement, in pleasure, in trust, in ways he'd never imagined possible with a woman, after knowing each other for so short a time. When she finally fell back exhausted, he smiled to think that the erotic hangings above the bed were tame by comparison with this.

'Do you never tire?' she asked when he stroked her into awareness again. Smiling into the pillows, she gave him an engaging sideways look. Curled up on the sheets like a contented pussycat, she made his stone heart long for the impossible, and so he took her again, turning his thoughts from complications to pleasure.

A long time later, he realised he was murmuring words in his own tongue to Lucy, and these were words he had never said to anyone. Whatever difficulties faced them, she was part of his life now. He had claimed her as she had claimed him, and, settling back with her safely nestled in his arms, he closed his eyes and they slept.

Dawn light woke Lucy when it streamed into the Golden Suite. Tadj lay sprawled across the bed. She had slept contentedly through the night in his embrace. He was so beautiful, she thought, staring down.

Hearing noises on deck, she was instantly alert. The consequence of being on board when the *Sapphire* left dock struck home forcefully, and, slipping out of bed without waking him, she went to peer out of the window. Her heart lurched as her worst fears were confirmed. The *Sapphire* was about to sail. Racing to drag on her clothes, she only knew that she had to get off before that happened, and there wasn't a moment to lose. Last night had been a wonderful dream, but she had always known she would wake up at some point. They both had their lives to live, and she didn't belong in this very different world. Tiptoeing back to the bed, she stared down wistfully, but some things could never be. Putting the past behind her had meant striving to move forward every day, and how could she do that if she stayed here? Wrenching her gaze away from the only man she could ever love, she left her heart with him, and hurried out of the room.

Tadj would move on when he tired of her, Lucy's sensible self insisted as she bolted down the gangplank. Life would continue as normal for the Emir of Qalala when the *Sapphire* sailed, while Lucy didn't have the luxury of taking time out.

Turning in response to the shouts of the sailors tossing ropes from shore to ship, she knew their strident voices were the death knell to the dreams she had so foolishly tucked away in her heart.

CHAPTER SIX

Three months later...

FROZEN TO THE spot on the tiled floor of the restaurant where she was working her second job on King's Dock, Lucy was stunned to see Tadj again. *How many more shocks could she take?*

As many as necessary, she told herself firmly after taking a few steadying breaths. Only an hour or so ago she had received a panicked phone call from her mother, to warn Lucy that her stepfather had unexpectedly received parole, and was due to be set free from prison, which meant they were both in danger. She had felt sick inside knowing there was an unborn child involved now.

And now this...

'Get away from here,' her mother had pleaded. 'It's the only way you can help me. You have to get out of the country, because if your stepfather finds you, he'll find a way to hurt me through you. Our lives are in danger, Lucy. I can't rest until I know you're safely out of his reach.' This was no exaggeration. Lucy knew only too well from past experience how dangerous her stepfather could be, and how utterly ruthless.

Holding Tadj's gaze steadily, she stamped on the urge

to tell him everything right away. She knew her eyes might give her away. Tadj had always been able to read her, and the fact that she was carrying his child couldn't be hidden for long. She didn't want to hide it—she was happy to think that in a few months' time there would be a baby—but she wasn't so certain how she felt about the fact that a child would bind them together for life, whether either of them wanted that or not.

'We meet again,' the Emir of Qalala intoned without a flicker of emotion on his dazzlingly handsome face.

She knew immediately that this was not the fun-loving guy from the café, but a very different animal, as Tadj regarded her as coolly as if they'd shared nothing more than a passing acquaintance. He'd drawn to a halt just a few steps away, and she could see nothing of the man she'd known in his eyes, yet somehow she must persuade this hostile stranger to take her away from here. This wasn't just a shock encounter, but a lucky quirk of fate that she must take advantage of. She'd go to Qalala, if she had to—whatever it took to keep her mother and baby safe.

All these thoughts were jangling in Lucy's head as they confronted each other. She would have liked more time to frame her argument and persuade him to take her with him, but there was no time.

With an almost imperceptible nod of his head, the Emir of Qalala summoned the maître d'. 'Lucy and I haven't seen each other for some time,' Tadj explained, 'and would appreciate your giving her the night off.'

This wasn't a question, but an instruction, Lucy thought as the maître d' gushed a response. Of course she could leave. 'Whatever suits you, Your Majesty,' he insisted.

The lift of one ebony brow was all it took for Tadj to

remind the maître d' that the Emir of Qalala was eating in his restaurant incognito, and that he didn't welcome reference to his royal status. This sent the hapless maître d' into a tailspin. 'I'll get your coat,' he told Lucy, rushing off.

At least fate was on her mother's side, Lucy thought as Tadj continued to stare at her. She'd had a genuine reason for leaving him three months ago, and could only hope that he didn't harbour grudges for long.

The distinguished gentleman who had been sitting with Tadj at the table made no complaint when his dining experience was brought to an abrupt end. Bowing politely over Lucy's hand, he excused himself, and within moments she noticed an official limousine sweeping away. So far, so good, she thought, as Tadj indicated that she should now sit down. 'We won't be staying long,' he told her. 'A glass of water, perhaps?'

If it hadn't been for her condition, a stiff brandy might have been more appropriate, Lucy reasoned, trying to dredge up some humour from what was a not so funny situation. Tadj's mention of leaving the restaurant was an additional reminder to keep a clear head. 'A glass of water would be nice,' she agreed, swallowing down her apprehension on a dry throat.

'Are you sure you're all right?' Tadj frowned. Cold as he was towards her, he was fundamentally a decent man. 'The shock of seeing me again hasn't been too much for you?'

The irony in his tone was the only warning she needed to be cautious, and she shot him a sharp look. Tadj's expression remained stony, while she remained silent. They had so much to say to each other, but the door of communication between them had slammed shut, and the mouth that had kissed her into oblivion remained set in a harsh line. Obviously, he was angry that she'd walked out on him. Who would do that to the Emir of Qalala? Who did that to anyone without a word of explanation? Lucy reflected unhappily, knowing she had to find a way to make this right, or the opportunity fate had so unexpectedly provided, to escape the country, and tell Tadj about their baby, would be lost.

She downed the water gratefully, and then plunged right in. 'I'm sorry I didn't say goodbye that night on the *Sapphire*, but you were asleep.'

'And you didn't think to wake me?'

He wasn't going to make this easy for her, and more than anything she wanted to tell him about the baby, but not here in a busy restaurant. It was such momentous news, she wanted to tell him in private so they could both take in what it meant.

'Perhaps you need something stronger than water?' Tadj suggested, in a way that warned he could read her easily.

Determined that she would not be bounced into blurting out the facts, she stated firmly, 'I never drink on duty, and I still have work to do.'

'You won't be working again tonight, so I don't see that's an issue.' His black stare dared her to disagree as he added, 'In my opinion a drink might settle you.'

'I hardly drink at the best of times,' she pointed out.

'And this isn't the best of times?'

Irony dripped off his every word. Sitting up straight, she came to a decision. No one could accuse her of being a coward. She had stood on her own two feet for long enough; she was about to become a mother. Not only had her stepfather failed to crush her spirit, she refused to run scared, and would do whatever it took to protect both her child and her mother, and when it came to defending herself she would fight. Drawing a deep breath, she said, 'I've got something to tell you.'

'You're pregnant,' Tadj stated without emotion.

Shock sucked the breath from her lungs. He'd guessed before she'd had chance to say anything. 'How did you know?'

'I know you,' he said. 'Three months?'

'Yes.'

'So my child,' he confirmed.

'Well, no other,' she said hotly.

The realisation that Lucy was expecting his child had hit him like a punch in the gut. He was about to become a father. What did he know about that? Precisely nothing. If he followed the example set by his socialite, uncaring father, the future of his child was grim.

Memories flooded back as he remembered how it felt to be the only child left sitting on his suitcase when the school holidays came around. Staff at the boarding school he'd attended had always done their best to make up for the neglect of his parents by calling Abdullah, a man who had cared for Tadj since Tadj was one of many in the nursery, to collect him from school. Being welcomed into Abdullah's happy family home had proved how children could live, not in palaces, but surrounded by love. How he'd longed for Abdullah to be his father, rather than to have been born a royal prince to parents who couldn't care less about him. Horror filled him at the thought that he could ever do that to a child. Stifling the dread, he moved on to practicalities that called for decisions, rather than maudlin recollections. He could have everything he wanted, including a ready-made family and a woman who had engaged his attention from the start, but this child would bind them together for life, which he hadn't planned for.

Lucy's face was pale and creased with worry as she waited for his reaction. His world had been jolted, but his logical mind had quickly kicked in. Safeguards must be put in place immediately for both mother and child. Three months ago, sex had been the only thing on his mind. He and Lucy had been lost in an erotic jungle, but they were back with far more than they'd set out with. He had no trouble accepting that he was the father of Lucy's child. No birth control was one hundred per cent effective. And on a positive note, the position of mistress was filled. He hadn't reckoned on a pregnant mistress, but putting Lucy and the child under his protection was vital, so the sooner he could get her away from here, the better.

Decision made, he stood. 'We're leaving,' he said, waiting for her to join him.

'Leaving?' Lucy flashed a glance outside, where another sleek black limousine had drawn up at the kerb.

'For my country house, and then on to Qalala,' he explained. 'We need to talk, and I'm not prepared to do that here.'

'Your country house?' Lucy queried, her voice shaking as if she was not quite in command of it. 'And then Qalala?'

Was he mistaken, or had she brightened at the prospect of leaving the country? No...she wasn't just pleased, she was relieved, he thought, as suspicion twisted inside him. 'We travel to my country house first, so that plans can be made for your arrival in Qalala. My staff need prior warning.'

Don't rock the boat, Lucy thought, though Tadj's tone

was chilling, and hardly boded well if she went with him now, but however cold he felt towards her for leaving him three months ago, and however shocked he might be about the baby, leaving the country was a priority, to keep her mother and her baby out of danger. What could be safer than leaving under the protection of the Emir of Qalala? Diplomatic protection would provide a safeguard from her vicious stepfather, leaving no loopholes for him to snake through.

Decision made, she stood, but then saw black-clad figures stepping out of the shadows. For a moment she thought her stepfather's thugs had found her, but when Tadj sent them off with a nod she realised they were his men. Out of the frying pan into the fire? she wondered.

'You don't need guards to make me come with you,' she told Tadj. 'I'll come quietly,' she added in a lame attempt at the humour they'd once shared.

Tadj said nothing, and seemed, if anything, more remote than ever. She had to give him a chance to get over the shock of learning she was expecting his baby, Lucy reminded herself. She wasn't the only one who'd been sent reeling with shock this evening.

'Now,' he prompted in a quiet, firm tone, glancing at the door.

She wasted a few more seconds, searching in vain for some sign of the warmth they'd once shared. Leaving the safe and familiar with a man she thought she knew, but suddenly couldn't be sure of, was quite an intimidating prospect. It was one thing knowing that Tadj was the Emir of Qalala, and quite another to feel the brush of his power.

'Get in,' he snapped when his chauffeur opened the door of the official limousine.

He joined her in the luxurious interior, but sat with his face averted as if he couldn't bear to look at her. Or, maybe he was deep in thought, Lucy reasoned. 'Are you kidnapping me?' she asked in an attempt to lighten the atmosphere.

'Are you over-dramatising?' he asked coldly as his driver closed the door.

No amount of luxury could soothe her in this confined space with a man who seemed so hostile. It takes two to tango, she wanted to tell him, but, so soon after her mother's alarming phone call, Lucy couldn't afford to rock the boat. This was the perfect opportunity to leave the country, and she couldn't allow anything to get in the way. His manner suggested that trust was a huge issue for Tadj, and if he suspected she was using him to escape her stepfather and keep her mother safe, she doubted he would ever forgive her.

'What have you been doing these past three months?' he demanded.

Jolted rudely back to the present, she turned to face him, and held his harsh stare steadily. 'I've been working...studying.' The moment she'd found out she was pregnant, she'd secured a second job at the restaurant close by the laundry, and was working hard to complete her studies at college. Her schedule didn't leave much spare time, but she'd needed the extra money for the deposit on a small garden flat she'd found close to King's Dock. With a tiny garden, this was where she had hoped to raise her child, but now her stepfather was free, she had to change her plans.

Everything had happened in such a rush, with Tadj appearing out of the blue and Lucy leaving with him. She would have to contact her employers, and talk to them both to explain that she was going away for a while. Luckily, college had broken up for the holidays, so that was one problem out of the way.

'Why, Lucy?'

'Why what?' Tadj's voice had shocked her tense and upright.

'Why did you walk out on me? Why have you taken so long to tell me about the baby? I thought we trusted each other.'

'We did—we do,' Lucy insisted.

Tadj's tone was harsh, and his black stare chilled her. She had the sense of clinging by her fingertips to any chance of having him take her out of the country where her stepfather couldn't find her, and use Lucy to blackmail her mother into allowing him back home.

Tadj's mouth twisted with scorn. 'Really?'

As he speared a disbelieving stare into her eyes, she hated the changes between them, and wished she could do something to bring back the man she'd met three months ago. He was so hostile she felt increasingly uncomfortable.

'You said we were going to your country house before we leave for Qalala. Is it much further?' She stared out of the window as the limousine sped along, only now realising how distracted she'd been, and how far they must have travelled.

'Does it matter?'

'Yes, of course it matters. People will miss me. They might call the police. I can't just disappear.'

Tadj's expression had blackened into a frown, making him appear even more intimidating. And alarmingly sexy, Lucy reluctantly conceded. The same attraction she'd felt three months ago still flashed between them like an unseen force.

'Why don't you call them, and reassure them?' he said.

'I would if I knew where we were going.'

Tone it down, Lucy thought. Arguing with the Emir of Qalala would get her nowhere. This wasn't the reasonable guy she'd met in a café, but someone else altogether. *And who was she?*

A mother, Lucy thought as she folded her hands protectively over her still-flat stomach. She might hate the role of schemer, but now this opportunity had dropped into her lap, she had to make the most of it.

'What are you hiding?' Tadj demanded suspiciously.

He knew her too well. Even after so short a time, he could read her like a book. 'Nothing.' Guilt stabbed her.

'You seem tense to me,' he observed, clearly not convinced.

'If you'd give me an address, maybe I'd relax. I don't think you'd like to be in this position.'

'I wouldn't put myself in your position,' he assured her coldly. 'And, if I did, I wouldn't make a song and dance about it. I'd find a way out.'

He was distracted by a phone call, which left Lucy to gaze out of the window as Tadj spoke in Qalalan, and the limousine picked up speed as it moved seamlessly onto the Motorway.

'Are you ready to tell me what's on your mind?' he said when he cut the call. 'Perhaps an apology for walking out on me?' he suggested cuttingly. 'I get that you have a job, college and responsibilities. What I don't get is why you couldn't wake me before you left. My take is that you got what you wanted and had no more reason to stay.'

'What I wanted?' Lucy queried, frowning.

'Sex with the Emir,' Tadj derided. 'Was that something to brag about to your friends when you returned to the laundry? Or were you going to sell your story to the press?'

'Clearly not or everyone would know by now,' she said tensely, finding it harder every minute to stay cool.

Even as his face twisted with scorn, her heart squeezed tight to think of everything they'd lost. *Everything?* She *had* got what she wanted that night, but not in the way that Tadj imagined. The explosion of joy she'd experienced in his arms would stay with her all her life.

'I mistakenly thought we had something worth pursuing,' he said in the same cold tone. 'You slept in my arms, but when I woke you were gone. How do you expect me to trust you after that?'

'The way I felt about you frightened me,' she admitted bluntly.

'So you walked away,' he said with a disbelieving shake of his head.

'If I hadn't felt an instant connection, I wouldn't have trusted you enough to stay, let alone have sex with you.'

'I trusted *you*.'

He made it sound like an accusation. 'I wish we could start over,' Lucy admitted, longing for a return to the ease they'd enjoyed when they'd first met.

'I'm sure you do,' he agreed coldly.

'So why am I here, if you're so angry with me?'

'You mentioned a child?' he gritted out.

His tone was like a file, grinding her down…if she allowed it to. 'I never meant to mislead you. I was trying to be realistic, and didn't want either of us to regret what happened that night.'

The limousine slowed and Lucy realised they must

have reached their destination. She stared out of the window to see towering gates illuminated by powerful security lights, opening onto a long, wide drive. She felt increasingly isolated and uncertain as the limousine began its stately progress towards a large and extremely impressive house. An awe-inspiring sense of history surrounded the building that only emphasised the fact that this was Tadj's territory. But she was about to become a mother, the most fearsome warrior of all, and there was no chance she was going to fail her baby, or her mother.

Issues had always been black and white in the past, Tadj brooded as they approached the house, but that was pre-Lucy. Nothing was straightforward now. The depth of his feelings when he saw her in the restaurant had stunned him, as had the discovery that she was pregnant. What else was she hiding? Why should he believe anything she said now?

Yes, he had trust issues. Being abandoned as a child had left its mark, and he doubted his ability to trust could ever be rebuilt. But where Lucy was concerned, was it his pride at stake troubling him most? No woman had ever refused him, let alone walked out on him. No woman had ever moved him enough to care if she had. Doubt nagged at him. When their child was born, would she make a good mother, or would she desert the child as she'd deserted him? He'd believed Lucy to be different: unique, special. Was his judgement flawed? As the limousine approached the house, he remembered a woman in his youth telling him she loved him, before walking out with every portable treasure she could carry, as well as his overly generous loan for her so-called business.

Lucy had asked for nothing, and had taken nothing, other than a surprisingly large chunk of his stone-clad heart.

'Did I hurt you? Was I inconsiderate in any way? Was that why you didn't tell me about the baby?'

'No,' she exclaimed so forcefully he believed her. 'I couldn't get hold of you—no one on your staff would put me through.'

'You didn't try hard enough.'

'Maybe,' she conceded. 'But neither did I want you thinking I was after your support. For all I knew, you might have forgotten that night. And I couldn't put my life on hold for you,' she added, in a reminder that Lucy was no one's for the taking, but would have to be won.

A line of uniformed staff was waiting to greet them. Lucy tensed at his side. He felt some sympathy for her being catapulted into this very different world, and also some admiration for a woman who judged him as a man, not a king. Lucy's brutal honesty was good for him. It was her reluctance to share information he found irritating. It made him wonder what she was hiding. He would make it his business to find out. What could possibly be bigger news than the baby?

His thoughts were put on hold as the driver opened the door, and the formalities of the meet-and-greet began.

CHAPTER SEVEN

LOVE WAS HARD when it was all one-sided. Tadj's formal manner chilled her as he introduced Lucy to his staff. There was no easy path, and she couldn't help the way she felt about him. If love came with blame and guilt and pain, as well as aching loneliness when it ended, she'd take that, for a chance to be with him. And if only it were that straightforward, she thought as she returned the smiles of his staff.

The last member of staff to greet her was Tadj's housekeeper, who invited her inside the Emir of Qalala's beautiful country home, making Lucy feel so welcome she could almost believe this was more than an escape route for Lucy and a necessary pause for Tadj during which time he could soak in the startling fact that she was pregnant with his child and make plans accordingly.

She had just been shown into the library. Tadj was waiting in the huge and very beautiful book-lined room, where the scent of old leather and a roaring fire created a deceptively relaxed setting. Lucy perched on the edge of a sofa, while the housekeeper said she would order tea. When the door had closed behind her, Tadj lost no time making his intentions clear. This wasn't the fun guy from the café, but the Emir of Qalala claiming his prize. 'I've missed you,' he said. 'I believe we have unfinished business.'

His look scorched her, and with a million and one things she could have said—and maybe should have said—what came to her lips was, 'Yes...'

His big stride ate up the room, and within moments he had raised her to her feet. Cupping her face in his hands, he stared deep into her eyes as if he would know every secret in her heart.

With only the thin stuff of Lucy's red dress dividing them, he could feel her heart beating against his chest like the thrum of a hummingbird's wing.

'Nervous?' he queried softly. 'Or guilty?'

'Neither,' she assured him with the spirit he loved.

The sweep of her eyelashes created crescent shadows on her cheeks, making her even more beautiful, if such a thing were possible. She was young and vulnerable, and he should have known better, but when he was committed to a certain path he had never been known to change direction. He'd missed her more than he'd realised, and not just the sex, which, admittedly, had been astonishing. He'd missed Lucy—the essence of Lucy, and every little thing about her that made her unique. No other woman had ever come close, and nor would they. The royal marriage mart was a bank of tedium, full of women who held no appeal. At least, not for him. Who could after Lucy? But he'd always worked in the best interests of Qalala, and he always would, and a state marriage was just one more thing expected of him. Finding a *suitable* wife was—

'Stop,' Lucy gasped, pushing him away as he drove his mouth down on hers. 'You're kissing me as if this is your last day on earth. Why?' she asked, her green eyes full of what he believed to be genuine concern.

'You,' he said honestly. 'You drive me to the edge of reason.'

'Funny,' she said without a smile. 'I've thought the same about you. Truce?' she suggested.

Tempting, he thought. Nothing had changed since their first night together. He still wanted her, and Lucy's response to him said she felt the same. The initial shock of learning he was about to become the father to her unborn child was fading. They were consenting adults with no restrictions, and a loving mistress would always be better than a compliant wife. He kissed her again, this time tenderly, and as he caressed her face he was convinced that a dynamic relationship such as this was infinitely preferable to a negotiated marriage. Savouring their reunion was becoming easier by the moment. They were good together, and good for each other.

'Are you seducing me?' Lucy asked when finally he let her go. 'You're doing a pretty good job,' she told him before he had chance to answer.

Nothing fazed her. Lucy kept his feet on the ground, which was a big plus in her favour, especially when he recalled some of the over-indulged princesses who were paraded in front of him on a regular basis, so he could assess them as potential brides. 'You don't sound too unhappy about being seduced,' he observed.

'Maybe because I'm not.' Her low, sexy laugh vibrated through him. 'Just not here in the library while we're waiting for tea.' She gave a sharp cry of pleasure as he teased her by rasping his stubble just below her ear.

'So, don't scream too loud,' he advised. 'Would you like me to lock the door?' When it came to choosing between a mistress like Lucy and an obedient wife, Lucy made it no contest. His hunt for a wife could wait.

I've missed you so much it hurts, Lucy thought as Tadj brought her into his arms. Heartache, she had discovered, was a real, physical pain. Would it ease, or would it have been better if they'd never met again? For Tadj, she was certain the answer to that was yes, but she must leave the country, and he was her best, perhaps her only chance, so, while this was everything she needed and wanted, guilt reminded her that it was also a form of deceit in its way. This magnificent mansion with its history and elegant architecture only emphasised the fact that it was just a fraction of Tadj's global wealth. Whatever she did or said, when he found out she was using him to leave the country, he could only think she was after his money like all the rest.

'We'll be leaving for Qalala in the morning,' he said, distracting her with kisses.

'So soon.' She knew she should be glad, but, though they'd shared the greatest intimacy of all, they didn't know each other that well, and with every step it seemed she was leaving the familiar behind, and moving deeper into a world she didn't know.

'Don't look so worried,' he said, pulling back to stare into her face. 'You'll enjoy every privilege that comes with the position of official mistress.'

She gasped at the gulf between them, and Tadj's lack of understanding for how that statement made her feel. He couldn't have heard her, as he went on, 'I accept the term mistress might sound quaint to you, but it's all I've got.'

If that was meant to be funny, it missed its mark. 'Your whore, don't you mean?'

Tadj's expression changed in an instant. 'I'm sorry you

see it like that,' he said stiffly. He moved away from her, as if putting space between them would somehow help.

How else was she supposed to see it? Lucy wondered as a polite tap came on the door. 'That must be tea,' she said, realising how close she had come to spoiling her chance to escape the reach of her stepfather. She had a baby to think about now, as well as her mother. This wasn't all about her and what her pride would allow.

Standing up, she crossed the room and opened the door to admit the smiling housekeeper. She even surprised herself with her acting skills as she made space on a low table for the tray. 'Thank you. This is just what we need.' Any distraction would do, even when it came in the form of scones and jam.

'So, you agree to my proposal?' Tadj demanded the moment the door had closed behind his housekeeper.

'To become your mistress? I can't say it's my career goal. If I accompany you to Qalala, it will be because I want to.' *And because I need to*, Lucy silently admitted, feeling conflicted and wretched as she added distractedly, 'And because it will give us chance to decide on visitation rights.'

'Visitation rights?' Tadj exploded. 'This is the child of the Emir of Qalala you're talking about.'

She must calm things down. Everything depended on how she handled this. 'I'll come with you, not because of any so-called privileges, but because I choose to come for the good of the baby.' She drew a deep breath, relaxing a little, because that much was true. 'I'm quite capable of earning my own living.'

Tadj said nothing. He'd turned his attention to some documents on his desk. 'No tea,' he said curtly when she filled a cup and put it in front of him. 'You might as well go to your room.'

She was being dismissed like a child? 'Before I go, I need this address, as well as our address in Qalala. I need to let people know.'

'Qalala?' He glanced up briefly. 'The palace, of course.'

'Fair enough,' Lucy replied, carefully staying calm. 'But I can't just say "country house in the middle of no-where", can I?'

He was silent for so long, she thought he intended to ignore her. This was proving harder than she'd imagined, but if he thought she was a commodity to be traded be-tween countries and palaces at the Emir's convenience, he was about to discover he was wrong.

'Tadj, I—' Her jaw dropped when he picked up the phone and started talking in Qalalan. She was tempted to ask the housekeeper to call a cab so she could leave, but how would that help her baby and her mother?

'Address,' he said curtly after he'd ended his call. 'That is what you asked for, isn't it?' he demanded as he scrib-bled something down on a piece of paper. 'You've got everything you need from me now, I presume?'

If he thought that, Tadj really was a changed man.

'Call the friends and employers,' he insisted as he held out the phone. 'Tell your landlady you're safe with me. What else does she need to know?' he demanded when Lucy stood dumbstruck in front of him.

Perhaps it was hysteria, but she began to laugh. 'You don't know Miss Francine.' Lucy's landlady, the owner of the laundry where she worked, was noted for defending the women beneath her roof like a tigress with its cubs.

'Just tell her we're at my place in the Cotswolds, and reassure her that you're safe,' Tadj rapped impatiently.'

Safe? Lucy doubted she knew the meaning of the word. How would Tadj feel when he found out about her stepfather? Would she be safe then, or would she be prevented from seeing her child and sent home when he realised she had criminal connections? However big the risk, she had to do this, she decided as she placed the first call.

'Your decision about becoming my mistress?' Tadj prompted when her conversation ended, and they were waiting in tense silence for the housekeeper to knock on the door.

'Hasn't changed,' Lucy confirmed, still wondering if this aloof stranger was the same man she'd kissed, and with whom she'd shared such an explosion of joy when they'd made love. When they'd first met he'd seemed so humorous, and approachable, but now her hackles rose. 'How would you feel if I asked you to be my official lover?'

'Pretty good,' he said without missing a beat.

Not so aloof now, she thought, still feeling needled and demeaned by Tadj's suggestion. 'It's different,' she said, shaking her head. 'You're suggesting I become the Emir of Qalala's concubine. Do you know how cheap that makes me feel?'

That's your problem, his look suggested.

'Let's turn this on its head,' she said. 'I ask you to be my lover, making it clear that all I need from you is sex and laughs, with no expectations on either side. When I'm tired of you, I ditch you. I'd like to say I'd give you a pension when you leave, but I'm afraid that won't be possible.'

'Lucy!' Tadj rapped impatiently, 'That is not what I'm suggesting.'

'Well, it sounds like it,' she flared. 'Can't you see how ridiculous your suggestion is in this day and age? No,' she warned when his eyes flashed with humour. 'This isn't a joke. Don't mock me. I need you to take this seriously.'

She was full of angry frustration. No one could frustrate her like Tadj. She never knew if he was being serious or teasing her. The only certainty was that sensible Lucy was nowhere to be found when Tadj was in the frame.

Picking up the phone, Tadj spoke to the housekeeper, asking that she delay taking Lucy to her room for another half an hour. 'Sit down,' he said quietly when he'd cut the line. 'I have something to tell you—to explain to you.'

'Oh?' She took a couple of steadying breaths, which gave her enough time to accept that it might be to her advantage to listen.

'You think I'm being autocratic, but what you need to understand is that Qalala is different, and, though you're expecting my child, the position of mistress is the only way I can have that child recognised in some way.'

'In *some* way?' Lucy exclaimed with affront. 'That's not enough. Either you recognise your child or you don't. There can be no half measures where children are concerned.'

'Please hear me out.'

She agreed with a curt nod.

'Thank you.' Coming to sit on a chair facing her, Tadj explained, 'The constitution of Qalala only allows the Emir to make a constitutional marriage, which is always arranged by committee.'

'You're joking!' Lucy cut in with disbelief.

'Actually, I'm not,' Tadj said in the same measured tone. 'There were many things I wanted to change when I inherited the throne, but the first thing I had to do was to set Qalala back on its feet in order to stop my people starving. My uncle ruined the country, so I hope you can understand that those vital actions were much higher up my agenda than dealing with the country's antiquated laws. These laws also allow for the Emir to take concubines, as you call them, and further allows for their children to be recognised and accepted into society. I imagine the thinking was that these state-arranged marriages might not always succeed, and so a provision was put in place to allow future rulers to find some happiness with their mistresses and children.'

'Wow,' Lucy murmured, utterly lost for words.

They were both silent for quite a while; now Tadj had been so frank with her, she felt she owed the same to him. 'Seems we both have something to confess,' she admitted.

As they stared at each other, she could see that Tadj was wondering what new bombshell was about to hit. Better to speak frankly, and hold nothing back. 'I need to get out of the country fast,' she admitted.

Tadj's expression didn't change, so, inhaling shakily, she told him the rest. 'My stepfather is a criminal and has just been released from jail.'

She expected a reaction, but Tadj's face told her nothing. 'He's a criminal boss with a very long reach, who made my mother's life a misery, and now he's threatening my mother through me. If she doesn't take him back, he'll come after me. That's why my mother begged me to get out of the country. I received the call from her quite literally minutes before I saw you in the restaurant. You gave me the perfect way out,' she admitted. 'So, there you are,' she said when Tadj remained silent. 'I need you to help me, and you want me to be your mistress, so your child will be recognised and not hidden away. If a compromise is possible, I have to consider it…' she waited. 'Please say something.'

Tadj picked up the phone 'I'm calling my housekeeper to show you to your room. Be ready to leave for Qalala first thing in the morning.'

CHAPTER EIGHT

LUCY GOT HER chance to call both her employers while Tadj was speaking to his housekeeper about the latest arrangements. Her second and most important call was to Miss Francine, a woman she had really come to care for. As she stood in the baronial hallway, she frowned as she waited for her elderly friend to pick up, thinking how to frame her news. She didn't want to cause any alarm, so it was crucial to find the right words. Tadj's suggestion that Lucy should become his official mistress was enough to send anyone into a tailspin, let alone a kindly octogenarian. As the log fire crackled, and the phone trilled in her ear, Lucy's thoughts returned to Tadj. Could a man insensitive enough to ask her to become his mistress in this day and age be expected to make a good father?

She didn't get the chance to progress the thought, and had to swiftly rejig her thoughts when Miss Francine answered. Having explained where she was and who she was with, Lucy explained that the Emir of Qalala had invited her to visit his country with a view to putting on an exhibition of the famous sapphires. It was almost the truth, and it was a relief when an excited Miss Francine took over from there. She'd read about the Sapphire Sheikhs, and believed the trip to Qalala to see the sapphire mines with an opportunity to display would make a wonderful addition to Lucy's CV. She chatted about Lucy's college course, and remembered that Lucy had always excelled at displaying various exhibits to their best advantage.

'Take all the time you need,' Miss Francine enthused. 'This is too good an opportunity for you to miss.'

That was one way of putting it, but then Lucy hadn't mentioned the complications. 'See you soon,' she said fondly as they ended the call.

'Maybe not so soon.'

She spun around to find Tadj standing behind her. 'Were you eavesdropping on my conversation?'

'No more than you're abusing your position as guest in my home.'

'I'm sorry—by doing what?' Lucy enquired.

'By talking about me as if I weren't here.'

'Well, you weren't here,' she said. 'And that's rich coming from the man who just invited me to become his mistress.'

Within moments, the battle lines were drawn. Emotions were running high between them, which was no surprise, Lucy conceded, when so much had happened in so short a time. If only there could be more than this, she thought as they stared at each other unblinking. The trip to Qalala was more than she could have wished for, but even that was tainted by the way it had been achieved. She hated this devious game-playing, when all she wanted was an honest relationship.

Between the Emir of Qalala and Lucy Gillingham? Dream on!

It was a relief to see the smiling housekeeper, ready to escort Lucy to her room.

'Mrs Brown will take good care of you,' Tadj said in a neutral tone that suggested Lucy was just another guest in his house. When did he plan the big reveal? she wondered.

'You'll find clothes in the dressing room in your suite,' he added in the same emotion-free tone. 'We'll meet later when you've had a chance to freshen up.'

For a trial run? Lucy's expression suggested coolly.

The housekeeper hadn't noticed, and was already heading across the hall. Tadj's mention of clothes in Lucy's dressing room made her think that he'd had this all planned out; whatever she'd said about becoming his mistress, his decision had been made. A chill ran through her at the thought that, once again, Tadj was in charge. He always had been in charge from the moment they'd met again in the restaurant, she accepted tensely.

'I expect to see you back in the library in one hour's time,' he called after her as he jogged up the stairs. She took his harsh tone of voice as more proof that the fun, uncomplicated man she'd met in a café had disappeared completely.

'You wouldn't be the first to stand and gaze around in wonder at all the treasures here,' the housekeeper said, misreading Lucy's expression. 'And I doubt you'll be the last,' she added with an encouraging smile.

'It's so beautiful here,' Lucy admitted, glad of the change of subject, taking in the stained-glass windows as they mounted the stairs, and intricate carvings on the bannisters and over the doors. 'I've never seen anything like this, except in stately homes that are open to the public.'

'The Emir is a very particular man,' Mrs Brown told her as she led the way.

So, where do I fit in? Lucy wondered. Furnishings, paintings, and more space than one man could ever use, even with a full team of staff, made her feel increasingly superfluous as Mrs Brown led her deeper into the wolf of Qalala's lair. Even the air smelled of money, though it was impossible to fault the restrained and classy décor. Deep-piled carpet soaked up their footsteps, while framed photographs made her pause and finally accept that this fabulous place was actually a home. Home to a very rich man, Lucy concluded, spotting a particularly striking image of Tadj, coated in mud after a polo match. Even in that shot, he looked amazing.

She stopped in front of another framed photograph, showing him seated on rough wooden benches. She assumed this must have been taken at the sapphire mine. Surrounded by working men, he appeared as one of them, relaxed and at home, in dust-covered jeans and a ripped top, his face streaked with dirt. The photographer had caught him in a pose with his arms outstretched to encompass the men on either side of him, and they were all smiling. How she longed to have that uncomplicated relationship. She could feel the warmth between them, even through the impartial medium of a camera. If only she could see more of that side of him, she thought as Mrs Brown led the way. They had reached a broad, light-filled corridor, where one more framed shot made her pause. This one was of Tadj with his friend Sheikh Khalid. Both men were grinning with pleasure, as well they might, as they were holding up handfuls of the biggest sapphires she'd ever seen.

'That photograph was taken in Qalala,' Mrs Brown explained when she noticed Lucy's interest. 'His Serene Majesty loves anything that reminds him of his friends and his homeland. Have you been to Qalala? It's very beautiful.'

As beautiful as here? Lucy wondered as she admired the craftsmanship around her that gave such a sense of history, of destiny.

'His Majesty treats his staff to a holiday in Qalala each year,' Mrs Brown continued as she walked on. 'His Majesty is so generous.'

And so distant from me, Lucy thought with regret as Mrs Brown paused in front of a highly polished mahogany door. 'It's no surprise people love him as they do,' Tadj's adoring housekeeper went on. 'You'll have a wonderful time when you go to Qalala—and I feel sure the Qalalan people will love you.'

'Oh, but I'm not—'

Too late. Mrs Brown had already entered the room, leaving Lucy to wonder if she'd been mistaken for more than she was. She couldn't imagine the Emir's official mistress had much of a public role, but what did she know?

A small yet luxuriously carpeted and decorated lobby promised a more than comfortable overnight stay at least. On top of a gilt and marble console table, one more photograph claimed Lucy's interest.

Mrs Brown heaved a sigh when she saw Lucy looking at it. 'His Serene Majesty asked me not to put so many photographs about, but I think it makes the place look homely.'

'I agree,' Lucy said politely, but with a warm smile for Mrs Brown. There was nothing remotely homely about the man in the photograph. Tadj sat astride a richly caparisoned black stallion. Wearing traditional robes, with his head and face partially concealed behind a flowing

black headdress, he looked more like a formidable con-
queror who took no prisoners than the genial employer
Mrs Brown had described, though the housekeeper's
opinion of her regal employer was to Tadj's credit, Lucy
conceded. She would have known him anywhere. His
eyes were unmistakeable, as were his bearing and uncompromising pose. A shiver of awareness ran down her
spine as it occurred to her that Tadj might not be prepared to compromise in any way at all when it came to
discussing the future of their child.

'Where does this door lead?' she asked to distract herself from such a troubling thought.

'It's a connecting door to His Majesty's suite,' Mrs
Brown explained. 'You can leave it locked, if you prefer,
or open the door, if that suits you better.'

Delicately put, Lucy thought. 'I see.' She did see, and,
though she might have stepped out of her world and into
his, the door between them would remain firmly locked.

As soon as Mrs Brown had left Lucy to her own de-
vices, she decided to freshen up first, and then change
her clothes before going down to the library. Stripping
off, she donned a robe, ready to take a shower before exploring her dressing room. She loved everything about
her accommodation, especially the outlook over the lake.
A lake…imagine that, she mused. This had to be one of
the most beautiful and fabulous houses in the country.
She found the pink marble bathroom and stripped off.
After a moment or two of awestruck stillness, she ran
the shower in a space that would easily accommodate
a rugby team, and stepped beneath the warm, soothing
water. She actually felt her shoulders sag as the tension
dropped out of them. Bliss, she mused happily, relaxing
for the first time since her shock encounter with Tadj in

the restaurant. Closing her eyes, she lifted her face to the warm, refreshing spray. And then heard an unmistakeable footstep.

'*Tadj!*' She spun around on her heels as he joined her in the steamy cubicle. He was stark naked too. 'You've got a nerve,' she exclaimed as her heart threatened to beat its way out of her chest.

'Don't I,' he agreed.

Powered by surprise, she pressed her hands against his chest. Tadj was rock hard, and didn't move. Tadj, hot, wet and hard, was enough to melt the firmest resolve. Animal instinct took over. Anger was a passion, and passion led to lust. They'd been too long apart, and she'd missed him too much. All they'd shared was too fresh in her memory. Yanking her close, he held her firmly against his hard length and kissed her, and within moments she was kissing him back.

There was no point trying to pretend she didn't want this. Pressed up against him with those skilful hands resting on her buttocks, she could only think of one thing. But it pleased her to put up a token struggle, just for the friction of his body against hers.

'Are you saying you don't want this?' he demanded harshly. Dipping at the knees, he teased her in the way she loved.

'Tadj...'

'Yes?' he murmured, knowing she would soon be past speech.

'What are you doing?' she gasped, wanting to delay the moment of mating to make it all the sweeter.

'Water saving?' Tadj's lips pressed down with irony. 'Auditioning for my new role as your lover?'

No need for that, she thought. She wanted to say,

'Hurry,' but refused to give him the satisfaction. And this was Tadj, the man she loved, the man she would always love. 'In your own time,' she said, matching his cynical tone.

He was on fire for her. She was perfection beneath his hands. Every curve of her body might have been designed with him in mind. He might be bigger than she was, but they fitted together perfectly. She matched him in every way there was. Right now, it was her breasts claiming his attention. When he caressed them, her nipples pressed imperatively against his palms. Lucy was all heat. Her familiar wildflower scent intoxicated his senses. Slipping his hands beneath her buttocks, he positioned her, while she gripped his arms as if her life depended on it. The desire to possess her grew stronger with every passing second, as did his wish for the novelty of serving— for now—as her all too willing lover. He was so turned on he was in agony. Remembering the last time they'd had sex didn't help, because it reminded him how big he was, how tight she was, and how it felt to be deep inside her. It was also a timely reminder to take things slowly so he didn't hurt her.

This consideration went no way to discouraging Lucy, who commanded, 'No, don't take your hand away. I like it where it is. If you're my lover, you have to do as I wish, which means following my commands to the letter.'

This was one instruction he had no difficulty obeying, and he laughed softly to see her reaction as he stimulated her the way she liked. 'I'm yours to command,' he said as he thrust her up against the wall. She wrapped her legs around him as he lifted her, and, with water cascading over them, he gave her what she wanted.

Some things would always overrule common sense,

and even pride, Lucy thought as Tadj brought her to the edge of reason, and this was one of them. As she rocketed into the first noisy release, she had to accept that she needed this—him—so badly that she wouldn't be able to think straight until he'd done with her. It was a long time before she quieted, then she realised groggily that Tadj was still kissing her, still moving, as he awakened her to the possibility of more pleasure.

'How did I do?' he asked dryly. 'Do I get the job?'

'I haven't decided yet,' she lied, smiling against his chest. She felt so safe in Tadj's embrace, she never wanted to move—never wanted this to end, but it would end; it must, because Tadj was the Emir of Qalala, while she was an independent woman, building her life and career, who had no intention of throwing everything away on a passion that must surely burn itself out. Becoming his mistress was a short-term arrangement, while being a mother was for life. She must remain free and self-sufficient, though it was all too easy to think they were meant to be together. Reality was harsh, she accepted as he nuzzled her neck and prepared to take her again. Tadj's life would move on, as would hers. 'No,' she whispered.

'No, until Qalala?' he suggested, the same irony colouring his tone, as if he doubted restraint was possible. 'You do well to conserve your strength.'

'I'm looking forward to visiting your country,' she said honestly, 'but I'm making one condition.'

Tadj's brows shot up. 'Which is?' he pressed.

'That no announcement is made about my becoming your official mistress.'

Tadj's expression darkened. No one had ever given the Emir of Qalala instructions before, Lucy presumed.

'You need to get away, don't you?'

'Yes,' she readily accepted, 'but I think more of you than to think you mean to hold me to ransom for that. I have a life, Tadj, as you do—Tadj, no!' she insisted as he dipped at the knees to take her again.

'Tadj, yes,' he argued in a soft, husky tone that tormented her senses to the point of no return.

'I need you to take me seriously,' she managed somehow to gasp out.

'Oh, I do,' he assured her as he did what they both needed, and with the most consummate skill.

CHAPTER NINE

IT WAS HARD to remain unmoved when you loved someone as much as she loved Tadj, Lucy realised as they kissed and touched. She felt safe in his arms as Tadj took her on a journey of pleasure; he made her forget everything, except arousal, which he increased by murmuring words in his own tongue. Even fears of the inevitable emotional fallout when this love affair ended, as it surely must when he returned to being the Emir of Qalala, and she was a working mother, stood no chance.

'Not done yet?' he whispered when she tried to steady her emotion-fuelled breathing. 'Then, use me as you want,' he invited.

'No energy left. You drained me completely.'

'I don't believe you.'

Tadj's darkly amused expression worked its magic, and she reached for him again, with the warning, 'You'll have to do all the work.'

'As your official lover, I expect to. It's my duty,' he said dryly.

'I'm glad you understand your responsibilities,' she agreed, longing for so much more. But Tadj was too good for her to ignore the sensation building inside her, and she groaned to encourage him as he continued. He brought her to the edge quickly, but kept her waiting, leaving her stranded on a plateau of pleasure, from which there seemed no way down. 'Please,' she begged.

'No,' he said flatly. 'In my own time, I seem to remember you instructing.'

He hissed through his teeth as Lucy reached for him. Had he forgotten that her appetite matched his? He took her again, firmly, slamming her against the wall as he dipped at the knees to thrust deep.

'Yes, yes! Please!' she responded in a throaty scream.

'I aim to please,' he said, relishing how tight she was as he set up a firm and regular beat.

'You *do* please,' she assured him, laughing with abandon as she moved vigorously in time with him.

He brought her to the edge and tipped her over, not once, but several times, until he was sure the marble must crack under the force of her screams of pleasure. When finally she lay quiet and relaxed in his arms, he swaddled her in a warm, fluffy towel and carried her to bed, where they made love again.

It was dark when Lucy finally surfaced, feeling very well used and as contented as a kitten.

Wake up! She was no kitten. Allowing her feelings for Tadj to grow was reckless. Giving herself body and soul, when nothing in the future was certain, was just building more trouble.

Stirring, he turned to look at her, hugging her knees and resting her chin on them as she brooded. 'Changing your mind about coming to Qalala with me?' he suggested. 'If you are I'll change it back again.'

Once more couldn't hurt, her body insisted as it overruled Lucy's sensible mind.

The next time she woke, daylight was streaming into

the room, and the bed beside her was empty. Turning her face into the pillows, she heaved a contented sigh and inhaled Tadj's warm, clean man scent. He must be in the shower, she thought. Sitting up, she grabbed a robe, and prepared to go exploring. The connecting door between their respective suites was open, and she could hear water splashing against the marble tiles. She pulled back on the thought that it was better to prepare for the day ahead than invade Tadj's shower, as he had invaded hers. She'd never be ready to leave if she joined him.

As uncomfortable as she felt rifling through all the high-end designer goods in the sumptuously fitted-out dressing room, she had to find something to wear. She settled on a simple outfit of trousers, shirt, and a sweater, then slipped her feet into the softest leather moccasins she had ever worn. They fitted perfectly. Everything fitted perfectly. Tadj had mapped her body with consummate skill, and whoever had gone shopping for him had the same understated taste as Lucy. The exclusive lingerie was the only exception to this rule as it was composed of the finest silk and lace, and far better suited to the mistress of the Emir than a casual guest, Lucy thought as she held up the flimsy garments, only to see light flooding through them. They were lovely and luxurious, but once again it seemed that Tadj was in control. How much stronger would his rule over her become in Qalala? There had to be a way to restore some balance between them, and it was up to Lucy to find it.

There were so many cosmetics, all brand new in their original boxes. It was as if the same person who'd bought the clothes had visited a high-end store and bought up every shade and product on the counter. Ignoring most of it, she drew a brush through her hair and slicked on some lip gloss. Carefully rolling up her red dress, she put it in a laundry bag to take with her. Leaving the suite, she found her way downstairs to breakfast by following the sound of clinking plates.

'Good morning.' Her heart flipped over as Tadj lifted his head as she walked into the light-filled room.

'Good morning,' she replied, trying to act cool, when his look was full of heat, and his husky tone was all it took to make her want him again.

'May I pour you some coffee?' he asked politely.

'That would be nice. Thank you,' she said.

Pausing for a moment in front of the floor-to-ceiling glass walls in the breakfast room, she admired the exquisitely designed gardens. The morning room was decorated in subtle shades that echoed the scene outside. Beyond the gardens, a lake as placid as a plate was home to swans that cruised in a stately white armada. She tore her gaze away as a hovering attendant pulled out a chair at the dining table. The unreality of the situation struck her forcibly as she sat down. Well, that was no wonder when she lived in a bedsit, and her usual breakfast was a rushed mug of instant coffee and a bowl of cereal, Lucy concluded with her customary good humour.

And then there was Tadj.

With his brutally muscular frame, and swarthy complexion, he didn't belong in these refined surroundings any more than she did, Lucy thought, until she remembered he was a desert king.

'I forgive you for sleeping through,' he said as the attendants came forward to offer Lucy countless selections from many different platters of food, 'but my flight plan is non-negotiable,' he added in a curt tone as soon as they were alone. 'We leave immediately after you finish breakfast.'

Should she bolt it down?

'No longer than half an hour,' he instructed.

Now the moment had come and her departure to Qalala was imminent, Lucy had to remind herself of all the reasons why this trip was necessary. Even so, she couldn't shake the feeling that she was jumping out of the frying pan and into the fire.

'Your clothes are being packed as we speak,' Tadj went on, 'so there's no need for you to rush your breakfast.'

'But—'

A single word was all he gave her chance to say before he left the room.

Sinking down in her chair again, Lucy reviewed her options. There were none. She was on holiday from college and had made calls to both her employers, so there was no reason why she couldn't go to Qalala. Apart from any advantage to Lucy and her CV, as Miss Francine had put it, there was a far more important reason to visit Tadj's homeland. Qalala was the other half of her baby's heritage, and Lucy owed it to her child to know something about the country. On top of that, the chance to be with Tadj and see the land he loved through his eyes would tell her more than anything about Qalala, and about the man she loved. Whether he would agree to be her guide, she supposed, would depend on whether she asked the question of the Emir of Qalala, or the man she knew as Tadj.

He was piloting the jet, so there was little chance for him to interface with Lucy. What? *Interface?* To be with her? To drink her in? To inhale and enjoy her familiar warmth

and scent. He wanted Lucy more than he could safely ex-
press, though after what he'd learned about her past and
Lucy's so-called family life, he doubted she would ever
be completely open with him. She wasn't completely open
with anyone. What was it about Lucy that took up every
available space in his brain? She tested his so far unchal-
lenged belief in his own judgement. Her stubbornness
angered and frustrated him in equal measure.

He was accustomed to controlling every situation and
should cut her some slack, he concluded. Lucy trod her
own path, because she'd had to, and was as intent on
doing the right thing, as she saw it, as he was.

Missing her had nagged at him every day they'd been
apart. Even now, seated in the comfortable area behind
the cockpit, she wasn't nearly close enough. He was impatient to introduce her to Qalala, so she could understand why he loved it so much. He was impatient to see
the country through her eyes. Making her feel comfortable in the desert was the first step to installing her as his
mistress. The constitution of Qalala allowed for nothing
more. And he wasn't about to let Lucy and his child slip
through his fingers.

Lucy might be everything he looked for in a mistress,
he accepted with a grim smile as he prepared to hand over
control of the jet to his first officer, but she still seemed
to need convincing of that.

'Take over, will you?' he asked his first officer.

It was a long flight to Qalala, which was an opportunity to further explain to Lucy that an official mistress
in Qalala enjoyed the same freedoms and privileges as a
wife. Slanting a grim smile, he expected his formidable
powers of persuasion to be put to their sternest test yet.

'Tadj...' Lucy smiled as he approached, as if she was

pleased to see him, which was surprising considering he'd been so abrupt with her this morning. She had her own games to play.

'My apologies. I was in a hurry this morning to make plans for our arrival.'

'Oh,' she said blandly with the faintest of smiles.

If he'd stayed any longer in the breakfast room, he would have dismissed the attendants and had her on the table, and that would definitely have delayed their departure.

'I thought you were flying this thing,' she said as he settled down on the seat next to her.

'This *thing* flies itself,' he assured her, 'and, of course, there's a first officer as well as an engineer on deck.'

'What if there's an emergency?' she demanded, cocking her chin to challenge him with this.

'My first officer is a fully qualified pilot. I'm sure he can handle things.'

'I'd prefer it if you were in charge.'

'Really?' He huffed a grim smile. 'Should I be flattered by this sudden reversal in your opinion?'

'Only if you're desperate,' she said.

They were back to the teasing banter. Good, that worked in his favour. Things would be so much easier if they were back on good terms.

'Stop frowning. My first officer will make sure we stay on course.'

'Are *we* back on course?' she countered fast.

'Shall we?' Losing no time to conversation, he jerked his chin towards the rear of the aircraft.

She stared at him for a moment and then left her seat.

'I have a suite of rooms at the back,' he explained as he led the way aft.

'Of course you do,' Lucy murmured with amusement.

'And a private study,' he informed her, 'as well as a rather comfortable bedroom, a sitting room, and a screening room—it's up to you.'

'The study?' she said.

'For a serious discussion?' he suggested.

'Absolutely,' she confirmed.

He'd had something else in mind, but if he learned more about Lucy's experience of her stepfather, it would be useful, not to mention that a part of him was very disturbed by Lucy's fear of the man. He also needed to reassure Lucy that as long as she was under his protection—and what greater protection could he offer than to make her his mistress?—she had nothing, and no one, to fear. And that protection would naturally extend to her mother. He'd had the man checked out, of course, but first-hand information was always welcome.

He opened the door on an informal and very comfortable seating area.

'This is your study?'

He indicated the desk. 'Relaxation as well as my business needs are provided for here. Take a seat,' he invited.

She had everything she wanted to say to Tadj set out in her mind, and it would be a relief to fill in the gaps, but as she dredged up facts about her stepfather she thought Tadj should know about, she was frustrated to notice her hands were shaking.

'That bad,' Tadj murmured as he propped a hip against the desk.

'You have no idea,' she admitted, knowing that they were on the same wavelength as always.

'I have some,' he said.

Dipping his chin, he left a space for her to fill, so she

told him everything: the violence, the fear, her stepfather's unexpected release from prison that had left her mother so vulnerable.

'She's in a refuge now,' Tadj stated calmly.

'How do you know?' she asked with surprise.

'With guards who'll look out for her,' he added. 'She'll come to no harm. I can promise you that.'

There was a tense silence as Lucy took this in, and then she guessed softly, 'Your guards are looking after her.'

'You didn't expect me to sit on the information and do nothing, did you? Your mother will be transferred safely to her own home as soon as I receive confirmation that your stepfather, who broke a court order to approach and threaten your mother, and, through her, you, is back in jail where he belongs.'

Lucy's mouth worked as she tried to take this in, but no words came out, until at last she admitted, 'I don't know what to say.'

'Don't say anything. Bullies have to be dealt with, and I'm lucky enough to have the resources to enable me to do that.'

'Thank you.' It didn't seem enough, when what Tadj had done without seeking any thanks at all had almost certainly saved her mother's life.

'No thanks are necessary,' he said in the same even tone. 'And now you're safe too,' he added.

And massively in debt to Tadj, whom she loved and believed she was starting to know. Tadj's brain was rigidly compartmentalised with the biggest section devoted to duty to his country and its people, and the next devoted to justice. He would never break the laws of Qalala, which left Lucy finely balanced between self-determination and gratitude. Needing time and space to think, she stood.

'Sit,' he insisted.

'I'd rather stand, if you don't mind.'

'And even if I do, I'm guessing,' he suggested dryly.

He towered over her, all-powerful and compelling, making her wish she had sketch pad handy to record the moment that Lucy Gillingham confronted the Emir of Qalala.

'You've been through a lot,' he said.

'So have many people.' Tipping her chin, she stared him in the eyes. 'The fact that we both have should make it easier to talk about the future of our child.'

Tadj made no reply, but this was a good place for them to talk, as there was no escape, Lucy thought. 'In six months time we'll be parents, responsible for a new life. I'm thrilled. I hope you are?'

'You want to know how I feel about becoming a father?' Tadj said in a voice she couldn't read. 'Ecstatic? Is that what you want to hear?'

Was this the Emir of Qalala or Tadj speaking? Lucy's emotions were so messed up, she couldn't tell. All she knew was that they were at an impasse with no tidy answers, and no way she could think of to make this right. There was only one constant, Lucy concluded as she folded her hands protectively over her stomach. She loved this man, and would always love him, and she grieved for the fact that they couldn't be like other couples, and share equally in this greatest joy of all.

CHAPTER TEN

HE WAS ECSTATIC at the thought of becoming a father, but there remained a lot for them to set in place to protect those he cared about. Lucy's expression was wounded. She didn't know what to expect of him. Perhaps that was for the best. He still had many facts and consequences to absorb and consider. The days of keeping royal lives private were long past, which was a good thing, in his opinion, and an idea was already starting to take shape in his mind.

'It's a long flight,' he said factually, 'and I think you should take advantage of the bedrooms on board.'

Was that an order, or an invitation? Lucy wondered as she rose to her feet.

'You mentioned we'd be staying in a palace in Qalala? I wasn't sure which one,' she admitted. 'I didn't realise you owned so many. I really should tell Miss Francine which one I'm staying in to reassure her...'

Tadj shrugged. 'We'll be visiting my fort in the desert. It isn't a prison,' he added when Lucy pulled a face, 'but a building of historic importance that has been completely renovated and refurbished, and I now consider it to be one of my most luxurious and well-equipped homes. Architects and historians worldwide seem to agree with me, as Wolf Fort has recently been designated one of the wonders of both the modern and the ancient world. I always find a stay there refreshing, and I'm sure you will too. It will give you chance to rest as you absorb another part of your baby's heritage.'

'Our baby,' Lucy said. 'Sounds great, but now, if you don't mind, I'd like to lie down…if someone would be good enough to show me to my bedroom.'

She was mentally exhausted and emotionally drained, Lucy concluded as Tadj picked up the phone, but at least everything was out in the open.

'One of the flight attendants will show you the way,' Tadj said coolly. 'I'll make sure you're woken up before we land.'

A moment of pure panic hit, when she realised that the Emir of Qalala could arrange for her to be hustled off the plane and locked away until she had her baby. She'd taken so much on trust, Lucy thought as she snatched a look over her shoulder to see if anything of the guy in the café remained.

'Go,' he said, glancing up from the documents he'd been studying. 'You look exhausted.'

Had she lost his trust along the way? She could only hope not. If this was it, and they could never be close again, there would be a big black hole in her life that nothing could fill.

The bedroom on board Tadj's jet was quite small but well equipped with the most comfortable bed, Lucy thought with a relieved sigh as she settled down on the crisp white sheets. But sleep didn't come easily, and she tossed and turned as she tried to work out what Tadj was thinking. When she finally drifted off to sleep there were worry lines between her brows, but she slept heavily, only waking when the promised knock came on the door.

Having taken a fast shower, she wrapped a towel around her and came out to find fresh clothes laid out on the bed. It was pretty much a replay of the clothes she'd been wearing when she boarded the aircraft. Who'd done this for her? she wondered, tracing the edge of the fabric with her fingers. Time to get her head around the fact that billionaires lived very different lives, with squads of people to anticipate their every need. The engine noise was already changing in preparation for landing, and with a shrug she pulled on the clothes.

Back in the main cabin, there was no sign of Tadj. He must have returned to the flight deck to take over the landing of the plane. She took her seat, and as the undercarriage went down she felt safe in his hands. Outside the window, a spectacular light show of pink, indigo, and gold was the most spectacular welcome to Qalala. The jet was on its final approach to what appeared to be a solitary airstrip in rolling miles of golden desert. By the time the wheels touched down, the purple light of dusk had settled over the land, but far from this being a sinister, or isolated location, Lucy could see vast crowds had gathered. The length of the runway was lined with bonfires, and people were already celebrating Tadj's return. Entire families seemed to have turned out to welcome him home. There were even riders on horseback, dressed in traditional robes, waving flambeaux in the air. The Emir of Qalala was home.

'Are you ready to disembark?'

Lucy turned to see Tadj standing behind her in the aisle. For a moment words escaped her. No more the conventionally dressed pilot, but in traditional black robes edged with gold, and a flowing black headdress wrapped around his head and face. The air of danger and exoticism he exuded was phenomenal. The photograph in his country house did him no justice at all.

'Lucy?' he prompted when she didn't move right away. 'People are waiting for us.'

Tempted to stubbornly refuse to rush, she remembered the countless people who had waited so long to greet their ruler, so she did rush, and was greeted on exit by warm gusts of spice-laden air, mixed with the astringent tang of aviation fuel.

'Shouldn't you go first?' she asked Tadj when he indicated that she should go ahead of him.

A flight attendant discreetly explained that the Emir would exit the aircraft last, which seemed strange to Lucy, but she didn't want to tread on any toes at such an early stage of the visit. Stepping out, she was blinded by lights, all of which were directed at the small platform at the top of the aircraft steps. She was just one of many being used to dress the stage, she realised, before the star of the show made his appearance. The cheers were deafening as the Emir of Qalala dipped his head to exit the jet. As he stepped out into the light his name was chanted repeatedly. With the sound vibrating through her body, Lucy had to remind herself that this man was the father of her child.

After descending the steps and greeting the official welcoming party, Tadj strode away towards the first in a fleet of sleek black SUVs. Lucy wondered if everyone who followed her onto the runway was heading to Wolf Fort.

Tadj's off-roader sped off before Lucy had chance to work out which SUV she was supposed to be travelling in. She had never felt more isolated than she did now, amongst this crowd of strangers, all of whom seemed to know exactly where they were heading. The sense of unreality only intensified as a gust of wind blew desert sand into her eyes. Everyone else was wearing protective headgear, she noticed. For once, it was a relief when a black-clad security guard, in a sharp suit, with a suspicious bulge beneath his jacket, ushered her towards one of the SUVs.

If only Tadj could have given her a few words of reassurance and explained what was happening.

Was this how he had felt three months ago?

Chastened, she climbed into the vehicle. No longer the lover, Tadj was the Emir of Qalala, and she would be a fool to forget it. She might be the mother of his child, but her future in this foreign land was unknowable and uncertain.

They'd driven for miles in the dark, sometimes on the highway, and sometimes on bumpy tracks, when suddenly lights appeared in the distance, and the ghostlike walls of an imposing edifice loomed out of the shadows. The fort was brilliantly lit and didn't appear sinister at all. Flags were flying in celebration of the Emir's return, and fireworks lit up the sky. Lucy's anxiety was quickly replaced by avid curiosity, and as the vehicle slowed to a halt she could see the official party greeting Tadj on the steps of the fortress. Everyone was dressed in the flowing robes of Qalala, and a guard of honour lined the route across a vast courtyard to an imposing stone entrance beyond. It was a disappointment to see Tadj disappear inside the ancient walls, but an elderly man who had stepped forward to greet her introduced himself as Abdullah as he bowed over her hand, and greeted her with warmth, saying politely, 'Welcome to Qalala. I hope you have had a good journey? As soon as I have seen you comfortably settled in your suite of rooms, I will take your order for food and drink, and hand over the agenda for your stay.'

'My agenda?' Lucy queried.

'His Majesty is leaving for the sapphire mines in the morning, and expects you to join him.'

Why couldn't Tadj tell her that? 'The sapphire mines?' she prompted, to the echoing clatter of their feet on the stone-paved courtyard. 'Are the mines far away?'

'No more than a day's ride,' Abdullah informed her with a gentle and reassuring smile. Bowing politely once more, he invited Lucy to go ahead of him into Wolf Fort.

Of course Tadj was busy, Lucy reasoned. He'd only just arrived home. She must be patient. But why did he want her to see the mines? Her surroundings distracted her. The historic fort was stunning and atmospheric, and called for more than one sketch to record this perfect blend of old and new. Behind its towering exterior, she found every modern luxury, even an elevator to transport her to her accommodation, which, it amused Lucy to find, was in a turret. If this was to be her home for the next unspecified number of days, Lucy thought as she turned full circle, it was going to be a magical stay, and she had the additional reassurance of knowing that her stepfather would never find her here.

'Do you like it?' Abdullah asked as she took in the fantasia of silk hangings, jewel-coloured rugs, and gilded mirrors.

'I love it,' Lucy enthused. 'Please thank the Emir for his kindness in allowing me to stay here, as well as all the staff who've prepared so thoughtfully for my arrival.' She was looking at the colourful exotic floral displays, the platters of delicious fruits, and jugs of squeezed juices. The turret suite was an unusual space with curving rough stone walls. These were softened by colourful and tasteful decorations, and beyond the windows she could see the crenellated battlements dressed for the Emir's return with a forest of flags.

'Your agenda, Miss Gillingham...'

Lucy turned in time to see Abdullah placing a document on top of a gilded console table. 'And your menu for tonight,' he added, placing a second sheet of paper on top of the first. 'Though, of course, the kitchen will accommodate anything you care for, and at any time you'd like to eat it.' His face broke into a smile, as if it delighted him to share the pleasures of the fort with Lucy.

'A chicken wrap?' she asked, mouth already watering at the thought as she returned his smile. Pregnancy cravings could pop up at the most unlikely times.

'With extra fries?' Abdullah anticipated with a grin.

'Wonderful,' Lucy enthused, relaxing for the first time since arriving in Qalala. 'Before you go,' she added as he turned to go, 'does His Majesty have a direct line?' She was done with hanging around, leaving the rest of her stay in the hands of fate and the Emir of Qalala.

'Didn't His Majesty write it down for you?'

If she told the truth, that Tadj hadn't offered to give Lucy his private number, she could be stranded in the turret until morning. 'I'm sure he meant to,' she said, 'but in the rush of coming here...'

'Of course...' Pulling out a pen from the pocket of his robe with a flourish, her gallant escort wrote Tadj's number on the top of her agenda.

The door had barely closed behind him when Lucy

pounced on the piece of paper. Reading the item immediately below the telephone number, she saw that she
should be ready to leave by helicopter for the sapphire
mines at dawn. She wanted to speak to Tadj before then.
The tension of not knowing how he really felt about the
baby was tearing her up inside. But his phone rang out.
She tried three times and could only conclude that he'd
decided not to take her calls. He was busy, she reminded
herself firmly.

Pregnancy hormones had a lot to answer for, Lucy
concluded when she paced up and down until she couldn't
resist calling him one last time. After another fail, she
flung the phone onto the bed and decided to call for
supper. After a bath she'd get some sleep. They had an
early start in the morning and plenty of time to talk during the journey to the mine, she reassured herself, until
it occurred to her that she might not be travelling there
with Tadj.

CHAPTER ELEVEN

FLYING IN A helicopter was more fun than she'd expected, though it took a moment before Lucy got used to seeing the ground dropping away beneath her feet through the clear bubble. She wasn't frightened with Tadj in control. He was a font of calm—when he wasn't driving her crazy in any number of imaginative ways. As the black aircraft, with its wolf, fangs bared, Tadj's insignia, emblazoned on the side in gold, soared away from the ground at an acute angle, she wondered if she'd ever seen anyone so focused, so sexy and confident, or so utterly and completely in control.

It was just a pity she couldn't read his mind. In the three months they'd been apart, they'd both changed. The man she'd thought such fun, and so dangerously easy to know, had turned out to be the hard-bitten ruler of a powerful country, while she was the woman expecting his child, a fact that had made her more stubbornly determined than ever to do the right thing for her baby, whatever that cost her in personal terms. She did miss the sexy, teasing guy in the coffee shop and couldn't help wondering what life would have been like with him.

'Okay?' Tadj demanded, his voice metallic and impersonal in her headphones.

'Fine,' she fired back.

She reassured herself that his insignia might be a wolf with its fangs bared, but Tadj cared deeply for his country and its people, and even if she were a passing novelty for the Emir of Qalala, and one he might dispense with once their child was born, she believed there was nothing to fear from him. He wasn't evil like her stepfather, a man whose wealth and power had been tainted by the misery he'd caused.

'Are you warmer?' he asked.

Did he care, or was he just being polite? 'I'm very comfortable,' she said honestly. She was looking forward to the adventure ahead.

They didn't speak again until the golden carpet of the desert gave way to a rough dun scrubland. The foothills of the mountains where the mines were located, Lucy guessed. Tadj confirmed this when she asked him if they were getting close.

'I have a project for you,' he added to Lucy's surprise.

'A project?' She followed his gaze through the floor to the rough terrain beneath them, and then flashed a questioning gaze across the flight deck.

'Your final assessment at college just took on a new and exciting slant,' he said, clearly loving the mystery he was causing.

'Did it?' Lucy frowned.

'Combining business with pleasure should be a bonus for you.'

What did that statement mean?

'Your stepfather's activities have prompted me to take certain steps.'

'Really?' Ice shot through Lucy at Tadj's mention of

a man who could inspire terror inside her like no one else. Besides, what more could he do? He'd already arranged for her mother to stay in a safe house and there was no way her stepfather's reach could extend to Qalala, was there?

Tadj's profile was fierce. This was the Warrior King. She could accept that the Emir of Qalala must protect his country, but what was this project he'd mentioned?

'Can I ask about the project?'

Her voice was tinny in his ear. Even so, he heard a quaver. 'Not now.' Preparations for landing took precedence.

Planning ahead was crucial. He was a forward-thinking man whose success drove the revival of Qalala. No one was allowed to disrupt his plans, not even the mother of his unborn child.

'Who are all these people?' Lucy asked with surprise, as the size of the crowd waiting to greet them became apparent.

'My team at the mine and their families,' he explained as he brought the aircraft down in a steady descent. 'Any excuse for a party,' he murmured dryly. His mood took an upturn as he spotted many familiar faces.

'They're very pleased to see you,' Lucy commented as she stared down.

He had brought Lucy here to the sapphire mines in Qalala, not so she could gauge his popularity, but so she could see the scope of his work, and appreciate the heritage their child would one day enjoy. There was no question that his heir, boy or girl, would experience a childhood away from Qalala. He was excited at the prospect of sharing all his desert lore, and introducing his child to their people, and to the glories of his beautiful country. Of course, as his mistress Lucy could be part of that. He wanted to keep her close. On a professional front, she'd be a positive asset, and he was a respecter of talent, who nurtured it wherever he found it. With the best cutters and polishers and jewellery designers working for him, he was keen to encourage new ideas when it came to displaying the jeweller's art. Lucy had recently won a prestigious prize at her college for work on the various exhibitions she'd arranged, making her an ideal candidate for him to draft into the team.

'We'll be staying here for the next few days,' he informed her. 'Roughing it,' he explained, 'so you'll get a chance to know the business—and me,' he added dryly. 'That is what you want, isn't it?'

'Yes,' she admitted, turning to stare at him.

Even allowing for the restrictions of the sound transmission on board, he detected tension in her voice, and by the time the aircraft had settled on its skids, silence was well established between them.

It was exciting to be here. There was a gritty reality about everything surrounding her, and, whatever project Tadj had in mind, she could only take things one step at a time. She had to make the most of this amazing opportunity to tour a sapphire mine with someone who could answer all her questions. That might not be Tadj, but, if nothing else, this trip would add gravitas to her CV. She had travelled to the source of the precious gems and was about to follow that journey through. With her baby's future to think about, there was no better building block for her career.

And her heart? Would have to take a back seat for now.

Tadj had talked about roughing it, Lucy remembered,

smiling ruefully as she looked around. If this was roughing it, she wasn't the only one who needed to get real.
Tadj could certainly do with a reality check. This particular shelter, situated on the fringe of a city of tents, was as
well equipped as any hotel. There was even a screened-
off area at the back, where she could swim in a rock-
shielded part of the lagoon. The biggest natural bathroom
in the world, Lucy concluded wryly as she pulled back
the hanging dividing tent from lagoon to peer outside.

'Do you like your new quarters?'

Her hand flew to her mouth as Tadj strode into the
pavilion. 'Don't you knock?'

He almost smiled. 'Fist on canvas is pretty useless.'

'You gave me a shock,' she admitted, straightening
up as she turned to face him.

'Don't slip and fall into the water,' he cautioned.

She could hear music in the distance, and its catchy
rhythm only seemed to highlight the tension in the tent.
'There's feasting and dancing tonight,' Tadj explained.
'At the wish of my people, I'll be attending, and I expect
you to be there too.'

Expect, she thought. What else did the Emir of Qalala *expect*?

'I'd love to come along,' she said, determined not to
be overwhelmed by Tadj's majesty at any point.

He shrugged, stinging her with his careless attitude.
She ached inside, missing the friendship that had sprung
up so easily between them on that first night. She missed
the camaraderie and banter they'd shared, but had no intention of grovelling to try to reclaim Tadj's favour. He
might be like a mountain, towering and inflexible, but
he had to move too.

'I'll bathe first,' she said, glancing in the direction of

the lagoon. The chance to refresh her mind as well as her body was well overdue.

'I'll bathe with you,' Tadj informed her. 'You should have someone with you when you swim.'

'I'm a strong swimmer,' Lucy protested as her pulse began to race off the scale.

'And pregnant,' Tadj said flatly. 'All open water holds risks.'

So much for solitude and time to think, but why antagonise him? She could shrug too, and, turning her back, she stripped down to her underwear. One good thing about growing up in gangland luxury was the unlimited use of a heated indoor pool at home, as well as a tennis court, and access to a string of ponies. When Lucy's father had been alive, the same property had been a simple hill farm where Lucy's parents had scratched a living. But they'd been such happy, uncomplicated times. When her father had died all that had changed. Lucy's mother had thought it a dream come true when a handsome stranger had whisked her off her feet, but that fairy tale had soon turned into a nightmare, and the simple hill farm had been transformed into a fortress, guarded by grim-faced men with automatic weapons.

'Lucy?'

The sharp note in Tadj's voice jolted her back to the present. Crossing her arms over her chest, as if he didn't know every inch of her body already, she glanced at him, wishing things could be different. Shielded by the tent, and by the towering mountain behind it, she had thought about swimming naked, but having Tadj join her in the black boxers he'd stripped down to was danger enough. She gasped when he put an arm around her waist. 'Sharps rocks,' he warned. 'Lean on me.'

The water was frigid with ice-melt from the mountains, but as they swam alongside each other Tadj steered her towards the cliff face where a waterfall was crashing down. *What?* She turned to look at him midstroke. If this was his idea of safety, she didn't think much of it. She should have known he'd guide her through to the other side of the pounding cascade where they were completely shielded from the outside world. Holding her in place with his hard, wet body pinning her against the smooth rock, he remarked, 'You swim well.'

Resting his forearms above her head, he made sure she wasn't going anywhere. 'And so do you,' she conceded, staring at him levelly.

She wanted this more than anything, and yet dreaded the moment when Tadj broke down the emotional barriers dividing them, because that meant laying her heart on the line for the Emir of Qalala to trample. Tadj lost no time in claiming his reward. As the freezing torrent thundered around them, he drove his mouth down on hers.

Tadj was a madness she could never refuse—never wanted to lose—and she responded with matching passion. He was as vital to her existence as air to breathe, food to eat, and the heat of his body, together with the chill of the icy water, created a force that went way beyond caution. Upping the stakes, she wrapped her legs around his waist. She gasped, knowing she would never get used to the passion between them. This might not be how she'd planned the immediate future to pan out, but if sex was all they had…

Tadj soon removed her bra and thong, and it was his turn to groan with pleasure as he mapped her naked body. 'Yes!' he hissed between his teeth, taking her firmly with one smooth thrust of his hips. From there it was a crazy race to the finish, while she worked with him, matching his force. They couldn't get enough of each other, so no sooner was one violent release achieved, than they were pursuing the next. Some wild force had possessed them, and as Tadj raked his sharp black stubble against her neck, she bit his shoulder, urging him on with words she barely recognised. They were like two animals in the prime of life, mating fiercely and unaware of anything else.

'Yes!' she screamed, not even trying to hold back when each shattering release had her in its grip. Sometimes sensation could be enough, and this was one of those times. Tadj had always been the consummate lover, and even here in the lagoon, with water crashing around them, he made sure that he extracted every available pulse of pleasure, and when she was quiet again, he teased her into awareness, by moving steadily and carefully, until her weary little bud had sparked back to life again.

'Oh, yes,' Lucy crooned as Tadj maintained a dependable and steady rhythm. Nestling her head against his chest, she let him do all the work, while she rested, floating in the water, concentrating on the place that had become the centre of her universe. He knew just what to do, how to stimulate and encourage, and it wasn't long before she was on the edge again.

'Now,' he instructed in a whisper against her ear.

'Oh, yes,' she groaned thankfully, as he pushed her over the edge into pleasure with a few firm thrusts.

'Once more, I think,' he said when she rested, gasping for breath.

'No, I'm done,' she said groggily, glad of his hands supporting her buttocks as she hung replete in his arms.

'I don't think so,' Tadj argued. 'I know you, and there's more. Shall I prove it to you?'

'Please,' she begged, loving the way his big hands tightened on her buttocks.

'You don't have to do anything, except experience pleasure,' he murmured in a low, husky tone.

How many lovers had used these cooling waters to sate their heated passion? She and Tadj were part of the lagoon's history now. That was Lucy's last thought before pleasure invaded her mind, and, for now, pleasure was enough.

They left the lagoon swimming side by side with long, leisurely strokes. Lucy's limbs felt heavy, and she felt sated. It was almost as if neither of them was in a hurry to return to dry land, where reality ruled. That sense of reality was challenged as soon as she climbed out of the water and spotted a pile of fresh towels left ready for them on the bank. This wasn't her usual reality, Lucy concluded as she wrapped a towel around her body, and the towels only emphasised the point that the Emir of Qalala was never completely alone; nor would his private life remain private for long.

But whatever else happened today, she had this to remember, she thought as Tadj secured a towel around his washboard waist.

Back in the tent, Lucy was surprised to find a silk tunic with matching silk trousers, in a soft shade of cerulean blue, waiting for her on the bed. It was the same style she'd noticed the Qalalan women wearing. Their fashions had intrigued her, as they were more active wear than purely decorative.

'Do you like them?' Tadj asked. 'It's a perfect outfit for the party,' he said, skimming a glance over the outfit.

'The party?' Lucy queried. 'I thought we'd get chance to talk. After all, we've got a lot to sort out…'

Tadj's stare was cool. He'd switched to Emir in an instant. Well, if he thought she was a candidate for his harem, he could think again.

'If my people organise a party to welcome me back, that takes precedence over everything else.'

Gritting her teeth, she reminded herself not to lose her cool. This was Tadj's kingdom, and she was his guest. 'Of course. I'll be proud to be your guest.'

'You'll be attending as my mistress,' Tadj rapped out.

'Do you intend to make an official announcement to that effect?' Lucy exclaimed with frustration. She'd never tacitly agreed that she would become his mistress. In fact she'd hoped he wouldn't hold her to that now everything about her stepfather was out in the open and he'd already put plans into place to deal with him.

Besides, she didn't fit the brief of any man's mistress, especially not the Emir of Qalala's. She was far too independent to be locked away in a fort awaiting His Majesty's pleasure—not to mention the fact that she'd been spared the flamboyant good looks she imagined must be necessary to hold down the post of official mistress. She didn't possess the sophistication, or the class to mix in high society. She was happiest with her friends at the laundry, or with her student chums at college, where she dressed as they did, in cheap tops and jeans. Above and beyond all that, she was about to become a mother, and with a child to support, as well as a career to plan, she didn't have time to waste swanning about.

'I won't need to announce anything,' Tadj informed her with a relaxed shrug, with about as much emotion as if they'd been discussing the weather. 'And, rest assured, I've no intention of embarrassing you.'

'Your people will guess when they see me at your side?' Lucy supposed.

'Correct,' he agreed.

CHAPTER TWELVE

'As we've discussed, arrangements have been made to keep your mother safe.'

'Thank you.'

'However,' he continued, brushing off her gratitude, 'until I receive certain reassurances, you will stay in Qalala.' Tadj's stare was penetrating. 'I understand that you had to get away, and would do anything—use anyone—to make sure that happened.'

'Please don't look at me like that. I never set out to get pregnant, but I'm glad that I am.'

'Can I believe you?'

'You must,' she insisted softly.

'For the sake of our child?' Tadj suggested. 'I suppose I'll never know what you were thinking three months ago. I can only make plans going forward from now.'

Anger surged inside her. They were both in the wrong, and she had no intention of being painted as the only sinner. 'How do you think I feel, when you ask me to be your mistress, to satisfy your sexual urges?'

'*My* sexual urges?' Tadj laughed out loud. 'That's rich, coming from you. Bottom line,' he snapped, before Lucy had chance to speak, 'you're under my protection, and there you will stay—and that includes you, your mother, and the baby.'

'Our baby,' she fired back. 'And my stepfather? What are you going to do about him? No one's safe while he's roaming free.'

'Your stepfather has been returned to jail where he belongs, and he won't be coming out of prison ever again, once my investigators have shared their information.'

Lucy was stunned into silence. She couldn't believe that her stepfather's tyranny was at an end. It meant she was free, and her mother was safe. Tadj had accomplished the seemingly impossible, by lifting a lifetime of fear and dread from her shoulders. 'It's really over?' she whispered as she marvelled at this fact.

'And always will be from now on,' Tadj confirmed. 'I wish you'd told me from the start.'

'We hardly knew each other,' she pointed out. 'I wouldn't burden you with that on the first day we met.'

'All the same, I wish you had,' Tadj told her.

'How can I ever thank you?' she asked.

'I'll think of something,' he promised with one of his dark, unreadable looks. 'But now you'd better get ready for the party. That's one way you can repay me tonight.'

By keeping up a good front, Lucy thought, longing for more as Tadj added, 'Call your mother. Let her know the good news, and then get ready. I'll return to collect you in half an hour.'

'Half an hour,' Lucy agreed tensely, knowing the phone call would take up every moment of that time.

What Lucy could never have expected was that several women would approach the tent just as she had tearfully ended the call to her mother and offer to help Lucy get ready for the party. It was impossible not to succumb to their warmth and friendliness. The way they had welcomed her to their community reminded Lucy of her first day at the laundry, where she'd made so many new friends. Just like them, these women were full of advice on how to wear her hair, and what make-up to put on. Language wasn't a barrier as several of them spoke English fluently.

'You should grow your hair,' one of the women insisted, and when Lucy asked why, she was told that a lover liked to run his fingers through long hair, while another, bolder woman, suggested other uses, when it came to teasing a man into a state where he would agree to anything. Lucy laughed with them, and said that her hair would have to do, and that whatever help they gave her, she would never be glamorous as they were. In Lucy's opinion, their exotic sloe-eyed beauty completely eclipsed her own Celtic complexion with its peppering of freckles. This statement was greeted by a chorus of disagreement, but what would Tadj think? she wondered when one of the women had directed her to a full-length mirror. Gone was the utilitarian outfit she had arrived in, and in its place was a two-piece of such exquisite workmanship she felt like a queen.

Queen for a night, Lucy reflected ruefully as the women tweaked and smoothed the delicate fabric of her trousers and matching tunic. There wasn't much they could do with her short haircut other than to place a single hibiscus blossom behind her ear.

So, hang me, I'm excited, she thought, imagining Tadj's expression when he saw her all dressed up for the party. Even after everything that had happened between them, the prospect of spending time with the sometimes forbidding Emir of Qalala made her face burn and her body sing hallelujah in four-part harmony.

'You look beautiful,' one of the older woman told her. 'The Emir won't be able to resist you.'

'He'll fall in love with you,' another insisted.

Lucy's shoulders slumped. Somehow, she doubted that.

'You're ready, I see.'

She whirled around to find Tadj standing behind her. He was silhouetted in the opening of the tent, backed by the blaze of countless campfires, and the sight of him dressed in traditional desert garb was enough to convince her that Lucy Gillingham was indeed a lost cause. Her pulse was racing, while her body was going crazy in the presence of her all-powerful fantasy desert Sheikh made all too heart-stoppingly real. In a simple black tunic, with loose-fitting trousers and a headdress wrapped around his fiercely handsome face, this desert king was sex on two hard-muscled legs. She was smitten all over again.

Love swelled inside her. As did doubt. The power of his presence was undeniably formidable, but did Tadj respect her as the mother of his child, or was she a convenient womb, to be dismissed as soon as their baby was safely delivered? For a woman who had seized control of her life and had been steering it in a steady and constant direction for some time now, it was unnerving to know that this was one situation over which she had no control.

Lucy's stepfather had been a problem, which Tadj had dealt with in his usual incisive way. She wouldn't be troubled again. Even after everything they'd been through, he wouldn't change a thing, Tadj concluded as he stared past the group of smiling women to the only woman who could turn his life upside down. Lucy looked stunning tonight, though he'd put her on show, and had expected her to behave a certain way, and that while she was vulnerable and her life was under the microscope. To her credit, she hadn't let him down. It remained to be seen how she would handle tonight's raw desert gathering.

Lucy proved to have a natural friendly way with everyone. How could he have forgotten that? he wondered, remembering her many friends at the laundry as he took in the crowd that had gathered around her on cushions in front of the open fire. With one of the older women acting as Lucy's unofficial interpreter, he wondered if the questions would ever end, though she fielded all of them with grace and humour, which was more than he deserved.

She felt his gaze on her, and stared at him in a way that made him want to join her immediately, but it was time for him to receive the fealty of the heads of tribes. He felt her continuing interest as he did this, and briefly wished he could offer Lucy more, but, until the law of the land was changed, Qalala expected him to make a politically advantageous marriage, and to please his people that would have to be soon.

When the formalities were over, he stripped off his top. Lucy seemed surprised when he dumped it onto the cushion next to her.

'Are we about to give a practical demonstration of my place in your world?' she asked discreetly.

Her words made him instantly hard, but he shot her a look, to warn her not to try his patience. No one addressed the Emir of Qalala in front of his people in a disrespectful way. 'I am preparing for the games,' he informed her.

Pulling her head back, she gave him one of her looks. 'Didn't I just say that?'

'The desert games,' he said patiently, though a betraying twitch of his lips might have given him away. No one could make him laugh at himself like Lucy.

'Indeed,' she said, flinching when someone handed him a sabre. 'Don't cut yourself with that.'

'I'll try not to,' he assured her. Dipping at the waist, he brought his mouth close to her ear. 'Rest assured, no one has lost their life at one of these gatherings yet.'

'There's always a first time,' she said brightly.

His warning look was completely wasted, though she did have the good grace to look alarmed when one of the tribesmen brought up his horse.

'Is that thing even safe to ride?'

With a brief ironic glance, he leapt onto the back of his black stallion. 'We shall see,' he murmured.

'Just remember,' she said, springing up and grabbing the bridle, 'you've got responsibilities now.'

'You're beginning to sound like a wife,' he commented as he wheeled his horse around.

'And you're the very spit of a delinquent husband,' she yelled after him as he galloped away.

He should be angry, but he wanted Lucy too much to be impatient with her for long, and, with the heat of competition on him, he was keen to get these games over with, and turn lust into reality. Whatever the outcome, Lucy would be in his bed tonight, where he'd be sure to make her pay, and in the most pleasurable way imaginable, for her unadulterated cheek.

Stay safe, you stubborn son-of-a-she-wolf, Lucy thought, clenching her fists with anxiety as she watched Tadj line up with the other riders, all of whom were mounted on spirited horses. There were women in the mix, she noticed with interest. So why was she sitting by the fireside? She was a damn good rider, and had been happy on horseback since her father had strapped her into a basket saddle on an old Shetland pony when she could barely walk. And these desert games weren't so much violent as skilful, she decided as a huge cheer went up. Riders raced down a torchlit track in pairs towards a gourd hanging from a pole. That was exactly the type of game she'd played with her friends. The first jockey to cut the gourd and return to the start line was the winner. Her gaze flashed to the pony lines, where several likely-looking animals stood waiting...

What the hell was she doing? Tadj's pulse rocketed as he spotted Lucy vaulting onto the back of a half-wild Arab pony. He yelled a warning, but, leaning low over the animal's neck as it broke into a flat-out gallop, she couldn't hear him.

And she accused him of taking risks!

Quitting the race, he wheeled his horse around and chased after her. The track was long and full of riders; so many that the youths whose job it was to hang the gourds could hardly keep up. Just as he reached her, Lucy seized a gourd, spun her pony around, and flashed past him. Brandishing the prize high in triumph provoked ear-splitting cheers from the crowd. She might be a stranger in their midst, but she was their champion tonight, and her surprise win had made her the spectators' favourite. Not his, he thought grimly as he urged his horse to catch up with hers. Seizing Lucy around the waist, he lifted her onto his galloping stallion, which provoked another round of cheers. Not surprisingly, Lucy was distinctly unimpressed.

'What the hell do you think you're doing?' she yelled at him in fury.

'Saving you from yourself,' he retorted grimly as he tightened his grip. Taking her back at a steady canter to the pony lines, he dismounted and carefully lifted her down.

'I don't know what you think you're playing at,' she said, throwing him off. 'I knew what I was doing. That was just an advanced version of the games we used to play when I was a child on the farm.'

'And were you pregnant at that time?' he remarked coolly.

'Don't you dare suggest I'd take risks with my baby,' she warned as he led her away.

'Well, you're not playing games on my watch,' he said, adding, 'especially not dangerous games,' as he escorted her back to her tent.

'Why not? Aren't rowdy games an appropriate pastime for your mistress?' Before he could answer, she added hotly, 'There were plenty of other women taking part— as well as children.'

'My interest is you—and *you*, in case you had forgotten, are pregnant.'

'Really? I'm your only interest? You could have fooled me,' she snapped. 'You ignore me most of the time, unless a particular type of carnal hunger strikes you, of course.'

'Which it never does for you,' he fired back, realising as he did so that, while no one could make him laugh like Lucy, no one could rouse every one of his carefully contained emotions as she could. He had never felt this heated before. Lucy's safety, and that of their child, were paramount.

'So, is it because I'm a woman that you object to my riding in the games, or because I'm your woman?'

'Because you're pregnant!' he roared, seemingly unable to get his point across.

'So now you care?' she mocked.

Pregnancy hormones, he thought as her eyes welled with tears. Upbeat one minute, she was on the edge of an emotional meltdown the next. He'd been doing some reading, as well as investigating, since Lucy had catapulted back into his life, and recognised the signs. 'Of course I care,' he insisted, then realised he was shouting. He never lost control—*ever*. Consumed by frustration, he snatched the sabre out of her hands, and tossed it to a waiting attendant.

'I'm pregnant, not sick,' she insisted as he ushered her inside the tent.

'You're a damn nuisance,' he spat out. 'What if you'd been hurt?'

'You could send me back as damaged goods,' she flashed, her eyes welling again, 'and recruit a new mistress.'

'Now you're being ridiculous,' he insisted with an impatient gesture.

'Am I?' she flared. 'You bring me here with one thing in mind, which is to be your official mistress. Knowing I wouldn't agree, you trump up excuses about some job or other—anything to get me here.'

'Which should tell you how much I care.'

'It tells me you're a complete control freak.'

'And what about you?' he argued. 'Deceit got you here, and has carried you through this far. Am I supposed to think better of you now?'

'I don't care what you think,' she railed, her voice shaking. 'I did what I had to.'

'You do care.' Grabbing her arms, he held her still.

'You care too much, which is why you're always trying to please everyone.'

'And failing miserably, I suppose.'

He couldn't bear to see Lucy hugging herself defensively. 'Yes,' he confirmed. The truth might be harsh, but it was preferable to how they'd handled things so far.

'All right,' she said. Straightening up, she lowered her arms. 'I will stay, but only on mutually acceptable terms.'

He dipped his head to stare into her eyes. 'You're setting terms now?'

'You bet I am,' she told him. 'What's so funny?' she asked. 'Just because you're not used to people standing up to you, doesn't mean I'm willing to fall in line. I need to work to support myself and the baby, but I'm extremely keen to learn as much as I can about our child's heritage, which is why I want to stay on in Qalala—at least while I'm on holiday from college.'

'So, being with me has nothing to do with your decision?'

Frowning deeply, she remained silent.

Shaking his head slowly, he stared into Lucy's fierce and determined eyes. She was as stubborn as he was. 'You are, without doubt, the most annoying woman I have ever met.'

'I would hate to come second,' she said.

'No chance of that.' Nudging her inside the tent, he dismissed their attendants. 'Sit,' he instructed.

'Sit yourself—or am I to be lectured like a child?'

Anything but a child, Lucy was a beautiful woman, who was carrying his baby, and he could think of no better mother. How to cope with Lucy's spirit was a question for another day, but did he want to clip her wings? Could he offer her enough to make it worth her while to stay?

Money didn't interest her, so for once in his charmed life he wasn't sure. 'As I mentioned on the flight here, I have a proposition for you—and it's something that doesn't hang on you becoming my mistress.'

'Well, that's a relief,' she said.

'Allow me to pause while I take in your compliment.'

'So, what is it?' she said, green eyes narrowing with suspicion.

'I'm offering you a job as part of my team in the sapphire division. You'd be paid the same as everyone else. Anything else is up to you.'

'And, what would the job entail?'

'Designing an exhibition for the best of the jewellery. I want to create a heritage museum here on site, as well as a touring exhibition.'

'Quite a small job, then,' she said dryly, but there was a distinct glint of interest in her eyes.

'Quite insignificant,' he agreed, acting stern.

'I'd be a tiny cog in a huge wheel,' she said thoughtfully.

'Correct. But each cog has something unique to offer, and, without it, the smooth running of the machine cannot be guaranteed.'

'You put it so persuasively,' she observed dryly.

'That was my intention,' he confessed with the hint of a smile.

'Are you serious?' she asked. 'I mean, this is like my dream job.'

'Never more so. Why waste your education?'

'If I agree, you can't treat me as if I'm made of glass.'

'I won't hesitate to pass an opinion,' he warned.

'And neither will I,' she countered with spirit.

'I would expect nothing less of you.' And, done with talking, he brought her into his arms.

'You've got a cheek.'

'Yes,' he murmured. 'And you have a beautiful body.'

'When can I see the mine and the museum?'

'When I say you can.'

'And when will that be?'

'You have to earn the privilege.'

As he held her still, she softened. 'When can I begin?' she asked, searching his eyes in a way that made him instantly hard.

'Right now?'

They only had to look into each other's eyes for understanding to spring between them. They were so well matched, and Lucy could always surprise him, he thought as she sank to her knees in front of him, not to bow in gratitude—oh, no, she'd never do that—but to wrap her mouth around him over the fine linen of his trousers until he couldn't think straight.

'Who's in control now?' she lifted her head to whisper.

Throwing his head back, he laughed, but shocked pleasure soon silenced him as she tightened her mouth around. Waves of sensation punched through him, and he groaned involuntarily as he opened his mouth to drag in some much-needed air. And this wasn't all she had in mind. Her nimble fingers were soon working on the fastening at his waist, and she freed him in no time.

The heat of Lucy's mouth on his engorged flesh was indescribable. Sufficient to say that the rasp of her tongue promised release like never before.

CHAPTER THIRTEEN

'YOU NEED THIS…we both do…'

'Witch,' he groaned as Lucy took control.

'Just to warn you, I'm no man's mistress,' she said as he laced his fingers through her hair to keep her close. 'I'm doing this because I want to.'

'Don't I know it,' he grated out.

Lucy's husky tone betrayed her arousal, but this was on her terms, and the challenge she gave him never failed to arouse.

She carried out her threat with surprising skill, but when he remarked on this, she said, 'I think I should know what you like by now.'

With a bellow of agony, he lifted her and dispensed with her clothes. Settling her onto him, he proved her right about them both needing this. Working furiously towards the inevitable conclusion, they brought each other to the edge efficiently, and within a few firm strokes they were plunged into pleasure so extreme it left them sated, and yet hungry for more.

'Not tonight,' Lucy said matter-of-factly. Sweeping up her clothes, she added, 'I'll give you my decision about the job tomorrow, after I've visited the sapphire mines, which will obviously impact on my decision to stay—so you'll get that too.'

'That's a lot of giving,' he commented as they locked eyes. 'Give yourself first,' he advised. 'You'll enjoy it, and it will help you sleep.'

She looked at him as if she couldn't quite believe he could match her for detachment. Whatever it took, he thought as they stared at each other.

Breath rushed from her lungs as he swung her into his arms, and she yelped when he dropped her on the bed. 'You're a very bad man,' she remarked with an expression that teased and tormented him.

'That I am,' he agreed. To pretend otherwise would mean a sleepless night for both of them, and what was the point in that?

Tadj was the most amazing lover. He made every part of her body sing, and he was right about her not being able to resist him. Why should she, when all she had to do was close her eyes and concentrate on pleasure? His steady breathing countering her hectic gasps made her all the more excited, and the crashing release that followed rocked her body and soul. She couldn't chart the moment when extreme pleasure turned to exhaustion, and finally sleep, but when she woke in Tadj's arms in the morning, it was the happiest moment of her life.

'I love you,' she whispered, safe in the knowledge that he was still fast asleep.

He grunted faintly, but didn't stir, which was a relief, because laying her heart bare put her entirely at Tadj's mercy. Tuned to her every mood, he wasn't long in waking. She was lying on her side with her back to him, which meant that Tadj only had to make the smallest adjustment to his position to take her from behind.

Arching her back, she raised her hips to make herself even more available for pleasure. Lazy lovemaking like this was the perfect way to start a day. Clutching a pillow, she concentrated on sensations, and nothing else.

'Better?' Tadj soothed when she tumbled noisily off the cliff edge. Moving convulsively to claim the last pulse of pleasure, she was incapable of speech. 'Is that what you needed?' he crooned huskily, with a smile of very masculine triumph in his tone.

She could only groan with contentment when he started again. 'See what happens when you're a very good girl,' he murmured.

'I can't be good all the time,' she warned.

'I noticed,' he said, seeming pleased.

'And I'm no pushover,' she insisted groggily, with a small contented smile.

'Of course not,' Tadj confirmed.

'Did I detect a faint mocking note in your voice?' she challenged, turning her head to spear a stare into his eyes.

'Did I detect some residual need here?' he countered, teasing her in the way she loved.

To hell with it! Thrusting her hips, she claimed him.

What a wonderful day, Lucy thought, feeling elated as she pulled on her jeans and top after bathing in the lagoon. Her body was still tingling from Tadj's expert lovemaking. She wanted more. She would always want more, where Tadj was concerned, though she was excited to see what came next when they visited the sapphire mines.

First, there was a short journey by helicopter, which Tadj piloted once again, and when they landed, he announced, 'We'll take the SUV from here.'

His excitement was infectious. Gone was the stern and

aloof Emir, and in his place *at last* was the guy she'd met in a café. 'Are you up for it?' he asked, nuzzling her neck.

'For everything,' she said, sharing a scorching look.

He was so hot, how was she ever going to concentrate? Lucy wondered as they climbed into the vehicle. Tadj's profile was all the more appealing for being so stern. He made her want his arms around her. With forearms like steel girders, deeply tanned and dusted with just the right amount of jet-black hair, there was no surprise there. Tadj was a stunning sight, in bed or out of it—but more complex than she had ever imagined.

'Some seams of sapphire are found in rock and call for conventional mining methods,' he explained in the low, husky tone that made her body thrill with pleasure. He glanced across, the heat in his gaze suggesting Tadj knew that Lucy's focus wasn't solely on the precious gems. 'Others turn up in streams, or even in the silt of a *wadi*, and need nothing more than a sieve to fish them out. What?' he asked.

'You,' Lucy admitted. 'I like you better up here in the mountains. You're a different man.'

'Than the one who was in bed with you a couple of hours ago?' His mocking frown teased every part of her as he leaned across to drop a kiss on her neck. 'I'm the same man with different interests,' he said, straightening up again.

What did the future hold? she wondered. It was all too easy to think that Tadj, in his banged-up jeans and a simple black top, really was the fun guy she'd met in a café, and it was tough remembering he was the Emir of Qalala, with a different life from hers.

The trip to the mine brightened things up again. It went much better than Lucy had hoped. She was fascinated by the work underground, where the air was warm and still, and on the ground where the mountain breezes whipped at her clothes as she watched the sapphires go through their initial sorting. Tadj had an enthusiastic team in place, and the very latest in equipment, and she couldn't help but want to be part of it, to the point where she was already working on some ideas for the exhibition.

'I think we could improve things here at your heritage centre,' she told Tadj frankly, when he invited comments from the team. 'You have some of the world's most spectacular jewels on display in what appears to me to be an uninviting warehouse. Visitors should be taken on a journey—a pictorial tour of all the various mining methods, where they can see examples of rough stones before they're cut, and then the polished jewels, both before and after they're set.'

As murmurs of agreement rose from his team, he knew he'd made the right choice in Lucy. Whether that was enough to persuade her to stay in Qalala was the big question, and remained to be seen.

'There needs to be a lush floor covering that creates a hushed atmosphere of wonder and awe,' she went on. 'And, of course, discreet lighting—and music to set the mood.'

'I can see your enthusiasm is infectious,' he told her as they left to smiling goodbyes, leaving his team to discuss the latest ideas.

His staff had arranged a picnic by the *wadi* where he and Lucy could spend time alone. It had rained recently, so the dried-up riverbed now provided a perfect swimming pool, where they could freshen up and cool down after a busy morning touring the mine. As the blistering heat of late afternoon slipped into the cooler lilac light of dusk they settled down to enjoy the feast his chefs had prepared, which was both simple and delicious, made even more so by freshly squeezed juice that his attendants had thoughtfully left cool in bottles they'd tethered in the stream.

Rolling onto his back, he stared up at the bowl of sky overhead, as it turned from a clear, cloudless blue to gold and crimson, as the day moved slowly into night. A chill breeze blew up as the lavender dusk, threaded through with smoky grey, lost its colour completely as the sun disappeared behind the mountains.

'This is even more beautiful than anything I've seen so far,' Lucy enthused softly at his side. 'You live in the most ravishing country. I'm not sure you deserve it,' she added, turning onto her stomach to stare at him with a cheeky sideways frown.

He laughed as he drew her into his arms. He was a man as well as an emir, but when he kissed Lucy Gillingham he felt like the king of the world. Seeing everything through Lucy's eyes had given him the greatest pleasure imaginable today. And she was right in that Qalala was beautiful. He found it even more so with Lucy at his side. 'So, you'll stay?' he whispered, feeling confident he knew her answer.

'For a fixed contract,' she agreed. 'I think that would be sensible, don't you?'

What he thought wasn't printable. Pulling back, he stared at her. That certainly wasn't the answer he'd expected. 'The jewellery you've seen must tour the world in the New Year, which means that time is at a premium.'

'It can't be organised exclusively to your timetable. I have a baby to consider.'

Anger and frustration propelled him up. Why was it that nothing was ever certain with Lucy?

'I have college to finish,' she reminded him as she clambered to her feet. 'I need my qualifications before I have the baby.'

'I have forgotten nothing,' he assured her coolly. 'And, as you have just so eloquently pointed out, the clock is ticking.'

'I'm going home for Christmas,' she informed him.

'Home?' he queried.

'Yes. Back to the laundry.'

'And if that doesn't suit me?'

'Look,' she said, obviously trying to be reasonable. 'I don't want to appear ungrateful for the wonderful offer you've made me here, or spoil what has been a memorable and very special day. I'm longing to work with your team. In fact, I feel quite passionately about it, as if it were meant to be.'

'But you're not passionate about staying with me?'

'I didn't say that. And it isn't true. It's just that some things are sacrosanct to me, and standing on my own feet is one of those things.'

'Even now when you've seen all this?' he said, spreading his arms wide to encompass everything he could offer. It wasn't just a job. He wanted Lucy to stay with him. And, yes, as his mistress to begin with, but things could always change. Like any other country, Qalala needed time to adjust, and in the meantime Lucy would have every privilege he could provide.

'Let me stop you there,' she said when he began to explain. 'I understand that a man like you can probably do anything he pleases, but that first you have to make sure your people are safe and Qalala's boundaries are strong.

I accept that those boundaries can be extended to Qala-la's advantage through marriage—which is exactly why I must plough my own furrow.'

'I care for you more than you know,' he said fiercely.

'Then, let me go,' Lucy said, her eyes welling with tears.

'I can't,' he admitted grimly. 'I want you and I want our child, *here* in Qalala.'

'But when it comes to your duty, you can't. Tadj, there is no easy way.'

'No quick way, certainly,' he agreed.

He could offer Lucy nothing at this precise moment, and he would not raise her hopes with empty promises. 'Whatever you decide,' he rapped out.

Now it came to losing her, reality had struck home forcibly, so that each word he uttered to ease her journey home was like a dagger in his heart.

'You will both be well provided for,' he added in a clipped tone to hide how that made him feel.

Lucy actually flinched as if he'd hit her. 'You're buying me off,' she said.

'I will do my duty by you,' he confirmed stiffly.

'If you can't see how that hurts me, I think we're both right; I must go. There's nothing left to say,' she added. 'But no money. I've never been interested in your material wealth. It's you I care about,' she admitted. 'And you care about Qalala, which is how it should be. We're both bound by promises we've made: you to your country, and me to myself. I don't want half a life like my mother endured, always hoping things will be better. I want to seize life and work hard to provide for my baby. Qalala wouldn't want half your attention, and neither do I. But I do worry about you.'

'You worry about me?' he queried sceptically.

'Yes. If you can't find a way to combine your personal hopes and dreams with what's best for Qalala, I worry that you'll never be happy. And I don't want to make things worse for you, by pulling you this way and that. Nor do I want our baby to grow up with parents at war. It's better that we live apart, and can be happy when we're with our child, than we live together and make each other miserable.'

He took a long time to answer, and then he said coolly, 'That decision is up to you. I would never keep you here against your will.'

'No,' Lucy argued gently, 'that's up to both of us. Because I know you can't change, I'm going to keep to my timetable, and go home as I said I would. I had imagined that when we'd toured the mine, we'd talk and plan for our baby, but you're not ready to do that yet, and maybe you never will be.'

'The sapphire mines bring prosperity to my people, and I won't apologise for focusing on them, because you need to understand what a vital part they play in Qalala's future. You could help with that. You say you want to understand this part of your child's heritage, so stay, and try to accept that my duty to Qalala and its people will always come before my own selfish personal desires.'

'But if you're not happy, how can your people be happy?' Lucy argued with her usual sound common sense. 'And where does our child fit into your master plan? A child changes everything.'

'Do you think I don't know that?'

'Changes everything for both of us, I mean,' she said.

He wasn't used to being lectured and he turned away. 'I suppose you expect me to take you home?' he declared when he was calmer.

'Back to King's Dock?' Lucy queried. 'I'm pretty sure I can find my own way back. I'm equally sure that my going home will be better for both of us. I'll send you my proposal for the exhibition as soon as I've got something to show you. And then, if you're agreeable, I'll take part in meetings online with the team. I don't see a problem handling things that way going forward.'

She was alone in that.

'And when it comes to putting my plans into practice,' she added, 'I'll happily travel anywhere necessary to make sure the team doesn't encounter any snags along the way.'

'With your baby strapped to your back?' he queried tensely.

'If I have to.'

'This is *our* child you're talking about. The child whose upbringing I will take full part in.'

Apprehension flashed across Lucy's face, but she rallied fast to add, 'Then, we'd better make time to talk. As you said, the clock is ticking.'

'I'm sure you've got it all worked out,' he commented bitterly.

'Don't be angry,' she begged. 'I want you to know how much I appreciate this opportunity—'

'Stop! Stop right now,' he insisted. He was done with the emotional battering. 'Make this project part of your final assessment at college.'

'I will,' she said, latching onto his cool tone with what he thought might even be relief.

They really wrung it out of each other, he thought as they stared unblinking into each other's eyes. The bond between them was as tight as ever, and would remain so when their child was born, but when it came to the most basic human feelings they were both hopeless communicators.

'I'll miss you,' Lucy said in a wry, offhand way, but her eyes were sad.

'You don't have to go home right away.'

'I do,' she insisted. 'I've got your brief for the exhibition safe in my head, and we'll keep in touch. We can talk online and make arrangements when my due date is closer.'

To discuss the future of their child via a screen over the internet reminded him of a child sitting on a suitcase, split between countries and two sets of people, one with generous hearts, who had wanted him to join them out of love they weren't afraid to show, while the others' social lives were more important. His worst nightmare was to be that type of parent. 'I'll be in touch regularly,' he said.

'Better that we get on with our lives,' Lucy told him.

Raising barriers so neither of them could see the future was as much his fault as hers, he supposed. His loathing for her stepfather and the damage that man had done to Lucy quadrupled as she turned away to hide her tears. Once hurt, never mended, he thought as they faced up to the long journey home.

CHAPTER FOURTEEN

LEAVING QALALA WAS AGONY. Leaving on a commercial flight, which Lucy had insisted on taking, only made things worse, because she had to hide her emotions and pretend her heart wasn't breaking. That shouldn't have been too hard for someone who had learned to guard her feelings growing up, but it was, because she might be as buttoned up as Tadj, but surely they should have been able to talk and make plans for their baby? Wasn't that more important than visits to a mine, and schemes for an exhibition?

They were both at fault, Lucy concluded. Tadj was duty-bound to Qalala, and refused to grant himself a private life, while she was equally inflexible when it came to remaining independent. Imagining Tadj marrying for the good of his country tore her up inside. It would destroy him, as well as his wife and any children they might have. Was that the reward of duty? If so, duty was a vindictive mistress, and it was up to Tadj to change things in Qalala. She couldn't help with that, and must concentrate on moving forward to build a stable base for her child. If Tadj wanted to be involved in their baby's upbringing, then so much the better, she would never stop him, but could she afford to put things on hold in the hope that he might?

As the aircraft soared high above the cloud line, she was sad for the things he'd miss. She wanted to share the first precious flutters of life with him, so he could feel the joy she felt at that moment. Maybe he'd had enough of her, and was glad to see her go. He hadn't exactly helped her to pack, but once they'd returned to the fort he'd done everything possible to smooth her journey home. On the one hand, she'd been relieved, because there'd been no ugly scenes between them, but right up to the last minute she'd hoped he'd ask her to stay, so they could somehow work this out.

That was a fantasy too far, Lucy accepted with a sigh as she stared unseeing out of the small window at her side. Tadj's position as the Emir of Qalala would always stop him following his heart. 'I'll get back to you,' he'd said at the airport, where they'd both held in their feelings, parting with a dispassionate kiss on both cheeks.

'About the job?' she'd pressed.

'About everything,' he'd said, and then he'd turned and strode away with a phalanx of royal guards surrounding him, keeping everyone, including Lucy, at bay. That was Tadj's life, his lonely life.

They'd have contact through their joint involvement in the Qalalan sapphire project, if nothing else, Lucy tried to reassure herself, and meanwhile she must concentrate on completing her studies and holding down her jobs. If Tadj delegated his side of the arrangements for their child to a member of staff, it would really hurt, but she'd have to get over that too. In this mood of absolute determination, she pulled out her sketch pad and started work on her initial design for the inaugural exhibition of the world-famous Qalalan sapphires.

* * *

Ruling Qalala ran through his veins alongside a rich vein of duty. Those two things had always been enough for him in the past, because he was devoted to his country and its people, but without Lucy in his life Tadj couldn't rest, he couldn't think straight, he couldn't sleep, he couldn't function.

After the longest span of loneliness in his life, action was called for. It was long overdue. If such a thing as a eureka moment existed, this was it, Tadj concluded as he slammed down the lid on the latest stack of royal papers. The most important document of all wasn't there. Hardly surprising, when it didn't exist yet. Now he knew what he'd lost, and what he stood to lose, he was ready to fight, not just for Qalala, but for Lucy and their unborn child.

Having called an extraordinary meeting of the royal council, he read out the marriage act, and when his twenty-first-century advisors heard the pronouncements of a bygone age, they had to agree with him that changes must be made.

'Do I take it that love is in the air?' Abdullah, his child-hood friend who sat on the council, and who had first shown Lucy around Wolf Fort, asked him with barely concealed excitement when the meeting had concluded.

'It means I will marry a woman of my choice,' he told Abdullah. 'If she'll have me,' he added dryly, with a hint of humility that was wholly unaccustomed.

'Lucy! I knew it!' Abdullah exclaimed, practically dancing on the spot with excitement. 'She's a challenging one,' he added as if that were the greatest praise, 'and just what you need.'

Tadj hummed as he strode away to put the change in the law into operation.

* * *

He grunted with impatience as he disembarked his jet. Lucy would be seven months pregnant by now. That was how long it had taken to 'speed along' the change to the law in Qalala. What had she done to him? *Was this love?* The thought hit him like a thunderbolt.

Thankfully, being the Emir of Qalala, as well as one of the richest men in the world, came with advantages, one of which was access to the royal fleet of aircraft as well as a royal yacht, added to which were the lack of formalities confronting him when he landed in a foreign country. His yacht was berthed at King's Dock, and he was soon on his way to join it.

He should never have let Lucy go, and he willed the limousine to travel even faster. Seven months pregnant. Only two months to go. Valuable time in a pregnancy. It wasn't too late for him to share the birth of their child, but they still had to discuss the details of what would happen next, and Lucy had steered every conversation they'd had towards talk of the exhibition she was planning with his team. A child mattered more, to both of them, he was sure. She was still suffering from the damage her stepfather had inflicted, and it was up to him to make a difference, so she could face the future with the happiness she deserved.

He had half expected to find Lucy still working at the laundry. He wasn't disappointed. Ruffled and sleep-deprived, with his collar pulled up against the awful weather, as he peered through the steamed-up window his spirits rose. Serving behind the counter, Lucy was as cheerful as ever as she chatted to customers in her usual friendly way.

Pulling back, he felt the loss of her keenly, as if he

were a child with his nose pressed against the window, viewing a treat he couldn't have, a gift he had forfeited for the sake of Mother Duty. He had to take a moment. Seeing Lucy again wrenched at his heart. There was no one like her, and there never would be. He'd never felt like this before. Laying his heart on the line was new to him. Raw sex and power, together with huge wealth and the mystique of royalty, had always been enough to open any door, but these things didn't mean anything to Lucy. She trod her own path, couldn't be wooed with promises of wealth or position. He would have to dig much deeper than that, or he'd lose her for ever.

The doorbell chimed with irritating optimism as he walked into the shop.

'*Tadj!*' Paling, Lucy gripped the counter.

Horror-struck that the sight of him might harm Lucy or the baby, he was holding her in a second. He should have warned her to expect him. Having plunged over the counter to grab her by the arms in case she fell, he held her in front of him to check she was okay. He could breathe again when the colour returned to her face. 'We have to stop meeting like this,' he murmured, drinking her in with all the fervour of a parched man in the desert.

With a hum, she broke free. The customer had left by now, so they were alone. Lucy had snapped back into work mode, pinning tickets on garments, before handing them through the hatch opening onto the steamy heart of the laundry. She was so graceful, so vulnerable, and desirable. Images collided in his mind of her cool hands on his body, and her soft lips on his mouth. 'Can you take a break any time soon?'

'I break for lunch in half an hour,' she said, glancing at the clock.

His spirits lifted, though he was careful to keep his tone casual. 'May I take you for coffee?'

'In the café where we first met?' she said, staring at him as if seeing him for the first time.

'I'll meet you there,' he confirmed.

'It will be busy at lunchtime,' she called after him as he left the shop. 'Bag a table if you get there first.'

Not the best offer he'd ever received from a woman, but, where Project Wooing was concerned, he thought it a reasonable start.

Lucy was late. Where the hell was she? Was she coming at all? He stared at the door, wondering if he'd been stood up, or if she'd run from him again, to some place where he'd never find her. The thought that he'd been stood up amused him, but if she'd gone—he couldn't even contemplate that, so, ordering another coffee, he told himself to use the time to plan and think. Impatience made that impossible. What use was planning, when Lucy was unpredictable? He had to find a way to pin her down, but he needed her here first... He stared with unblinking attention at the door, as if that could make her appear. She was more precious than he'd realised, which was why he hadn't come here with a better offer, but with the ultimate offer, and one he was confident she couldn't refuse.

If she turned up, that was.

Tadj's arriving at the laundry unannounced had really thrown her. What did he want? Did he think she'd changed her mind about becoming his mistress? She racked her brains to think if there was a single problem where work was concerned, but she couldn't think of one. As she'd thought all along, they could communicate perfectly well over the internet, and plans for the various exhibitions of the Qalalan sapphires were progressing well. Hopefully, he was here to talk about the baby. She longed for a compromise, her heart picking up pace just thinking about Tadj, and discussing with him the most important topic in their lives. The prospect of that was like all her Christmases and birthdays come together. *But* he mustn't think he could rule them as he ruled Qalala.

She hurried to take a shower, and, as she was seven months pregnant, getting dressed meant exchanging one shapeless sack for another. Staring at herself in the mirror brought an image of Tadj into her mind. How could he possibly find her attractive in this condition? And why should she care? Surely that meant he wouldn't want her as his mistress, so that was one hurdle she'd jumped over.

The fact that they hadn't exchanged a single personal word since Lucy had left Qalala was as much her fault as his. She'd thought it better to let things cool down, but that meant he'd missed scans, and hearing the heartbeat of their child. She felt bad about that, but he couldn't walk back into her life and think that nothing had changed. She hadn't been sitting around doing nothing these past few months; if he thought that, he was due a surprise.

Snow flurries were settling on the ground as she prepared to leave. It would soon be Christmas. Before then, she'd stop work and concentrate on getting ready to welcome the baby. Her mother had booked a cruise over the holidays, and Lucy planned to spend the time alone. Several friends had offered alternatives, but enjoying the

festivities in the midst of a happy family would only remind her how much she missed Tadj.

Anyway, enough of that, she thought, mashing her
lips together to blend in the lip gloss. If only she weren't
so pregnant and unwieldy—but she was pregnant, and
she was unwieldy, Lucy concluded with a wry smile, so,
suck it up!

She strode to the café with her head bowed against
the wind. Otherwise, she was in no way bowed, but was
striding to this meeting loud and proud. And, instead
of a shapeless sack, she had shoehorned her body into a
figure-hugging dress she'd been saving for Christmas.
She didn't want Tadj to think her weak, just because
she was pregnant, and she was proud of her baby bump.
Which was just as well, Lucy concluded, catching sight
of her reflection in a shop window. There was no hiding
her condition now, and why should she? With an Hon-
ours accreditation in her back pocket, and the promise of
a great career ahead, she was doing okay without Tadj.
If he wanted to be part of her life, he would have to…

He would just have to ask, Lucy thought wryly as she
reached the café and spotted him waiting inside.

The day was transformed from grey and dismal to something vibrant as Lucy breezed in. Her presence cheered
everyone up, and turned every head in the café. She approached the table he'd 'bagged' as instructed, in a flurry
of flying scarf and watchful eyes. Her cheap red coat refused to fasten over her baby bump, which made her seem
even more vulnerable to him than she had in the shop.
The bitter wind had turned the tip of her nose the same
colour as her coat, which he found endearing.

Standing, he held out her chair. 'How've you been?' he asked as soon as she was settled.

'Pregnant.' Her gaze was steady and long. 'And busy,' she added, softening her tone. 'Did you see the latest drawings I sent?'

'Not only have I seen them, I've approved them,' he confirmed. His team had agreed that Lucy had a real talent when it came to capturing a person's interest before leading them through the story of a sapphire, from its discovery as a rough, unpolished stone, to a glowing gem that added lustre to some of the world's most beautiful women. 'But that isn't what I'm here to talk about,' he said. 'I want to know about you.'

'Me? I feel fantastic,' she said, 'and very excited about the baby.'

'And ready to talk?'

'I am,' she confirmed.

He wanted her alone so much it was eating him up inside. 'I gather you've taken the rest of the afternoon off?'

'I'm not being awkward,' she said, 'but, no, I haven't. I really need this job, and the money it brings in.'

Fortunately, the waitress chose that moment to arrive with coffee, as well as the slices of toasted cheese he'd ordered, anticipating Lucy's pregnancy craving for food. 'I took the liberty of—'

'Brilliant,' she exclaimed. 'I'm famished. But *you* decided *what* I should eat?' she added, frowning deeply. Then she burst into laughter. 'You should see your face. But, seriously, thank you. I'm hungry all the time, and this does look delicious.'

'Tuck in,' he encouraged.

'It won't make any difference,' she assured him as

she polished off the first piece of toast, wedging the last chunk in with her fist. 'Excuse me while I munch this—the baby eats everything before I get a chance. Or, at least, that's what it feels like,' she said, laughing again.

'Take your time, finish up. Are you sure you're getting enough to eat?' he asked with concern as she devoured every scrap of food on her plate, then picked off the crumbs with the pad of her forefinger.

'Haven't you heard about eating for two?'

'Are you sure you're not eating for a litter?'

They both laughed this time, and it felt as if the sun had just come out.

'Quite sure,' she said. 'I've seen the scans. Just me and one baby.'

Carried away on a wave of euphoria, he insisted, 'I still think you need someone to look after you.'

'Do you now?'

He'd been too fast, he thought as she lost the smile, and he would have to be more measured to stand a chance of winning Lucy's trust. Unfortunately, with Lucy sitting there, smiling her challenging smile, that proved impossible.

'Have you finished? Shall we go?' he pressed, standing up, ready to leave.

'Impatient to the last,' she commented as she stared up at him.

'Remember that clock ticking,' he said.

To his relief, she stood too. 'Where were you thinking of going for this talk? I've only got half an hour before I have to be back at the laundry.'

'My yacht's berthed in the marina.'

'Of course it is…' There was a pause and then she said, 'You're not kidding, are you?'

He shrugged. 'Do I ever?'

'Well, I'm not going on your yacht. I don't have time, or the inclination to risk you sailing away with me still on board.'

He curved a smile. 'Why would I subject myself to that?'

'Fair point,' she conceded. 'So, you're really here to talk about the baby.'

'I really am,' he confirmed. 'And talk about us.'

'There is no us,' she said as he ushered her out of the café. 'And I haven't changed my mind,' she added the moment the door to the busy café closed behind them. 'I won't agree to becoming your mistress,' she informed him. 'And I can't be late back, because they're giving me a bit of a send-off tonight—'

'A *send-off*?' he cut in, feeling as if a cold hand were clutching his heart.

'Yes,' Lucy told him matter-of-factly. 'I've decided to set up a small design company—just one team player, namely me. I've managed to save enough from my jobs for the deposit on a small rental property, so I can work from home when the baby arrives. It's all thanks to the start you gave me. News spreads. As soon as the press got wind of the part I'm playing in the tour of the Qa-lalan sapphires, it was all over the news, and the phone never stopped ringing. By the time one becomes two,' she added with a beatific smile as she cupped her hands protectively over the pronounced swell where their baby resided, 'I should be well into my next contract.'

'Bravo,' he said flatly, 'but as you won't be working once the baby arrives I can't see how that's relevant.'

'I'm sorry?' she said.

'Just that,' he said curtly. 'Once our child is born, I'll support you both.'

She stopped dead in the street. 'Maybe I should get back now.'

'No—please,' he added in a more conciliatory tone. 'Just give me half an hour, and I'll explain.'

'I could give you all week, and you still couldn't say anything to change my mind.'

'Hear me out,' he insisted quietly.

She stared at him for a few moments, and then conceded, 'I agreed to make myself available to talk about our baby, and I will.'

'Thank you.'

Available? He seethed in silence as they walked on towards the marina. He had come here to take care of Lucy and the baby, and to do his duty by them, not to have Lucy set the rules.

'I understand how busy you are, so you don't have to do this,' she said. 'You can leave me here.'

'And we'll communicate via our monitor screens? I don't think so,' he said.

'What, then?' she said, throwing her arms wide. 'As you can see, I'm managing very well without you—'

'But you don't have to,' he broke in. 'That's why I'm here. Will you listen to my proposal or not?'

'Not.'

'I beg your pardon?'

She shrugged. 'We need some cooling-off time. I'll be free from around eleven tomorrow.'

'You'll see me now, or not at all,' he insisted as he linked her arm through his.

'You can't just frogmarch me onto your yacht,' Lucy protested as he strode with her towards the marina. 'I have my own life, and free will.' Steel gates swung open at his approach. 'No, Tadj,' she said firmly, pulling back.

Feelings roared inside him, and for a moment he felt like a youth again who'd been played. 'Must we do this in the middle of the street?'

'No,' Lucy said in a maddeningly reasonable tone. 'We can meet again at eleven o'clock tomorrow, when we've both had chance to calm down.'

CHAPTER FIFTEEN

TADJ WAS GRIM-FACED as he returned the salute of his officers as he boarded his yacht. Events had not unfolded as he had anticipated.

This was Lucy, so why expect them to?

The past with all its uncertainties was in his face again, thanks to a woman who had done nothing to deserve his disapproval. In fact, the opposite was true. Rather than wait for him to save the day, Lucy had continued to build a successful future for herself and her child. It was the surprise element of the rain check that got under his skin.

Examining his conscience, he found a few gaps. Had he been completely open with her? Hadn't he filled her in on what he'd been doing? A word or two would have sufficed—would have changed everything between them. Had he expected Lucy to blithely go along with whatever he decided? When had she ever done that? Seething with impatience to see her again, he glanced at his watch. The countdown to tomorrow had begun.

Had she gone too far turning Tadj down? Would she even see him again? Lucy wondered as she got ready for the party. He was the Emir of Qalala, after all, not the guy in the café who'd taken whatever she'd thrown at him in the spirit it was intended. They'd both changed, and no wonder Tadj had lost his sense of humour. She'd had no idea on that first encounter what a rigidly structured life the ruler of a powerful country was forced to lead. Surely Tadj had earned some downtime? No one could ever accuse him of short-changing Qalala. Perhaps it was time to allow the people of Qalala to do something for him. Freeing him to be happy would be a start, and the country could only benefit. No slave of duty could ever give their best, in Lucy's opinion, and she was sad to think Tadj couldn't love where he chose, or enjoy the freedoms she enjoyed. It was duty first, duty always for the Emir of Qalala, she reflected, putting on a sunny face as she came down the stairs and her friends gathered round. They were keen to find out what had happened when she met up with Tadj. There were no secrets in the workplace.

'I didn't want to miss this,' she said honestly, 'so we're meeting again tomorrow morning.'

'You blew out the Emir of Qalala for the chance to be with us?' one of her friends demanded with amazement.

'I wouldn't miss this for the world.'

That same friend looked at her with concern, and then someone else changed the mood as she exclaimed, 'Lucy—Lucy—look at all the gifts for the baby. Can we start to open them now?'

'You shouldn't have spent your money on me,' Lucy exclaimed as she confronted the mountain of carefully wrapped gifts. 'You've gone to far too much trouble.'

'No more than you deserve,' Miss Francine chimed in firmly. 'You're always doing things for us, and now it's our turn to make a fuss of you.'

Excited exclamations greeted the revelation of each

new gift, many of which were painstakingly home-made. She would rather have these genuine tokens of love than all the sapphires in the world, Lucy concluded as she unwrapped them. If only Tadj could understand that.

He had never been more certain that something was right, or that it could slip through his fingers so easily. Losing Lucy was unthinkable. It would spell disaster for them and for their child. She had every quality he'd been searching for in a queen. The only surprise was that he, with his reputation for decisive action, had remained blinkered for so long. Lucy's strength and determination set her apart from the so-called *suitable* princesses. With her natural flair and warmth, she was everything he could wish for. If this were a straightforward business deal, he would have secured her long before now. But this wasn't a straightforward business deal.

Inside his suite on board his yacht the *Blue Stone*, he studied the priceless sapphire in his hand. Everything hinged on his next move. Tucking the precious gemstone into the back pocket of his jeans, he railed at the thought that he must wait. If he attempted to bounce Lucy into a decision, she'd bounce the other way. As a lover his credentials were sound; as a man in love, he had so far proved to be pretty useless. It was time to sort that out.

So, this was it, Lucy thought. Still glowing from the party her friends had thrown for her the previous night, she'd slept fitfully, waking long before dawn had brightened her bedsit. And then she'd spent ages pacing and fretting, instead of getting ready to meet Tadj. She should have drawn up a list—an agenda—something he would understand. Frowning as she chewed her lip worriedly, she stared out of the window at the distant shape of the *Blue Stone*, which was floating like a slumbering leviathan at anchor just a few hundred yards away. It was almost eleven o'clock on a cold grey winter's morning. Even the sky looked like a sheet of ice. Wrapping up warmly would do nothing to protect her heart, she mused wryly as she wound a scarf around her neck. Even her much vaunted common sense couldn't help when Tadj was in the frame. She loved him unconditionally, which made her more vulnerable than she would like. Grabbing her cross-shoulder bag, she checked the contents before leaving the room.

'Call me stupid,' she told her friends and Miss Francine as they gathered around her to wish her well, 'but I'm really excited at the thought of seeing him again.'

'Not stupid,' Miss Francine insisted as she brought Lucy into her arms for a hug. 'A woman in love could never be called stupid in my book.'

Lucy's friends chipped in with their own raucous suggestions, drowning out Miss Francine as Lucy gave her elderly friend an extra hug. 'We make our own luck,' she said as she made her way to the door. 'So I'd better get out there, and get busy making some.'

'Just don't let him walk roughshod over you,' a friend called out.

'Who's going to protect the Emir?' Miss Francine countered.

There was no protection against love, Lucy thought as she said goodbye to her friends and left the shop.

As she fell beneath the shadow of the *Blue Stone*, she could see Tadj waiting out on deck. Her heart went crazy, but when he jogged down the companionway to greet her, they exchanged nothing more than polite kisses on both cheeks. Her lips still tingled from contact with his warm, firm skin, and from the lightest rasp of his stubble. She missed the wildness of their passion, and knew that might never return. Even if it had, she reflected with amusement, on this huge vessel surrounded by officers in crisp whites, it would hardly be appropriate to greet the Emir of Qalala with anything but discretion and reserve. Well, maybe a little more than that, she conceded as she stared deep into Tadj's unreadable eyes. She wouldn't have cared who was watching if things had been normal between them.

'Welcome on board the *Blue Stone*,' the Emir of Qalala intoned stiffly. 'After you,' he invited politely.

So it was going to be formality all the way, Lucy thought with a heavy heart. Once inside the *Blue Stone*, her disappointment was soon forgotten.

'Goodness, this is amazing,' she exclaimed. Talk about leaving one world behind and entering another. This *was* amazing. She felt shabby in contrast to her surroundings. Everything was pristine and polished. 'I thought your friend Sheikh Khalid's yacht was amazing, but this is—'

'Doubly amazing?' Tadj supplied.

'Yes,' she said, staring directly into his eyes. Was that a hint of humour? Was Tadj back?

'Are you expecting someone?' she asked as they walked deeper into the floating palace. Maybe he was expecting more guests, she thought, taking in all the fabulous floral displays dressing the grand salon. It was a blow to think he might cut their meeting short. 'Unless this is just how the other half lives?' she suggested.

'It could be how you live,' he said.

'I believe we've already had that discussion.'

'I believe we have,' he agreed with a look that reduced her to a lustful crisp.

She barely had chance to register this fact before Tadj yanked her hard against his body. 'I'm mad to have waited so long,' he said.

'To shanghai me?' she demanded, shivering with excitement and dread.

Stepping back, Tadj lifted up his hands. She felt the loss of him immediately. He knew what he was doing. Nothing Tadj did was ever unintentional.

'Sit,' he invited in a voice she couldn't read.

'Better not—pregnancy? I might fall asleep.'

'How flattering,' he commented with the lift of one brow.

The tension between them was unsustainable, Lucy thought as she quickly explained, 'I just tire easily.'

'And must be hungry, I'm guessing.'

Before she could answer this, he tugged a bell pull on the wall. 'And then a siesta, I think.'

'Oh, no,' Lucy protested. 'I'm not staying that long.'

A discreet knock on the door heralded the arrival of a parade of stewards, carrying all sorts of tempting delicacies into the room. And she was starving.

Somehow eating made everything seem normal again, and the tension between them evaporated, leaving them free to discuss the future of their child. Tadj was keen that both cultures were given equal weight, and that they must both have a say in every decision.

'A say?' Lucy queried, worrying that her opinion might carry no weight. Tadj held all the financial cards, making it impossible for her to fight him through the courts.

'Don't look for trouble,' he warned. 'You're the child's

mother, so of course your views will be listened to and implemented if we agree they're beneficial. And, yes, I did use the word *we*,' he confirmed.

This was a massive adjustment for Tadj, and he hadn't finished surprising her yet. 'What's this?' she asked as he handed her a document.

'Read it and you'll see.'

Tadj would uphold Lucy's right to independence in deciding how best to mother her child. 'You're giving up all your rights,' she said.

'Because I trust you,' he stated frankly.

Her heart clenched tight, but she had to be sure of his motives. 'Does this mean you don't want the responsibility?'

'Quite the opposite. I intend to take a full part in the upbringing of our child, but it's important that you feel secure. You mustn't ever feel threatened at any point. Carry on working for as long as you feel able to—do everything that makes you *you*.'

She didn't need anyone to tell her what this must have cost Tadj in time and effort when it came to changing things in Qalala, or how far he'd come in personal terms.

'I just have one question,' he said. 'Do you trust me?'

This was such an important moment, crucial for Tadj, yet an image chose this moment to pop unhelpfully into her head. She had never imagined making such a vital pledge while heavily pregnant with grease around her mouth, having scoffed every bit of food in sight.

'Lucy…?'

Turning away, she mopped her mouth with a napkin, which gave her chance to draw a deep, steadying breath. 'Yes, I trust you,' she said with absolute certainty. 'I trust you with my life. And, more importantly, with the life of our child.'

'Then, I have something to say.'

He sounded so formal now, more like the Emir than Tadj.

'Can you say it after that siesta you mentioned?'

Tadj seemed surprised. 'I'm not sure I can wait.'

She stared into his face and a quiver of arousal ran through her. 'You could join me.'

'If that's what you want.'

He sounded so stern, but as he picked up her bag and coat she saw a look in his eyes she recognised. 'It is what I want. We could share the bed?'

Tadj threw her a look that sent her senses into freefall. 'How accommodating you can be.'

'When the offer promises so much, why would I hesitate?'

'Good news for me,' he said dryly.

He was back. The man she'd fallen in love with was back. 'What was it you wanted to say to me?' she remembered as they left the room.

'It can wait,' he said, and, linking their fingers, he led her to his suite.

He'd barely shut the door, when he brought her into his arms and kissed her. 'Marry me,' he said while she was still gasping for breath.

'Are you serious?' Lucy exclaimed, taken completely by surprise.

'What do you think this is?' Tadj growled as he backed her towards the bed.

'Evidence that you're pleased to see me after all?'

He laughed, and with a new freedom, she thought as he demanded, 'Can you be serious for a moment?'

'If I must.'

'I think you must.'

'Marry me, and all this—' he glanced around '—will be yours.'

'I don't want anything but you.'

But he didn't appear to hear her. 'The *Blue Stone* is only one of many assets I own across the world—take your pick.'

I choose you, she thought. The rest is unnecessary. I don't need it. The type of riches he was describing were better suited to a princess, or an heiress, not a working single mother with no time on her hands to appreciate them. They should belong to a woman with expectations, and all Lucy wanted was love.

'I'm sorry. I can't marry you,' she said. 'I can't allow you to do this, when we both know I bring nothing to Qalala's benefit.'

'You bring everything,' Tadj argued fiercely. 'You're everything I've ever wanted and everything Qalala needs.' Cupping her face in his hands, he stared deep into her eyes. 'I'm bringing Qalala into the modern age, and with you at my side I can achieve that faster. And I know you don't expect an easy ride.'

'I never have,' she said. 'But marriage is a step too far. You don't need to feel sorry for me.'

'Sorry for you?' he said. 'I know what you're capable of, which is why I'm asking you to be my wife.'

Lucy shook her head. 'I love you too much to see you sacrifice everything for me.'

'I don't have to. If you love me, it's enough.' Tadj went on to explain how the constitution of Qalala had been amended to allow the Emir to marry a wife of his

choosing, rather than accept a bride chosen by committee. 'You do love me?' he confirmed.

'More than life itself,' Lucy admitted with her customary bluntness.

They stared at each other, and then Tadj said, 'So
you'll marry me.'

'Is that any way to ask?'

The tension broke and they laughed.

'Excuse me, my lady,' he said, making her a mock
bow. But as he got down on one knee, he made a fatal
error. 'As our marriage is already arranged, I should, I
suppose, ask you formally.'

'What?' Lucy exclaimed, in no mood to hear anything more. 'If our marriage is arranged, you'd better
unarrange it.'

'And have our child raised out of wedlock? Surely,
you understand I can't allow that.'

'I don't see that it makes any difference at all,' Lucy
said as he sprang up. 'Our child will be brought up with
love—what else matters? A child needs to feel loved,
and secure and happy. Do you think it cares about a
piece of paper?'

'A royal child will be under scrutiny.'

'True, but you could have asked me first—warned
me that plans for our wedding were already under way.
It is usual.'

'Do you expect me to be patient now?'

'You?' she queried with a glimmer of grim humour.
'No. But I do expect you to grant me an equal say over
everything we do. That is what you promised.'

He should have paced things differently, given Lucy
more warning and a better build-up to his proposal. He'd
be there for her and their child whatever her answer now.

But her answer had to be in the affirmative 'This *is* the best,' he said. 'How can it be otherwise? Do you propose to live on the opposite side of the world?'

'So your concern for appearances has driven this proposal?' she exclaimed. 'Silly me, when I thought you were in love and being romantic.'

'I am being romantic,' he blazed, or he was doing his best, anyway. 'What about you and me? Don't we deserve happiness?'

'No one deserves happiness,' she countered hotly. 'It has to be earned. And never at the expense of anyone else.'

'You can play the saint all you want,' he exploded, 'but please don't expect me to do the same!'

Frustration was hammering at his brain and Lucy was equally heated. Grabbing him, she wrestled hard, rubbing her body against his in her passion. If this was fate, he was destined to get the best workout every single day of his life.

Fate had thrown them together, and now demanded action, Lucy thought as she ripped at Tadj's clothes.

'Slow—careful—don't forget your condition,' he insisted as she battled to get him naked.

'I haven't forgotten anything!' she flared. Pregnancy had made her mad for sex, mad for him. Knowing pleasure was only a few deep thrusts away made her fiercer than ever.

'No,' Tadj said firmly. Standing back, he refastened his jeans. 'Not here like this…'

Hormones snapping left her ready to scream he couldn't frustrate her like this, but, scooping her up, he carried her to the bed. 'Now,' he murmured with that annoying half-smile of his tugging at one corner of his mouth. 'Where were we?'

Stripping her efficiently, he positioned and controlled her buttocks with his big, slightly roughened hands, and then took her with the utmost care, but with the utmost thoroughness too, she was happy to report. One deep thrust with a sensational massaging motion of his hips at the end of it was all it took to tip her over the edge into screaming pleasure. While she responded in time to each powerful spasm, Tadj continued to move steadily, ensuring the next release was upon her before the first had even ended.

'So, what's your answer to my proposal?' he demanded the moment she was quiet.

'It hasn't changed,' she said, dragging in some much-needed air. 'You belong to Qalala and I belong here—well, as close as damn it when I move.'

'Move?' Tadj demanded. 'Move where?' Releasing her, and withdrawing, he swung her around. Horns locked, they glared at each other, until something changed in Tadj's eyes. Had he finally accepted the gulf between them was too wide?

She should have known better. Lifting her, he carried her into the bathroom, where, stripping off, he switched on the shower. 'I need an answer, Lucy.'

His eyes were black, and his body was magnificent. And she, unusually, was lost for words, so she shrugged. 'I'm moving out of my bedsit,' she managed finally. 'It's too small…' She gasped as he backed her into the shower. Turning her to face the wall, he nudged her legs apart with his, and made sure that this was the very best shower she'd ever experienced.

CHAPTER SIXTEEN

MUCH LATER, WHEN they lay entwined on Tadj's bed, Lucy turned her head to say, 'Even after everything you've told me about the changes in the constitution of Qalala, I can't marry you.'

'Because?' Tadj queried, his voice made husky by the exertions of love.

'I can't because I'm not equipped to be the wife of an emir.'

'I beg to differ,' he said, reaching for her. 'I'd say you were extremely well equipped. And as for your use of the word *can't*? It doesn't suit you. I've never known you to give up so easily.'

'You've never known me in love before,' Lucy confessed. 'I can't agree to anything I think might hurt you.'

'You'll hurt me if you don't marry me. Who else will I have to argue with?'

Swinging her beneath him before she could answer, he pinned her hands above her head in one big fist. Teasing her stubborn lips apart, he kissed her, and remained looming over her. 'You're everything to me,' he said bluntly. 'You don't hurt me. You challenge me, and I need that. You opened my eyes to more possibilities for Qalala. The country needs you more than it needs my money.'

'As I do,' she said. 'So stop offering me castles and country homes, when all I want is your heart.'

'You've got it,' Tadj said fiercely. 'My people need love, and that's what you give them.'

'How do I do that?'

'By being you. You make people happy. I've seen you in action, remember?'

'At the party in the mountains?'

'Everywhere. People trust you—as I do,' Tadj admitted.

'And is this how you intend to persuade me?' she demanded as he rasped his stubble against her neck.

'Yes.' And showing no sign of remorse, let alone tiring, Tadj took her again.

Tightening her muscles around him, she evened things up, bringing him to a thundering climax within…um, maybe half an hour. A long time later when her limbs were so heavy with contentment she could barely move, Tadj asked her to marry him again.

'I haven't changed my mind. You've made a good case, bringing Qalala into the modern world, and raising our family together, but—'

'But nothing,' he said. 'We belong together. And if you want me to prove it again…'

'You're not exhausted?'

'Should I be?' Binding her close in his arms, he said, 'Now it's your turn to listen to me. Neither of us has been idle while we've been apart, and I've made the choice of my bride.'

'Do I have a say in this, or is that a command, Your Majesty?'

'Well, it isn't a humble request,' Tadj admitted.

'I imagine not,' Lucy agreed dryly. 'That would be so unlike you. But I do have one request.'

'Name it.'

'I get to organise my own wedding.'

'Granted,' he said, acting stern. 'Though the royal ceremony—'

'Will require expert input,' she agreed. 'That's where you come in.'

'Don't tempt me. Oh, okay,' Tadj conceded. 'I'm tempted…'

There was quite a lengthy interlude before they got back to talking business. 'Be warned, you'll be taking on a lifetime of duty,' he said.

'Don't forget love,' Lucy added. 'Right now my heart feels ready to explode.'

'Indigestion?' Tadj queried.

'Love,' Lucy said firmly, thinking how sexy Tadj looked when he narrowed his eyes like that. 'Love,' she repeated softly, knowing she would stand by this man through thick and thin.

'I ask nothing more of you,' he said.

'Will you marry me for love?' she asked softly.

'Is that a proposal?' Tadj asked, eyes glinting with amusement as he tipped his head to one side.

'Could be…'

'I have something for you,' he said when he'd kissed her.

'What a coincidence,' Lucy replied. 'I have something for you.'

'Show me,' Tadj insisted.

Slipping out of bed, she grabbed a throw, and, padding across the bedroom, she entered the stateroom where Tadj had left her bag.

'What's this?' he asked when she returned and handed him an envelope.

'Open it and see...'

Tadj stilled as he recognised the significance of the black and white image in his hand. 'It's your baby...our baby,' Lucy explained.

'And this is the only time you'll ever see me cry,' Tadj assured her.

'Are you pleased?' She came to join him on the bed.

'You should have warned me,' he said.

'I don't think anything can prepare you for that,' Lucy murmured as she stared over his shoulder at the blurry image of their unborn child.

Tadj couldn't tear his gaze away from it, but finally he looked up. 'You've made me the happiest man on earth,' he murmured. 'I said I had something for you, but it seems worthless compared to this.'

Holding the fragile image to his hard-muscled chest, as if he couldn't bear to part with it, he reached for a small velvet box in the drawer in the nightstand.

Guessing what it might be, Lucy protested, 'But I really don't need anything else, when I've got you, and our child.'

'Which is a hell of a lot more than you must have expected when you walked into that café that day.'

Lucy's heart overflowed with love as Tadj stole another glance at the black and white image. Placing it on the nightstand, he brought her into his arms. 'I think we both got a lot more than we bargained for that day.'

And every day from now on, Lucy thought as Tadj teased her lips apart and kissed her again.

'No. Absolutely not. I can't accept this!' Lucy protested many hours later, when they had showered and dressed, and Tadj's arms were loosely linked around her waist as they stared out across the winter scene on the marina. He had just slipped the most amazing ring onto her finger.

'You must,' he insisted as she stared in disbelief at the fabulous lustrous blue sapphire with its circle of flashing diamonds. 'If you don't, the world will think the Qalalan sapphires aren't good enough for my bride.'

'What a line,' she said. 'If you think you can convince me.'

'I can and I will,' Tadj assured her.

The ring was very beautiful—stunning, in fact, Lucy mused as she stared into its rich blue heart. Qalalan sapphires were as blue as the ocean on a sunny day, and the diamonds around its blue depths sparkled like sunlight on the waves.

'I really can't,' she insisted. 'This ring is the centrepiece of the touring exhibition. We open on Valentine's Day in London, remember?'

'How clever of you to have this most amazing sapphire and diamond engagement ring as the highlight of the tour,' Tadj commented straight-faced.

'You don't even sound surprised,' Lucy noted with suspicion.

'I'm not. Clever of my craftsmen to ask you to try it on, don't you think?'

'You—'

'I intend to stay one step ahead of you,' he informed her with a wicked grin.

'I wish you joy of that.'

'Something tells me I'm going to need it,' Tadj agreed.

'The ring stays with the exhibition,' Lucy insisted. 'And I won't change my mind,' she added as Tadj sank to underhand tactics when he rasped his sharp black stubble against her neck.

'I designed the ring for you,' he explained. 'There isn't another like it in the world. We'll choose something else to take centre stage in the exhibition…something huge and heart-shaped in celebration of Valentine's Day, and far too cheesy for you.'

'You arranged this all along, didn't you?' Lucy accused softly.

'Guilty as charged,' Tadj admitted, lips pressing down as he gave a casual shrug.

'Is it always going to be like this?' Lucy demanded with a mock warning frown.

'I certainly hope so.'

Tadj's mouth had curved in an irresistible grin that warned Lucy to be on her guard. 'I will definitely need to keep my wits about me,' she said, trying to sound stern.

'But not your clothes, I hope…'

It was only a short stride for a strong man to carry his bride-to-be to the bedroom.

EPILOGUE

LUCY AND TADJ's first wedding ceremony had been a small, intimate ceremony at King's Dock on board the *Blue Stone*. They had delayed their marriage until the warmer, more optimistic days of spring had allowed everyone they were close to to attend, including Lucy's mother, who had been home from her cruise and had looked at least ten years younger. The day had been everything Lucy had ever dreamed of, as well as a thrill for Miss Francine, whose laundry had received a complete overhaul, thanks to Tadj's generosity. Miss Francine had taken a full part in the ceremony as one of Lucy's maids of honour, and had been most ably escorted by Tadj's courtly aide, Abdullah.

On that first wedding day Miss Francine had fussed over Lucy's simple wedding gown, until Lucy had been sure it would be steamed out of existence. Much the same was happening today with a much grander dress, as Lucy and her friends and family prepared for the big public ceremony in Qalala. The youngest, and most important bridesmaid, was Lottie, as Princess Charlotte was known. A Christmas Day baby, Lottie had been delivered by Tadj, when she'd proved as impatient as her father. A turkey dinner would never be the same again, Lucy reflected with loving amusement as her mother held up Lottie for a kiss.

The streets of Qalala were packed with locals and visitors from across the world. Who could resist what had been dubbed 'the love match of the century'? Lucy thought, smiling as she counted the minutes until she'd see Tadj. And then she did see him—reflected in her mirror. 'You're not supposed to be here,' she scolded as he strode into the room.

Dismissing everyone, he embraced his wife. 'You didn't expect me to wait, did you?'

'No,' Lucy admitted, thinking what a magnificent sight he was in his robes of state.

'You're not supposed to be so beautiful,' he teasingly complained, drawing her into his arms. 'How am I supposed to resist you?'

'You're not,' she said. 'What's this?' she added as he handed over an official-looking sheaf of documents.

'Your next commission,' he said. 'I intend to keep you working. My fellow Sapphire Sheikhs are jealous of my exhibition, and have asked if you would arrange something similar for them. You'll be kept busy,' he promised. 'Though, not too busy...'

'Tadj,' she exclaimed, guessing that his intentions were far from honourable. 'In a tiara and wedding dress?'

'If that's what it takes,' he said with a shrug. 'Though, please try not to move, or your crown might drop off...'

'I hope you're joking?'

'Joke when I make love to my wife?'

Some time later, Lucy was forced to take a quick dip in the bath, complete with crown, before Tadj helped her to dress again in the fabulous gown he'd insisted on buying for her in Paris on one of their many trips.

'You look beautiful,' Lucy's mother breathed, standing back to admire the daughter she knew would take care of her wherever she lived.

'More than beautiful,' Miss Francine added.

Tadj could only agree with everyone's opinion of his stunning bride, and as Lucy walked towards him on her mother's arm, down the long aisle that led to their future, he knew without doubt that he was the luckiest man on earth.

'It seems like only yesterday that we were sitting across a Formica table, teasing each other,' Lucy told him, long after the wedding feast had ended, and they were alone at last in Tadj's apartment at the royal palace.

'What's changed?' he growled as he dragged her close. 'All this—' he glanced around at the formal gilding and decoration, the marble pillars stretching up to colourful frescoes on a vaulted roof above the royal four-poster bed '—is just the icing on the cake.'

'Are you suggesting I'm crumby?'

'Anything but,' he said, laughing as he removed her tiara and necklace.

In just her high-heeled white satin shoes and a skimpy lace basque, with fine silk stockings, Lucy had to ask the obvious question. 'Would you like me to order coffee to go with your cake?'

'Why waste time?' Tadj demanded as she wriggled out of the rest of her clothes.

There were occasions when it felt good to assert her authority, and others times she was quite happy to let Tadj do all the work…and this was one of those times.

'I love you,' Tadj whispered later, much later, when she was sated and they were snuggled up in bed.

'And I love you,' she whispered, staring deep into his eyes.

'For ever,' Tadj murmured.

'Not long enough,' Lucy complained in a groggy, smiling whisper against his mouth.

'My wife.'

'My husband.'

'My world.'

* * * * *

THE VIRGIN'S
SICILIAN
PROTECTOR

CHANTELLE SHAW

For Rosie and Rob.
You are both amazing.
Just keep swimming!

CHAPTER ONE

THE PICTURE SPLASHED across the front page of the newspaper was damning. Arianna focused her bleary gaze on the photograph of herself, almost spilling out of a tiny bikini top and swigging champagne from a bottle, and shuddered.

Once she would not have given a damn that she'd made the headlines yet again. But that had been before she'd had an epiphany on her twenty-fourth birthday, just over a year ago, and realised that nothing she did would make her father take any notice of her. The only thing he was interested in, besides making money, was controlling her, as he had controlled her mother.

Arianna regularly spent the summer at the family villa in Positano and, although she'd never bothered to learn the language properly, she'd picked up enough Italian to be able to translate the paragraph beneath the newspaper picture.

The return of the Brat Pack!
Once again the offspring of many of Europe's wealthiest families have flocked to the Amalfi coast to spend the summer partying.
Heiress Arianna Fitzgerald was clearly enjoy-

*ing herself with close friend, reality television star
Jonny Monaghan, aboard his luxury yacht.*

*Arianna is the daughter of billionaire fashion
designer Randolph Fitzgerald and has been fa-
mously described in the British press as 'the most
privileged and pointless person on the planet'.*

That particular comment had been reprinted so often
that Arianna was bored of reading it. She dropped the
newspaper down on the patio tiles, feeling too disori-
entated to wonder who had left it where she was bound
to see it, and rolled over onto her back, trying to remember why she had spent the night on a sun lounger
by the pool. Her head was thumping and her mouth
was parched. She had no recollection of how she had
come to be on Jonny's boat, or how she had arrived at
Villa Cadenza. Nor could she remember tying a sarong around her to cover up the miniscule gold bikini
that had been a regrettable impulse buy when she had
been in Australia.

God, she felt awful. But it couldn't be a hangover
because she'd barely drunk any alcohol. She wondered
if someone could have spiked the bottle of champagne
she'd taken a sip out of. Jonny and his crowd—who
had once been *her* crowd—used cocaine and other so-
called recreational substances to alleviate their termi-
nal boredom. But, although Arianna had partied as hard
and as frequently as her peers, she'd never taken drugs,
because she had seen the devastating effects they'd had
on some of her friends.

As she lay there trying to summon the energy to
get up off the lounger and go into the house, she heard
footsteps on the marble tiles, and the aroma of coffee

assailed her senses. Good old Filippo. The butler had been kind to Arianna when she'd been a child—unlike most of the temporary nannies her father had employed to look after her during the school holidays. She had attended an exclusive English boarding school but her refusal to accept any kind of authority had led to her being expelled when she'd been fifteen.

Filippo was one of the few people who had not seemed to disapprove of her when she'd been a surly pre-teen and then a rebellious young adult. She could also testify that the butler's secret recipe for a hangover cure worked. But what she craved right now was strong black coffee.

The footsteps halted and Arianna frowned. It was true she had never paid any attention to Filippo's footwear before, but she was sure he did not usually wear heavy-duty black leather boots. Or faded denim jeans. She lifted her gaze and discovered that the waistband of the jeans sat low on a pair of lean hips, above which was a black T-shirt stretched tight over a flat stomach and a broad, impressively muscular chest.

The man, who was definitely too tall to be Filippo, was carrying a tray. Had her father employed a new butler? She craned her neck so that her gaze reached the man's face and her heart crashed against her ribs.

'Who are you? And where's Filippo?' Her voice sounded husky because her throat was dry, not because the stranger's stunning good looks had taken her breath away, she assured herself.

'My name is Santino Vasari. I'm your new bodyguard.' The deep rumble of his voice, as sensuous as dark molasses, had a peculiar effect on Arianna's insides. 'Your father said he would let you know that he had hired me.'

'Oh, yes.' The fog around her brain was clearing and she remembered the text she'd received from her father yesterday when she had arrived in London on a long-haul flight from Sydney. Stupidly, her heart had leapt when she'd seen Randolph's name flash up on her phone's screen. She'd wondered if he'd missed her while she had been in Australia for six months. But the message had simply said that a bodyguard would meet her at Villa Cadenza, and that Santino Vasari was an ex-soldier who had turned to private protection work after he'd left the army.

His incredible physique certainly suggested that he had been in the armed forces. Arianna licked her dry lips with the tip of her tongue and flushed when his gaze focused on her mouth. She felt at a disadvantage sprawled on the sun bed while his eyes roamed over the silk sarong that had become bunched up around her thighs before he continued a leisurely inspection of her bare legs. She was used to attracting attention. Indeed, she had spent much of the past decade seeking notoriety and scandal. But something about Santino Vasari and her unexpected reaction to him made her sit up and swing her legs over the side of the lounger.

She winced as the movement exacerbated her pounding headache and the smirk on Santino's lips sent a sizzle of temper through her.

'I did not ask for a bodyguard. You have had a wasted journey here,' she said abruptly. Her cut-glass English accent was as sharp as a razor. 'I don't want you, Mr Vasari.'

'Is that a fact?' There was disbelief in his lazy drawl.

An arrogant, almost cocky confidence that every woman who laid eyes on him wanted him. His self-assurance was probably not misplaced, Arianna acknowledged. 'Handsome' did not come close to describing the ruggedly masculine beauty of his chiselled features: the slashing lines of his cheekbones that emphasised the harsh angles of his face and the square, worryingly determined jaw, covered with dark stubble the same colour as the almost black hair that curled rebelliously over his collar.

Santino Vasari did not appear to be fazed by her frosty attitude. He strolled towards her, moving with a loose-limbed grace that reminded Arianna of a prowling lion—silent, purposeful and decidedly dangerous. His manner was relaxed but his eyes—startlingly green eyes that gleamed as brightly as peridots—were watchful and unsettlingly perceptive.

Her heart gave another hard kick in her chest when he dropped his gaze to the swell of her breasts. Heat surged through her. She felt her nipples pucker but managed to resist the urge to glance down to see if they were visible through her bikini top. No other man had ever had such a potent effect on her. Not one. She'd come to the conclusion some time ago that she had a low sex drive—or maybe she was frigid, as an ex-boyfriend had told her when she had refused to have sex with him.

Arianna lifted her chin and forced herself to meet Santino's mocking look with cool indifference. But when he placed the tray on a low table, before he pulled a chair up close to her sun bed and sat down, her heartbeat accelerated. Her senses seemed more acute and she breathed in the spicy sandalwood scent of his aftershave carried on the warm, early morning air.

'You see, Arianna…' he murmured, and she quickly tore her gaze from his mouth. 'May I call you Arianna? "Miss Fitzgerald" is frankly a bit of a mouthful when we are going to be spending a lot of time together.'

'The hell we are!'

He ignored her angry outburst. 'Whether you like it or not your father has hired me to be your protection officer, which means that I will accompany you every time you leave the house.'

She drummed her long, perfectly manicured nails on the arm of the sun lounger. 'Why has Randolph developed a sudden urge to protect me when he has never shown any concern for me before? And why does he think I need protecting while I'm here? Positano has a low crime rate, and I'm well known in the area. I've been coming here every summer since I was a child.'

'You certainly announced your arrival in Amalfi,' Santino said in a dry tone. He picked up the newspaper. 'You were still asleep when I brought you a copy of today's paper. The picture of you fooling around with your sailor boyfriend made the front page of many of the English and European tabloids, as well as the local press here on the Amalfi Coast. Anyone who wants to find you won't have to look very hard.'

Arianna shrugged to hide her discomfiture that she'd been unaware of his presence while she'd slept. It made her feel vulnerable, somehow, knowing that he was the only man who had ever seen her asleep. 'I don't suppose anyone will be looking for me. Most of my friends are aware that I spend the summer in Positano.'

She wondered why Santino had sounded terse, but as she stared at the newspaper she suddenly understood.

'I'm not stupid, Mr Vasari. I am aware of the reason why my father hired you.'

She thought that he tensed, although she couldn't be sure. His eyes narrowed on her face but his tone bordered on uninterested as he murmured, 'And what reason is that?'

'Randolph employed you to make sure that I keep out of trouble and out of the papers, didn't he?'

'You have a well-documented history of getting into trouble.' Santino flicked his gaze back to the newspaper photo, and the look of contempt that crossed his hard features filled Arianna with an emotion that she was startled to realise was shame.

She had never cared what other people thought of her, or at least that was what she had tried to convince herself. The scathing words of the headmistress who had expelled her from her school—that she would amount to nothing in life unless she changed her attitude—still stung ten years later. But, Arianna assured herself, she absolutely did not care what a man who made a living from looking menacing, and who was probably all brawn and no brains, thought of her.

'Drinking yourself to oblivion and flaunting your body like a hooker seems like pretty stupid behaviour in my opinion,' Santino Vasari said, and something in his tone made her feel as small and insignificant as she'd felt all those years ago in the headmistress's office.

Her jaw dropped. No one had ever spoken to her quite so bluntly before, and the thought struck her that if her father *had* criticised her just once it would have been an indication that he cared about her. But Randolph's lack of interest had led to her running wild throughout her teenage years and she'd behaved like the spoilt brat that the tabloids, and the odious man who was sitting too close to her and invading her personal space, believed she was.

'I did not ask for, nor am I the least bit interested in, your opinion,' she informed Santino icily.

The glitter in his green eyes sent a frisson of excitement through her when she realised that he was struggling to control his temper. At least she made him feel *something*—which she had never achieved with her father.

'I expected you to arrive at Naples airport on a flight from London yesterday. But, when I went to meet you, you didn't show up,' he said curtly. 'How did you get to Positano?'

She shrugged. 'At Heathrow I bumped into a friend, Davina, who was about to fly to Amalfi on her father's company jet and she invited me to go with her.' It was all coming back to Arianna now. The private jet had landed at an airfield near to the Amalfi coast and Davina had arranged to join Jonny and a group of friends on his yacht *Sun Princess*.

By then it had been something like thirty-nine hours since Arianna had left Sydney and she had hardly eaten or drunk anything in that time. She'd been too tired to argue when Jonny had pulled her onto the yacht, saying that he would take her along the coast to Positano. All she had wanted to do was sleep, but with a party in full swing it had been impossible. At least sunbathing on the deck had allowed her to close her eyes, and she had worn the gold bikini for the first time without realising how inadequately the tiny triangles of material covered her breasts.

When someone had passed her a bottle of champagne, she'd taken a sip to quench her thirst. It was bad luck that just then a speedboat had raced alongside the yacht and the paparazzi on board had taken the photograph which had made it onto the front page of the newspapers.

She glanced at Santino's arresting face. He was not handsome in a pretty sense, unlike some of the male models with whom she had worked on fashion shoots. Featuring on the front covers of upmarket glossy magazines was her only claim to a career, she acknowledged ruefully.

Santino's hard-boned features and powerfully muscular physique exuded a raw masculinity and brooding sensuality that evoked a visceral longing deep in Arianna's pelvis. Her reaction shocked her. For all of her adult life she had flirted and acted the role of a siren, tempting men with her beauty. But she'd never felt desire or chemistry, or whatever this wild heat in her blood was called.

Inexplicably she found herself tempted to explain the true version of what had happened on the yacht. Even more oddly, she considered telling him the truth about herself: that she had finally grown up and wanted to make something good out of her life. But he probably wouldn't believe her, and he would not care anyway. No one ever had. Not her business-obsessed father or her mother who, when Arianna had been a child, had abandoned her for a lover and a new life on the other side of the world.

She watched Santino press the plunger down on the cafetière and pour coffee into the single cup on the tray. Eagerly she reached out her hand to take the cup but he lifted it to his lips and took a long sip.

'It's good coffee,' he murmured appreciatively. 'I suggest you go and get yourself some. You look as though you could do with a dose of caffeine.'

She flushed, wondering if she looked as bad as he had implied. She ran her fingers through her tangled hair and guessed she looked a wreck after she'd travelled from one time zone to another. Her body clock had gone haywire and she wasn't suffering from a hangover but severe dehydration. 'I assumed that Filippo had asked you to deliver the coffee to me,' she said sharply.

'The butler was whizzing up a concoction of what looked like raw eggs and spinach in a blender.' Santino gave a shrug. 'Filippo told me he usually makes the smoothie to cure your hangover after you've had a heavy night of partying.'

He removed the cover from a plate to reveal Arianna's favourite breakfast that the cook, Ida, always prepared for her of freshly baked rolls and thin slices of ham. Her stomach growled with hunger as she watched him pick up a roll and bite into it. With any luck he would choke, she thought sourly.

'The cook told me she is preparing *agnello arrosto con fagioli bianco* for dinner—roast lamb with white beans,' he said after he had polished off a second roll. He leaned back in his chair and stretched his arms above his head, causing the hem of his T-shirt to ride up, revealing a strip of his bronzed torso and a sprinkling of black hairs that disappeared beneath the waistband of his jeans. 'I can see I'm going to enjoy staying at Villa Cadenza.'

The glimpse of his taut, tanned abdomen had a strange effect on Arianna's insides and she felt hot all over imagining where his body hair grew more thickly beneath the zip of his jeans. She knew she was blushing, and when she dragged her gaze away from Santino's crotch up to his face the gleam of amusement in his eyes added fuel to her simmering temper.

'You won't be staying here,' she told him furiously. 'I'm going to call my father and put an end to this ridiculous situation.'

Arianna spied her handbag and suitcase on the floor close to the sun bed. Vaguely she remembered that one of the crew on Jonny's yacht had brought her and her luggage to the villa in the early hours of the morning. The front door had been locked and she hadn't wanted to wake the butler so she had slept on a sun bed for the rest of the night.

She dug out her phone and called her father's private number. But inevitably it was his personal assistant, Monica, who answered and gave the usual excuse that Randolph was busy and did not want to be disturbed. 'I'll tell him you phoned and I'm sure he'll be in touch when he has time,' the PA said smoothly, although she must know that Randolph had never in living memory returned one of his daughter's calls.

'I'd like to leave a message for him.' Arianna watched Santino pour out the last of the coffee from the cafetière and gulp it down, and her blood boiled. 'Will you tell my father that I have no need of a bodyguard and I have fired Mr Vasari?' She gave Santino a haughty look. 'He will be leaving Villa Cadenza immediately.'

Santino let his eyes roam over Arianna as she leaned back on the sun bed while she talked on her phone. Her long, tanned legs went on for ever and the silk sarong tied around her body did not hide the fullness of her breasts. Desire spiked sharp and urgent in his groin and he was thankful that the newspaper on his lap hid the betraying bulge beneath his jeans. He had known before he'd agreed to be her bodyguard that she was beautiful, but he had been unprepared for the hunger she aroused in him, the white-hot lust that surged through his veins.

She had recently starred in an advertising campaign for a famous perfume brand and pictures of her on bill-boards wearing sexy, black lace underwear had ignited a fire inside him. Sex was used indiscriminately by advertisers to sell products, and no doubt every red-blooded male who looked at the photos of Arianna wanted to run their hands over her lush curves and kiss her sensual mouth that was both an invitation and a challenge. But it was a challenge he must ignore, Santino reminded himself.

When he had found her asleep on the sun lounger earlier he'd realised that a camera could not capture the true essence of her beauty. Fine-boned and slender, she'd looked as fragile as a porcelain figurine, and she was quite the loveliest thing he had ever seen. It was those exquisite cheekbones and the delicate perfection of her elfin features, he thought broodily. Photographs did not do justice to the luminosity of her English rose complexion.

She had woken a few minutes ago and her long, curling lashes had swept upwards as she'd surveyed him with her big brown eyes flecked with gold. He told himself he must have imagined he had glimpsed a haunting vulnerability in her gaze. The sulky pout of her mouth was too sensual, too provocative, for her to be anything other than the brazen temptress beloved by the tabloids and gossip columns.

Santino rubbed his hand around the back of his neck to ease a knot of tension in his muscles. His fingers automatically slipped beneath his shirt collar and traced the ten-inch scar from a bullet wound he'd received while he'd been serving in Afghanistan. The bullet had entered just below his shoulder blade and ripped open his body before exiting his neck at the base of his skull. It was incredible that he had survived, and, like the images in his mind of war, the scar would never completely fade. Nor would his guilt.

Eight years ago he had come close to death on a dusty, blood-spattered desert road. His life had been saved by his best friend and fellow SAS member, Mac Wilson, who had dragged him out of the line of fire. But that act of immense bravery had cost Mac his legs when an IED had exploded beneath him.

Restlessly, Santino stood up and walked across the terrace, aware that Arianna's gaze followed him. His thoughts flew back to six months ago when Mac had requested his help to bring down a gang of drug smugglers believed to be responsible for his sister's death. Mac was determined to bring Laura's Italian boyfriend to justice but he had no proof that the man, Enzo, had supplied her with the cocaine which had killed her. Mac had asked Santino to infiltrate the gang who had links to the Calabrian mafia, known as the 'Ndrangheta. He had not needed to remind Santino that he was unable to do so himself because he was confined to a wheelchair.

Working undercover, Santino had discovered that, as well as drug smuggling, the gang had carried out several high-profile kidnappings and been paid millions of pounds of ransom money. Their next target was the

English heiress Arianna Fitzgerald. The kidnappers had kept her under surveillance for some time and knew that she spent the summer at her father's villa on the Amalfi coast. Santino had alerted the Italian police, but they had been unable to contact Arianna, so had warned her father of the threat to his daughter.

Santino recalled his meeting with Randolph Fitzgerald a week ago at the billionaire's Kensington home Lyle House.

'You are the best person to protect my daughter when she returns from Australia, Mr Vasari. Name your price. What will it take to persuade you to accept the job of Arianna's bodyguard?'

Santino had been irritated by the other man's arrogant assumption that everything could be bought and everyone had a price, but he guessed that those things were probably true for one of the richest men in England. 'I am not a CPO,' Santino had reminded Randolph. 'I have given you the names of several security agencies who can provide close protection officers and will arrange for your daughter to receive round-the-clock protection.'

'Your training and experience with the SAS gives me confidence that you will be able to keep Arianna safe. After all, it was you who found out that a mafia gang are planning to snatch her from my villa in Positano and demand a multi-million-pound ransom for her release. The Italian police are hunting for the gang but, until they are arrested, the threat to Arianna remains.'

It was true that the in-depth knowledge Santino had amassed about the gang members while he had pretended to be one of them meant he knew how they operated and could be one step ahead of them. But it was also true that he had no desire to babysit a spoilt socialite who, by her own father's admission, was headstrong and difficult.

Even if only a fraction of the reports about Arianna Fitzgerald's party lifestyle were true, she had earned her reputation as a good-time girl. For years her face and her stunning body—invariably poured into figure-hugging dresses—had regularly appeared on the front pages of the tabloids. One social commentator had sarcastically observed that Arianna would turn up to the opening of an envelope if it gave her an opportunity to pose for the cameras.

'I left the army a long time ago and since then I have established a successful career. I don't need a job,' Santino had told her father bluntly. 'It could be months before all the gang members involved in the kidnap plot are apprehended. I can't take that amount of time away from my business interests.'

Randolph nodded. 'I believe your chain of delicatessens under the brand name of Toni's Deli has outlets across the UK and in many European cities. You sold the business eighteen months ago and since then you have concentrated on growing your investment portfolio.'

Noticing Santino's surprise, Randolph had added drily, 'I did my homework about you, Mr Vasari, and I have a proposition that might interest you.'

Despite himself, Santino had been curious. 'I'm guessing that your proposition is dependent on my agreement to protect Arianna?'

'Preparations are underway to float Fitzgerald Design on the stock market and a price has been set at thirty-five pounds per share.' The fashion designer handed Santino a piece of paper. 'The top figure is the valuation of the company, and the figure beneath it is the number of shares I am prepared to give you in return for you taking on the role of my daughter's bodyguard until the kidnap threat is over.'

Santino lifted his brows when he looked at the figures. 'It would cost you a lot less to employ a CPO through a security agency.'

'As I have already stated, I believe you are the best man for the job.' Randolph leaned back in his chair. 'You are no doubt aware that my daughter frequently appears on the front pages of a certain type of newspaper. For some reason Arianna seems to enjoy courting notoriety, but the publicity surrounding her is likely to have brought her to the attention of the gang who intend to kidnap her. An important element of your job will be to shield her from the paparazzi and keep her out of the headlines.'

Randolph was clearly confident that the offer of a significant number of shares in Fitzgerald Design would persuade him to agree to be Arianna's bodyguard, Santino had mused. Why shouldn't he accept the shares as payment for protecting a pampered young woman who, quite frankly, sounded as if she was a pain in the backside?

Originally, he had set aside some time to try and help Mac gain justice—in some form or another—for his sister's death. But Arianna Fitzgerald was being threatened by people who had no respect for life. The 'Ndrangheta were ruthless and Santino did not like to think what they might do to her if they seized her.

Randolph leaned across the desk and, as if he'd read

Santino's mind, said, 'I have faith that your SAS training makes you the ideal person to protect my daughter.
What do you say?'

There was only one thing that Santino could say.
'All right, I will be Arianna's bodyguard until the gang
members have been caught.'

'There is one problem.' Randolph hesitated. 'Arianna
must not be told the real reason why I have hired you
to be her protection officer.'

When Santino frowned the billionaire quickly continued, 'My daughter is prone to volatile emotions. She
has seen various experts—psychologists and so forth.'
He gave a dismissive shrug. 'I don't pretend to understand the reason for Arianna's histrionics but a year ago
she overdosed and spent several weeks in hospital. I am
concerned about how she might react to the news that
a mafia gang are planning to kidnap her. For the sake
of her emotional stability it will be better if the gravity
of the situation is kept from her.'

'I will find it a lot harder to protect Arianna if she is
unaware of the danger she is in,' Santino had argued.

'That is why I chose you for the job,' Randolph replied slickly. 'I suggest you allow her to think that the
reason I hired you is because the launch of Fitzgerald
Design as a public company will attract a huge amount
of publicity. I trust that you will keep my daughter safe,
Mr Vasari.'

Santino pulled his thoughts back to the present and
cursed beneath his breath as he stared at Arianna's
scantily clad figure sprawled on the sun bed. His fantasy of undressing her and cradling her pert breasts
in his hands would have to remain in his imagination.

When he had been in the army a sense of duty and honour had been ingrained in him. Arianna's father had put his faith in him, which meant that the delectable Miss Fitzgerald was definitely off-limits.

CHAPTER TWO

'I'M AFRAID YOU can't dismiss Mr Vasari,' Randolph's PA said in her calm, slightly patronising manner which Arianna found intensely irritating. 'I have his employment contract which both he and your father signed here on my desk.'

'I don't care about any wretched contract.' Too agitated to sit still, Arianna jumped up from the lounger. 'This is intolerable. I don't *want* a bodyguard. Randolph can't force me to have one.'

'Your father told me to inform you that if you do not accept Mr Vasari's protection services then your monthly allowance will be stopped,' the PA said crisply. 'While you are in Positano, Mr Vasari will stay at Villa Cadenza and he will accompany you at all times when you go out.'

For a few moments shock rendered Arianna speechless. It was not the first time her father had used money to try to control her and anger surged like boiling lava through her veins. A year ago she had resolved to start her own fashion-design business so that she could earn her own money and not be reliant on the—admittedly generous—allowance that arrived in her bank account every month. However, her dream of being independent was as yet unfulfilled. Her lack of business skills and serious doubts that her designs were any good had prevented her from turning her dream into reality. Recently she had taken another step towards her goal, but she would need every penny of the money she had inherited from her grandmother to cover the start-up costs of establishing her business. It meant that she would have to rely on the allowance from her father for a little while longer.

But she would not tolerate having her privacy infringed by the constant presence of a bodyguard. Especially not the arrogantly self-assured man who had resumed his seat close to her sun bed. Santino leaned back in the chair and folded his arms behind his head while he trailed his eyes over her and looked unimpressed.

'Unimpressed' was not a reaction Arianna was used to receiving from men. She had attracted male attention since she'd been thirteen, when her body had started to develop from that of a skinny, coltish girl into a curvy young woman with a face and body that men lusted after. At first she had been scared by her power, but as she'd grown older she had learned that she could use feminine wiles to her advantage.

Against her will, her eyes were drawn to Santino's and she glimpsed a fire in his brilliant green gaze that caused heat to unfurl in the pit of her stomach. But she told herself she must have imagined his predatory look when his eyes narrowed and his expression became unfathomable.

She turned away and spoke into her phone in a low tone, conscious that he was within earshot of her conversation. Monica had worked as her father's assistant for years and guarded him fiercely. In truth, Arianna had often felt jealous of the close relationship the other woman had with him. 'Please let me speak to Randolph,' she muttered, feeling a familiar sense of betrayal at her father's indifference.

'I'm sorry. He has meetings for the rest of the day, but I'll let him know that you want to talk to him,' Monica said and ended the call before Arianna could respond.

Angrily she chucked her phone down on the sun bed but it bounced off the cushions and landed on the tiles with an ominous clatter. She picked it up and cursed when she saw a crack across the screen.

'You want to be more careful.' Santino's mocking voice was the last straw and Arianna spun round and glared at him.

'What I *want* is for you to get out of my house!' she snapped, aware that she sounded petulant, but her anger was mixed with a growing sense of panic at the realisation that her father was once again trying to exert his influence over her life.

Santino strolled towards her. His steps were unhurried, yet Arianna sensed that if she bolted towards the house he would move with the deadly speed of a big cat pursuing its prey and catch up with her before she'd gone any distance.

'This isn't your house. Your father owns the villa, and more to the point he pays my wages,' he drawled. 'I have been given instructions from Randolph to stay close to you when you go out shopping or meet your friends in bars or at the beach.'

Santino had not specified that his orders were to monitor her behaviour and prevent her from attracting the paparazzi's attention, but Arianna was certain that was the reason her father had insisted on her having a bodyguard. She knew that Fitzgerald Design was about to be floated on the stock market, and no doubt Randolph was anxious that she did not create any bad publicity before the launch that might affect the share price.

'You're loving this, aren't you?' she accused Santino angrily. Her fingers itched to slap the mocking smile off his handsome face.

He gave her an impatient look. 'I can't say that I relish the prospect of babysitting a spoilt socialite who has no idea how privileged she is. Your father believes that some of your friends are seriously into the drugs scene and he is concerned about you—'

'My father,' she interrupted him, 'doesn't give a damn about me and he is only concerned with protecting the Fitzgerald Design brand name. It's true that I can't force you to leave, but you will be housed in the staff quarters, and there is no reason for me to have to see you around the villa.'

'Randolph invited me to enjoy the facilities at Villa Cadenza and make myself comfortable. I'll be sleeping in the guest suite next door to your room.' Santino grinned when she glared at him. 'You'll soon get used to me being around and who knows? You might even enjoy my company. I was thinking of having a swim in that amazing infinity pool. Do you want to join me?'

'No,' she said through gritted teeth. She wanted to scream and shout as she'd done as a teenager—when her temper tantrums had been worse than those of a three-year-old, the governess her father had hired after Arianna had been expelled from school had told her.

'The truth, my dear,' Miss Melton had said crisply, 'is that the more you behave like a spoilt brat the less your father will want to have anything to do with you. Mr Fitzgerald is a very busy man and his time is precious.'

The implication had been that Randolph had more important things to do than pay attention to his difficult daughter. Nothing had changed, Arianna thought angrily. Santino Vasari's job was not to protect her but to control her.

He had walked over to the pool and was standing with his back to her, perhaps admiring the clever illusion that the water was pouring over the edge of the terrace. Or maybe he was enjoying the view of the azure sea through the huge glass window in the wall, beyond which was the villa's private beach. There was something so arrogant about his relaxed stance—as if he owned the place—that infuriated her.

Without pausing to think—a trait that had got Arianna into trouble on numerous occasions—she ran up to him and stretched out her hands to shove him into the pool. Her bare feet made no sound on the tiles, yet Santino must have sensed she was behind him, as he leapt out of her path with startling agility for such a big man. With nothing to slow her momentum she teetered on the edge of the pool and let out a yelp as she fell in and the water closed over her head.

She came up coughing and spluttering. The water wasn't cold, but it jolted her to her senses, and for a moment she felt a familiar sense of panic before she realised that she could feel the bottom of the pool beneath her feet. She felt like an idiot for her childish behaviour, and Santino's laughter told her that he shared her opinion. She waded over to the edge of the pool and clambered up the steps, ignoring the hand he held out to assist her.

'I see you changed your mind about having a swim,' he taunted.

Arianna stepped onto the poolside…and discovered that she was no longer wearing the sarong. It must have come loose in the pool and she saw the length of cerise silk floating in the water. 'Go to hell,' she snapped.

'I've already been there.' The amusement had disappeared from his voice. 'Helmand province was a hell on earth that few people, especially someone as privileged as you, could begin to imagine. When I was in Afghanistan I saw good men, some of them my close friends, die in the line of duty.'

'I don't know much about the war in Afghanistan,' she admitted.

'No, I don't suppose you do. Battle reports and casualty figures are not the sort of thing to feature in gossip columns, which I imagine is the only kind of news you read. But I assure you that hell would be a picnic in the park compared to desert warfare.'

Of course he had to be a war hero, Arianna thought, feeling another stab of shame that she had done nothing in her life to be proud of. Being chosen as the face of a perfume advertising campaign was utterly irrelevant compared to Santino risking his life on the battlefield.

She gathered up her long, wet hair in her hands and wrung out some of the water before she flicked it behind her shoulders. Santino made a rough sound, as if he had released his breath slowly, and when Arianna looked at him her gaze was trapped by the hard gleam in his eyes. He was staring at her as if he wanted to devour her and the stark hunger etched on his face evoked something fierce, bright and *electrifying* inside her.

She was supremely conscious that her body was no longer hidden beneath a sarong and her tiny gold bikini was not much more than three triangles of material held together with narrow ties. The action of pushing her hair back had lifted her breasts and, glancing down, she saw the hard points of her nipples jutting provocatively through the clingy, damp bra top.

There was a pile of freshly laundered towels by the side of the pool. Santino strode over, picked up a towel and returned to offer it to Arianna. 'Here, you had better cover yourself up. I can see that you're cold,' he said, resting his gaze deliberately on the betraying hard points of her nipples. The mockery in his voice was mixed with something darker that prickled across her skin and made her breasts feel heavy.

She felt scorched by his glittering gaze, by the heated desire she saw in those green depths. Triumph swept through her with the realisation that he wanted her but she sensed that he resented the attraction he felt for her.

'I'm not cold,' she murmured, ignoring the towel he held out to her. Tipping her head to one side, she regarded him through half-closed lashes, enjoying a sense of feminine power as she gave him a teasing smile, and his jaw hardened. 'I may as well go in the pool with you now that I'm wet.'

She saw his gaze drift over her body, following the droplets of water that she could feel trickling down her stomach to her thong-style bikini pants.

'Are you wearing swim-shorts under your clothes? It doesn't matter if you're not,' she said archly. 'I often sunbathe naked out here on the terrace. I hope that won't make you feel uncomfortable.'

Santino's eyes narrowed. 'I know you like to play games, Arianna, but don't think you can play them with me.' His lips curled sardonically when she opened her eyes wide and gave him a look of pure innocence. 'I've read the tabloid stories about your countless affairs with celebrities, and seen the pictures of you falling out of nightclubs and flaunting that incredible body of yours in revealing clothes that would make a whore blush. You can try all the tricks you like but you won't distract me from doing the job your father hired me to do.'

'And of course the tabloids always tell the truth,' she said abruptly. Her voice was sharper than she'd intended. Santino's scathing tone made her feel grubby and *cheap*. She had spent the best part of ten years trying to punish her father for his lack of interest in her, and she'd actively encouraged the paparazzi's attention with the wild behaviour that had earned her the label of 'spoilt little rich girl'. But the truth was that the only person she had hurt was herself.

There was no reason why the contempt in Santino's eyes should make her feel as if he had peeled away a layer of her skin, leaving her exposed and raw. What right did he have to judge her? He acted like Mr High and Mighty but she had discovered his weakness. How amusing that she was Santino Vasari's Achilles' heel, she thought, hiding her hurt feelings behind a wall of bravado the way she had learned to do since she'd been eleven years old.

She took the towel out of his hand and dropped it onto the floor before she stepped closer to him. A smile played on her lips when he folded his arms across his chest in what could only be described as a defensive gesture, which intrigued her.

'You sound worried, Santino. How do you think I might distract you?' she murmured, running her fingers lightly along his forearm. His skin was like warm silk and beneath it she felt the tensile strength of hard sinews and muscles.

His face hardened, the skin drawn taut over the slashing lines of his cheekbones. 'I'm warning you, Arianna,' he said harshly. 'I'm not one of the pretty boys who flock around you. Don't test my patience too far.'

'How could I do that, I wonder?' she purred. Common sense told her that she should walk into the house right now, taking what was left of her pride with her. But the dismissive tone in Santino's voice clawed at her lifelong sense of insignificance.

Her father had never paid her any attention, but at eighteen she had discovered that the paparazzi swarmed to take pictures of her when she stumbled out of nightclubs looking wild-eyed and the worse for drink. She had been dubbed 'the party princess' by the tabloids and, as her notoriety grew, she was invited to all the best parties. Restaurant openings, theatre first nights, art gallery exhibitions: anyone with a new business to promote included Arianna Fitzgerald on the guest list, knowing that her presence would ensure the event received maximum publicity.

She would show Santino that he could not dismiss her as if she was an irrelevance. He *would* take notice of her. 'Am I testing your patience now?' she asked softly as she trailed her fingers up his arm to his shoulder, feeling his bunched muscles beneath his T-shirt.

His breathing slowed and her heart raced as she continued her exploration, running her fingertips over the rough stubble on his jaw before she traced the sensual shape of his mouth. She pressed her body closer to his and tilted her head up to meet his gaze.

The feral gleam in his eyes caused her heart to lurch. But she could not back down now without making even more of a fool of herself. Cupping his cheek in her palm, she stretched up on her toes and covered his mouth with hers. He made no response. Not a flicker. His arms were still folded across his chest and he was as solid and unmoving as granite. His lips were unyielding, and it occurred to Arianna that in a lifetime of embarrassing herself Santino's rejection was her crowning humiliation.

Desperate to elicit some sort of reaction from him, she nipped his lower lip with her teeth. He made no sound but his chest rose and fell swiftly. 'Don't say I didn't warn you,' he said then, his voice a low growl that resonated through her.

Abruptly he unfolded his arms and clamped his hands on her shoulders. While Arianna was wondering if he intended to push her away from him he jerked her forward so that her soft breasts were pressed up against the hard wall of his chest. His gaze narrowed and she saw fire and fury glinting in his green eyes beneath his thick black lashes. But then his head swooped and he captured her mouth with his in a searing kiss that felt as if he had branded her with his unique potency.

Nothing had prepared her for the devastation he wrought on her mouth or on her soul as he forced her lips apart with the bold flick of his tongue. The heat of his body was dangerously addictive and, when his arms closed around her like bands of steel, trapping her against him, she melted in the inferno.

His kiss was all her fantasies rolled into one. Masterful and merciless, he demanded a response that she was powerless to deny him. She closed her eyes and her senses sang to the slide of his lips over hers and the taste of him on the tip of her tongue. He made her ache *everywhere*.

Needing to be even closer to him, she pressed her pelvis against his. They fitted together like two pieces of a jigsaw. But, before she had time properly to register the shockingly hard bulge of his arousal beneath his jeans, he lifted his mouth from hers at the same time as he withdrew his arms from around her waist and returned his hands to her shoulders.

This time he did push her away from him, so forcefully that she would have stumbled if he had not tightened his grip on her shoulders, and she feared her bones might snap.

'So, what is your plan, Arianna?' he drawled, no sign in his voice or his sardonic smile of the tumultuous passion that had exploded between them seconds earlier. 'I suppose you think you can accuse me of sexual harassment to give you a legitimate reason to fire me? But it won't wash, princess. It will be your word against mine.'

She sensed the suggestion in his scathing tone that his testimony would hold more credence than hers. After all, she was the darling of the tabloids, renowned for her outrageous behaviour with a string of celebrity lovers. It took every ounce of her willpower not to let him see how much his jibe had hurt, or how vulnerable she felt, still reeling from the kiss that patently had not affected him.

'Of course I wouldn't make a false allegation,' she said stiffly. 'It would be a terrible thing to do when too many women genuinely suffer sexual harassment.'

He looked at her curiously, as if she had surprised him, but then he shrugged. 'So why did you come on to me? I am under no illusions about you, Arianna. I warned you not to play games and I meant it. Your father hired me to be your bodyguard and I will not allow you to distract me. Nor, I should make it clear, do my duties include keeping you entertained with sex. So, if that is what you were hoping for when you kissed me, you're out of luck.'

Arianna wished that the ground would open up and swallow her, but pride came to her rescue and she gave a tinkling laugh as brittle as thin ice on a frozen pond. 'I can hardly bear the disappointment,' she said with a theatrical pout. 'At least you don't need to worry about drowning in the pool, Mr Vasari. That over-inflated ego of yours should help to keep you afloat.'

Santino dropped his hands down to his sides and clenched them into fists as Arianna spun away from him and marched across the terrace. *Well done*, he congratulated himself sarcastically. It was crucial that he gained her trust but all he had succeeded in doing was alienating her.

If he had any sense he would tear his gaze away from the perfect, peachy roundness of her bottom cheeks sassily displayed by her daring choice of swimwear. But his common sense, like his self-control, had gone up in flames when she had put her mouth on his. It occurred to him as he stared at her delectable derriere that it was unlikely she would actually swim in that miniscule bikini and that its purpose instead was to allow her to flaunt her incredible body.

She stepped through the open glass doors into the house and only when she had disappeared from view did he realise that he had been holding his breath. His nostrils flared as he inhaled deeply, but even though she was no longer standing in front of him the lingering scent of her perfume—an intriguing blend of exotic floral notes and something spicier and boldly sensual—inflamed his senses.

Why the hell had he kissed her? Telling himself that technically she had kissed him first did nothing to appease his conscience. He should have pulled his mouth away from hers, but there had been something curiously innocent about the tentative brush of her lips over his that had surprised him. Because he knew all about Arianna Fitzgerald—and 'innocent' was not a word ever associated with her.

The truth, Santino acknowledged grimly, was that his usual, logical thought process had deserted him the instant he'd set eyes on her and he'd felt a jolt of lust in his groin so intense that it had *hurt*. It had felt like a punch, as though he'd been winded and he couldn't catch his breath.

His reaction puzzled him. He was no stranger to beautiful women and he enjoyed an active sex life uncomplicated by emotional entanglements. The women he dated were intelligent professionals—elegant, discreet and unlikely to be plastered over the gutter press half-undressed, he thought, glancing with distaste at the picture of Arianna on the front of the newspaper.

Everything he had heard about her reinforced his belief that she had been over-indulged by her long-suffering father. Every picture of her when she was actually dressed showed that she had expensive tastes in designer clothes, shoes, handbags and fabulous jewellery—presumably all paid for by her doting daddy. In short, Arianna was the kind of woman he despised, but frustratingly his libido did not care that she was a spoilt socialite and his erection was uncomfortably hard pressing against the zip of his jeans.

The turquoise pool looked inviting with sun glinting on the surface. Earlier he'd pulled on a pair of swim-shorts beneath his clothes, thinking there would be time for him to swim while he waited for Arianna to wake up. His jaw clenched as he remembered her remark that she liked to sunbathe naked. Knowing that Arianna was a flirtatious tease did nothing to ease the throb of his arousal. Cursing himself for his weakness, he stripped off his clothes and dived into the pool. He swam as if his life depended on it—thirty lengths, fifty—until his shoulders ached and his chest burned and his rampant libido was subdued.

Later he made a detailed check of the villa's grounds and was concerned by the lack of security. The butler had explained that he locked the front door at night but that Arianna liked to leave her bedroom window open while she slept. The easy access to Villa Cadenza from the private beach was another problem. It would be feasible for kidnappers to climb over the wall and jump down onto the terrace. They could take Arianna at gunpoint through a door in the wall that led to the beach and force her onto a waiting boat without any of the villa's staff noticing or raising the alarm.

As Santino walked into the house he heard the sound

of a car's engine. Hurrying back outside, he glimpsed the tail lights of the sports car that he'd seen parked in the garage disappear out of the courtyard. He knew the car belonged to Arianna. Damn her! Her insubordination was infuriating, but he was more furious with himself for not keeping a closer eye on her.

'Did Arianna say where she was going?' he asked Filippo.

The butler shook his head. 'No, but she often visits the beauty salon in the town, and Giovanni's Bar next to the beach is a popular venue where she meets her friends.'

There was also a four-by-four parked in the garage and fortunately the keys were in the ignition. Santino jumped in and fired the engine. The road outside the villa was not overlooked by any other houses for part of the way down the mountain and he was worried that the kidnappers could be waiting to ambush Arianna as she drove away from Villa Cadenza. Moments later he drove out of the gates and was soon hurtling around the hairpin bends, speeding along the road that wound down to the coast.

Despite his simmering temper he could not fail to appreciate the spectacular scenery. The towering grey cliffs were covered with lemon groves that sloped down to the coast. Dominating the skyline was the azure Tyrrhenian Sea sparkling in the bright summer sunshine. The coastline here was similar to his birthplace and the place he thought of as home, Sicily. The difference was that Positano, the same as most of the other towns on the Amalfi coast, had become a chic and expensive tourist destination favoured by the glitterati.

Rounding another bend, the town was revealed in all

its picturesque beauty. Pink, peach and terracotta-coloured houses clung perilously to the cliffs and looked as though they were in danger of tumbling into the sea. At the heart of the town stood the Church of Santa Maria Assunta, with its eye-catching dome made of blue, green and yellow tiles. But Santino's eyes were fixed firmly on the silver sports car ahead of him on the road. He saw the car's brake lights flash on as Arianna's progress was impeded by a bus trundling along in front of her.

There was no possibility of overtaking on the narrow road and it was another five minutes before the bus pulled into a bus stop. After another mile or so Arianna turned up a narrow road and Santino followed her. Most of Positano was a pedestrian zone and tourists had to park in one of the garages on the edge of the town. But she drove down a back street where there was parking for local residents and swung her car into a vacant space.

Santino parked behind the open-top sports car and jumped out of the four-by-four. He strode up to the car, leaned over and snatched the key out of the ignition before Arianna had a chance to stop him.

'You really are the most tedious man,' she said languidly, although he sensed the effort it took her to control her temper.

'That's not the impression you gave when you kissed me earlier.' He felt a spurt of satisfaction when she bit her lip, and dismissed the odd idea that her air of vulnerability was not an act.

Her eyes were hidden behind oversized designer sunglasses and he was frustrated that he had no idea what she was thinking. She looked expensively chic in tight white jeans and a blue-and-white-striped Breton top. A red silk scarf kept her long chestnut hair back from her face. Her lips were coated in scarlet gloss and he felt a crazy urge to kiss her until he had removed all traces of lipstick from her mouth.

'Why didn't you tell me you were coming into town?'

'Because I'm going to the beauty salon,' she told him in a bored tone, nodding towards a shop with the name Lucia's Salon over the door. 'I don't need a bodyguard while I'm having my nails done.' She threw her hands up in the air. 'Look around you. There are no paparazzi here to report on my wild behaviour that might embarrass my dear daddy.'

She started to walk towards the salon and glared at him when he fell into step beside her. 'You can't come in. If you insist on staying, you can wait outside, but don't blame me if you get bored, Mr Vasari.'

'I doubt I could ever get bored around you,' he said drily. 'And I thought we had agreed to drop the formality, Arianna.'

She spun round to face him and jabbed her finger into his chest. 'I didn't agree to anything, certainly not to my every move being watched by one of my father's sycophants. I demand that you give me some space.'

Despite his intention to try and win her trust, Santino felt riled by her withering tone. He was tempted to tell her that, far from being her father's sycophant, Randolph had begged him to be her bodyguard.

'You're not really in a position to make demands, are you, Arianna? If I were you I would remember that your father promised to stop your allowance if you refuse my protection. How would you survive?' he taunted. 'It's not as if you have a successful career to fund your extravagant lifestyle. You simply leech off your father.'

'If I want your advice, I'll ask for it,' she snapped, jabbing her finger into his chest a second time.

'Do that again and I guarantee you won't like the consequences.'

'What will you do?' Her husky voice was laced with amusement. 'Will you put me across your knee and spank me?'

Desire kicked hard in his groin at the erotic images her words evoked. His nostrils flared as he inhaled deeply. 'Would you like me to? Are those the kinds of games you like to play?' he drawled, fighting an unbearable temptation to pull her into his arms and cover her sulky mouth with his. She was the most infuriating woman he had ever met, and he could not comprehend why she made him feel more alive than he had felt in years.

He stretched out his hand and removed her sunglasses. She blinked in the bright sunshine and the flecks of gold in her brown eyes gleamed with temper.

'Give those back immediately.'

He made a tutting sound. 'Try saying "please". Didn't your parents teach you better manners when you were a child?'

Something flickered in her gaze that surely could not be sadness, Santino told himself. Arianna was a beautiful, rich heiress and she wanted for nothing.

'My mother cleared off to the other side of the world with her lover when I was eleven,' she told him in a hard voice. 'My father didn't know how to deal with my "difficult behaviour" when I cried every night. He was so desperate to send me back to boarding school that he drove me there himself—the first and last time he took any interest in my education. I didn't see him again for months. Every school holiday, he used to send me out to Villa Cadenza with a nanny.'

She snatched her sunglasses out of Santino's fingers and replaced them on her nose. 'The only thing I learned from my parents is to put *me* first, and look after myself, because no one else gives a damn.'

CHAPTER THREE

ARIANNA WISHED SHE could speak Italian better as she tried to explain to the receptionist in the beauty salon that, if the tall man who was standing in the street came into the salon and asked for her, she was to tell him that Miss Fitzgerald was having her legs waxed in one of the treatment rooms.

'You have *appuntamento*?' the girl asked, studying the appointments book on her desk.

'No.' Arianna opened her purse and took out a wad of notes. 'I haven't booked any treatments. I just want you to pretend to the man outside that I will be here in the salon for a few hours—*per favore*,' she added, remembering Santino's jibe about her manners.

She handed the confused-looking receptionist the money before she walked to the back of the building and exited into a small courtyard that she had discovered by chance on a previous visit to the salon. A door at the rear of the building adjacent to the beauty salon led to a flight of stairs, and at the top she entered a large workroom. There were several tables with sewing machines and around the room were tailor's dummies draped with material.

'So you are here at last. But you are late.' The woman

who greeted Arianna was small and round, with jet-black hair swept into a severe bun and fierce black eyes. 'If you want to learn to sew from the best seamstress on the Amalfi coast, I expect you to be here at the time we arranged.'

'I'm sorry…*mi dispiace*,' Arianna said meekly.

Rosa handed her a length of muslin. 'Probably you have forgotten everything I taught you last summer, but we will see. You can begin by showing me that you can construct a French seam.'

Arianna nodded and immediately set to work. For years she had fought against the idea of becoming a fashion designer. She had been determined to distance herself from her father, not follow in his footsteps. But a year ago she had acknowledged that ignoring her creativity was making her unhappy. She had a natural flare for designing and sketching clothes, and she loved playing around with different materials, textures and colours. She knew instinctively when an outfit looked right or wrong, the importance of how a material draped and the need for precision tailoring to create a truly beautiful garment.

Last summer while she'd been staying in Positano she had commissioned an evening gown from local designer and dressmaker Rosa Cucinotta. Rosa had shown her around her workroom and it had been a defining moment for Arianna, confirming her decision that she wanted a career in fashion design. But although she had good drawing skills she needed to learn how to sew, make patterns and know how to construct a garment.

She had dismissed the idea of applying to study fashion design at a college in England for fear that the press would find out. It was important to keep her hope of one day owning her own fashion label a secret, especially from her father. If she did make a successful career, she wanted it to be on her own, without Randolph's money or influence.

She had persuaded Rosa to give her sewing lessons, and when she'd returned to London last autumn she had studied with Sylvia Harding, a famous fashion designer who, before she'd retired, had been a couturier to royalty. During the six months that Arianna had spent in Australia, she had worked with a couple of funky young designers in Sydney. For the first time in her life she had had to work hard, and she'd loved it.

For the next hour she concentrated on pinning and cutting the material, before using a sewing machine to make a neat seam that she hoped would be up to Rosa's high standards. Finally she looked up, feeling reasonably happy with her efforts. She was sitting next to the window that overlooked the street and had a perfect view of Santino seated at a table outside the café opposite the dress shop and the beauty salon next door.

The constant presence of a bodyguard following her around was going to make it difficult to spend a few hours every day at Rosa's workshop, she thought with a frown. It would be easier if she told Santino that she was having sewing lessons, but she was reluctant to reveal her dream of establishing her own fashion label.

Her stomach squirmed with shame as she remembered how he had called her a leech who relied on her father for money. At the age of twenty-five she knew she should be independent, although many of her peers in her social circle—the offspring of super-rich parents—lived off trust funds and vast inheritances. But she wanted to be her own person—whoever that was,

Arianna thought wryly. She had spent her teenage years and early twenties hating her father, but the result was that she'd become someone she did not like or respect.

As she stared at Santino she felt that strange breathless sensation that only he had ever induced in her. His long legs were stretched out in front of him and his impressive biceps showed beneath his short-sleeved T-shirt. She had noticed earlier that he had a tattoo of a snarling tiger on his upper right arm. He glanced at his watch. No doubt he was bored waiting for her but he would have to get used to it. It occurred to Arianna that she would not need to fire Santino—all she had to do was behave so badly that he was bound to resign from his post as her bodyguard.

'Are you sewing or admiring the scenery?' Rosa asked drily.

Arianna quickly jerked her head round and felt her face grow warm when the dressmaker moved closer to the window and looked at Santino. 'Is he your lover?'

'No! Definitely not.'

'A pity.' Rosa shrugged her ample shoulders. 'He is very handsome.' She picked up the length of fabric that Arianna had been working on and inspected the neat seam. '*Eccellente.* You have improved a lot since last summer when you began sewing lessons with me. You still have much to learn, of course, but I can see you have a natural skill.'

'Thank you.' Arianna blushed again. She was not used to being praised, which was partly her own fault, she acknowledged. As a child she had sought attention from her various nannies by misbehaving, and she'd done the same with her father. At least when Randolph had been angry with her it meant that he'd actually noticed her. But mostly her father had treated her with crucifying indifference on the rare occasions when they met. He travelled extensively for his work, and Arianna had felt the same sense of abandonment that had been so devastating when her mother had left her behind to start a new life in Australia.

Meeting Celine in Sydney after they had not seen each other for more than a decade had been a strange experience, Arianna mused. She had been shocked to discover that she had a half-brother, Jason, who was nearly fifteen. Her mother had explained that she'd been pregnant by her Australian lover when she'd left her husband and daughter. She had wanted to take Arianna to Australia with her, but Randolph had refused to allow it, and he had offered Celine a large amount of money in return for her agreement not to seek custody of Arianna or contact her.

Celine had sacrificed a relationship with her daughter and accepted the pay-off from Randolph, which had allowed her to bring up her son. Arianna understood her mother's reasons but it hadn't hurt any less to hear that she had been used as a pawn in her parents' bitter divorce.

At least she was back in touch with Celine and, although they would never have a close mother-daughter bond, Arianna had promised to visit her mum in Australia and get to know her stepbrother. She was about to start a new chapter in her life and launch her career. For the first time ever she had a sense of purpose and she had surprised herself with her fierce determination to succeed as a designer.

Her unexpected fascination with Santino Vasari was as annoying as it was inexplicable. Once again, Arianna's gaze was drawn to the window, and as she stared at Santino she unconsciously traced her tongue over her lips where his mouth had branded hers. She could still taste him, and she could remember in vivid detail the hunger in his kiss—the glorious, blazing heat of it that had burned through her and pooled, molten and yearning, low in her pelvis.

It made no sense that she was attracted to one of her father's minions. She was certain that Santino had been hired by Randolph to police her behaviour and she didn't understand why she was tempted to tell him that most of the stories about her had been fabricated by the paparazzi. She had pretended to be a social butterfly, aimlessly flitting from one glamorous party to another and from one celebrity lover to another, to punish her father and remind him of her existence.

But admitting those things would be akin to ripping away the mask she had hidden behind the whole of her adult life to reveal the real Arianna Fitzgerald—the vulnerable, un-confident woman…the lonely girl who expected everyone to let her down. She could not be side-tracked by a man who said he was her protector but who, her instincts warned, was dangerous to her peace of mind. She was just starting out on a journey of self-discovery and she was not ready to deal with the disturbing effect that her bodyguard had on her. Deep down, she suspected that she would never be ready for Santino Vasari's devastating sensuality.

'I swear your nail polish is the same colour it was before you went into the beauty salon two hours ago,' Santino said tersely when Arianna walked over to where he was sitting outside the café.

He stood up as she approached and she had to tilt her head to look at his face. She hated that she felt small and ridiculously fragile when he towered over her. He was easily several inches over six feet tall, but more than his impressively muscular physique he exuded a latent power and an air of command that she guessed came from his time in the army.

She dropped her phone into her bag and gave a care-less shrug. 'They're acrylics and need to be replaced every two weeks. I did warn you that you would get bored,' she murmured with a saccharine-sweet smile that evidently did nothing to lighten his black mood.

His heavy brows drew together. 'Seriously, can't you think of anything more interesting to do than spending hours having your body pampered?'

'Seriously, you need to remember that you are an employee, and not my spiritual guide whose job is to lead me towards enlightenment and a better life,' Ari-anna told him furiously. She spun round and marched along the street, straight past where her car was parked. 'I've just had a call from my friend Jonny, inviting me to spend the afternoon on his yacht. I won't require a bodyguard,' she said to Santino over her shoulder. 'You might as well go back to the villa and I'll call you later this evening when I want you to collect me.'

She increased her pace and walked swiftly through the pedestrianised streets, past pretty restaurants, art galleries and clothes shops with brightly coloured dresses displayed on rails outside. In midsummer Pos-itano was full of tourists and she had to weave her way through the crowds on the steps down to the beach. She had almost reached Giovanni's' Bar when she sensed someone close behind her, and she turned her head and glared at Santino.

'Go away,' she hissed. 'I can't enjoy a drink with my friends when you are hanging around. I don't want to admit that you are my...' She had been about to say 'minder', but he interrupted her.

'Babysitter,' Santino mocked. 'Don't worry, I'll be discreet,' he drawled as he followed her into the bar.

Most of the crowd who Arianna had met the previous day were in the bar and she joined Davina Huxley-Brown at a table and ordered a drink. What she really wanted to do was go back to Villa Cadenza and work on her designs. But it was Filippo and Ida's afternoon off. She'd felt uncomfortable at the prospect of being alone with Santino at the villa, which was why she had accepted Jonny's invitation.

'Jonny is sending the motor launch over to collect us,' Davina told her. 'Who's the hunk that you arrived with?'

Arianna pretended to be puzzled. 'I didn't arrive with anyone.'

'Shame. I was hoping you could introduce me to the gorgeous guy over there.'

Arianna followed her friend's gaze across the bar and saw Santino chatting to the Dutch twins Poppy and Posy Van Deesen. He was about as discreet as a nuclear explosion, she thought, gritting her teeth when she watched him flirting with the two attractive blondes. Of course he had to glance over in her direction at that exact moment and caught her staring at him. Hot-faced, she turned her head away and took a gulp of her gin and tonic before she remembered that she hadn't eaten breakfast or lunch.

The launch drew up alongside the wooden jetty on

the beach and Arianna and some of the others climbed aboard. She immediately put on a life-jacket, although most people did not bother. Minutes later the dingy was zipping over the sparkling sea to where the luxury motor yacht *Sun Princess* was anchored some way off shore.

'You look better than you did yesterday.' Jonny greeted her when she boarded the yacht. He beckoned to a steward who stepped forward and handed her a glass of champagne. It would be churlish to refuse, but she definitely did not need any more alcohol, Arianna decided as she strolled along the deck, looking for somewhere to put down her drink. She felt an odd sensation that she was being watched, and when she glanced over her shoulder she saw that the steward was staring at her. For some reason a shiver ran through her. She did not remember seeing that particular steward on board the yacht yesterday, but she'd been so jet-lagged that most of the day was a blur.

She whirled round at the sound of a familiar voice, and anger fizzed inside her when she saw Santino step onto the deck of the yacht, followed by the Van Deesen twins. The launch had returned to pick up the remaining guests from the beach and bring them out to the *Sun Princess*, and evidently he had managed to get himself included. Poppy Van Deesen linked her arm though his and her twin sister clung to his other arm.

'This is Santino,' Poppy announced. 'He was all alone in the bar, so we asked him if he would like to hang out with us. I hope no one objects?'

'No objection from me,' Davina murmured. 'I'll be happy to hang out with him any day. She looked at Arianna. 'You are rather over-dressed, darling. Aren't you going to get changed?'

'I forgot to bring a bikini with me.' Arianna had not planned to spend the afternoon on the yacht and she was feeling hot and uncomfortable in her skinny jeans.

'I have a spare you can borrow.' Davina fished into her bag and pulled out a turquoise bikini. 'You're bigger up top than me so the cup size may be a bit small.' She shrugged. 'But it might mean you get noticed by our sexy new guest.'

Attracting Santino's attention was the last thing she wanted to do, Arianna thought darkly when she returned to the deck wearing the borrowed bikini. The top was strapless and she was scared to move in case her breasts spilled out. She looked across the deck and saw him surrounded by a group of girls, including the twins and Davina.

Following her out to the yacht was taking his bodyguard duties too far. But his real job and the reason her father had hired Santino was to make sure she stayed out of the newspaper headlines, she reminded herself. She lay back on a sun lounger and flicked through a magazine but it was difficult to ignore Santino's sexy, accented voice mingled with the high-pitched laughter of the girls who flocked around him.

Evidently he was too busy enjoying himself to take any notice of her. Arianna felt a hot rush of jealousy that made her furious with herself. She was no longer that person who needed to be the centre of attention. She'd grown up and taken charge of her life, or at least she had made a start. Santino made her revert to the old Arianna, the person she hadn't liked, the person she had vowed never to be again.

Cursing beneath her breath, she jumped up and walked along the deck away from Santino and his fan club of adoring females. At the stern of the yacht she saw Hugo Galbraith, whom she had dated briefly, about to take one of the jet-skis out.

'Hop on,' he called to her. 'I'll take you for a ride.'

Arianna glanced over her shoulder and saw Posy Van Deesen perch herself on Santino's knees. The Dutch beauty was all over him like a rash. Not that Santino seemed to mind, she thought irritably. On impulse she grabbed a life-jacket and stepped down to the docking platform so that she could climb onto the jet-ski. She sat behind Hugo, but as she fastened the straps on the life-jacket she realised that it was too big. Hugo had already started the engine and he opened the throttle to send the jet-ski skimming over the sea.

'Go back,' she shouted, but the jet-ski was moving fast and her words were whipped away on the breeze. She held on tightly around Hugo's waist, hoping he would make it a short trip. They were already a good way away from the *Sun Princess*. Personal watercraft were not allowed close to the beach but this far out from the shore there were a few jet-skis and speed boats racing around.

Arianna suddenly saw a jet-ski moving rapidly over the water heading towards them. She tapped Hugo's shoulder to alert him to the danger and he pulled the handlebars round to turn their jet-ski in a different direction. But they were moving too fast to make such a sharp turn. Everything happened so quickly that Arianna barely had time to cry out as she and Hugo were thrown off the jet-ski.

The shock of landing in the cold sea made her gasp,

and she choked as she took a mouthful of water. The ill-fitting life-jacket did not support her properly and her face was partially submerged. A little way off the rider-less jet-ski was still hurtling round in circles, causing a whirlpool effect that was dragging Arianna under. She realised that Hugo must not have attached the kill cord which would have stopped the jet-ski's engine when he had been thrown off.

Terrified, she gasped for breath and her mouth filled with water again as waves created by the out-of-control jet-ski crashed over her head. Memories of when she had almost drowned as a child flashed into her mind and she thrashed her arms and kicked her legs to try to keep afloat.

The other jet-ski that moments ago had been racing across the water now slowed down and came up close to Arianna.

'Signorina!'

The rider held out his hand, indicating that he would pull her onto his jet-ski. But she could not move and she felt numb with shock and fear as her face slipped beneath the surface again and her nostrils filled with water.

'Arianna, hang on. I'm coming for you.'

Startled to hear a familiar, commanding voice, she turned her head and saw Santino in the motor launch that was being driven by one of the yacht's crewmen.

'Signorina, take my hand.'

The stranger on the jet-ski leaned down and tried to grab hold of Arianna's shoulder. She heard a splash, and when she looked back at the launch she saw that Santino had dived in to the sea and was swimming to-wards her. In a matter of seconds he was beside her and

wrapped his arms around her, lifting her up so that her
face was out of the water.

'I've got you, baby.'

His voice was oddly rough, almost as if he was concerned for her, as if he cared—which obviously was a
figment of her imagination, Arianna told herself. But
she curled her arms around his neck and clung to him,
weak with relief that her life was not going to end at
the bottom of the ocean. She was vaguely aware that
the stranger on the jet-ski turned his craft around and
raced away. Santino hooked his arm around her beneath
her breasts and towed her to the launch where the crewman helped to pull her on board.

Reaction set in and she hugged her arms around her
and fought off a surge of nausea. Santino had climbed
back onto the boat, and he draped a towel around her
shoulders. He hunkered down in front of her, and even
in her shocked state she noticed that he had stripped off
his jeans and T-shirt before he'd dived in to the sea and
his wet boxer shorts clung to his hips.

'Next time, make sure you wear a life-vest that fits,'
he growled.

Arianna couldn't stop shivering. 'Where's Hugo?'
she asked through her chattering teeth.

'Another crewman managed to jump from the launch
onto the jet-ski and take control of it before he picked
your boyfriend up.' Santino frowned as a shudder ran
through her. He lifted his hand and smoothed her wet
hair back from her face. 'You had a bad scare, but you're
safe now, *piccola*.'

The gentle endearment—she knew that the English
translation was 'little one'—was her undoing. She had
been so afraid, and without Santino's quick actions it

was very likely that she would have drowned. Arianna bit down hard on her lip but her emotions overwhelmed her and she burst into tears. 'I thought I was going to drown,' she choked. 'The life-jacket didn't keep me afloat and I can't swim.'

Santino swore as he put his arms around her and pulled her close. His wet chest hairs felt soft beneath Arianna's cheek and the powerful thud of his heart reverberated through her. She heard him speaking in Italian and was aware that the launch was moving, but even though she was safe she couldn't forget those terrifying moments when her mouth had filled with sea water. She wanted to be able to shrug off what had happened as another stupid scrape that she had a reputation for getting herself into. But she couldn't pull herself together and she pressed her face into Santino's chest to muffle her sobs.

CHAPTER FOUR

SANTINO WAS NOT good with tears. They made him uncomfortable and reminded him too much of when his mother had died and his father had wept like a child. Antonio Vasari's outpouring of raw emotion had seemed shameful to his fifteen-year-old son. Santino had not known how to cope with the stranger his father had become.

The once strong, cheerful man whom Santino had idolised had been destroyed by grief as surely as Santino's mother's life had been destroyed by an aggressive brain tumour. The specialist had given Dawn Vasari a year to live, but she'd lasted barely six months, leaving behind a heartbroken husband, teenage son and eight-year-old daughter.

Santino had begged his father to take the family back to Sicily, from where they had moved to Devon a year before his mother's illness had been diagnosed. But Antonio had refused to leave the place where his wife had been born and had died unfairly young. Santino's memories of his late teens were of roaming over desolate Dartmoor for hours, often days, at a time, trying to make sense of life and loss and the realisation that *love* was not worth the agony.

He had cried on the day of his mother's funeral, alone in his bedroom, while his father and sister and his mother's relatives had been downstairs, united somehow in their grief. But he'd felt like an outsider and he hadn't wanted their sympathy. He'd wanted to punch something. His tears had not helped to ease the pain in his heart and he hadn't cried again. Ever.

He understood fear. He'd seen it in the eyes of some of the men from his patrol in Afghanistan when they had been ambushed and for a while it had looked as if none of them would survive. He knew what it was like to look death in the face. He tightened his arms around Arianna's trembling body and let her cry it out.

Grimly he acknowledged that he had failed to protect her. He'd jumped into the launch as soon as he'd seen her on the back of the jet-ski, and witnessing the accident when she'd been thrown into the sea had caused his heart to miss a beat. He frowned as he recalled the dangerous behaviour of the other jet-skier. The rider had appeared deliberately to drive towards the craft that Arianna and her friend had been on. It was almost as if he'd wanted to cause an accident. And then he'd tried to pull Arianna onto his jet-ski. Had the jet-skier wanted to rescue her, or had there been something more sinister behind his actions?

Santino ran his hand around the back of his neck and over his scar. The kidnappers must be aware that Arianna was in Positano after she'd appeared on the front page of the newspapers. But how could they have known that she had gone out on the jet-ski unless they had been close by—perhaps on one of the other yachts anchored in the bay—and had been watching her through binoculars? The incident with the jet-skis was probably nothing to worry about, he tried to reassure himself. But his instincts warned him that the threat to Arianna was very real.

The launch stopped in the shallows close to a small, secluded beach that was not often discovered by tourists. As Santino had hoped, it was empty. After giving instructions to the crewman, he scooped Arianna into his arms and carried her up the beach, depositing her carefully on the sand and dropping down onto his knees beside her.

'Lie back while I check you over,' he ordered after he'd helped her out of the life-jacket. To his surprise she did not argue. 'Are you hurt anywhere? Your body took quite an impact when you came off the jet-ski at speed and hit the water.'

'I'm okay.' Her eyes were closed and she spoke so softly that he had to lean closer to hear her. 'I'm just shaken up.'

'I'm not surprised.' He felt a knot of tension in his gut when he thought of how easily she could have drowned if he hadn't reached her in time.

Her lashes flew open and he stared into her big brown eyes, watching the golden flecks on her irises reflect the gleam from the sun in the cobalt-blue sky above them. She was so god damned beautiful. He pushed the thought away, determined to remain professional as he ran his hands over her arms and down her legs, checking for any broken bones.

'Why did you go on the jet-ski if you can't swim?'

'Because I'm an idiot. That's what you think, isn't it?' she said flatly. 'It's the opinion my father has of me— when he thinks of me at all, which isn't very often.'

Santino didn't know what to make of this different

Arianna with hurt in her voice and that air of vulnerability that he'd assumed was an act when they had been
at the Villa Cadenza. He'd felt certain that he had her
measure. Spoilt and privileged with little of substance
beneath her exquisite packaging. He frowned as he remembered that he'd found Randolph Fitzgerald a cold
and arrogant man when he had met him.

'I don't think you are an idiot,' he said roughly.
'How come you never learned to swim when there's
that amazing pool at Villa Cadenza?'

'I nearly drowned when I was a young child. I must
have only been three or four and the incident left me
with a fear of being out of my depth in water.' Catching his questioning look, she explained, 'I was with my
parents at a hotel somewhere. I don't remember where.
My father travels around the world for his business, and
before my parents' marriage broke up my mother and I
occasionally went with him.

'On the day that it happened my father had taken me
to play in the shallow part of the pool. But while he was
talking on his phone I must have waded deeper. I was
terrified when I realised that I couldn't feel the floor
of the pool beneath my feet. I remember calling to my
father, but he was some distance away, and because he
was on his phone he didn't hear me.'

Arianna sat up and hugged her knees to her chest.
'I remember the sensation of my mouth filling with
water. I was choking and couldn't breathe. Luckily another hotel guest arrived at the pool and jumped in and
saved me from drowning. When my father finally finished his phone call, he told me off for misbehaving.'
She gave a humourless laugh. 'I learned two valuable

lessons that day. The first to be fearful of deep water, and the second that my father has little interest in me.'

'It's true that a traumatic event in childhood or teenage years can affect people in their adult lives,' Santino said, remembering the anger that had eaten away at him for a long time after his mother's death. Joining the army had given him a sense of belonging and purpose and he'd learned to deal with his anger. But fighting in a brutal war that had cost the lives of a couple of his close friends had reinforced his wariness—he refused to call it fear—of emotional attachments.

'I tried hypnotism once to try to get over my fear of drowning, but I panic when my face is in the water,' Arianna admitted. 'When my father sent me out of his way to Villa Cadenza every summer, a few of my nannies tried to teach me to swim, but I made such a fuss that they gave up.'

'In future I suggest that you don't allow your boyfriend to take you for a ride on a jet-ski,' Santino growled. He could not understand why, when he had seen Arianna climb onto the jet-ski and wrap her arms around the fair-haired Englishman, he'd felt as though he'd been punched in his stomach. The feeling could not have been jealousy, he assured himself, because no woman had ever evoked that emotion in him—or indeed any emotion other than sexual desire.

Arianna sent him a quick glance. 'Hugo isn't my boyfriend.'

'Your friend Lady Davina something-or-other told me that you're involved with this Hugo guy.'

'She probably said it because she fancies you and wanted to take me out of the competition.' Arianna gave one of those maddeningly nonchalant shrugs that, for

reasons he was unable to explain, Santino found infuriating. 'But Davina needn't have worried. I'm not interested in you.'

'No?' The word hung in the hot summer's afternoon
air, an unintentional challenge—or maybe not unintentional, Santino acknowledged self-derisively as his
eyes locked with Arianna's. Adrenalin was still pumping through him after rescuing her from the sea, and
his relief had been mixed with an indefinable emotion
when she'd wept in his arms.

Tears still clung to her lashes, but he watched her
eyes darken, the pupils dilating. Sexual tension had
simmered between them by the pool at Villa Cadenza.
Santino had taken one look at her and something had
shifted deep inside him. He had told himself it was
lust, for how could it be anything else, anything more?

Here on the secluded beach it was as if only the
two of them existed. Like the biblical Adam tempted
by Eve's sensual promise, he could not take his eyes
from Arianna wearing another sexy bikini that showed
off her stunning figure. He was conscious of his heart
pounding in his chest and the heat of the sun on his back
as he slowly bent his head.

Her breasts rose and fell, and he heard her swiftly in-
drawn breath, but she did not move—she simply stared
at him with her brown eyes lit with gold. She was an
irresistible temptation and with a low groan he claimed
her mouth with his.

He tasted salt from the sea on her lips and when
he dipped his tongue into her mouth her sweet breath
mingled with his. She hesitated for a heartbeat that felt
to Santino like a lifetime. With a sense of urgency he
had never experienced before he increased the pres-

sure of his lips on hers, and his heart clattered against his ribs when she tipped her head back and opened her mouth to him.

Her surrender shattered the last remnants of his self-control. Santino forgot the rules he had set himself as he deepened the kiss and explored the sensual shape of her lips before he delved into her mouth and tangled his tongue with hers. It was hot and intense. He was blown away by Arianna's passionate response as he felt a shudder run through her when he trailed his lips over her cheek and gently nipped her ear lobe with his teeth.

He kissed his way down her elegant neck and along the fragile line of her collar bone. Her skin was like satin and her breasts felt soft against the hard wall of his chest when he slid his arms around her and pulled her into his heat. She moved her hands up to his shoulders and he eased her down onto the sand, stretching out beside her so that he could skim his fingertips over the tantalising dips and curves of her body.

Her narrow waist fascinated him, the gentle flare of her hips even more so. He was so hard it hurt. He thought he might explode if he did not have her, if he did not sink between her silken thighs and drive his shaft home. The feminine scent of her arousal was the sweetest fragrance and he was certain that her hunger was as intense his. Her breathing was as unsteady as the erratic thud of his heart.

Driven by a need greater than he had ever known, Santino traced his fingers over Arianna's skimpy bikini pants that sat low on her hips. He felt her stomach quiver but, when he slipped his hand between her legs, she tensed.

'No.'

The word detonated inside his head and catapulted him back to reality. *What the hell was he doing?* He could not make love to Arianna. Love played no part in what he wanted, Santino acknowledged. He was desperate to have sex with her, but he must not give in to the desire that ran hot and wild in his veins. He was appalled by his lack of finesse. He'd behaved like a hormone-fuelled teenager and almost lost his self-control. It had never happened before and he was rocked by the effect that Arianna had on him.

He levered himself so that he was sitting upright and lifted his hand to shield his eyes from the glare of the sun while he scanned the empty beach. It was his job to protect her, but if the kidnappers arrived at the secluded bay he would stand little chance of keeping her safe from a ruthless and probably armed gang.

Arianna sat up and ran her fingers through her hair that was drying into tangled curls around her shoulders and made her look younger than did her usual sleek style. Her eyes were huge and dark in her delicate face. Santino dragged his gaze from her pert breasts half-spilling out of her bikini top. 'I guess this is not the time or the place,' he muttered.

Her eyes flashed fire at him. 'You guess right. There isn't a time or a place when I would agree to have casual sex with you.'

Stung by her snippy tone, he said curtly, 'That's not the impression you gave a few moments ago. You wanted me.' His eyes narrowed. 'Or is that the kind of game you like to play? There is a word for women who deliberately lead men on.'

'Are you saying that I'm not allowed to change my mind?' Her voice was sharp, but Santino noticed that her mouth trembled and something tugged in his chest. 'I admit I got carried away, but I hadn't expected you to kiss me.' She looked around the secluded beach and back to him, biting her lip. 'Why did you bring me here instead of taking me back to the yacht? And why did you send the launch away?' Her tension was tangible. 'Did you intend to seduce me? Maybe you think I owe you for rescuing me?'

'Of course I don't think that,' he denied roughly. 'You were in an emotional state after the incident with the jet-ski and I thought you might want some time to pull yourself together before we returned to the yacht.'

Santino's jaw clenched as shame rolled through him. He prided himself on his integrity but Arianna's accusation had hit a mark. She had been traumatised after being thrown off the jet-ski and the accident had brought back memories of how she had nearly drowned as a child. Once again he had been struck by her vulnerability, but that had not stopped him coming on to her. His body still ached to possess her and with a curse he jumped up and ran down the beach, diving into the waves and striking powerfully through the water.

A few minutes later he heard a boat's engine and saw the launch returning to the little cove. It ran up onto the sand and he waded through the shallows and spoke to the crewman. When he looked back up the beach, he couldn't see Arianna, and fear gripped him. It would be impossible for the kidnappers to have snatched her in the few minutes that he hadn't been with her, he told himself.

To his relief he spotted her over by some rocks, but as he walked towards her she backed away from him. 'I can't face going on the launch.' She hugged her arms around her body and her mouth crumpled. 'I know you must think I'm stupid.'

He frowned. 'Why do you put yourself down?' For reasons he could not explain to himself, Santino wanted to take her in his arms and comfort her as he had done after she'd been thrown off the jet-ski. 'Your fear of drowning is perfectly understandable after your childhood experience. I don't think you are an idiot, or stupid.'

Santino had a suspicion that Arianna was far more astute than she allowed people to think, but now was not the time to wonder why she played to the tabloids' opinion of her as an empty-headed socialite. He held out her bag containing her clothes. 'I sent the crewman back to the yacht to collect your things. Get dressed. We can return to the town via the stairs that climb up the cliff from the beach.'

She stared at him with wide, wary eyes, but then she suddenly smiled. Not the carefully choreographed smile he'd noticed she kept pinned to her face when she had been with her jet-set friends aboard the yacht. The smile she gave him was spontaneous and warm, and it stole his breath. 'Thank you,' she said softly.

There were three hundred steps winding up the steep cliff. Santino counted every one of them in an attempt to keep his mind and his gaze from Arianna's sexy derriere covered in tight-fitting, white denim jeans. They walked back to the car in silence and she didn't argue when he slid behind the wheel. Earlier he had called Filippo and arranged for someone to collect the four-by-four.

On the way back to the villa he glanced at Arianna and saw that she had fallen asleep. No doubt she was still shocked by the accident with the jet-ski, he thought grimly. The breeze blew strands of her chestnut-brown hair across her face. He recalled those moments on the beach when her body had trembled beneath his touch and his jaw tightened as he forced his gaze back to the road.

Fifteen minutes later he parked in the courtyard at the front of Villa Cadenza and touched her shoulder. 'Wake up, Sleeping Beauty.'

Her long lashes swept upwards and she regarded him sleepily with her velvet brown eyes. Santino could not bring himself to look away from her, from her mouth that was a sensual temptation even before she ran her tongue over her bottom lip. And the crazy thing was his feeling that it had been a wholly unconscious invitation, as if she was unaware of the effect she had on him.

He ran his hand around the back of his neck and felt the scar left by the bullet that had nearly claimed his life. A permanent reminder of the frailty of humankind. 'What happened earlier was a regrettable mistake,' he said curtly. 'I should not have kissed you.'

Her brows rose. 'Aren't all mistakes, by definition, regrettable? And surely you mean two mistakes? You kissed me by the pool this morning and then again on the beach this afternoon,' she reminded him.

'The first kiss was instigated by you.'

'I didn't hear you complain,' she said mildly.

He scowled at her. 'The point I am making,' he growled, 'is that it can't happen again.'

Arianna stepped out of the car and flashed him a brittle smile that made him wonder what had happened to the girl on the beach whose smile had lit up her lovely face, or if she had even existed outside of his imagination.

'You would be more convincing if you stopped staring at me as if you're visualising me naked in your bed,' she murmured, before she sauntered into the house, leaving Santino with a mental picture of her that instantly made him hard. He clenched his hands on the steering wheel while he fought the temptation to go after her and demonstrate that she was nowhere near as immune to him as she pretended to be.

The discordant sound of voices arguing broke the almost cloistered quiet of the workroom above Rosa's dress shop. Arianna glanced at her watch and was startled to see that she had been engrossed in her work for the past three hours.

After she'd shown Rosa some sketches of a cocktail dress that she had designed, the seamstress had suggested she should make a *toile*—a rough model of the dress made from muslin. Usually the *toile* would be placed on a tailor's dummy to see how the garment draped. But Arianna planned to make the dress for herself out of mulberry silk, and she had tried the *toile* on to check the fit before she worked with an expensive fabric.

She moved away from the mirror to look out of the window at the rear of the workroom and her heart sank when she saw Santino standing in the courtyard below. He was having a heated conversation with the manageress of the beauty salon. Damn the man, Arianna thought as she took off the *toile* and hurriedly pulled on her skirt and top.

At the villa the previous evening she had been furious when she'd discovered that he had confiscated the keys to both of her cars. But her accusation that she was a prisoner in her own home had elicited no sympathy from Santino. 'You can drive either of your vehicles as long as I accompany you to wherever you are going,' he'd told her.

But Arianna doubted that he would fall for her excuse of visiting the beauty salon again while she was actually at Rosa's workroom. Determined that Santino should not find out about her sewing lessons, she had slipped out of Villa Cadenza early in the morning and caught a bus into the town. Using public transport was a novelty that she would need to get used to in the future when she would have to rely on earning her own income from her fashion business.

Santino must have realised that she was missing from the villa and had driven into Positano to search for her. Although her Italian was limited, Arianna gathered that he had accused the manageress of the beauty salon of being involved in her disappearance. As she ran down the staircase from the workroom she fumbled to pull up the zip on her skirt and emerged into the courtyard flushed and breathless. 'What are you doing here?' she asked Santino crossly.

He jerked his head in her direction, and she was shocked by his strained expression. His skin looked grey beneath his tan, and his hair was dishevelled, as if he'd run his fingers through it many times.

'Arianna.' He strode over to her. 'Are you all right? I feared—' He broke off abruptly.

She was puzzled. 'You feared what, exactly?'

He did not reply and there was no clue to his thoughts

on his chiselled features. She grimaced. 'I suppose you were worried that I was up to no good.'

'Again,' Santino said drily, and the contempt in his voice brought a flush of colour to her cheeks. His eyes narrowed and she had an odd feeling that he wanted to say something else, but at that moment the door behind her banged shut in the breeze.

Santino looked up at the window of the building that she had exited from and frowned. 'Why did you leave the villa without me? I told you, it is your father's wish that I should accompany you whenever you go out.'

'And I told you that I need some privacy. I'm sick of my father's attempts to control my life,' Arianna said bitterly. She stiffened when Santino flicked his hard gaze over her.

'Did you get dressed in a hurry? Your shirt is buttoned up wrong.'

She looked down at her sleeveless cotton shirt and saw that she had misaligned the buttons in the button holes.

'Why all the secrecy?' he demanded. 'The woman in the beauty salon told me that you didn't have your nails done yesterday and you weren't even in the salon. So where did you go?'

He moved towards the door behind Arianna, and she knew that if he opened it he was bound to climb the stairs and discover Rosa's workroom. She stepped in front of him to bar his way, but he was so much bigger than her, and he would easily be able to push past her. With a deep sense of reluctance she decided that she would have to tell him about her sewing lessons.

'I came here to meet someone,' she muttered.

Santino's gaze lingered on her wrongly buttoned

shirt before moving up to her hair that had come loose from her chignon. Strands of hair curled around her face. It had been warm in Rosa's workroom, and Arianna could feel that her cheeks were pink. He looked up at the window again. From the outside of the building there was no indication that the room on the second story was a workroom. It could be a private apartment above the shop. Santino watched her fasten her shirt properly and his jaw hardened.

'By "someone" I assume you mean a lover,' he said harshly. 'Did you get up from his bed and dress in a hurry before you came down to meet me?'

Arianna was so taken aback by his accusation that she said nothing. Santino continued in a clipped voice, 'So, did you spend yesterday afternoon with this guy while I sat outside the damn café, drinking endless cups of coffee, and waited for you?' His green eyes glittered. 'I suppose that's why you sneaked out of the villa today?'

'I did not sneak out.'

Santino had given her a convenient excuse for her trips into Positano and Arianna was under no obligation to tell him the truth. She felt a little pang in her heart, thinking that she must have imagined the gentle concern he had shown her on the beach the previous day. He was constructed of iron and granite and there was no chink in his armour. 'My personal life is my business and I can do whatever I like, with whomever I like,' she told him coolly.

'As your bodyguard, I need to know where you are going and who you are meeting.'

Arianna's temper simmered. He made her feel like a naughty schoolgirl and she was incensed that he would report her every action to her father. Santino was effectively spying on her and she knew why. No doubt Randolph was anxious to avoid a scandal like the one she had been involved in a year ago, when the tabloids had printed graphic details of her alleged wild night of sex with a famous footballer.

The story had been pure fabrication. She'd danced with the footballer at a nightclub and they had been spotted by the paparazzi leaving the venue together. What hadn't been reported was that Scott Hunter had flagged down a taxi for her, and she had returned home alone with a blinding headache that had turned out to be the start of a severe bout of the flu.

She lifted her chin and fixed Santino with an icy glare. 'Do you seriously expect me to give you a list of my lovers?'

'From what I've heard, it's a long list,' he said bitingly.

For a split second it crossed Arianna's mind to tell him that the rumours and gossip about her were untrue. But why would he believe her? It was obvious that he believed the tabloid stories. And why did she care what he thought of her? She didn't, she assured herself.

'Can I assume from your judgemental tone that you are a virgin?' she asked him sweetly. 'You have never had a lover because you are saving yourself until you fall in love and decide to marry the lucky recipient of your affections?' He obviously did not like her sarcasm, and his dark brows drew together in a slashing frown when she continued, 'Or is this a case of double standards? It's fine for you to have any number of sexual partners, but if I do the same thing I must be a whore?'

'This is a pointless conversation,' he said through

gritted teeth. 'For the record, I don't have any intention of falling in love, and in my opinion marriage is an out-dated institution.' His jaw was rigid and Arianna's heart gave a jolt when she realised that he was struggling to control his temper. Common sense warned her not to antagonise him further, but the hard gleam in his eyes sent a heady rush of adrenalin through her.

'Maybe you're frustrated because you can't have me?' she taunted.

He moved faster than she could blink and caught her by her shoulder, pulling her towards him so that her breasts hit the hard wall of his chest and her breath was expelled from her body. She stared into his eyes and re-alised too late that she had been a fool to play with fire. The heat of his gaze scorched her and the contemptuous curl of his mouth hurt her more than it should.

'We both know that I could have you any time I wanted,' he bit out.

She opened her mouth to deny his arrogant claim, but the words were trapped in her throat. His face was so close to hers that the stubble on his jaw scraped her cheek. His warm breath grazed her lips and a quiver of desire ran like molten fire through her as she tilted her head in readiness for his mouth to claim hers. She was unaware of how utterly she betrayed herself. Her entire being was focused on Santino, on her need for him to kiss her, and she stared at him with wide-eyed incomprehension when he muttered something in Ital-ian and thrust her away from him.

'Somehow the thought that you have come straight from another man's bed lessens your appeal. It's like turning up late to a feast and finding only pickings left,' he drawled. But Arianna sensed from his harsh inhalation of breath that it had cost him to speak in that dismissive manner.

She was tempted to take him upstairs to Rosa's workroom to prove that he was wrong about her—that there was no mystery lover—and she would enjoy watching him grovel. The satisfactory scene that unfolded in her imagination was spoiled by the realisation that, if she revealed to Santino her plans to establish her own fashion label, he was likely to tell her father.

So she gave an airy shrug of her shoulders and put her hand on the door that led to the stairs to the workroom. 'You seem to be under the misapprehension that I care what you think about me, Santino. But here's a news flash—I don't give a damn.' She opened the door and threw him a haughty glance over her shoulder. 'I'll be busy here for another hour and you can wait for me in the car.'

CHAPTER FIVE

IT WAS ONLY because the party was for Jonny's birth-day that Arianna decided to attend. Jonny was a good friend, and there were few enough people who she con-sidered to be true and trustworthy friends, she acknowl-edged ruefully. Having a billionaire for a father meant that she'd had to learn to spot hangers-on and those so-called friends who hoped that an association with her would boost their career or their bank balance. A few times she had been burned, and she would be the first to admit that she had an issue with trust.

The party was a black-tie event taking place at the hottest nightclub on the Amalfi coast. Indira Club was in Amalfi town, along the coast from Positano, and the venue had been hired out exclusively for the party. The guest list was a mix of the great and good—wealthy so-cialites from across Europe and A-list celebrities who Jonny knew from his reality television show, *Toffs*. It was inevitable that the paparazzi would be present out-side the club in droves—the pap pack hunting the brat pack with their long-lens cameras.

Arianna had made the decision a year ago to step away from the glitzy world she had been part of since she was eighteen. Her brush with death when a bout of the flu had developed into a serious case of pneumonia had led to her re-evaluating her life. It was ironic, she mused, that the best way to get her designs noticed when she launched her fashion company would be to grab the media's attention any way she could. But establishing her own fashion label was not a whim. She was serious about starting her business, and she had to hope that if the clothes she designed were good enough they would speak for themselves.

The dress she had chosen to wear to the party was one of her own creations. Made of gold silk organza with a tulle overlay, the ball gown had a tight-fitting bodice with narrow shoulder straps and a full skirt. The design was unashamedly romantic and had been inspired by stories of fairy-tale princesses from Arianna's childhood.

All she needed was a handsome prince, she thought wryly as she dabbed perfume on the pulse points at her wrists and neck. She loved the exclusive fragrance that had been created for her by a famous Parisian perfumer, but she would no longer be able to afford bespoke perfume when she launched her fashion business. It would be a small price to pay for her independence from her father though.

Buoyed by that thought, Arianna collected her evening bag and pashmina and headed out of her bedroom. Halfway down the villa's sweeping staircase she saw Santino walk across the entrance hall and her footsteps faltered. He halted at the bottom of the stairs and seemed riveted by her appearance.

'You look exquisite,' he said thickly.

'Thank you.' She tried to sound cool and composed but her voice was annoyingly husky, and she felt herself blush beneath his intense scrutiny as she descended the last few steps. His green eyes gleamed and she glimpsed a feral hunger in his gaze that felt like a kick low in her belly.

He looked incredible in a tuxedo, white silk shirt and black bow tie. The stubble on his jaw had been trimmed and his dark-as-night hair was tidier than usual but still curled rebelliously over his collar.

'Don't you think you are rather overdressed for a bodyguard-cum-chauffeur?' she murmured, feeling a stab of jealousy as she wondered if he intended to meet a woman in Amalfi once he had delivered her to the party.

'The invitation states black tie.' Santino took a gold-edged card out of his jacket pocket. 'Your friend Jonny invited me to the party when I met him on his yacht, after I explained that you and I are *very* good friends.' The suggestive wink he gave infuriated her even more.

'Why on earth did you tell him that?'

'I thought you might prefer that the other guests to-night don't realise I am your bodyguard.'

She glared at him. 'I told you, there is no need for you to be at the Indira Club. The party is invitation only and the paparazzi will be prevented from entering the club. If you must, you can escort me to the door to make sure I don't do anything outrageous that would guarantee my photograph appearing on the front of to-morrow's tabloids.'

'But this—' Santino waved the invitation in front of her '—means that I can attend the party with you. Rather than you having to explain to your friends that I am your minder, it makes sense if I pretend to be your date.'

She shook her head fiercely and her hair, which

she'd allowed to dry into its natural, loose, silky curls, bounced on her shoulders. 'No way.'

'You can explain to anyone who asks that we got together after I rescued you when you came off the jet-ski,' Santino continued smoothly, as if she hadn't spoken.

Arianna opened her mouth to tell him that she would rather go to the party with Jack the Ripper than with him. Except that it wasn't true. The glitter in Santino's green eyes intrigued and excited her, and when he offered her his arm she hesitated before she placed her hand on his forearm. Beneath the sleeve of his jacket she felt the latent strength of sinews and muscles. His snarling tiger tattoo was hidden beneath his clothes but Santino was a dangerous beast and she must not forget it.

Tonight, however, the tiger was at least giving the appearance of being tamed. Santino escorted her outside and held the car door open while she climbed in and layers of gold tulle frothed around her. 'Would you like the sun roof open or closed?'

She grimaced. 'Closed, please, or my hair will look like I've been dragged through a hedge.'

'I doubt you could ever look anything other than perfect.'

Arianna glanced at him when he slid into the driver's seat, startled by the deep timbre of his voice. His eyes met hers and that feeling between them that she dared not examine too closely pulsed hard and hot. She swallowed and turned her head to stare out of the window.

'I'm sure Davina will be delighted to see you again, as will Poppy and Posy—the very attractive blonde twins you flirted with on Jonny's yacht,' she reminded him drily when he looked bemused.

'There is no need to be jealous, *cara*. I will only have eyes for you at the party.'

'I'm not *jealous*.' She jerked her head round to glare at him and felt certain that his lips twitched.

As he drove away from the villa she maintained a dignified silence while she struggled to regain her composure. The powerful sports car ate up the miles and soon they were flying along the Amalfi coast road, full of twists and turns and hairpin bends that Santino negotiated with skilful assurance. The scenery was dramatic, with the cliffs towering above the road on one side and a terrifying drop down to the coast on the other. The sun sinking below the horizon cast pink-and-gold streaks across the sky which were reflected on the dark, glassy sea.

Arianna was too pent up to notice the view. 'I'm not your *cara*,' she muttered, angry with herself for the way her heart had given a jolt at his careless endearment.

She had kept out of his way when they'd returned to the villa after he had found her in Positano and tension had simmered between them. But eventually boredom and loneliness had sent her down to the kitchen. Some of her happiest childhood memories were of when Ida had allowed her to help make bread, or she had sat at the table and watched Filippo, whose hobby was mending watches and clocks.

But when she'd entered the kitchen she had found Santino seated at the table, his long legs stretched out in front of him while he sipped a beer and chatted to the elderly couple. Their conversation was in Italian, and Arianna had felt like an intruder when the three of them had fallen silent. She'd quickly poured herself a glass of fruit juice and left.

It reminded her of when she'd been a teenager, on the rare occasions when she had been at home with her father and had walked into a room where he was entertaining guests. Randolph had never introduced her to his friends or asked her to join them and she had felt like an unwelcome visitor in her own home.

When she'd exited the kitchen and closed the door loudly behind her, she had heard Santino resume talking to Filippo and Ida, and her resentment of him had grown. But her conscience had pointed out that if she'd handled things differently instead of behaving like a spoilt brat he might have invited her to stay.

Silly tears stung Arianna's eyes as she recalled how alone she had felt when she'd returned to her bedroom. The rich princess in her ivory tower. She looked at Santino's tanned hands holding the steering wheel, before moving her gaze up to his strong profile, and asked herself why his opinion of her mattered.

'You have an Italian name and speak the language like a native, so how were you able to serve in the British army if you are Italian?' She gave in to her curiosity about him.

'I have dual nationality. My father was Sicilian and my mother was English. I was born in Sicily and lived there until I was a teenager, when we moved to the south west of England.'

'We?'

'My parents and younger sister, Gina. My mother's family are farmers in Devon. She met my father when she was on holiday in Sicily. Apparently they fell in love at first sight, were married within a month and I was born a year later. Madre had seemed happy living in Sicily. Sometimes I've wondered if she knew she was ill and wanted to go back to the place where she had grown up,' Santino said half-beneath his breath. He glanced at Arianna. 'My mother died from a brain tumour eighteen months after we moved to England.'

'I'm sorry,' she said softly. 'The tragedy must have been even harder for you and your father and sister to bear when you hadn't lived in England for long.'

'Yes.' His voice was devoid of emotion but she noticed that he flexed his fingers around the steering wheel and his knuckles whitened.

'Did your father take you and your sister back to live in Sicily after your mother's death?'

'No, he wanted to remain in Devon to be near to her grave. My father never really recovered from her death, and when he died a few years ago I believe it was a release from his unhappiness.'

'That's sad, but also very poignant that he loved your mother so much.'

'Do you think so?' Santino's jaw clenched. 'My father numbed his grief with whisky and left my English grandparents to more or less bring up my sister. Gina was only eight when our mother died. She is a credit to the grandparents who took good care of her, although it is down to her own hard work that she has a successful career as a senior fashion buyer for a top department store in New York.'

Had that been a dig at her lack of a career? Arianna wondered. Santino's sister must have been affected by the loss of their mother, but at least she'd had other family members to fill the void and give her affection. When Celine had moved to Australia and left Arianna behind, no one had paid her any attention, certainly not her father.

'Did your grandparents take care of you too?'

'They did their best, but I was an angry young man and I don't suppose I was particularly likeable.' Santino braked as he steered around a steep bend. 'I felt like an outsider living in a tiny Devon village and, at school, my odd-sounding name and my accent made me different from the other kids. My grandparents tried to get me interested in their farm but I missed my old life and my friends in Sicily.'

He glanced at Arianna and admitted, 'I hated spending hours every day in a cold milking shed with a bunch of cows.' His rueful grin lit a flame inside her and she smiled back at him.

'What made you decide to join the army?'

'By the time I was seventeen, I'd begun to seriously go off the rails, and I'd been in trouble with the police a couple of times for minor offences. There was an army recruitment day at school, and I signed up, because being a soldier seemed a better option than getting a criminal record.' He was silent for a moment. 'Being in the army made me feel that I belonged somewhere and gave me some self-respect.'

'I understand what it's like to feel lost,' she admitted, wondering as she spoke why she had opened up to him when she had never felt an inclination to do so with anyone else.

He frowned. 'How have you ever felt lost, Arianna? You grew up with immense privilege, you are stunningly beautiful and you have the world at your feet. If you feel lost, you only have yourself to blame,' Santino said harshly. 'You could use your wealth, and the media's fascination with you, to great effect by raising money for charities or bringing awareness to social issues. But instead you do nothing better than drift from one party to another and one meaningless affair to another.'

'Not everything you have read about me in the newspapers is true!' she snapped, stung by his criticism. A lot of rubbish had been printed about her, but she felt a sick sense of shame when she remembered various photos of herself falling out of clubs, and on more than one occasion out of her clothes. There had been a time when getting drunk had been preferable to dealing with her emotions, and she'd sought popularity to prove to herself that she wasn't lonely.

She turned her head away from Santino and a tense silence replaced the camaraderie that had briefly existed between them. They arrived in Amalfi, and out of the car window she saw a crowd of photographers in front of the Indira Club. Instead of stopping outside the entrance, Santino turned up a side road, and minutes later he parked the car in an alleyway at the back of the club.

'It will be best if we enter the building through the back door,' he said in answer to her questioning look.

'To avoid the paparazzi, presumably. Has my father offered to pay you a bonus if you keep me out of the tabloids until after Fitzgerald Design's stock market debut?' she asked sarcastically.

'Arianna…' He seemed about to say something else, but when he put his hand on her arm she shrugged him off.

'Randolph manipulates people. It's all part of his control strategy. I should know, because he has tried to control me all my life,' she told Santino bitterly before she swept past him, gathering up her long skirt in her hands to avoid brushing against a stack of empty beer crates

by the back door to the club. She didn't look round to
see if he was behind her as she marched through the
kitchens, ignoring the startled looks of the staff. The
voice of the DJ led her to the main area of the club,
where the dance floor was already packed with party
guests and she spotted Jonny leaning against the bar.

'I didn't see you arrive,' he said as he handed her a
flute of champagne and watched her take several long
sips. 'That's vintage Krug that you're knocking back
like lemonade, darling.' A faint frown crossed Jonny's
pleasant features. 'What's wrong, Arianna?'

'Nothing,' she lied. 'I just needed a drink. Do I get
to dance with the birthday boy?'

'Only if you can assure me that your ex-army boyfriend won't rip my legs off,' Jonny said wryly. 'He
mentioned while we were on the yacht yesterday that
he had served in the forces.'

Arianna followed Jonny's gaze across the room to
where Santino was leaning against a pillar and was evidently the focus of interest of a group of women nearby.
His height made him easy to pick out, and the brooding
expression on his devastatingly handsome face caused
her heart to give a jolt. She remembered that her father
had said in his text message that Santino had been in
the SAS. It would account for the steel core that she
sensed ran through him. 'It's not what you think,' she
muttered to Jonny.

'Maybe you should let Santino know that, if the hungry way he's looking at you is an indication of what
he's thinking,' Jonny murmured as he led her onto the
dance floor.

For the next few hours Arianna sparkled. She flit-
ted from one dance partner to the next like a golden

butterfly, and laughed and flirted and drank too much champagne, just as everyone expected of Arianna Fitzgerald, the party princess. She congratulated herself on not looking over her shoulder for Santino, but a sixth sense told her that he was watching her, and she laughed louder and flirted more outrageously with the men who flocked around her. They seemed young and crass compared to Santino's smouldering sensuality, and her breath rushed from her lungs when he appeared in front of her and smoothly took the place of Hugo Galbraith, with whom she had been dancing.

'My turn, I think you'll find,' he told Hugo. His smile did nothing to disguise his dangerous tone and the Englishman stepped back from Arianna with alacrity. She hardly noticed Hugo walk away as her gaze tangled with Santino's green eyes, glittering with what she belatedly realised was fury. He clamped one arm around her waist and his other hand captured hers and held it against the lapel of his jacket, just as the DJ slowed the tempo and played a haunting ballad that had topped the music charts for weeks. 'You are obviously enjoying yourself,' he growled.

'Why wouldn't I have a good time at the party?' she countered, flashing him a brittle smile. 'Socialising is what I do best, after all.'

She felt the muscles in his arm flex as he pulled her closer so that her cheek was pressed against the soft silk of his shirt, and his shockingly hard arousal nudged the junction between her thighs.

'Is he here? Was he one of the pretty boys I saw you dancing with?'

Startled, her lashes swept upwards. 'Who?'

'Your lover.'

'I don't have a lover.' Too late she remembered Santino's assumption that she'd spent the morning with a man when she had actually been in Rosa's workroom. 'Um…what I mean is, no…he isn't at the party. Would it bother you if he was here?'

'Everything about you bothers me, *cara*.'

His rough voice sent a curl of heat through her. She told herself that she must have imagined he'd sounded possessive, or that the hard gleam in his eyes softened a fraction. But she did not imagine that he dipped his face closer to hers, so close that she was mesmerised by the sensual shape of his mouth as he brought it within a millimetre of her lips.

'You can no doubt feel how bothered I am by you,' he drawled. There might have been a hint of self-derision in his voice, but Arianna was only aware of his potent masculinity when he moved his hand to the small of her back and exerted pressure to bring her pelvis into burning contact with his. Feeling the solid ridge of his erection beneath his trousers elicited a flood of molten heat between her legs.

She shivered in the heat of his fire, but when his warm breath grazed her lips she whispered, 'You said you couldn't kiss me again.'

'I lied,' he muttered. And then he proved it by covering her mouth with his.

It was wild and hot. Santino's lips moved over hers with devastating assurance, sipping her, tasting her, and she trembled at the onslaught of his fierce passion. It did not occur to Arianna to try to resist him. She pressed her body against his, needing to be closer to him. Her hands were flat on his chest and she felt the heat of him through his shirt. Between kisses she snatched a breath and the spicy scent of his aftershave that assailed her senses sent another lick of fire through her.

His kiss transported her to another universe where only they existed—where there was only the hard wall of his muscular chest against her breasts and the sweet intoxication of his mouth on hers. She was lost instantly and utterly to his mastery, and she kissed him back mindlessly as the fire inside her became an inferno.

'We need to get out of here, *cara mia*.' Santino lifted his mouth from hers and whispered the words in her ear before he nipped her earlobe with his teeth.

She shivered with pleasure, but the spell he had cast on her broke, and reality hit like a sharp slap. It was bad enough knowing that his husky endearment was a lie and she was not his darling. But, worse still, they had been all over each other like a pair of teenagers while they'd been on the dance floor, in full view of four hundred or so party guests. Once again she was the centre of attention and it was a small mercy that the paparazzi were not around to snap pictures of her shameful behaviour. It was that thought that made her stiffen and pull out of Santino's arms.

'Aren't you worried that some of the other guests might post pictures of us on social media?' She was pleased that she managed to inject a note of mocking amusement into her voice to disguise the shame and hurt that coiled through her like a poisonous serpent. 'And if the tabloids got hold of the photos I'm sure my father wouldn't be too impressed, as he is paying you to keep me out of the limelight.'

Santino frowned. 'Arianna...'

'Leave me alone.' Tears stung her eyes and she blinked hard. She would rather die than let him see that if he cut her she would bleed the same as any other mortal. She heard him swear, but she'd already spun away from him and was weaving a path through the crowded dance floor, heading for the exit.

Outside the front of the club the paparazzi had dispersed. Behind her she heard Santino say urgently, 'Arianna, wait…' But she ignored him and hurried away from the brightly lit street.

Humiliated and desperate to be alone, she headed past the harbour, which at the height of the summer was full of yachts and motor cruisers. As she walked farther away from the town, the clinking sound of the yachts' rigging was a strangely mournful sound. A figure detached from the shadow of a doorway and walked past Arianna. She caught sight of the man's face in the light from the street lamp and had an odd feeling that she had seen him before somewhere.

When she reached the little beach area at the far end of the harbour, she took off her high-heeled sandals and walked along the shoreline, where the waves rippled over her feet. Her lips were still stinging from Santino's kiss and her insides squirmed as she recalled her wanton response to him. She hated him, she thought angrily, and she didn't understand why he affected her so much.

'*Signorina, per favore*, you have a light for my cigarette?'

The voice that came out of the darkness was strangely familiar. She whirled round to see the man who had passed her on the street a few moments ago. Now she recognised him as the jet-skier who had caused the accident the previous day. With him was a second man, and as the moon slid out from behind a cloud she realised that he was the steward from Jonny's yacht who had made her feel uncomfortable.

'No, I don't smoke,' she said loudly, hoping that there might be other people nearby who would hear her. The two men did not move away and Arianna's heart beat a frantic rhythm in her chest with the realisation that she was alone on the dark, deserted beach. She stumbled as the waves swirled around the hem of her ball gown. The men were both stockily built and rough-looking, and when they moved menacingly towards her she took another step backwards into the sea. 'What do you want?' she demanded fearfully.

CHAPTER SIX

SANTINO'S FEET POUNDED on the road, echoing the pounding of his heart as he raced towards the harbour. He hadn't seen which way Arianna had gone when she'd left the club, but he had been alerted by her scream, and as he ran he cursed himself for allowing her out of his sight. Again.

'Arianna, where the hell are you?'

In the moonlight he saw her tearing across the beach and relief hit him like a punch in his gut. He jumped down onto the sand and ran towards her, catching her when she threw herself into his arms. Her breath came in harsh gasps and her slender body shook as she burrowed into his shirt front.

'*Cara*, what happened?' He slid his hand beneath her chin and tilted her face up. The shimmer of tears in her eyes tugged on emotions he'd buried inside him when he had stood at his mother's graveside and vowed never to allow himself to care so deeply ever again.

She struggled to draw a breath. 'Two men approached me, and one of them grabbed my arm, but I managed to get away. I hid behind some boats on the beach, and the men must have heard you shouting my name, and they ran off. He tore my dress.' Arianna's voice wobbled and Santino saw that the shoulder strap on her dress was hanging by a thread. Violent anger surged through him but he ruthlessly controlled it and stroked his hand over her hair as if he were soothing a frightened colt.

'I'm sure the man who grabbed me was the jet-skier who ran into me and Hugo,' she said shakily. 'The other man works as a steward on Jonny's yacht. I noticed yesterday that he kept staring at me.'

Santino peered across the dark beach. A storm was brewing and the moon had disappeared behind clouds. Luckily Arianna had managed to hide from the men. But the scar on the back of his neck prickled and his instincts warned him that her safety was still threatened. He held her tighter when he felt a shudder run through her.

'Thank goodness you arrived when you did.' She managed a faint smile and Santino was struck by her courage. He would have expected her to be hysterical, but although clearly shaken she remained calm. 'It's the second time in two days that you've rescued me. Maybe I do need a bodyguard to keep me out of trouble after all,' she said ruefully.

His jaw clenched. He had promised Arianna's father that he would not tell her about the plot to kidnap her, but he had compromised her safety. He could not risk taking her back to Villa Cadenza—and he was grimly aware that his lack of control when he had kissed her had sent her running out of the nightclub and into danger.

Pulling his phone from his jacket, Santino made a brief call to Paolo, an old friend from his childhood. Earlier in the day he had arranged for Paolo to bring his boat across to the Amalfi coast from Sicily in case the kidnap threat escalated and he needed to get Arianna away quickly. That scenario had just become a reality, and once again he was furious that he had allowed himself to be distracted from his duty of protecting her.

'Come on, we should go,' he told her, trying to hide his concern that the two men—maybe there were more of them—could be close by.

'I left my shoes on the sand.' She resisted his attempt to lead her away from the beach. 'They're designer and cost a fortune. Why can't I go and find them? The men have gone, and I don't suppose they meant any harm. I allowed my imagination to run away with me,' Arianna argued when he clamped his arm around her waist and half-carried her along the jetty, past the boats moored on either side.

Behind him Santino heard the screech of tyres on the road, and when he looked back over his shoulder he saw four men jump out of a car and sweep a powerful flashlight over the boats in the harbour. He swore. 'Forget the damned shoes. We need to go now.'

'Go where?' Arianna's eyes were huge in her pale face when he halted next to a motor cruiser. 'Santino, what is going on? I'm not getting on a boat. I want to go back to Villa Cadenza.'

'It's too dangerous for you to return to the villa.' He heard footsteps walking fast along the jetty and realised he had no choice but to act. '*Cara*, you have to trust me,' he said before he scooped her off her feet and leapt aboard the cruiser with her in his arms. Paolo had already untied the ropes that secured the boat to the jetty and was waiting in the cockpit with the engine running. Santino called to him, and moments later the boat headed towards the harbour exit.

'Put me down!' Arianna thumped her fists on his chest when he carried her down the steps into the salon. He swore as he deposited her on the sofa.

'Take it easy, you little wildcat.'

The gold flecks in her eyes gleamed with temper. 'What do you mean "take it easy"? This evening I have been physically assaulted by two strangers and kidnapped by my bodyguard.'

Santino dragged his gaze from the jerky rise and fall of her breasts framed so perfectly by her gold dress. 'I'm not kidnapping you,' he said gruffly. 'I'm taking you to my home in Sicily where I will be better able to protect you from the mafia gang who are determined to kidnap you and demand a multi-million-pound ransom from your father for your release.'

She stared at him, the disbelief on her face turning to something warier when he held her gaze. 'That story sounds very far-fetched.'

'Why? Your father is immensely wealthy and your regular appearances in the tabloids made it easy for the gang to track your whereabouts. They have watched you for more than a year and know that you spend every summer in Positano. They know who your friends are, and one of the gang applied for a job as a steward on your friend Jonny's yacht. When you went out on the jet-ski yesterday, the steward alerted the other gang members, who were on a boat near to where the *Sun Princess* had dropped anchor.'

'How do you know all this?' Arianna bit her lip, drawing Santino's attention to her mouth, and he remembered how soft it had felt beneath his when he'd kissed her. Adrenalin was still pumping through his body, heightening his senses and inflaming his desire for her.

Cursing silently, he stripped off his jacket and loosened his bow tie before he crossed the salon to the bar. 'I don't know about you but I could do with a drink.' Alcohol might anaesthetise him to her sensual allure.

She shook her head when he held up a bottle of whisky. 'Could I have some water, please?'

He took a bottle of water from the fridge, poured himself a large whisky and walked back to sit down next to her on the sofa that ran along one wall of the salon. The single malt was smoky and mellow, and he took a long sip.

'I found out about the plot to kidnap you while I was working undercover to infiltrate a gang of drug smugglers in southern Italy. The authorities were unable to contact you to warn you of the threat, so they alerted your father, and Randolph subsequently hired me as your bodyguard. The Italian police are doing their best to hunt down the gang members and arrest them, but until that happens you are in danger.' He raked his fingers through his hair. 'The best way I can protect you is to hide you in Sicily where the kidnappers won't think of looking for you.'

'Why didn't you tell me?' She looked stunned, but almost immediately her chin came up and she glared at him. 'You had no right to keep that information a secret from me.'

'Your father thought it best that you did not know. He was concerned about how you would cope with the kidnap threat because he thinks you are emotionally fragile following the drug overdose you took a year ago.'

'I did *not* take an overdose,' she said sharply. 'At least, not the way my father implied.' The gold flecks in her eyes flashed again. 'I accidentally took too much of a strong flu remedy and was admitted to hospital after the housekeeper found me unconscious. I ended up in intensive care when I developed pneumonia. I was in hospital for five weeks, including for my birthday, but Randolph didn't visit or phone me once. I doubt he was even aware of how ill I was.'

The tremor in her voice tugged on something deep inside Santino that he was determined to ignore. He tore his gaze away from Arianna's mouth and drained his glass before he stood up and went to pour himself another drink.

'My father's indifference was proof, if I'd needed it, that he doesn't care about me,' she said dully.

'If that was true, why did he hire me to be your bodyguard?'

'If I was kidnapped it would create negative publicity likely to affect the value of Fitzgerald Design's shares when the company is floated on the stock market. Also, my father would loathe having to pay a ransom. Money is the only thing he cares about.' Her mouth trembled and she quickly pressed her lips together. 'I'm not even certain that he *would* pay the kidnappers to secure my release.'

'Of course he would,' Santino said roughly. 'Your father is not an ogre.'

'I recently discovered that he had bribed my mother not to seek custody of me after my parents divorced. Not because he wanted me, but because he is obsessively controlling.' She gave a bitter laugh. 'Randolph can be charming when he wants something. It would certainly suit him to hire an ex-SAS serviceman to foil a plot to kidnap the daughter he regards as a nuisance.' Her expression became speculative. 'I would be interested to know just how my father persuaded you to take the job of my bodyguard.'

She jumped to her feet and her temper exploded. Even the gossamer layers of her gold dress seemed to shimmer with fury. 'You should have told me the truth instead of treating me like a child.'

'You behaved like a child,' he countered harshly, trying to ignore the stab of guilt in his gut that she was right. 'You were determined to defy me.'

'Because I believed you had been sent by my father to control me. And maybe *that* is the truth here. I only have your word that a mafia gang are plotting to kidnap me.'

'What do you think the men on the beach wanted, Arianna?'

She paled, and guilt corkscrewed through him again. She had been through enough tonight, and he didn't know why he felt an overwhelming need to take her in his arms and comfort her. 'I can show you the email I received earlier this evening from the Italian police,' he said. 'I thought I recognised one of the stewards on Jonny's yacht. The police ran a check on him and confirmed that he is one of the gang members.'

'I see.' She sank down onto the sofa as if her legs would not hold her up. Her teeth gnawed her lower lip, making him want to lean forward and soothe the place with his tongue. She had driven him crazy all evening when he'd watched her dance with an endless stream of young men at the party. Popinjays all of them, insulated from the harsh realities of life by wealth and privilege, as Arianna herself was. It was odd, then, his idea that she did not fit in with her crowd of friends. That sense of alienation was something Santino remembered when his family had moved from Sicily to a small Devon village.

He swirled the amber liquid in his glass and asked himself why he was looking for hidden depths to Arianna that might indicate there was more to her than the spoilt party princess and tabloid darling. Why did he even care? He frowned. The insights she'd given about her relationship with her father had been surprising. Could it be that her attention seeking was a deliberate ploy to disguise the vulnerability that he'd glimpsed occasionally?

Annoyed by his train of thought, and more by his damnable fascination with her beautiful body, he stood up. Arianna was searching for something in her evening purse and pulled out a packet of pills.

'They're painkillers,' she explained when his eyes narrowed. 'I suffer from migraines, often brought on by stress,' she said pointedly. 'Do you have any idea how long I'll have to stay in Sicily?'

He shrugged. 'It could be a few weeks before the Italian police are able to arrest all the gang members.'

'Weeks! I assumed it would be a matter of days. It's crucial that I return to London by the middle of September for Fashion Week.'

'Your attendance at a fashion show is, of course, crucial,' he said sardonically. 'I'll tell the police they need to work faster so that your hectic social life isn't disrupted.'

As Santino strode up the steps and onto the deck, he wondered why he had thought that there might be more to Arianna than vanity. She was a beautiful, empty shell, and he couldn't understand why he was disappointed or what he had hoped for.

He stepped into the motor cruiser's cockpit and chatted with Paolo. It was good to catch up on news about old friends, and he admitted to himself that he was glad of an excuse to return to Sicily. His family home, Casa Uliveto, was the only thing that he permitted himself to love, apart from his sister.

Santino regarded the first fifteen years of his life as a golden time before everything had changed. His mother had died and his father had sunk into a deep depression. It had scared him when he was a teenager to see how love and grief had destroyed Antonio. In truth the idea that love could have such a powerful effect still scared him far more than when facing his own mortality on the battlefields in Afghanistan.

Restlessly he headed back down to the salon, assuring himself that this need he had to be near Arianna was simply because she was his responsibility. His mouth twisted as he thought how much she would hate that. Her fierce independence surprised him as much as her fiery temper excited him. She was beautiful when she was angry and exquisite when she was asleep. Santino came to an abrupt halt in the doorway of the salon and stared at her slender form stretched out on the sofa.

She was lying on her side and the upper slopes of her breasts were pushed above the neckline of her dress, reminding him of perfect, round peaches that he longed to taste with his tongue. The side split in her long skirt had fallen open to reveal one slender, silky-smooth thigh. Her sensuality called to him like a siren's song, but the way she slept with her hand tucked beneath her cheek and her lips slightly parted was curiously innocent.

Even while Arianna was asleep she sent out conflicting messages, Santino thought grimly. Was she the shameless It Girl who played to the paparazzi? Or was that the lie, and was the ethereal creature who aroused his protective instincts—and aroused a lot more besides, he acknowledged self-derisively—the real Arianna Fitzgerald?

He looked over at the bar. The single malt offered a tempting escape from the mess inside his head but he resisted. Memories of seeing his father slumped in a chair, surrounded by empty cider cans and too drunk at three o'clock in the afternoon to be able to collect Gina from school, had taught Santino that alcohol did not provide salvation. He picked up his jacket and draped it over Arianna to keep her warm—not to save himself from the temptation of her delectable body.

And that, he thought grimly, was the biggest lie of all.

Sunlight slanting through the shutters cast stripes across the bedspread. Arianna opened her eyes and looked around the unfamiliar room, and her memory slowly returned. She was at Santino's villa in Sicily and this was his sister's bedroom. He had told her that Casa Uliveto had been his childhood home and his father had kept the house when the family had moved to England. Santino had explained that Gina lived in New York and was not planning to visit in the next few months.

She sat up cautiously. Her head still felt delicate after the migraine attack that had started on the boat that had brought her and Santino to Sicily. The strong painkillers she'd taken had knocked her out and she remembered little of the journey. She vaguely recalled that Santino had carried her off the boat and across a beach to some steps that led up to the house. But she had been half-asleep and hadn't taken much notice of her surroundings, although she had been aware of his strong arms around her as he'd carried her, and the steady thud of his heart beneath her ear when she'd rested her head on his chest.

He had brought her to the bedroom, and she'd been sufficiently awake to take off her dress before she'd climbed into bed and immediately fallen back to sleep. She squinted at her watch and was shocked to find that it was nearly eleven a.m. No wonder her stomach felt hollow. Her feet met the cool floor tiles when she slid out of bed. The room's décor of whitewashed walls, dark wood furniture and soft blue bedding was simple but pretty, and the muted colour scheme was repeated in the en suite bathroom.

Arianna caught sight of herself in the mirror above the sink and grimaced to see her tangled hair and smudges of mascara on her cheeks. She never went to bed without first removing her make-up and using a variety of expensive potions on her skin. But the only items she'd brought with her in her little gold evening bag were a toothbrush, a mini perfume spritzer and a lip gloss. She didn't even have any shoes, she thought, remembering her beautiful designer sandals that she'd left behind on the beach in Amalfi.

It felt strangely liberating to have no possessions. At Lyle House and at Villa Cadenza her wardrobes were bursting with clothes, many of which she'd never worn. Shopping had filled the empty hours of every day, but the truth was that all the clothes, shoes and luxury toiletries that she'd paid for with a swipe of her credit card hadn't eased the emptiness inside her.

A shudder ran through her when she thought of the two men who had approached her on the beach after she'd run out of the nightclub. It had been a frightening experience but she'd assumed that the men were drunk and hadn't meant any real harm. Learning that they belonged to a mafia gang and had intended to kidnap her made the incident much more terrifying. If Santino had not found her in time, she could have been kidnapped and her life would have been in danger. The recent news story about a well-known footballer's wife, who had been snatched and then murdered by her kidnappers after her husband had involved the police, was a grim reminder that the mafia was utterly ruthless.

Her shoulder was stinging, and when she looked in the mirror she saw a jagged red weal on her skin. She remembered that the man who'd grabbed hold of her had been wearing a ring and she'd felt it cut into her. Nausea swept through her. She felt dirty and tainted, and with another shudder she hurried into the shower and scrubbed every inch of her body with a bar of lemon-scented soap.

Santino had told her that his sister kept a few items of clothes at the house and wouldn't mind if Arianna borrowed them. It was that or wear her ball gown, she acknowledged as she put on a pair of bleached denim shorts and a sleeveless cinnamon-coloured top made of a silky material that clung rather too lovingly to her breasts. It was lucky that she and Gina Vasari were the same dress size, she thought.

A pair of leather flip-flops that she found in the wardrobe fitted her. The lack of a hairdryer or straighteners meant that her hair dried naturally into loose curls. Studying her reflection in the mirror, she felt oddly vulnerable with her face bare of make-up. She felt naked without her favourite scarlet lipstick, and annoyingly she found herself wondering what Santino would think of her now that she looked ordinary instead of glamorous.

Arianna's heart skipped a beat when she went downstairs and found him in the kitchen. Like her, he was wearing denim shorts, and his black T-shirt was moulded to his impressive six-pack. She had followed the smell of bacon frying and her stomach growled as she watched him load two plates with bacon, eggs and mushrooms.

He gave her a searing look as she hovered uncertainly in the doorway. 'The only thing I liked when I moved to Devon as a teenager was an English cooked breakfast,' he told her as he pushed a plate across the table towards her. 'Help yourself to coffee.'

'I'm starving,' she confessed, pulling out a chair.

'Me too,' he drawled. The blatant suggestion in his voice brought her skin out in goose bumps, and the gleam in his eyes made her blush as he raked his gaze over her and she felt her nipples tighten. She hadn't worn a bra beneath her ball gown yesterday evening, and there hadn't been one among Gina's clothes for her to borrow. The silky material of the shirt brushing against her bare breasts with their taut, sensitive peaks felt deliciously sensual and made her intensely aware of her femininity.

Santino took his place opposite her at the table and picked up his knife and fork, but his eyes did not leave her face. 'You look very lovely this morning, Arianna,' he said gruffly.

Was he joking? Self-consciously she ran her fingers through her riot of curls. 'I'm not wearing make-up.'

'You don't need it. Your skin is beautiful.' He broke off abruptly and she had the impression that he was annoyed with himself. Flustered and agonisingly aware of him, she dropped her gaze from his harshly handsome face and tried to concentrate on eating her breakfast.

'This is good,' she murmured after a couple of mouthfuls of crisp bacon. Where did you learn to cook?'

'The army taught me to be self-sufficient, but I'm not an expert chef by any stretch of imagination. My sister is a much better cook than me.'

She speared a mushroom. 'Why did you leave the army?'

'I'd served in the Parachute Regiment for ten years, including three tours of duty in Afghanistan, and I felt it was time to do something different.' He picked up his cup and took a gulp of coffee. 'A good friend of mine had been badly injured and Mac was invalided out of the army at the same time as I left. We decided to go into business together.'

'Doing what?' she asked curiously.

'My father had opened a delicatessen in Devon, specialising in selling olive oil that comes from the olive groves here at Casa Uliveto. Dad took little interest in the shop or anything else after my mother died. It was close to bankruptcy when I took it over but I managed to turn the business around. Mac and I ran it together until he left to pursue other interests.'

Arianna found it hard to picture Santino running a shop. It seemed rather ordinary for such an extraordinary man. 'I know from my father that you were in the SAS,' she murmured.

He shrugged, and she sensed he was reluctant to talk about his time in the special forces but she couldn't stem her curiosity. Her eyes were drawn to the tattoo of a snarling tiger on his arm. 'Does your tattoo have special significance?'

He nodded. 'I took part in a special mission in Helmand, codenamed Tiger. Those of us who survived had the tattoo done in honour of the men who lost their lives or suffered life-changing injuries.' His voice was flat and devoid of emotion but Arianna noticed a nerve jump in his cheek.

'The scar on your back.' she murmured. 'Did you receive it in Afghanistan?' She had been shocked when she'd seen the jagged scar that ran from his shoulder blade up to his neck and disappeared beneath his hairline.

Santino had stiffened when she'd mentioned his scar, and she thought he wasn't going to answer, but then he said, 'My patrol was ambushed by sniper fire,' he said at last in a taut voice. 'I was hit. It was bad luck that the bullet struck me at a point where I wasn't protected by my body vest. I would certainly have died if Mac hadn't dragged me out of the line of fire. But the area was strewn with landmines and one step in the wrong place could be fatal. In Mac's case, both his legs were blown off when an explosive device detonated.'

'It must have been terrible.' Arianna did not know what to say that wouldn't sound inane.

'Helmand was hell,' Santino told her savagely. 'You can have no idea of the guilt I feel knowing that my best friend can never walk again.'

Startled by the rawness in his voice, she murmured, 'You can't blame yourself. It was Mac's decision to go to your aid.'

His jaw clenched and Arianna sensed that he controlled his emotions with an iron will. 'Of course I blame myself,' he told her grimly. 'Mac didn't even know that I was alive when he ran across to me. If he had left me where I'd fallen he wouldn't be confined to a wheelchair for the rest of his life.'

Impulsively, Arianna reached across the table and covered Santino's hand with her own. Her eyes softened with compassion. 'What would you have done if the roles had been reversed? I don't believe that you would have left your friend to die.'

He frowned. 'Of course not.'

'If you had lost your limbs while saving Mac's life, would you blame him for your injuries?'

'No, I would be glad that he was alive.' He exhaled heavily. 'I see where you are going with this.' He moved suddenly and caught her fingers in his. 'I had not expected such insight from someone who spends her life shopping and socialising.' He looked down at her small hand in his much larger one and rubbed his thumb over the pulse that was beating frantically in her wrist. 'I am intrigued to know, who is the real Arianna Fitzgerald?'

'Just because I go to a lot of parties doesn't mean that I can't feel sympathy.' Desperate to hide the hurt she felt at his comment, Arianna said flippantly, 'Perhaps if the tabloids knew there was another side to me they would label me "the tart with a heart of gold".'

She snatched her hand out of his and continued to eat her breakfast, but her appetite had faded. Santino refilled both their coffee cups and leaned back in his chair, studying her intently, as if he was trying to fathom her out.

'Why was a Devon shopkeeper trying to infiltrate a gang of drug smugglers in Italy?' Arianna asked him. Something about his story did not add up.

He laughed. 'As a matter of fact I sold the delicatessen business a while ago. Prior to that Mac had left the business to set up a private investigation agency. He's fifteen years older than me, and before joining the army he had been in the police force.' Santino's expression turned serious. 'Mac's younger sister died suspiciously and Mac was convinced that Laura's drug-dealer boyfriend was involved in her death. He discovered that the guy had links to the mafia in southern Italy and he asked me to infiltrate the gang with the aim of breaking up their drug-smuggling operation.'

'Wasn't that an incredibly dangerous thing to do? If your cover had been blown the gang might have killed you.'

He shrugged. 'There was an element of risk. But Mac was devastated by his sister's death, and I owed him. When I learned that the gang intended to kidnap a wealthy English heiress, your safety took precedence over Mac's desire for revenge on his sister's killers. But if the Italian police are successful in arresting the gang members there will hopefully be justice for Laura.'

Arianna swirled the coffee grounds around in the bottom of her cup while she mulled over everything he had told her. From the sound of it Santino's only intention had been—and still was—to protect her from the mafia gang who wanted to kidnap her. He hadn't been trying to control her behaviour and keep her out of the media spotlight as she had accused him of doing. Her problem was that she believed every man was a control freak like her father, she thought ruefully.

Santino was brave and honourable. He had risked his life to help his friend Mac, and he had been there to protect her every time she had needed him. It made her stroppy attitude towards him when they had been in Positano seem even more childish.

At least now the subterfuge was over. She couldn't even blame him for withholding the truth about the kidnap threat when he had been given misleading information from her father that she had supposedly taken a drug overdose. The weeks she had spent in hospital with pneumonia had been a horrible, frightening time and the fact that Randolph hadn't contacted her at all had forced her to accept that he would never be interested in her.

She looked over at Santino and her breath caught in her throat when his gaze trapped hers. He was impossibly handsome and his chiselled features—those slashing cheekbones and square jaw—were cruelly beautiful. The only slight softening was his sensual mouth, tilted upwards at one corner in a wry smile that made her wish he would walk around the table, pull her into his arms and kiss her with all the heat and hunger she could see in his glittering green eyes.

He had said he was intrigued to know who she really was. And here at his house in Sicily, away from her old crowd and the photographer's lenses, she did not have to pretend any more. Maybe she could prove to him that she was not the party princess and darling of the tabloids. What if she told him that she didn't want to be that person any more, and that actually she had never been the wild child with a scandalous reputation?

Would he even care? And why did his approval matter so much to her?

The answer caused her heart to give a jolt. She was falling in love with Santino. She had known the moment she had met him that he could be dangerous to her peace of mind and she'd sensed that he had the power to hurt her. But he also made her feel more alive than she had ever felt, and that feeling was as dangerously addictive as she suspected the enigmatic man who had stolen her heart could be.

CHAPTER SEVEN

'I NOTICED SOME art folders in my bedroom,' Arianna said, pulling herself together and replacing her coffee cup on the saucer. 'Do they belong to your sister?'

Santino nodded. 'Gina took a combined art and business degree before she moved to America to become a fashion buyer.'

She felt envious of Santino's sister. She wished she had studied art, but at eighteen she'd lacked the confidence to apply to universities after her governess had told her that she did not have the commitment to work for a degree. Typically, she had decided to fulfil Miss Melton's low opinion of her and had spent the next six years partying in those playgrounds of the super-rich— Monaco, St Bart's, Verbier and Aspen.

Her lack of business qualifications was something else she needed to consider before she launched her own fashion label, Arianna acknowledged. She had never had to live within a budget before but she would need to make big financial decisions. A familiar sense of worthlessness descended over her. Setting up her own company seemed daunting and maybe she would fail. *But isn't failure better than never trying?* whispered a stubborn voice inside her. It was the conclusion she had come to a year ago when she had been in hospital fighting for her life. She had been given a second chance and was determined to make her life worthwhile.

'There's an empty sketchpad with your sister's art portfolio. Would it be okay if I used it?' She kept her voice casual. 'I might do a bit of drawing to pass the time.'

'I don't suppose Gina would mind if you use some of her old art stuff. But don't think that you can swan around while you are staying here,' Santino told her bluntly. 'Unlike the luxurious way of life you are used to, I don't employ an army of staff to cater to your whims, and I'm not going to run around after you. I'll expect you to pull your weight. I don't suppose you've spent a lot of time in a kitchen or learned how to cook, but you can wash the dishes. No, there's isn't a dishwasher,' he said drily when she glanced around the room. 'Welcome to the real world, *cara*.'

'I'm not completely useless,' she snapped, stung by his mocking tone. She certainly wasn't going to admit to him that she had never washed the dishes in her life. When she ate alone in the vast dining room at Lyle House, the butler whisked the plates away immediately after she had finished eating.

Santino seemed to have used every pan in the kitchen, no doubt on purpose, she thought darkly as she filled the sink with hot water and started on the mountain of washing up he had created. But after she'd washed the copper pans and dried them with a tea towel until they gleamed, before she hung them on hooks above the stove, she realised that she was enjoying pottering about. There was a sense of achievement in turning the disorder back into a clean and tidy kitchen. It gave her confidence that she would manage just fine when she moved into her own home in London, probably a rented flat, as she wouldn't be able to afford to buy somewhere while she was trying to establish her business.

Through the window she saw Santino chopping the wood that was used to fuel the kitchen stove. He had stripped off his T-shirt and his broad shoulders glistened with sweat. Arianna felt a melting sensation low in her belly, an ache that throbbed insistently as she imagined him holding her against his muscular body, touching her, kissing her...

She blushed furiously when he glanced towards the window and caught her watching him. But she didn't look away and neither did he. The unguarded expression in his eyes made the ache inside her pulse harder, hotter. Even when they were not in the same room sexual tension simmered between them and she had no idea how they were going to live together, possibly for weeks, without that tension exploding into raw passion.

She released her breath on a shaky sigh when Santino finally resumed chopping logs. She could stand there all day watching his rippling muscles beneath the sheen of his olive-gold skin but it seemed wiser to keep out of his way—although not because she was afraid of him. He had proved that he was committed to protecting her. It was her reaction to his smouldering sensuality that scared her.

He evoked a longing in her that she'd never felt for any other man, she admitted to herself as she walked back up the stairs to her bedroom. She needed something to distract her, so she settled down with the sketch pad and pencils she'd found. It was some time later when she heard a knock on the door, and her heart clattered against her ribs as she scrambled off the bed and crossed the room to open it.

Santino braced his arms on the door frame and scowled at her. 'Do you intend to hide up here and sulk for the rest of the day?'

For some reason his bad mood made her feel better, knowing that he was as disturbed by her as she was by him. 'I didn't realise I'd been working for so long.' A glance at her watch revealed that she had been absorbed in sketching designs for a good part of the afternoon.

His brows rose and he said sardonically, 'Working? I didn't realise you knew the meaning of the word.' He looked over her shoulder at the pages of sketches scattered on the bed and his scowl deepened. 'You mean you've been drawing pretty pictures of dresses.'

'They're sketches of designs that I plan to create back at my fashion studio in London,' she told him, irked by his mocking tone. She stood aside to allow him to enter the bedroom and he walked over and picked up a few of the sketches.

'I know nothing about art or fashion but these look very detailed.' He gave her an intent look, as if he was trying to fathom her out. 'So, you have a studio?'

It sounded more glamorous that it actually was, but Arianna wasn't going to explain that she had recently signed the lease on a space in an old warehouse. She was paying the rent with money she'd inherited from her grandmother and she was excited that it was the first step towards independence from her father.

Santino's expression became speculative. 'Are you trying to emulate your father or merely playing at being a fashion designer until you grow bored of it?'

'Certainly not. Randolph won't be involved in any way in my fashion business. He doesn't know anything about my plans.' She bit her lip. 'No one does. You are the first person I've told.' She was already regretting that she'd given away her secret, but she had been angered by Santino's assumption that she could not do anything by herself and was reliant on her father.

'I'm hoping to launch my fashion brand "Anna" at London Fashion Week in February next year—if I can find a financial backer prepared to invest in my business.' She was unaware of the flicker of doubt that crossed her face. 'The reason I want to attend Fashion Week this September is so that I can see what is trending in the fashion world and hopefully make some contacts.'

She waved her hand at the sketches on the bed. 'These are ideas I'm working on for the mid-season shows, known in the industry as Pre-Fall, which are held around the end of November. The British Fashion Council are offering an opportunity for new designers to present their work. It will give me a chance to gauge the reaction of fashion journalists and buyers to my designs, but I'll have to work fast to be ready in time. And it won't help if I'm stuck in Sicily for weeks,' she said ruefully.

She leaned over the bed to gather up the loose pages of her sketches and the wide neck of her shirt slipped down, baring one shoulder. Santino swore softly.

'How did you get that cut? It looks sore.'

'It's nothing,' she muttered. 'One of the men on the beach was wearing a ring and the edge of it scraped my shoulder when he tried to grab me.' She felt sick remembering the incident, and perhaps she paled, be-

cause Santino put his hand on her uninjured shoulder
and pushed her gently down onto the bed.

'Sit there while I find some antiseptic lotion,' he
commanded.

Once his self-assurance had seemed threatening to
her lack of confidence but now she accepted his strength
instead of resenting it. He strode into the bathroom and
returned almost instantly carrying a first-aid kit, from
which he took out a tube of cream.

'Hold still.' He unscrewed the cap and squeezed a
little of the medication onto her shoulder. His touch
was surprisingly gentle when he spread the cream over
the cut.

Arianna had a sudden memory of when she'd been
a little girl and her mother had cared for her grazed
knees after she'd fallen off her bike. She had adored
Celine, but the close bond between them had lessened
when her father had insisted on sending her to a boarding school when she'd been eight. The older pupils had
teased the younger ones who cried if they were home-
sick, and even at that young age she'd learned to hide
her feelings behind a wall of bravado.

She could not understand why Santino's unexpected
kindness made her eyes fill with tears. She tried to blink
them away but a trickle of moisture slipped down her
cheek.

'Does the cut hurt?' His concern tugged on her heart.
She couldn't remember the last time someone had actually cared about her. Arianna shook her head, not
trusting herself to speak. He sat beside her on the bed
and trapped her chin in his fingers, tilting her face up
so that she could not evade his gaze. Something inde-

finable flickered in his green eyes as he brushed a tear away with his thumb. 'Don't cry, *piccola*,' he said softly.

She stared at his mouth as he brought it closer to hers and felt that inexplicable pull that had always existed between them. From the start there had been a connection, a mutual awareness, that they had both tried to deny. But she didn't want to fight him any more, Arianna admitted to herself. She wanted to throw herself into his fire and burn in the blaze of his smouldering sensuality.

He moved his hand from her jaw to caress her cheek and she felt his other hand slide into her hair. Her heart was beating so fast that she felt breathless, and something hot and urgent unfurled in the pit of her stomach when she glimpsed the hunger in his gaze seconds before he claimed her mouth with his and the world spun off its axis.

She tasted of honey, sweet and utterly addictive, and Santino could not resist her. He told himself that he had kissed her simply to comfort her, conveniently pushing aside the knowledge that *caring* was an emotion he avoided. The vulnerability he glimpsed in her chocolate-drop brown eyes stirred something inside him that he refused to acknowledge, much less define. Perhaps that air of loneliness about her was another illusion created by the smoke and shadows that was Arianna.

Right now she was real enough. Her lips were soft and moist beneath his and her warm breath filled his mouth. He wanted more, wanted her closer, and he lifted her across his lap and nearly lost it when her bottom pressed against the painfully hard ridge of his arousal. Her perfume teased his senses. She smelled of exotic flowers on a hot summer's day, and the lemon groves in his beloved Sicily, but her fragrance was as frustratingly elusive as the woman who curled her arms around his neck and wantonly pressed her breasts up against his chest.

He could feel the hard tips of her nipples, tight and hot, burning through his T-shirt. It didn't matter what Arianna was or what she was not. Right now she was in his arms and kissing him with a hunger that matched his own, and there was not a chance in hell that he would deny himself what he had wanted from the moment he'd set eyes on her. Arianna beneath him, on top of him. His fantasies about her had kept him awake at night, and he was done with trying to figure out why she fascinated him more than any woman ever had.

Without lifting his mouth from hers, he pushed his hand between their bodies and slipped it beneath her silky top, skimming his fingers over her stomach and up to capture one breast. He tested its weight in his palm and felt her shudder when he dragged his thumb over her nipple. Her skin was as soft as a peach and he had to taste her. Easing away from her a fraction allowed him to lift her shirt up and over her head, baring her breasts to him.

He gave a low growl of appreciation. She was perfection. Her creamy skin was satin-smooth and her breasts were round and firm, each pert mound adorned with a dusky pink nipple that tilted provocatively, inviting him to run his tongue over the tip. He was shocked to find that his hands were unsteady when he sank them into her glorious hair and let her silky curls slip through his fingers. Desire pounded an insistent drumbeat in his blood, and he knew from her rapid breathing and the slumberous heat in her eyes that her need was as great as his.

He shoved away the strange idea he'd had on previous occasions that her air of innocence was real. Stories of her excesses had filled too many gossip columns. Not that Santino cared. He enjoyed sex with women who were sexually confident. The sight of the cut on her shoulder made him hesitate, and perhaps he would have heeded the reminder that it was his duty to protect her if she hadn't dragged the hem of his T-shirt up his torso and run her hands over his chest.

'Witch,' he said hoarsely when she scraped her nails across his flat nipples, making him even harder, even hungrier for her. Unable to control his impatience, he tugged his shirt off before he bent his head to her breast, closing his mouth around her nipple and sucking. Hard. The effect on her was instant, but the audible catch of her breath…surely she could not have sounded startled? Once again Santino pushed the odd thought away and concentrated on pleasuring her breasts, rolling one nipple between his fingers while simultaneously lashing the other turgid peak with his tongue.

She arched backwards, offering her breasts to him, and he had never seen anything more beautiful than Arianna with her cheeks flushed with passion and her long hair—shades of chestnut and cinnamon—tumbling in a riot of loose curls down her back. The heat between them burned hotter and the world disintegrated. He tumbled them both down onto the mattress and propped himself up on one elbow while he skimmed his other hand down to the waistband of her denim shorts.

'Look at me,' he commanded, a question in his eyes when her lashes swept up and she met his gaze. She answered him by pulling his face down to hers and parting her lips with an eagerness that caused his heart to give a jolt as he kissed her again and again. He would never have enough of her. She was a siren luring him to his doom, but he didn't care about anything other than his need to possess her gorgeous body and seek salvation between her silken thighs.

He fumbled with the button and zip on her shorts, impatience making his movements uncharacteristically clumsy. Finally, he tugged the denim shorts down her legs and sat back on his knees to admire the graceful lines of her slender figure, almost naked but for the tiny black knickers that hid her femininity from him.

Her eyes were huge and dark with desire, and Santino's gut clenched at the soft sound she made—half-protest, half-plea—when he leaned over her, braced his hands on either side of her on the bed and pressed his mouth against the scrap of black lace. The scent of her arousal filled his senses as he pushed the panel of her panties aside and ran his tongue over her slick, wet opening. Her molten heat was the sweetest nectar and he felt a quiver run through her when he delved deeper into her feminine core, lapping her, tasting her.

Arianna's husky gasps of pleasure almost sent Santino over the edge, but somehow he still retained enough control to remember that they were not in his bedroom, where he kept contraceptives. But his sister and her fiancé had stayed in this room when they had visited earlier in the summer. His heart kicked in his chest when he pulled open the bedside drawer and found a packet of condoms. He was so hard he thought he might explode, and he bit back a groan when his denim shorts snagged on his erection as he yanked them off, followed by his boxers.

He knelt back on the bed and looked down at Arianna. She was more beautiful than anything he had ever seen with her silky hair spread over the pillows and her big brown eyes lit with gold flames. The elegant lines and sensual curves of her body were a work of art, and his gut clenched in anticipation of her long, lissom legs wrapped around his back. Her pert breasts were firm yet soft, the colour of pale cream, each topped with a cherry-red nipple, and he bent his head and feasted on them, smiling when she bucked and moaned.

Next time he would take things more slowly and indulge in leisurely foreplay, he promised himself. But right now he was desperate to be inside her and he swiftly donned a protective sheath. He pulled her panties down her legs and ran his fingers over the neat vee of soft brown curls he'd exposed before he pushed her thighs apart. Supporting his weight on his elbows, he positioned himself over her and lowered his head to claim her mouth in a hungry kiss.

'I should probably tell you...' she whispered against his lips.

Dio! Had she changed her mind? His heart was thundering in his chest but somehow he held himself back. 'The only thing you need to tell me, *cara*,' he growled, 'is if you want this. One word—yes, or no?'

'Yes,' she said without hesitation.

Relief surged through him, adding to the potent heat in his groin. He didn't wait—couldn't, if he was honest. His desire for her consumed him and he slid his hands beneath her bottom to lift her hips towards him.

At last he was where he wanted to be—on the edge of heaven.

He surged forward and thrust into her. And stilled.

His shock turned to incomprehension and disbelief when she went rigid beneath him. The sharp cry she'd given at the moment he'd penetrated her had been of pain.

How the hell could Arianna be a virgin?

Guilt seared through him even as he felt the tension slowly seep from her body as her internal muscles stretched to accommodate him. He felt as though his aching shaft was encased in a velvet glove. Her slick heat enticed him to slide deeper into her. But he held back, just, his throat working as he swallowed hard. The craziest thing of all was the swift, fierce rush of triumph that swept through him, a possessiveness that shook him to his core and which he rejected absolutely. Sex and emotions was not a mix he had ever sought.

He withdrew from her, even though it was the hardest thing he had ever done. He did not know if it was disappointment or relief that darkened her eyes, and when she bit her lip the beast inside him roared. Cursing beneath his breath, he propped himself up beside her and trapped her gaze with his. 'Why?' he demanded tautly.

Something flickered on her lovely face, that hint of vulnerability that he now knew was real, he thought, guilt clawing through him again. 'Why was I a virgin, I suppose you mean?' she said in a low voice.

He gritted his teeth. 'You suppose right, *cara*. How could it be so, when stories of your affairs have littered the gutter press for years and provided cheap titillation for anyone who is interested?'

Colour ran along her exquisite cheekbones but she

said defiantly, 'No one believes the rubbish printed in the tabloids.'

The implication that anyone who did was a fool was not lost on Santino, and with a flash of insight he realised that he had wanted to believe the worst of her to keep her at arm's length. 'What about when you defied me and left Villa Cadenza to go and meet your lover in Positano?' He recalled the scalding jealousy he'd felt, imagining her in bed with some guy.

'I was having sewing lessons with a seamstress in her workroom next door to the beauty salon.' She shrugged when his brows lowered. 'You were convinced that I must be having an affair because you believed my reputation as a tart was true.'

Santino sighed heavily, unable to deny her accusation. 'Did you never consider denying the things that were written about you or demand a retraction from the newspapers?'

She glanced at him from beneath her long eyelashes. Her wariness that he had assumed was an act now tugged on emotions he did not want to acknowledge. 'You'll laugh if I tell you the truth.'

'Try me,' he said gruffly.

'The only times my father ever phoned me were when some scandal or another about my private life made the headlines. He hated my notoriety, not because he cared about me, but because he feared it could have an adverse effect on the only thing he does care about, which is Fitzgerald Design.' She bit her lip. 'When I was a child, Randolph only noticed me when I behaved badly, so I carried on. But a year ago I decided that I can't spend the rest of my life seeking my father's attention.' Her rueful smile did not reach her eyes. 'I suppose I finally grew up.'

Santino ignored the complicated feelings that Arianna evoked in him. 'I haven't seen much evidence of that,' he mocked. 'You should have told me it was your first time.'

'I tried to…'

He swore, and colour ran under her skin, but her eyes flashed gold with temper. 'Would you have believed me?' she came back at him, fiery and proud. She sat upright and pushed a hand through her hair, drawing his eyes to the silky brown curls that tumbled over her breasts. Desire corkscrewed through him but he couldn't succumb to his hunger for her that made him feel hollow and aware of the gaping emptiness inside him. An emptiness that Arianna of all people could not fill. Whatever she thought of her father, Randolph had hired him to protect his daughter, and he would do his duty, Santino vowed silently.

'Why me?' he demanded.

She did not pretend to misunderstand him and her reply set off alarm bells inside his head. 'I knew I would be safe with you,' she said softly.

Safe! The word mocked him. 'Arianna…'

She interrupted him. 'From the start you have taken care of me.'

'It is my job to protect you,' he growled.

She shook her head. 'It's more than that and you know it. There is a connection between us.' Before he could deny it, she said fiercely, 'I wanted you to be the first.'

'And because you are Arianna Fitzgerald you decided that it is your unassailable right to have what you want, with no thought of the consequences,' he said furiously. 'You should have been honest instead of dumping your virginity on me and expecting—what?—that I would fall in love with you?'

He swung himself off the bed and pulled on his shorts, hardening his heart against her stricken expression. When had his *heart* got involved? he wondered blackly, feeling a beat of fear. He had decided a long time ago when his mother had died and his father had become a broken man that he was better off alone.

'A few minutes ago you wanted to make love to me.' Arianna's voice pulled him from the past. 'I didn't think you would realise it was my first time, but I hadn't expected it to hurt as much as it did,' she admitted wryly.

Truly, she was going to kill him. 'I don't do love,' he told her bluntly. 'I wanted to have sex with you, and why wouldn't I? You are beautiful, and I thought you were experienced.' He tried to ignore his conscience that reminded him that he'd sensed an innocence about her that had baffled him.

He bent down to retrieve his shirt from the floor and pulled it on. When he turned back to face her he was relieved that she had tugged the sheet around her, hiding the temptation of her gorgeous body from his eyes, although nothing could erase the memory of how she had felt beneath him, so soft and pliant. Cursing silently, he strode across to the door.

'I understand what has happened,' he told her curtly. 'It's not uncommon for a client to develop a crush on the bodyguard assigned to protect them. It is my responsibility to take care of you until the kidnap threat is over. But you have a romanticised view of our relationship. Hopefully the situation will be resolved soon. I received an update from the Italian police that they are closing in on the gang, and when you leave here and return to your old life you will forget about me.'

'Do you really believe that, Santino?' From the other side of the room the gold flecks in Arianna's eyes flashed fiery bright. She knelt up on the bed and lowered the sheet, baring her breasts. Tossing her hair back over her shoulders, she put her hands on her hips, and the sheet slipped down to reveal her slim thighs and the sexy triangle of tight curls that hid her femininity. 'I know you want me.'

Despite himself, and his determination to resist her, Santino could not take his eyes from her. 'Beautiful' did not come near to describing her lush curves and the brazen, seductive promise of her exquisite body. But, as with everything to do with Arianna, that promise was a lie. She was innocent—or she had been, until he had taken her virginity, he thought grimly. *Dio*, she was something else for him to feel guilty about.

His muscles ached with tension as he fought an internal battle with himself. He could cross the room in four strides and pull her into his arms, finish what he had started. Temptation pulsed hard and hot in his blood but he fought it. *It was his duty to protect her.* From herself if necessary, and especially from him, because, whatever Arianna was looking for, Santino knew he could not give it to her.

'You're wrong,' he told her impassively. 'I want a woman who understands the concept of sex without strings. Not someone who is needy and immature and who is looking for some sort of father figure to give her the attention she craves.' She blanched and he reminded himself that he was being cruel to be kind. The quicker he disabused Arianna of the idea that he was a heroic figure, the better for both of them. He stepped into the corridor and spoke to her over his shoulder. 'I suggest you put your clothes on and we will forget that any of this ever happened.'

CHAPTER EIGHT

SHE WAS SUCH an idiot! Fiery colour scorched Arianna's cheeks, making her feel even hotter than she already was, squashed into the overcrowded carriage on the Tube. It was more than four months since Santino had rejected her and decimated her pride. It had taken a long time for her to scrape herself off the floor, and she still had regular flashbacks to how she had wanted to die of embarrassment when she'd dragged a sheet around her naked body after he had turned her down.

A few moments ago, the sight of a tall, dark-haired man standing on the station platform had made her heart lurch, until he had turned around, and her stomach had swooped with disappointment that it wasn't Santino. She searched for his ruggedly handsome face everywhere, even though she knew it was pointless to look for him in London. Presumably he was at his villa in Sicily, or in Devon, where he had owned a delicatessen shop. He hadn't told her what he did for a living since he'd sold the shop but maybe he had taken over his grandparents' farm.

Her heart gave a pang as she remembered his sexy grin when he'd confessed that he hadn't enjoyed milking cows. She had smiled back at him, her heart soaring because he'd shared something of himself with her, something that perhaps he had never told any of those women with whom he enjoyed sex without strings. She had stored every snippet of information she had learned about him in her mind, like a magpie hiding golden treasure in its nest. And at night her imagination ran riot as she pictured Santino's naked body, a masterpiece of powerful muscles and satiny, olive-gold skin, his broad chest covered with whorls of dark hairs that arrowed over his flat stomach and grew thickly around the base of his manhood.

The train pulled into the underground station and Arianna was glad to escape from the carriage before the heat inside her made her combust. But she could not stop her mind flitting back to the awful, awkward days at Casa Uliveto when she had been desperate to avoid Santino. Forgetting what had happened between them was impossible.

In the past, when her friends had talked about sex, she had tried to imagine a scenario when she finally lost her virginity. Ever the romantic, she had dreamed of giving herself to a man she trusted, and she'd thought she had found that person. But Santino's cruel rejection had blown apart her fantasy that he felt something for her. That he *cared* about her. He had reminded her that it was his job to protect her, and insisted that what she felt for him was a crush, as if she'd been a silly teenager mooning over pictures of her favourite pop star.

Repressing a shudder of shame, Arianna joined the queue of rush-hour commuters shuffling towards the escalator at London Bridge station. She checked the time, and her stomach nosedived as she realised that she was in danger of being late for the most important meeting of her life.

Her thoughts flicked back to Sicily. Thankfully her ordeal of living with Santino, and cringing with embarrassment whenever she'd walked into a room and found him there, had only lasted for a week. Early one morning he had knocked on her bedroom door, and she'd despised herself for the way her heart had leapt with hope that he had come to claim her because he could not resist her.

Instead he had informed her in a clipped voice that the Italian police had swooped on the mafia gang and arrested them. The kidnap threat was over, and he had chartered a private jet to take her to Positano or London, whichever she decided. It had been painfully obvious that he couldn't wait for her to leave, and Arianna had told herself that she'd imagined she'd glimpsed a feral hunger mixed with regret in his eyes before he had turned and walked out of the room.

She snapped back to the present as she emerged from the station and was met by an icy blast of wind that carried a mixture of rain and sleet. December had heralded the start of winter, and her elegant champagne-coloured skirt and jacket and matching four-inch stiletto heels offered no protection against the elements. She regretted that she hadn't taken a taxi across London, but now that she was living on a tight budget she couldn't afford luxuries such as taxis.

Fortunately, The Shard was close to the station, and as she hurried towards the building's entrance she looked up at the iconic skyscraper clad with glass that reflected the sullen grey skies above. Tiger Investments' offices were on the seventeenth floor, and Arianna took

a deep breath and tried to calm her nerves when she
exited the lift into the company's minimalist and very
stylish reception area.

'I have an appointment to see Rachael Martin,' she
told the stylish blonde receptionist after she'd introduced herself.

The young woman smiled. 'I'll let Rachael know
you have arrived.'

While she waited, Arianna mentally ran through
her presentation. She had been contacted by Tiger Investments after she had applied for funding for her
fashion business through an angel investor network.
She knew that angel investors were essentially private individuals or companies who provided capital
for new businesses in return for equity. This was her
chance to secure money that she needed to cover the
huge costs involved in showing her designs at London
Fashion Week.

She wondered how Rachael Martin, who she assumed headed the investment company, had become a
successful businesswoman. Not for the first time Arianna was beset by doubts that she could establish her
own fashion label in a highly competitive market place.
But a stubborn belief that her designs were fresh and
innovative meant that she pinned a smile on her lips
when she heard her name.

'Miss Fitzgerald? I'm Rachael. If you would like
to come with me, I'll take you to your meeting.' The
woman who greeted her possessed a self-confidence
that Arianna envied. She could do this, she told herself
as she followed the other woman along a plush carpeted
corridor, lifting a hand nervously to check that her chignon was in place before she stepped into a large room

with glass walls and floor-to-ceiling windows. It was like being in a goldfish bowl, and heading straight for her was a predatory shark.

'What are you doing here?' Her heart slammed into her ribs as she stared at Santino. He looked different from the bodyguard she had known in Italy but no less handsome. Instead of jeans he wore a charcoal-grey suit, pale-blue shirt and a navy silk tie. The superbly tailored jacket emphasised the width of his shoulders and he was so devastatingly attractive in his formal clothes that she sucked in a sharp breath. 'Don't tell me that you work for Tiger Investments? The coincidence would be too ghastly,' she murmured, striving to sound flippant to disguise her shock.

'I *own* Tiger Investments,' he corrected her coolly.

'But... I thought that Rachael Martin...' Arianna glanced over her shoulder and discovered that the other woman had left the room.

'Rachael is my PA,' Santino told her. 'I asked her to arrange your visit because I thought you would refuse to meet me.'

In her mind Arianna pictured the tattoo of a tiger on Santino's bicep. There had been a clue in the name Tiger Investments, but honestly she had never expected to see him again. Thinking of his tattoo evoked memories of his naked, aroused body, which did nothing to restore her composure.

'You were right. We have nothing to say to one another.' Disappointment thickened her voice with the realisation that Santino had brought her here on false pretences. 'Is this another example of your cruelty—to get my hopes up that you would offer funding for my fashion company?'

His eyes narrowed on her face. 'You gave yourself to me, *cara*. Don't try to make out that you were a martyr,' he said softly.

She flushed as erotic images swirled in her mind of his whipcord body poised above her and his erection pushing between her legs. Molten heat pooled low in her pelvis and she hastily dropped her gaze from his.

Santino walked over to the sleek black-and-chrome desk that took up the whole of one corner of the office, but instead of sitting behind it he leaned his hip against the top and indicated the chair in front of the desk. 'Please, sit down—unless you prefer to stand while you give your presentation.'

'Is there any point?' Arianna felt a flare of frustration that she'd had a wasted journey. 'I'm looking for at least five hundred thousand pounds to launch my business, and I doubt that the proceeds from the sale of your delicatessen in Devon would allow you to make that level of investment.'

'My company, which traded under the brand name of Toni's Deli, was valued at two hundred and seventy-five million pounds when I sold the business.'

She sank down onto the chair. '*You* owned the Toni's Deli chain of shops? The brand is huge in the UK and Europe.'

He nodded. 'I built the company up from one poorly performing outlet that my father had opened in Exeter to over two thousand stores in seventeen international locations. I'd dabbled in investing in start-up companies, and eventually sold the delicatessen business so that I could set up Tiger Investments. The question is not whether I have enough money to invest in your business,' he said sardonically. 'You will have to prove to

me that you have a product and business strategy that
I believe will be successful.'

He straightened up, but instead of moving to sit behind his desk he pulled up a chair next to Arianna. She
felt a betraying heat spread across her cheeks. Being this
close to him made her heart race, and the spicy scent
of his aftershave evoked memories of when she had
been in his arms and he had kissed her with fierce passion. Seeing Santino again had been shocking enough,
and learning that he was a millionaire entrepreneur had
completely thrown her.

She fired up her laptop and opened the PowerPoint
file containing her pitch deck that Jonny had helped her
to create for her fashion label, Anna. 'You want to give
a brief overview of your business model. Ten to fifteen
slides that will make a great first impression,' Jonny had
told her. 'Don't read from your script or you'll sound
like a robot. And make eye contact with the person you
are hoping to impress.'

No doubt it was sound advice, but Arianna's mind
had gone blank. She bit her lip when she accidentally
brought up the wrong file. 'Sorry, just bear with me,'
she muttered. She couldn't bring herself to look at Santino let alone make eye contact with him. The first slide
flashed up on the screen and she dropped her pages of
notes on the floor. Flustered, she leaned down to pick
them up at the same time as he did, and their hands
brushed, sending a sizzle of heat through her.

She had assumed that nothing could be more hu-
miliating than when she had offered her body to Santino only for him to tell her that she was needy and
immature. But she had been wrong, Arianna thought
miserably fifteen minutes later, when she had finished

delivering her presentation and stumbled to answer the questions he fired at her. She was angry with herself for making such a hash of it, and his silence shredded her nerves even more. 'Well, what do you think?' she asked nervously.

'I think that was the worst presentation I've ever sat through.' His blunt reply made her heart sink and, when she forced herself to look at him, she saw impatience glittering in his green eyes. 'Your marketing skills are, at best, questionable, and you seem to know nothing about PR and creating a brand.'

He leaned back in his chair and hooked his ankle across his other thigh, looking the epitome of a hard-nosed, highly successful entrepreneur. 'Your *only* saving grace,' he said curtly, 'is that I believe you have a good product. My sister saw your Pre-Fall collection last month at a show arranged by the British Fashion Council to present emerging designers. I think I mentioned that Gina is a senior buyer for a New York department store. She knows the fashion industry, and she was genuinely excited by your designs.'

Arianna's spirits, which had sunk to the pointed toes of her designer heels, cautiously lifted. 'Does that mean you will consider investing in Anna?'

Santino stood up and strode over to the window. The usually spectacular view across the city was shrouded in thick cloud, and the rain beating against the glass made him long for the heat and sun of a Sicilian summer's day. But his beloved Casa Uliveto was no longer the restful bolthole where he could relax.

After he had sent Arianna away he'd assumed that he would forget about her fairly quickly. But she had constantly been in his thoughts, and at night he'd been kept awake by memories of how she had knelt on the bed—naked and so goddamned beautiful that he ached thinking about her—and offered herself to him. There had always been a danger, when he'd arranged to meet Arianna today, that he would think with a certain part of his anatomy that was as hard as a spike beneath his trousers, rather than with his head, he acknowledged.

Her business plan was laughable, and he should send her packing, but his instincts told him that her fashion label Anna had huge potential. He had noticed Arianna's name when he'd reviewed start-up companies on an angel investor network. When his sister had come to London last month he had asked Gina to attend the Pre-Fall shows and give an opinion on Arianna's designs.

'She is the most exciting new designer this year, perhaps this decade,' Gina had assured him. 'Arianna Fitzgerald has phenomenal talent, which I suppose is not surprising, when you consider that her father is one of the greatest fashion designers in the world.'

Santino swung round from the window and studied Arianna, irritated by his body's involuntary reaction to her as desire corkscrewed through him. She was even lovelier than he remembered. His eyes were drawn to her long legs encased in sheer tights. Her vertiginous heels added at least four inches to her height. The fitted jacket of her elegant suit emphasised her narrow waist that he remembered he could span with his two hands. She had unfastened the jacket's buttons, and her breasts were high and firm beneath her silk blouse.

So much for his belief that he had managed to get her out of his system, he thought grimly. One reason for meeting her had been to test his immunity to her sensual allure. The ache of his arousal was mocking proof that he had failed.

'I don't understand why your presentation did not include the fact that your father is Randolph Fitzgerald,' he said abruptly. 'Or for that matter why you are seeking investment in your business when your father could bankroll your fashion label.'

She stiffened at his mention of her father. 'I've had no contact with Randolph since I returned to London, and he is not involved in any way in my business plans.'

'Linking your fashion label to Fitzgerald Design would be an excellent way to promote Anna. It doesn't make sense not to utilise your association with your father.'

'No.' Arianna jumped to her feet. 'Anna is *my* label. The designs are entirely my work, and if I succeed it will be on my own merits, not because of who my father is.'

'And what if you fail?'

'I won't fail.' The gold flecks in her eyes flashed with determination. 'I know my designs are good. My Pre-Fall collection received excellent reviews and my Autumn/Winter collection for next year, that I am working on to showcase at London Fashion Week in February, is even better,' she said passionately.

Dio, he wanted to burn in her fiery passion. The throb in Santino's groin intensified as he imagined Arianna's naked, creamy pale limbs spread across the black glass surface of his desk. It would be easier if he could dismiss her business ideas as unlikely to succeed. Then he could simply invite her to dinner and take her to bed, and he was confident that within a month he'd have grown bored of her, which invariably happened with the women he bedded.

But his gut told him to put his money into Anna, and his instincts had always proved right in the past, which was how he had become a self-made millionaire. He walked back across the room, picked up her presentation notes that she had left on the desk and dropped them into the wastepaper bin.

'That's what I think of your business plan,' he told her, trying to ignore the inexplicable tug he felt in his chest when he studied her crestfallen face. 'I am prepared to make an investment of half a million pounds in your fashion label, but I want a forty percent stake in the company.'

He watched her eyes widen. The flush of rose-pink that winged along her exquisite cheekbones made her prettier than ever, and Santino threw himself down into the chair behind his desk to conceal the bulge of his arousal beneath his trousers. 'Also,' he said gruffly, 'you will have to improve your marketing skills. I'll expect you to meet me twice a week so that we can work on business strategies and promotion ideas.'

'I won't have time,' she argued. 'I was planning to employ staff to deal with PR and the business side of the company, to allow me to focus on my role as creative director.' Her mouth turned down at the corners and Santino didn't know whether he wanted to shake some sense into her or kiss the sulky pout from her lips. The latter was a serious contender, he acknowledged heavily.

'You can't just do the fun stuff,' he told her impatiently. 'What I learned from running my delicatessen company is the necessity to know and understand every aspect of the business. Creating a product, whether it is clothes, cars or dog food, is the easy part. The hard work is persuading people to buy your product rather than a competitor's.' He stood up to indicate that the meeting was over. 'I'll have my legal team draw up a contract for you to sign, and money will be transferred into your business account.'

Arianna also rose to her feet. She was poised and elegant, making him long to ruffle her and unearth the passionate woman he had discovered in Italy. 'I realise that I need a better understanding of running a business, and I am willing to learn everything you can teach me,' she said softly.

Dio, had he imagined there was a double-edged meaning in her words? Erotic images filled his mind of the things he would like to teach her in his bed. She smiled and Santino's breath was squeezed from his lungs. It was not the perfunctory smile that had graced the tabloids when she had been endlessly photographed by the paparazzi. It was the smile he had seen once before when they had been on the beach in Positano. Open and unfeigned, it lit up her face and made the gold flecks in her brown eyes gleam with the warmth of the Sicilian sun.

It hit Santino with the force of a meteor strike that it wasn't Sicily he had missed for the past four months but Arianna. She held out her hand and, as he curled his fingers around hers, a jolt of electricity shot up his arm and he cursed silently.

'So we have a deal,' she murmured. 'Thank you. I promise you won't regret it.'

Too late, he thought grimly. He was already regretting his decision to get involved with Arianna's business. But he could not make it personal, and he was determined to keep their relationship on a professional footing. He didn't want to feel the confused emotions that she evoked inside him. He did not want to *feel*, full stop.

He watched the sexy sway of her bottom beneath her tight-fitting skirt as she walked out of his office and ordered himself to get a grip. But the scent of her perfume lingered in the room for the rest of the day, heating his blood so that he could not concentrate on work. He reminded himself that he could retract his offer to invest in her fashion label. She would find another investor, and he would go back to being comfortably numb, which was how he preferred to live his life.

Santino's jaw clenched. The SAS had the motto 'Who Dares Wins'. Was he seriously considering pulling out of a good investment opportunity because he was afraid of getting involved with Arianna? He was confident he could handle his inconvenient attraction to her—and if not, if all else failed, he would have to get his hands on her and resolve his fascination by taking her to bed.

CHAPTER NINE

THREE FRUSTRATING WEEKS later Santino was forced to admit that he had made a serious error of judgment. However, the problem was not his investment in Arianna's fashion label.

The official launch of Anna would be the debut runway collection at London Fashion Week's spring show, early in the new year. There had been a buzz of interest from fashion journalists in the wake of Arianna's Pre-Fall showcase, and her client list was growing quickly. So much so that Santino had suggested she should move into a larger studio so that she could employ pattern cutters and seamstresses. At the moment she did everything from designing clothes through to making the final product, and he knew that she often worked until eight or nine o'clock at night.

In all honesty he had been impressed by her work ethic and drive to succeed. At their twice-weekly meetings, where he was giving her a crash course in business operations and marketing strategy, she had shown that she was fiercely intelligent and quick to learn. Santino realised that he looked forward to those meetings. Arianna's dry wit often made him laugh. She was also a good listener and he'd found himself opening up to her in a way that he had never done to anyone else.

He'd told her things that he had buried deep in his subconscious about what he had witnessed in Afghanistan, his ever-present sense of guilt that Mac had lost his legs and other friends he'd served with in the army who had lost their lives.

'I don't suppose you want to hear all this stuff,' he'd said gruffly one day the previous week when he'd glanced at his watch and discovered that their meeting had overrun by two hours.

'You should talk about what happened to you in Afghanistan instead of bottling it up.' Arianna's gentle reply had made him feel raw inside, and the temptation he felt at every one of their meetings to take her in his arms and kiss her soft, inviting mouth almost overwhelmed him.

He wondered when she had changed from the spoilt heiress with a scandalous reputation in the press to the hard-working, funny, compassionate woman he had got to know. And then it occurred to him that she hadn't changed, that this was the real Arianna Fitzgerald, and the shallow socialite he had believed her to be when he'd been assigned as her bodyguard had only existed in the tabloids.

Santino brooded over this one Friday evening, four days before Christmas, as he drove through an area of London that had the dubious honour of being known as the most underprivileged borough in the capital. The problem was Arianna herself. Or, more specifically, his obsession with her. He thought about her all the time and it couldn't continue. Having an affair with her seemed the only solution. Admittedly another solution would be for him to take a step back. He could appoint one of his executives at Tiger Investments to teach her about business and marketing instead of doing it himself. His chief finance officer had a Master's degree in economics. But he'd seen the way that James Norton looked at Arianna. The guy practically salivated over her. Santino flexed his hands on the steering wheel when something hot and corrosive unfurled in the pit of his stomach.

He did not understand the possessiveness he felt for Arianna, and the truth was it unsettled him. In the past, women had come and gone from his life leaving no mark on him. He had enjoyed their company fleetingly, enjoyed the sex more, and had never thought of them again after the affair ended. Which brought him full circle, he brooded. The solution to his problem with Arianna was to sleep with her. When they were together in his office he had noticed the loaded glances she sent him when she thought he wasn't looking at her. Their sexual chemistry had always been off the chart, but in Sicily he had held back because he'd felt responsible for her.

Following the directions on the car's satnav, Santino parked in a narrow street lined with Victorian houses that had evidently been turned into flats. He checked the address that the butler at Lyle House had given him when he'd gone to Kensington, hoping to find Arianna. He'd had to cancel their usual Friday morning meeting because he had been delayed on a business trip to Germany. Their next meeting was scheduled for when he returned from New York after the Christmas break. His excuse for wanting to see her was so that he could discuss a promotion idea. But he had been informed by the butler that Arianna had moved out of her father's house when she had returned to London from Italy at the end of the summer.

Some youths swigging lager out of cans were hanging around the front door. They eyed Santino suspiciously, but his height and build gave him an obvious advantage, and they stepped back to allow him to pass. Loud rock music pounded from one of the flats, and his mouth thinned as he clambered over a ripped-open rubbish bag on the stairs on his way up to the top floor.

Arianna opened the door when he knocked and looked cautiously round the safety chain. Her eyes widened when she saw him. 'What are you doing here?'

'I was going to ask you the same question,' he said tersely as he followed her into the dingy bedsit. There was a bed, a sofa and an old television in the main room and a tiny kitchen and shower room off the passage. 'Why are you living in this dump?'

She shrugged. 'It's all I can afford. Rents in London are astronomical and I was only able to afford the deposit on this place with some money I inherited from my grandmother. I pay the rent for my design studio from my business account, but the money you have invested in my business is not for my personal use.'

'I don't expect you to live here,' he said grimly. 'Why did you move out of your father's house?'

'Because I want to be free from Randolph's attempts to control my life. No one will be able to accuse me of relying on my father or using his money to establish my business. It's important that my fashion label Anna is completely independent from Fitzgerald Design.'

He prowled around the cramped room. When he glanced at Arianna, the wary expression in her eyes threw him back to Sicily, when she had crept around Casa Uliveto like a timid mouse. Guilt twisted in his gut as he acknowledged that he'd been excessively harsh because he had felt honour-bound to fight his desire for her.

'Did you want something?' she murmured. 'Only it's late, and I was about to go to bed.'

Her hair was piled on top of her head and a few stray, damp curls framing her rose-flushed face were an indication that she had recently showered. He lowered his eyes to the man's shirt she was wearing and wondered if she was naked beneath it. The oversized shirt came down to mid-thigh, and Santino felt a lick of heat run through him as he let his gaze roam over her long legs. He wanted to feel them around his hips. He badly wanted to press his mouth to the fragile line of her collar bone and undo the buttons on her shirt one by one so that he could cradle her bare breasts in his hands.

'Come to New York with me for Christmas,' he said abruptly. His jaw tightened when she looked startled, and part of him wondered what he was doing. But another part of him that was uncomfortably hard beneath his jeans seemed to be in control of his thought process.

'I—I can't,' she faltered. 'I've made other plans for Christmas.'

Acid seared his insides. 'What kind of plans? Or perhaps I should ask who you will be spending Christmas with. Is it the lover whose shirt you wear in bed?'

The gold flecks in her eyes flashed but she replied coolly, 'Jonny gave me a few of his shirts that he was throwing out. He knows I find them comfortable to sleep in. Not that it is any of your business, but I don't have a lover.'

'I had dinner with a client at The Dorchester on Tuesday night, before I flew to Germany, and I saw you there with Jonny Monaghan.' Santino's breath whistled between his teeth as he remembered how he had been tortured by the idea that Arianna had spent the night at the hotel with the aristocratic Englishman.

'Jonny is my oldest friend. Again it is not your business, but he has been in love with Davina for years.' She put her hands on her hips and her eyes challenged him from across the room. 'You know quite well that it was my first time with you. To be honest, I haven't felt tempted to repeat the experience with anyone else after that unsatisfactory encounter.'

'Unsatisfactory?' The word felt like a slap and he clenched his hands to stop himself for reaching for her.

'Well, yes, frankly. I don't know about you but the earth definitely didn't move for me.' Beneath her flippant tone there was something else that made Santino furious with himself. He'd known that he had hurt her and now he saw the proof in the faint tremble of her lips before she pressed them tightly together. 'I don't know what you want,' she said in a low tone.

'Don't you?' He was unaware that he had moved towards her, drawn by some force of magic that he could not resist. He was so close to her that he could feel the warmth of her skin from her recent shower. The evocative scent of her perfume made him feel drunk with desire. He watched her eyes darken when he stretched out his hand and removed the clip from her hair so that her chestnut curls tumbled around her shoulders. She did not resist him when he pulled her into his arms.

'Then let me show you,' he growled against her lips before he covered her mouth with his and kissed her as he had longed to do since he had put her on a plane in Sicily.

Arianna knew she should not open her mouth to Santino's demanding kiss but she couldn't help herself. It was madness, but she didn't care. Months of missing him so much that it had been a permanent ache in her heart, and the last three weeks of frustrated longing for his touch, meant that she was helpless beneath the onslaught of his passion. The fierce glitter in his green eyes revealed a hunger that he could not hide. The hard length of him pressed up against her pelvis made her arch into him, needing to be even closer to the power and glory of his muscular body.

She told herself it was the shock of his unexpected visit that clouded her judgement and made it impossible for her to think when her entire being was focused on the feel of his lips sliding over hers. When he pushed his tongue into her mouth she shook with a need that only this man had ever evoked in her. She slid her arms up to his shoulders, anchoring herself to his strength while her heart soared.

His kiss was everything she had dreamed of on the lonely nights since she had left Sicily. He was everything she wanted—so handsome it hurt her to look at him, so strong and yet so exquisitely gentle as he feathered kisses over her cheek and nuzzled the sweet spot behind her ear.

Her breasts felt heavy and molten heat pooled between her thighs. He tasted like heaven and when she held his face between her hands the rough stubble on his jaw felt abrasive against her palms. He sank a hand into her hair and clamped his other arm around her waist as he lifted her off her feet and carried her the short distance over to the bed.

'I want you,' Santino said hoarsely. 'And I know you want me. Your body betrays you so beautifully, *cara.*' He ran his hand down the front of her shirt and unerringly found the hard point of her nipple. She shuddered when he rubbed his thumb over the taut peak. But the arrogance she had heard in his voice sent a chill through her as she remembered how he had rejected her with brutal indifference.

What kind of a fool was she to allow herself to be so vulnerable again? Where was her self-respect that she had fought so hard for?

She stiffened and pulled out of his arms. 'I do want you, it's true,' she said huskily. It was pointless to deny it after she had kissed him so eagerly. 'But I'm fairly certain, taking into account my limited knowledge of these things, that I don't want sex without strings. I'm sure it works for some people, but I waited until I was twenty-five to lose my virginity, and I want something more than casual sex.'

The stunned expression on Santino's face would be hilarious, Arianna supposed, if she didn't feel like crying. If she achieved nothing else in her life, at least she could claim the accolade of being the only woman to have turned him down. It didn't feel as good as she might have thought.

He made a frustrated sound. 'What are you hoping for, Arianna? A declaration of love?' His tone was scathing. 'Or are you holding out for a ring on your finger?'

She gave his questions serious consideration. 'Not the first necessarily, and then only if it was an honest declaration. As for marriage...' She grimaced. 'My parents' miserable attempt at marriage was not a good advertisement. I stopped believing in fairy tales a long time ago. But friendship, mutual liking and respect are things I will hope for in any relationship I might have.'

'I do respect and like you,' he insisted. His tone was so grim that he might have been announcing the outbreak of a war. 'But I don't wear my heart on my sleeve, and I have no intention of ever falling in love.'

Arianna tried to ignore the pang her heart gave. 'Why not?' She wished she knew what he was thinking but his chiselled features gave nothing away. 'What are you afraid of?'

He swore. 'Love is a pretty word for lust. What we have going on between us is real and honest.'

His hands reached for her again and the gentle brush of his fingers down her cheek almost made her weaken. Almost. But she would not respect herself if she succumbed to the hard gleam in his eyes, even though she longed to let him show her how good they would be together. Instinctively she knew that sex with him would be amazing. But she also knew that it wasn't enough for her. It would never be enough. She would want more from Santino than he was prepared to give, and he would destroy her.

She stepped away from him and hugged her arms around herself to replace the warmth of his touch when he dropped his hands down to his sides. 'I think you should leave,' she said huskily. A spurt of pride made her repeat the words he had said to her in Sicily. 'We'll forget that tonight happened.'

His eyes glittered. 'I'll go, if you are sure that's what you want. But I won't ask you again, *cara*.'

She stared down at the threadbare carpet when she heard him open the door. The sound of it closing brought her head up and she ran across the room and pressed her cheek against the wood, listening for his footsteps on the stairs. The silence stretched her nerves and she was tempted, so very tempted, to fling the door open and call him back. She would love to spend Christmas with him in New York instead of alone in her horrible bedsit. Since moving out of Lyle House, she'd been on a steep learning curve about how to fend for herself. A little part of the old Arianna longed for the luxurious lifestyle she had taken for granted. But she could not allow Santino to save her. She had to save herself.

Finally she heard him walk across the landing and the thud of his footsteps on the stairs faded away. Arianna continued to stand with her palms pressed flat against the door, telling herself that she had done the right thing to send him away. But it felt like a hollow victory.

Christmas was hectic, and Arianna spent the first few days of the New Year moving into her new design studio off Bond Street. The premises comprised a large workroom on the upper floor with a showroom below. She was glad to be busy so that she did not have time to think about Santino. But at night she lay awake, torturing herself with visions of him enjoying the festivities in New York with some gorgeous and no doubt sexually experienced woman—or women.

She missed their meetings at his office, which usually extended to them having lunch together. He was generous with his time when he explained business strategies to her, and his marketing ideas were quite brilliant. It was easy to see how he had become a millionaire tycoon, although she suspected that the real key to his success was his stubborn determination and a willingness to work eighteen-hour days. He had admitted that his busy schedule left little time for a private life, and Arianna wondered if it was an excuse to avoid personal relationships.

Why couldn't she just accept that he did not want a relationship with her? she asked herself angrily. Instead of mooning over him like a lovesick teenager, she needed to focus on establishing her fashion label. She was excited about her new studio. The bigger workshop meant that she had been able to employ a seamstress and pattern cutter, while in the store she stocked a range of ready-to-wear clothes and offered a personal consultancy service. The rent on the premises in a prime central London location was exorbitant, but Santino had advised that she needed a visible presence in order to attract high-end customers.

She wished he were here with her for the opening day of the Anna store, but she hadn't heard a word from him since he had stormed out of her flat ten days ago. She missed him desperately and asked herself why she had turned him down, when all she wanted was to be in his arms—and in his bed, she admitted. She could not forget the wild passion that had blazed between them in Sicily. Although Santino had pulled back, she was certain that the fire had burned as hotly for him as it had for her. But he had felt responsible for her when he'd discovered that she was a virgin. She *should* have told him, she thought guiltily.

The jangle of the bell over the door sent her hurrying through from the back office into the store, thinking that she had her first customer. But instead she was handed a delivery by a courier. Mystified, she opened the box and discovered an exquisite winter bouquet of white lilies, pale lilac-coloured freesias and delicate snowdrops. The perfume of the freesias in particular filled the room with a heavenly fragrance.

With the bouquet was an envelope, and Arianna's heart missed a beat when she pulled out an invitation to a charity fundraising dinner and ball at a top London hotel as the plus-one of Mr Santino Vasari. The event tomorrow evening was being hosted by the prestigious Society of Business Entrepreneurs, and she told herself that Santino must have asked her to accompany him because he had a financial stake in her business.

She turned the invitation over and read the few words written in his bold hand on the back.

I will pick you up from your studio at seven p.m.
Please come.
Yours, Santino.

Her breath caught in her throat as she wondered why he hadn't simply signed his name. She warned herself not to read too much into why he had written 'yours' when he patently wasn't hers. But when she had put the flowers in water she propped the invitation against the vase and smiled every time she looked at it.

By the following evening she was a mass of nervous tension. Santino hadn't phoned during the day to check if she would be going to the ball, and his arrogance—she supposed that he'd assumed she would jump at the chance to go on a date with him—made her question what she was doing.

It made sense for him to collect her from her new business premises, as it was near to the hotel where the event was being held. Arianna was wearing another of her own creations: a strapless black velvet ball gown with a tight-fitting bodice and a full skirt overlaid with black and silver tulle. Once again, the dress bore the hallmark of her romantic, fairy-tale designs. Her hair fell in loose curls, caught back from her face with a narrow velvet ribbon, and there was a sparkle of diamonds at her throat.

She stopped fiddling with her hair when she heard the ring of the doorbell, and her heart was thudding painfully hard when she ran downstairs from the studio and invited Santino into the store.

'Hello,' she said breathlessly, blushing when she realised how gauche she sounded. Like a teenager on a first date rather than the sophisticated woman she wanted him to think she was. He looked mouth-watering in a tuxedo, and she could see through the fine silk of his white shirt the dark shadow of his chest hairs.

He let his gaze roam over her, and the fierce glitter in his green eyes set her pulse racing. '*Bellissima,*' he said softly.

She pretended to misunderstand him and lifted her hand up to her necklace. 'They were my grandmother's diamonds.'

His sexy smile stole her breath. 'I wasn't sure if you would come.' His oddly rough tone eased her doubts and she smiled back at him.

'I'll just get my coat.'

'Wait. Give me your wrist.' He slid his hand into his

jacket pocket, and Arianna tensed when he fixed a diamond bracelet around her wrist. It was an exquisitely delicate piece of jewellery, and she was aware of how much it must have cost.

She bit her lip. 'I can't possibly accept this.'

'It's your Christmas present, and also an apology for behaving like an ass the other night.' He hesitated, his eyes narrowing on her face. 'Did you have a good Christmas?'

'A busy one. I volunteered at a homeless shelter and lost count of how many portions of plum pudding I served up.'

He was still holding her wrist, and moved to capture her hand, lifting it up to his mouth and pressing his lips against her fingers, sending a shockwave of heat through her. 'I wonder if anyone knows the real Arianna Fitzgerald,' he said wryly. His husky voice caressed her senses like a velvet cloak as he murmured, 'I'd certainly like to be given the chance.'

Did he mean it? While she was trying to formulate a reply he took her coat from the hook and held it while she slipped it on. The frosty night air cooled her hot face when she followed him out to his car.

'Did you have fun in New York?' she asked in a determinedly casual voice as he drove them to the hotel. 'I suppose you went to loads of parties?'

'Not one, as it happens. I stayed with my sister and her fiancé. Gina is in the early stages of pregnancy, and suffering from morning sickness, so I was roped in to cook the lunch. Immediately after Christmas I flew to Devon to visit my grandparents and try to persuade my grandfather to employ someone to help him on the farm. He is nearly eighty and still milks the cows by himself.'

'Will you take over the farm one day?'

He shook his head. 'I suppose it will be sold eventually, unless Gina decides to take it on. The plan had been for my parents to run it, but after my mother died Dad had no interest in anything and spent the next ten years drinking himself to death,' he said grimly.

They had arrived at the hotel and there was no chance to continue the conversation. But Arianna had heard an emptiness in Santino's voice that made her realise how hard it must have been for him as a teenager, when his happy family had been torn apart by the loss of his mother, and because of his father's decline into depression and alcoholism. Perhaps it explained his aloofness, she mused. The deep affection in his voice when he spoke of his sister showed that he did have emotions, but he kept them under tight control.

Arianna had attended many high society functions, but it was hard not to be impressed by the hotel's magnificent banqueting room, which had been decorated with stunning floral displays. Five courses of the finest food were served at dinner, but she was too aware of Santino sitting beside her to do justice to the meal. She drank a little champagne, but the bubbles of excitement inside her were caused by the smouldering glances he sent her, and the brush of his thigh against hers beneath the table burned through her dress.

After dinner there were speeches by representatives of various business organisations and from the heads of the charities that would receive money from the fundraising event. Santino excused himself from the table— Arianna assumed to visit the restroom—and she was surprised when he walked onto the stage.

Standing behind the podium, he explained that he

had set up a charity that provided help for injured ex-servicemen and women to find jobs. The charity, called Can Do, offered practical training in new skills, along with psychological support for people living with the mental and physical effects of war. Santino spoke movingly about his co-founder Mac Wilson, who had lost his legs in an explosion, and of the many other service personnel who had been invalided out of the armed forces and needed to find new careers.

Later, in the ballroom, he drew her towards him, one hand resting on her waist and the other at the small of her back as they danced together. The music tempo slowed, and Arianna's heart raced when Santino pulled her even closer and she felt his lips brush across her brow. Their bodies moved in complete harmony, and with a soft sigh she gave herself up to the music, the moment and the intriguing, infuriating, irresistible man who was holding her in his arms as if she were infinitely precious.

She did not want the night to end, she acknowledged when the ball finished at midnight, and they were in the car driving through the brightly lit city streets. Perhaps he had read her thoughts and he shot her an intent look. 'Do you want to come back to my place for a drink?' he murmured.

She took a swift breath that did nothing to slow the frantic pounding of her heart. Instinctively she knew that if she declined his invitation he would not put pressure on her, but it would be the last time he'd ask her.

What did she have to lose? whispered a voice in her head. Sexual chemistry had fizzed between them all evening, and the way that Santino had been so attentive and charming hadn't been an act. His desire for her was there to see on his gorgeous features and in the burning intensity of his gaze. He was no longer her bodyguard. She understood that his sense of honour had stopped him from making love to her when they had been in Sicily. But now she did not need his protection.

They had pulled up at some traffic lights and she turned towards him, her eyes finding his in the dark car. 'All right,' she said steadily. 'But I've had enough to drink for one night.'

His slow smile sent a quiver of anticipation through her. 'We will have to think of something else to do then, *cara mia*.'

CHAPTER TEN

ARIANNA EXPECTED SANTINO'S apartment to be as minimalist and edgy as his black-and-chrome office in The Shard. But his penthouse close to Tower Bridge was a stylish yet comfortable home, with beautiful wooden parquet floors and muted gold soft furnishings that reminded her of Casa Uliveto in Sicily. The huge bi-fold glass doors that ran the length of the apartment looked over the river Thames and across to the historical Tower of London.

'Let me take your coat,' he murmured, coming up behind her as she stood in front of the window and pretended to study the view of the city lights reflected on the black river. She allowed him to draw her coat from her shoulders and watched his reflection in the glass as he placed it over the back of a chair. He slipped off his jacket and bow tie and unfastened several of his shirt buttons, revealing an expanse of olive-gold skin and a scattering of black chest hairs.

The spicy scent of his aftershave made her senses tingle and a shiver prickled over her skin when he came back and placed his hands on her bare shoulders. The heat from his body was tantalising and she was aware of the inherent strength of his broad chest when he drew her against him. She felt the solid ridge of his erection press against her bottom, and her insides melted. His warm breath feathered along her collarbone as he murmured, 'Have you changed your mind about that drink?'

She sensed he was not going to push her into anything she did not want to do and that he was waiting for a sign from her. Pulse racing, she turned around to face him. 'I haven't changed my mind,' she told him huskily. 'I don't want a drink. I want you to make love to me.'

Something feral and fierce blazed in his eyes but he said in a measured voice, 'I don't do love, *cara*.'

The warning was loud and clear: *Don't expect more than I'm prepared to give.* And she wouldn't, Arianna assured herself. She would abide by Santino's rules. But she knew she would regret it for the rest of her life if she didn't explore the feelings he aroused in her, the hunger that coiled tight and hot in the pit of her stomach. She stood on her tiptoes and brushed her lips over his. 'Then show me what you *do* do,' she challenged him softly.

'*Dio!* You drive me insane.' The rasp of his voice sent flames across her skin as he pulled her into his arms and lowered his head. He claimed her mouth with a possessiveness that caused her heart to slam into her ribcage as he slid a hand beneath her hair to cup her nape, and angled her head so that he could plunder her lips.

The hunger in his kiss dissolved the last of her doubts. She sensed the moment his iron control snapped, and met the demands of his mouth with demands of her own as their scorching passion ignited into an inferno.

'You are so beautiful,' he said hoarsely when he lifted his lips from hers and trailed hot kisses along her jaw, then down her throat, moving lower still to explore the slopes of her breasts above the neckline of her dress. Her nipples were tight and hot, and she shuddered when he ran the zip down her spine and freed her breasts from the velvet bodice, cradling her firm flesh in his palms.

She arched backwards in mute supplication, offering her breasts to him, and could not restrain a gasp of pleasure when he closed his mouth around one taut peak and laved it with his tongue, before moving to do the same to her other nipple. The sensation of him sucking each rosy tip in turn evoked an ache in her pelvis, a primal need that consumed her and made her impatient for him to assuage the throb between her legs.

'Do you have any idea how many nights I have been kept awake by fantasies of doing this?' he growled. 'I wanted you with me in New York.'

'I wished I'd gone with you,' she admitted. 'I want you to show me everything, Santino.'

He swore softly and pulled her zip all the way down so that her dress pooled at her feet in a froth of black and silver tulle. His eyes glittered as he studied her slender body, naked except for her tiny black silk panties and sheer black hold-up stockings with bands of lace around her thighs.

'Beautiful,' he said again, in a low tone that resonated with desire, before he scooped her up in his arms and carried her through to the bedroom. Arianna barely noticed the ultra-masculine décor of brown and gold. She only saw the huge bed as Santino tossed back the covers and laid her down on the cream satin sheets. She watched him strip off his clothes and felt a sharp tug of anticipation in the pit of her stomach when he pulled his boxers down his hips and his erection jutted thick and hard from the mass of black hairs at his groin.

The bedside lamps emitted a golden glow that high-lighted the angles and planes of his face and gave a sheen to his bronzed skin. He was a work of art, so handsome that she felt weak looking at him, and weaker still as she imagined him driving his solid shaft inside her.

'I want to touch you,' she whispered when he knelt over her. She ran her hands over his chest, and explored the ridges of his powerful abdominal muscles, but when she skimmed her fingers over the tip of his arousal he groaned and captured her hand.

'Not this time, *cara*. I want you too badly.' Sitting back on his haunches, he slid one stocking down her leg, followed by the other, and then hooked his fingers into her panties and pulled them off. His eyes gleamed as he pushed her thighs apart and ran his finger over her opening, his mouth crooking in a sexy smile when he put the same finger into his mouth. 'You taste sweet,' he murmured, returning his finger to her moist folds, gently parting her so that he could slide in deep. All the while he trapped her gaze with his, and the feral gleam beneath his half-closed lashes made her heart thunder.

'Do you like it when I do this?' He rotated his finger inside her until she gasped and trembled, and then he slipped a second finger into her, moving his hand in an erotic rhythm while she curled her fingers into the sheet and made a guttural sound in her throat.

'Please,' she croaked. She was a slave to his mastery as he caressed her with consummate skill, flicking his thumb over the sensitive nub of her clitoris so that she arched her hips towards his hand, desperately seeking something that she sensed was near yet was frustrat-ingly elusive.

When he withdrew his fingers from her, she felt a flicker of dread that he was about to reject her again. She closed her eyes, unable to bear the humiliation she had felt in Sicily.

'Arianna, look at me,' he bade her, his voice like rough velvet. Swallowing hard, she obeyed him and her heart missed a beat at the intensity of his gaze. 'I have never wanted anything in my life as much as I want you right now,' he said, and it was as if he was making a vow. She watched, dry-mouthed, as he unrolled a condom over the length of his erection, and understood why he had stopped caressing her momentarily. Her pulse rate accelerated when he lifted himself over her and nudged her legs open with his thigh.

And then he pressed forward so that the tip of his manhood pushed slowly, so slowly, into her as he claimed her inch by exquisite inch, filling her with his hardness. The size of him made her catch her breath, and he waited, his eyes burning into hers, while her internal muscles stretched to accommodate his powerful penetration.

'Sei mio,' he muttered, his mouth against hers, before he kissed her with an eroticism that made her tremble anew as he tangled their tongues. Distantly in her mind she seemed to recall that the Italian words meant 'you are mine'. But then he withdrew from her a little way, and she lost the ability to think as he thrust deep and repeated the action again and again.

He took her with long, steady strokes and increased his pace when she lifted her hips to meet each devastating thrust. He drove her higher, higher, and she dug her nails into his back as the pressure inside her built to a crescendo. His mouth claimed hers again and the unexpected tenderness in his kiss crept around her heart.

'Let go, *cara mia*,' he whispered at the same time as he slipped his hand between their sweat-slicked bodies and unerringly found the tight nub of her femininity. The effect was shattering, the caress of his clever fingers combined with the relentless rhythm of his possession sending her up and over the edge. She cried out as she flew into the flames and burned. The intensity of her orgasm was indescribable, and when moments later Santino gave a harsh groan and collapsed on top of her, his big body shuddering in the throes of his climax, Arianna felt their souls connect as profoundly as their bodies were entwined.

Santino rolled onto his back, breathing hard, his heart still pumping like a piston in his chest. He had known that sex with Arianna would be good. The chemistry between them had always been white-hot, and all it had taken was one spark to set off an explosive reaction.

Initially he had been driven by his piqued male pride to demonstrate that there was nothing *unsatisfactory* about his skill as a lover. But somewhere along the way her ardent response, coupled with a faint uncertainty that revealed her inexperience, had blown him away. He'd found that he could not control his urgent desire. His blood had pounded in his veins, and when he'd entered her and felt how tight she was he had almost come right then. It had never happened to him before, and in the aftermath of their wild passion he wanted to understand why Arianna's mix of innocence and sensuality turned him into putty in her hands.

Not quite putty, he thought self-derisively as he felt

himself harden again. A ripple of tension ran through him. He'd had the best sex of his life with Arianna. But it was just sex, he reassured himself. His emotions were not involved, nor would they ever be. He had learned when he was a teenager that he was better off alone. Safer.

He turned his head and studied her when she sat up. The flush of rose on her cheeks was repeated on the tips of her breasts where his mouth had suckled her. He ached to curl his tongue around her pouting nipples, but the wariness in her big brown eyes stopped him from reaching for her. She lifted her hand to push her tumble of silky curls back from her face and the diamond bracelet twinkled in the light from the bedside lamp.

'You should only ever wear diamonds, *cara*,' he murmured, running his finger over the sparkling stones around her neck, before he cupped one breast in his hand and succumbed to the temptation to close his lips around its tender peak. The faint gasp she gave fuelled his desire even more and he frowned when she swung her legs over the side of the bed.

'I should go.' She scooped up her knickers and dress from the floor, and stood there looking decadently sexy and oddly vulnerable, holding armfuls of tulle. 'Taxi drivers often refuse to drive along the street where I live after midnight. Apparently it's a no-go area controlled by drug dealers.'

'I don't want you to go back to your flat tonight.' As he spoke, Santino decided that he did not want her to live in a notoriously rough part of London. He would find a place for her closer to his apartment, somewhere with a good security system and a concierge. His thoughts raced ahead. When this thing he had with

Arianna had burned itself out, he argued with himself, he would still want her to live somewhere where she would be safe.

'You are not my bodyguard and I am not your responsibility,' she told him firmly. He recognised the glint of battle in her eyes and realised that she needed careful handling. Throwing back the sheet, he walked over to her, his heart contracting when he noted the pink stain on her cheeks deepen as she seemed transfixed by his unashamedly naked and aroused body.

'You said you wanted me to teach you everything,' he reminded her softly as he took her dress from her and threw it onto the chair before he lifted her into his arms and carried her back to bed. 'We have barely started your lessons, *cara mia.*'

'Oh.' Her eyes widened when he laid her down on the sheet and proceeded to take a condom out of its wrapper and roll it down the length of his erection. 'Do you... Do you want to do it again?'

That husky uncertainty in her voice was going to kill him, Santino decided. 'What do you think?' he drawled, kneeling over her so that his swollen tip pressed against her moist opening. He shoved her legs wide apart. She bit her lip and the beast inside him growled.

'I think I'm ready for my second lesson.' Her tremulous whisper increased his urgency. But, just to be sure that she was absolutely ready for him, he bent his head to the feminine heart of her and bestowed an intimate caress with his tongue that had her writhing as she sank her fingers into his hair. 'Please...' she moaned when at last he positioned himself over her.

She was so beautiful lying there with her legs open, utterly exposed to his hungry gaze. As he slid his shaft between her silken folds and drove deep inside her, he felt again the odd sensation of a hand squeezing his heart. But then she wrapped her long legs around his back, as he had so often imagined her doing, and he pushed everything out of his mind as he gripped her hips and began to move, taking them both to the edge of ecstasy, and they flew into the fire together.

Afterwards she curled up against him while her breathing, and his, gradually slowed. When she tried to move away he clamped his arm around her waist. 'Stay,' he murmured, 'and in the morning I'll cook you breakfast.'

She stretched like a sleepy kitten. 'All right, but I need to take my necklace off. The clasp is delicate and I'm worried it could break.'

He unfastened the clasp and dropped the string of diamonds into her hand. 'It clearly means a lot to you. Were you fond of your grandmother who gave you the necklace?'

'I adored her. Grandma Charlotte died when I was twelve, a year after my mother went away. She was the only person who understood that my brattish behaviour was a result of missing my mum when she moved to Australia without me. I felt confused and angry.'

Santino remembered that he had felt those same emotions after his mother had died. 'Surely your mother came back to visit you, or you visited her?'

'No. My father paid her to stay out of my life and I had no contact with her until earlier this year. When we did finally meet again, we were strangers.'

While Santino went to the bathroom to deal with the condom, he found himself wondering if any of the tabloid editors who had labelled Arianna a spoilt so-

cialite knew or cared that her childhood had been unhappy, despite the wealth and privilege she had grown
up with. The hurt in her voice, when she'd spoken about
her mother who had abandoned her and her father's indifference, made him furious on her behalf.

Returning to the bedroom, he was unsurprised that
she had fallen asleep. It was two a.m., and he had been
awake since six the previous morning, but he wasn't
tired. Arianna made him feel alive in a way he had
never felt before. He did not make a habit of asking his
lovers to stay the night, but he couldn't find it in him
to regret her presence in his bed when he slid in beside
her and she immediately curled up against him. Her glorious hair rippled over the pillows and her long lashes
made dark fans on her cheeks. Tomorrow he would deal
with the complicated emotions she aroused in him and
lay down some ground rules, he promised himself. But
for now he was content to draw her soft, curvaceous
body against him and count her eyelashes one by one.

When Santino woke the next morning it was to an
empty bed and, he quickly discovered, an empty apartment. Checking his watch, he was astounded to find
that it was nine forty-five. He never slept in. Even on
the rare occasions when he asked a woman to stay over,
he was always up early for an hour in the gym before
his morning shower—his usual routine. Invariably he
was keen not to prolong the night before for longer than
he could help, and he was adept at evading awkward
questions about future dates.

But Arianna had left without waking him or even
leaving a note. As he slammed around the kitchen
making coffee, he told himself he should feel relieved

that she obviously understood the no-clinging and no-crowding rules that he insisted on in an affair.

Two cups of strong black coffee and a shower later, his mood had not improved and, when he arrived at his office and glared ferociously at a junior secretary who spilt a jug of water over his desk, he called Arianna simply to make sure she had got home safely.

'I'm at my studio. I had to unlock the store this morning to let my assistant in,' she explained in an airy voice that made him grit his teeth. 'I didn't want to wake you when I left your apartment.'

He waited for her to ask when they would see each other again, or at least drop hints that it would be lovely to meet up. 'Look, I have to go.' She sounded distracted. 'I'm about to have a consultation with a client who wants several outfits for a cruise she is going on.'

'Have dinner with me tonight?' he said quickly. 'I'll pick you up from the studio at seven.'

'I can't I'm afraid.'

Santino's jaw clenched. Was she playing games, playing hard to get? And, if so, why wasn't he prepared to walk away? There were plenty of other attractive women he could invite to dinner. But there was only one Arianna, and she was the only woman he wanted, he acknowledged.

'A client is coming for a fitting at seven-thirty this evening because it's the only time she has available, but I should be free by nine o'clock, if you want to meet me then,' Arianna told him.

Some of the tension drained out of him. 'I'll see you at nine.'

'Okay.' Her voice became husky. 'I think I will be ready for my next lesson by then.'

Dio! He stared at his phone when she ended the call, not sure if he wanted to swear or laugh. She was a minx, and he spent much of the day devising suitable punishments, which involved him kissing every single inch of her body while she writhed and pleaded for his possession.

By nine that evening, when Santino parked his car outside the Anna store, he had got himself back under control, and he was determined to take control of his affair with Arianna. She would have to understand that he called the shots in their relationship—which wasn't even a relationship. They shared an intense physical attraction, but passion like theirs couldn't last, and he gave it a month before it burned itself out.

Her assistant seamstress was just leaving when he entered the shop, and after the woman had gone he locked the door and walked up the stairs to the design studio. Despite the late hour Arianna was still working and Santino paused in the doorway to admire the sight of her delectable derriere covered in tight black jeans as she bent over one of the big cutting tables. She must have heard his footsteps and she spun round, pushing a wayward curl off her face and giving him a wide smile that did odd things to his insides.

'Guess what?' she said, dropping her dressmaker's scissors and running across the room to launch herself at him. He laughed as he caught her in his arms, fascinated as ever by her spontaneity. Her perfume teased his senses and he pressed his face into her hair as she wrapped her legs around his hips. 'I had two new clients visit the store today and they placed orders for dresses. You were right about the importance of a visible presence on the high street. I wouldn't have the

Anna store and design studio without your financial support through Tiger Investments.'

She tipped her head back and the gold flecks in her brown eyes glowed. 'You look very macho in black leather,' she murmured, running her hand over his old biker jacket. 'What will you do if I kiss you?'

The tug of desire in his groin was so sharp it made him catch his breath. 'Why don't you find out?' he said thickly, and couldn't restrain a low groan when she covered his mouth with hers and kissed him with a sensuality that made him shake with need. 'Do you have any idea what you do to me?' he muttered against her throat while his fingers deftly unfastened the buttons on her pink silk blouse. The black bra beneath it was semi-transparent and her dusky pink nipples were visible through the sheer material.

She pressed her pelvis up against his painfully hard erection as he carried her over to the worktable, moving her hips sinuously to create a burning friction between their bodies. 'I have some idea,' she murmured and caught her breath when he sucked her nipples through her bra.

'Good, then you will understand that I have to have you now. I can't wait, *cara*.' He set her on her feet and swiftly dispensed with her blouse and bra, cradling her bare breasts in his palms and flicking his thumbs over the taut peaks. He had never felt such an intensity of need as he did with Arianna.

A warning voice inside Santino's head reminded him that he was supposed to be in control and establishing the rules and boundaries of their affair, but he shoved the thought away and slid his hand into the stretchy material of her jeans, rubbing his fingers over the panel of her panties and then slipping inside them to caress her wet heat.

Arianna was breathing hard, and when he eased back a fraction he saw that her eyes were half-closed and her mouth slightly open, her pretty face flushed with passion. 'I want you too,' she whispered, placing her hand on the bulge of his arousal beneath his jeans. 'But how can we do it here?'

'Like this.' He kissed her hard on her mouth and then turned her round and gently pushed her down so that she was bending over the table.

'Santino?' She looked over her shoulder at him, her eyes wide with excitement and faint uncertainty that he was anxious to dispel.

'It will be good, baby, trust me.'

'I do trust you,' she said softly, and something fierce and unexpectedly tender tugged in his chest. He feathered kisses down her spine and then gripped the waistband of her jeans, pulling them and her knickers down her hips. She kicked off her shoes and he helped her to step out of her trousers before he ran his hands greedily over the smooth, pale contours of her bottom. Hand shaking, he freed his rock-hard erection from his jeans and nudged her thighs apart. He surged into her, feeling the faint resistance of her vaginal muscles at first as he drove in deep and filled her.

It was wilder and hotter than anything Santino had ever experienced, but it could not last. Jaw clenched, he held her hips tightly while he established a devastating rhythm, faster, harder, the soft moans of pleasure she made shattering his tenuous control. He thrust again, and her thin cry mingled with his harsh groan as they climaxed together, and the power of it sent shudders of aftershock through him.

Afterwards he held her in his arms and claimed her mouth in a slow, deeply sensual kiss that somehow seemed even more intimate than the mind-blowing sex they had just shared.

'You're coming back to my apartment tonight,' he told her after he'd driven her back to her bedsit and clamped a protective arm around her shoulders as they walked past the gang of youths hanging around the front of the building. 'You can't possibly like living here,' he said when she looked mutinous.

'I don't like the flat or the area,' she admitted. 'But at least I am independent of my father. Hopefully my label will start to sell and I'll be able to afford a nicer place to live.'

'You can take a salary out of the money I have invested in your business to pay for your living costs. In the meantime you need to stay with me so that we can continue your lessons,' he murmured, pulling her into his arms and kissing the pout from her lips until she melted against him.

After she had packed a bag he took her back to his penthouse, and while she had a bath he ordered Thai food from his favourite restaurant. Of course, the sight of her all pink and flushed, smelling divine after her bath, aroused a different hunger in him and he had to have her again. It was nearly midnight when they finally ate the food straight out of the plastic containers it had been delivered in.

'This is fun,' Arianna said happily as she sat cross-legged on the sofa, eating noodles as gracefully as if they were dining at a five-star restaurant. Her smile faded and Santino discovered that he would give away everything he owned if he could put the smile back on her lips.

'What's the matter, *cara*?'

'Oh, there was a spiteful piece written about me in one of the fashion magazines. You would think I'd be hardened to bad publicity by now,' she said flatly, revealing a vulnerability that made his insides clench. 'But the journalist who wrote the article suggested that my father is the creative and financial force behind Anna and Randolph must help me with the designs.'

He rubbed a hand over his jaw. 'We need to devise a great PR campaign in the run-up to London Fashion Week. You could give a couple of interviews to explain your concept of Anna as a fashion brand for contemporary women. It would also be a good idea if we gave a joint press statement about Tiger Investments' involvement in your company.'

'Would you be prepared to do that?'

He nodded. 'I have a vested interest in wanting Anna to succeed as I own a forty percent share of the business,' he reminded her. 'Leave the PR campaign to me while you concentrate on producing a runway collection that will blow the fashion world away.' He untied the belt of her bathrobe and cupped her breasts in his hands. 'But right now I think you should concentrate all your attention on me,' Santino said thickly as he scooped her into his arms and carried her back to his bed.

CHAPTER ELEVEN

ARIANNA'S KNEES ACHED from kneeling on the floor in front of a mannequin while she sewed the hem on a cocktail dress that she planned to include in her collection at London Fashion Week's spring show. Her back was stiff, her fingers were sore from sewing sample pieces—her seamstress could not do all the work alone—and with less than a week to go until the show she was beset by self-doubt.

After weeks of preparation, the actual amount of time during which her designs would be paraded on the runway by the models she had hired was minutes. But she knew that those moments could make or break her fledgling career. Fashion editors, writers and bloggers would scrutinise her work and their verdict of her debut collection was crucial to the future of her Anna label. She wanted to succeed as a designer, not just for herself, but to prove to Santino that the faith he had shown by investing in her business had been justified.

'I thought we agreed that you would not work past 9:00 p.m.' Santino's gravelly voice had its usual effect on her heart, making it flutter like a trapped bird in her chest. She removed a couple of pins that she'd been holding between her lips before she stood up and turned to see him stroll across the studio. He had changed out of the suit that she'd watched him put on that morning into black jeans and a grey cashmere sweater topped by his black leather biker's jacket that gave a dangerous edge to his devastatingly sexy looks.

'I just need to finish this,' she explained, grimacing when he shook his head.

'No, *cara*, you need to come home for some food, a relaxing bath and bed.'

A shiver of pleasure ran through her at his use of the word 'home'. Technically, of course, the penthouse near Tower Bridge was Santino's home, but for the past month she had lived there with him. She was still paying the rent on her bedsit, while she was supposed to be looking for a new flat to move into, but she had been so busy preparing for the fashion show, and the few places she had viewed online hadn't met with Santino's approval.

If she was not careful she would start to believe that he was as happy with their current living arrangements as she was, Arianna thought. Her good sense warned her not to hope he felt something for her that went deeper than the sex-without-strings affair he'd insisted was all he wanted. But when he smiled at her the way he was doing right now, and when he kissed her with passion and an inherent tenderness that played havoc with her heart rate, she dared to wonder if he might love her a little. It would be too good to be true, because she loved him a lot. With all her heart, in fact. The voice in her head that cautioned that she could get badly hurt was way too late.

She glanced back at the mannequin. 'The show is in three days and I still have tons to do. It will only take me another five minutes to finish this. I'm not tired,' she insisted.

'All the more reason for us to have an early night,' he drawled, with a glint in his eyes that caused her stomach muscles to clench with anticipation.

As it was, they did not even make it to the bedroom at his apartment. He pulled her into his arms and kissed her hungrily while the lift took them from the underground car park up to the penthouse. Once inside, they tore each other's clothes off, and he tumbled her down onto the sofa and made love to her with a fierce intensity so that she shattered once, twice, before he let out a harsh groan and collapsed on top of her.

It was early the next morning when Arianna woke with a start to the sound of Santino shouting. She sat up in bed and switched on the bedside lamp. He was sprawled next to her, the sheet tangled round his hips, his head moving restlessly on the pillow. His eyes were closed and he was breathing hard so that his chest rose and fell jerkily. When she touched his shoulder his lashes flew open and he stared at her blankly.

'You were having a nightmare,' she told him softly.

He shoved a hand through his hair. 'I'm sorry if I woke you.'

She bit her lip. His desperate cries had ravaged her heart. 'Was it about when you were serving in Afghanistan?'

'No.' He exhaled heavily. 'I was dreaming about my father.' Arianna waited, and after a moment he said roughly, 'I've mentioned before that after my mother died Dad sank into a deep depression and became reliant on alcohol.' A nerve jumped in Santino's cheek. 'One evening he disappeared from the house. I knew he'd been drinking all day, and I was worried when I couldn't find him. I went down to the beach that had been a favourite place he used to go to with Mum.'

'Did you find him?'

'Yes, I found him. He had walked into the sea fully clothed. It was winter and the waves were huge. By the time I waded into the sea, he had been under the water for a few minutes and he was a dead weight. I was scared that we would both be swept against the rocks but I finally managed to drag him back to the beach, and he punched me.'

'He *punched* you? Why?'

'Because I'd saved his life. He wanted to die and be with my mother.' Santino's jaw clenched. 'He loved her so much that nothing else mattered to him, not his children or his business. For my father, death was preferable to living without the woman he loved.' He gave a grim laugh. 'What does that say about love?' he asked savagely. 'When I was a boy I looked up to my father, respected him. But I watched him become a pathetic drunk. Love weakens and destroys.'

Arianna stared down at the sheet that unconsciously she had been pleating between her fingers. 'Perhaps that's true for some people, but for others love strengthens and empowers them,' she murmured.

She took a deep breath, aware of the painful thud of her heart beneath her ribs. Santino's story made her ache for him, for the teenage boy who had risked his own life to save his father. His mother's death had robbed him of both his parents and it wasn't hard to understand why he had a deep mistrust of strong emotions.

But she was sure he felt something for her. They had grown so close these past few weeks, and every time they made love it felt like a complete union that was much more than the physical act of sex. Hearing what had happened in his past gave her an insight into why he kept tight control of his emotions, but the fact that he had opened up to her surely must mean he trusted her?

'Love has made me stronger,' she said softly. I love you, Santino.'

'Then you are a fool,' he bit out coldly. 'I made it clear from the start that all I wanted was a no-strings affair.' His green eyes were as dark and wild as a stormy sea. 'Whatever romantic notions you have about me are a fantasy. I don't believe in happy-ever-after, and I am not in love with you.'

A knife sliced through her heart but she clung desperately to hope. 'You can't deny that we have been happy these past few weeks,' she said huskily.

'Sure, we have amazing sex, but it won't last.'

'Only because you don't want it to last.' She put her hand on his arm. 'I understand...'

'No, Arianna, you don't get it.' He shrugged off her hand and swung his legs over the side of the bed. She watched him yank open the wardrobe and grab a T-shirt and jogging pants. 'It was always going to end between us because I can't give you want you want. I don't want to fall in love with you or anyone else.'

His words fell like hammer blows, smashing her dreams to pieces, but she was not prepared to give up on him, on them. What she had learned since she had vowed to take charge of her life eighteen months ago was that you had to fight for what you wanted.

'I know you love your sister,' she argued. 'I think you are afraid to allow yourself to fall in love with me. You're scared to give us a chance.'

'There is no *us*,' he told her curtly. He had pulled on

his clothes and strode over to the door. 'I should have guessed that you would want more.' His voice was as hard and uncompromising as the expression on his granite features. 'Women always do.'

Arianna stared at the door after Santino had slammed it behind him, feeling numb. His parting shot played on her deepest insecurities—his implication that she was one of a long list of women he'd had affairs with who had hoped for more from a relationship with him than he was willing to give. She had no idea where they went from here. But, having given him her heart and had it thoroughly trampled on, she could not bear to be humiliated by him again—and she could not continue to live in his apartment.

Tears stung her eyes but she angrily blinked them away. The old Arianna might have curled up in a ball and cried, but she had a fashion show to put on, a business to run and, she remembered with a jolt, she and Santino were supposed to be holding a joint press conference later that day to promote her Anna label. She could take the easy way out and make up an excuse for why she couldn't attend. But *she* was not a coward, she thought grimly.

She bit her lip. Santino was a war hero and couldn't be accused of cowardice, which must mean that he had told her the truth when he'd insisted that he wasn't in love with her. She must have imagined she'd seen a tender expression in his eyes that had given her false hope.

His PR team had arranged for the press interview to be held in Tiger Investments' hospitality suite. Arianna felt sick with tension at the prospect of seeing Santino again, but her pride insisted on her hiding her broken heart.

As she had done so often in the past, she disguised her feelings behind a wall of bravado, and when she sauntered into his office—wearing a scarlet suit with a very short skirt and four-inch heels, black patent stilettos that made the most of her shapely legs—she had the satisfaction of seeing dull colour streak along his cheekbones.

'You're cutting it fine,' he said brusquely as he glanced at his watch, and she had a strange feeling that he was desperate for an excuse to look away from her. 'The interview is at twelve, and it's five to.'

No way was she going to admit that she had arrived at The Shard fifteen minutes ago and had paced up and down the cloakroom trying to control her nerves. Santino held open the door, and as she walked past him the evocative scent of his aftershave almost made her crumble. But she lifted her chin and gave a confident smile to the group of journalists assembled in the hospitality suite.

She sat down on a sofa facing the journalists and tried not to stiffen when Santino sat next to her. She'd prepared a short speech outlining her ideas and aspirations for her fashion label, which she delivered perfectly without glancing at her notes.

'You stated that your only financial backing comes from Tiger Investments and that your father, the celebrated designer Randolph Fitzgerald, has no involvement in your fashion label,' a journalist said.

Arianna nodded. 'That's right. Anna is entirely independent from my father's fashion business.'

'That is not entirely true,' the journalist persisted, looking at Santino. 'Isn't it the case, Mr Vasari, that you were given a significant number of shares in Fitzgerald Design by Arianna's father when his company was floated on the stock exchange last summer?'

'No, you have been misinformed…' Arianna began. Beside her Santino shifted in his seat.

'Yes, I received shares in FD when it became a public company.'

Arianna's stomach hit the floor.

'So there is a link between Randolph Fitzgerald and Anna.' The journalist gave Arianna a triumphant look. 'Mr Vasari owns shares in your father's company and Tiger Investments provides financial backing to your business. Did your father give Mr Vasari the shares to persuade him to back your fashion label? And is Randolph in fact the creative genius behind Anna?'

'Absolutely not,' Santino answered the journalist tersely, but Arianna barely heard him. Her head was pounding and she felt horribly sick at the shocking news that Santino had shares in Fitzgerald Design. She pressed her hand to her brow, feeling as though her head was about to explode.

'Arianna, are you all right?' Santino asked urgently. His fake concern battered her already bruised heart.

'I have a migraine. I'm sorry, but I can't continue with the interview.' She lurched to her feet, and hurried out of the hospitality suite. She flinched when Santino caught up with her and put a hand on her arm. Anger joined the host of violent emotions swirling inside her and she couldn't hide her sense of betrayal. 'Don't touch me, Judas,' she hissed, before she spun away from him and stalked down the corridor with her head held high and her heart in tatters.

A cruel wind whipped across the Devon beach where, twenty years ago, Santino had dragged his father out of the sea. He shoved his hands deeper into his coat pockets as he stood, watching the waves crash onto the shore. White spray flew up and mingled with the mist that slicked his hair against his skull, but the freezing temperature was not as cold as the lump of ice in his chest.

He was sure he would never feel warm again, that he would never smile again. For what was there to smile about when he had lost the one thing in his life that he cared about more than anything else—the one person who had briefly melted the ice inside him and filled him with light and laughter?

'Arianna.' He whispered her name and the wind whipped it away. He could not forget the shock and devastation on her face when the damned journalist at the press conference had revealed that he had accepted shares in her father's fashion business. *Dio*, he should have seen it coming and prepared her. It should not even matter. The journalist had made more of the link between his interests in Fitzgerald Design and Anna than really existed. He had not kept the shares, and had donated them to the charity he had set up. But Arianna did not know that, and she hadn't given him a chance to explain. He knew he had hurt her badly, perhaps even more than when he had brutally rejected her for a second time.

He rubbed his hand over his eyes and discovered that his lashes were wet. It must be the mist or the salt spray from the sea. These could not be tears sliding down his cheeks, he assured himself. As he walked along the beach, the mournful cries of the wheeling gulls echoed the silent cry of pain inside him. Had his father felt this miserable when he had tried to drown himself all those years ago? Santino halted and kicked a lump of sand with the toe of his boot. His father had wanted to die rather than face life without the woman he loved. Now *he* was facing a lonely, pointless life without the woman who had captured *his* heart.

Arianna's accusation that he was scared to fall in love with her taunted him. He had been commended for his bravery when he'd served with the SAS in Afghanistan, but in truth he was a coward. Since he had been a teenager he had supressed his emotions and turned his back on love. But where had that got him? Santino asked himself painfully. He was alone on an empty beach and hurting like hell. He did not want to walk into the sea. There was only one place he wanted to be, only one woman he wanted to be with. As he tore back up the beach, he could only pray that he hadn't left it too late finally to come to his senses.

The days leading up to London Fashion Week were crazier than Arianna could have imagined. It was a good thing that she'd had no time to eat or sleep because she didn't feel like doing either. Since she had walked out of the press conference and away from Santino, her appetite had been non-existent. Luckily she had been so exhausted from dealing with last-minute preparations and problems for the show that when she had crawled up the stairs to her bedsit at night she'd slept for a couple of hours without dreaming of him. But his treachery was the first thing she remembered when she opened her eyes, and her heart felt like a lead weight in her chest.

Tonight she should be feeling on top of the world and celebrating at one of the celebrity-packed parties she had been invited to. But instead she was alone at her studio, where she had escaped to after the show. Her runway collection had received a standing ovation and

Anna was the buzz word on the lips of every fashion editor, blogger and fashionista.

Such recognition and excitement for an emerging brand was unusual and she felt proud of her debut presentation. But it all felt meaningless without someone to share her success with. Jonny had been at the show with Davina and some of her other friends, but the only person she longed to see had not been there. Santino's absence had reinforced the message that he wasn't interested in her.

Arianna stiffened when she heard footsteps on the stairs. She was sure she had locked the shop door, and only she and Santino had a key. She whirled round and her heart collided with her ribs as she stared at him.

'You look terrible,' she burst out. 'What's happened?' His face looked ravaged. There was no other word to describe the deep grooves on either side of his mouth and the tormented look in his eyes as he walked towards her. There was only one person he cared about. She swallowed. 'Is it your sister? Has something happened to the baby?'

He shook his head, his gaze riveted to her face. 'Gina said that her pregnancy is progressing fine when I spoke to her an hour ago. She told me that I'm an idiot, but I already knew that.' He halted in front of her and raked his hair off his brow with an unsteady hand. 'The fact that you can show so much compassion after everything I have done is proof, if I needed it, that I am the greatest fool in the world.'

He did not really look terrible, of course, she acknowledged as she raked her eyes greedily over him. He looked dangerously gorgeous in faded jeans, a black sweater and the leather jacket that she loved almost as much as him. Arianna looked away from him and released her breath slowly. 'I don't understand, and to be honest I don't really want to. I'd like you to leave.'

Something almost desperate flashed across his hard features. 'Will you at least listen to me? And then you can throw me out if you want. God knows, it's nothing more than I deserve.'

Stupid tears filled her eyes and she blinked them away angrily. 'Did my father give you shares in Fitzgerald Design to persuade you to be my bodyguard?'

He held her gaze unflinchingly. 'Yes.'

She choked back a sob, devastated anew by his betrayal. 'You should have told me when I applied to Tiger Investments for funding for my fashion label. You *knew* how important it was to me that Anna was in no way linked to my father.'

'I didn't keep the shares,' he said quietly. 'Initially they were paid into Tiger Investments' accounts but I transferred them over to the charity I set up to help exservicemen train for new careers. No link exists between your fashion company, my investment company and your father, and I have given a statement to the press to that effect.'

'You know what some journalists are like. They would love to see me fail,' she said bitterly. 'They won't believe that the clothes in the Anna brand are entirely my designs, and they'll think that my father must have something to do with my company.'

'The fashion editors I spoke to after your presentation at London Fashion Week were in raptures over your work.'

She stared at him. 'How do you know?'

'I was there. Of course I was there,' he said softly.

'I was so proud of you this evening, Arianna. You are incredibly talented and you work damned hard. You deserve to be the huge success that I am confident you will be.'

His praise only made her heart ache even more. 'If you were at the fashion show why didn't you come and join me? I wouldn't have had the chance to take part in the show if you hadn't invested in my business.'

'Tonight was your night and I wanted you to enjoy the acclaim.' He hesitated and a nerve in his cheek flickered. 'I was scared to approach you in case you told me to go to hell,' he said roughly. 'I am a coward as well as a fool, and I couldn't face the possibility that I might have driven you away for good.'

'I thought that was the plan. You wanted to drive me away.' She couldn't hold herself together. Seeing Santino again was tearing her apart and a tear slid down her cheek. 'You could not have made it any clearer that you don't feel anything for me,' she whispered.

'I love you.'

Another tear slipped down her cheek, and another, and another. She didn't know what hurt most—his lie, for it *must* be a lie, or the terrible darkness in his eyes that made her think, made her hope, that he actually meant it.

'You don't do love.' She threw the words he had said to her back at him. 'You want to go through life untouched by emotions, unloving and unloved.'

'I love you,' he repeated, his voice thick, as if his throat was constricted. His eyes were fiercely bright and her heart stopped when she saw that his lashes were wet. 'I know what I said, and for a long time it was true. I didn't want to feel the level of emotions that had destroyed my father. But then I met you, Arianna.'

His hand shook as he reached out and brushed a stray curl back from her face. 'The most beautiful woman I have ever seen. I took one look at you and my wonderfully ordered, controlled existence was blown apart. You infuriated me with your defiance and captivated me with your loveliness, which I quickly discovered is much more than skin-deep. You are beautiful all the way down to your compassionate heart.'

Her mouth trembled. 'How can I believe you? You sent me away—*twice*. You broke my heart, Santino. I spent most of my life wishing that my father would love me and it nearly broke me. I can't do that again.' She scrubbed her wet eyes with the back of her hand. 'If you can't love me the way I want to be loved, the way I love you, then I'm better off without you.'

'Tesoro mio—' His voice cracked. 'If you give me the chance, I will spend the rest of my life showing you how much I love you. You are everything, Arianna—' he swallowed convulsively '—and without you I am nothing.'

Hope unfurled inside her, a tentative happiness that she wondered if she could dare to believe in. 'Truthfully, you love me?' she whispered.

'Perhaps this will convince you.' He slipped his hand into his jacket pocket and pulled out a small velvet box. Her heart juddered to a halt when he opened it to reveal an exquisite cluster of diamonds set on a white-gold band. 'I had better do this properly so that you can tell our grandchildren the story of when I proposed,' he murmured as he dropped down onto one knee.

'Santino,' she said faintly.

'Will you marry me, Arianna? Will you have my babies, and will you love me for ever, as I will always love you?'

More tears slipped down her cheeks, but they were tears of joy as she looked into his eyes and saw the blaze of emotions in his glittering green gaze. 'I don't know what to say.'

'Say yes, *cara mia*,' he pleaded, 'and make me the happiest man in the world.'

Arianna smiled and heard him catch his breath. 'Yes,' she said softly, holding out a trembling hand for him to slide the engagement ring onto her finger.

'I said you should always wear diamonds, and now you always will,' he murmured as he stood up and drew her into his arms. His mouth claimed hers in a kiss that stirred her soul with its tender devotion.

'I love you.' She looped her arms around his neck as he lifted her off her feet. 'I think you should make love to me right now.'

Santino's soft laugh was husky and hesitant, as if he too could not quite believe that love was theirs for the taking, theirs for all time. 'Try and stop me, baby,' he murmured against her lips. And then he worshipped her with his body so beautifully, so *lovingly*, that Arianna discovered fairy tales could come true.

* * * * *

COMING SOON!

We really hope you enjoyed reading this book. If you're looking for more romance, be sure to head to the shops when new books are available on

Thursday 13th December

To see which titles are coming soon, please visit
millsandboon.co.uk

MILLS & BOON

Coming next month

THE SECRET KEPT FROM THE ITALIAN
Kate Hewitt

'Maisie.'

Antonio looked up at the sound of her name on another man's lips. The man was standing by the entrance to the hotel, a smile on his face as he held out his arms. Slowly Antonio turned and saw Maisie walking towards the man, a tremulous smile curving her lush lips, a baby nestled in her arms.

A baby.

Antonio stared as the man took the baby from her, cuddling the little bundle as he cooed down at it.

'Hey, sweetie.'

Jealousy fired through Antonio, although he couldn't even say why. So Maisie had moved on, found a boyfriend or husband, and had a baby pretty darn quick. That was fine. Of course it was. Except...

They'd spent the night together a year ago, and although Antonio wasn't an expert on babies by any means, the child nestled in the man's arms looked to be at least a few months old. Which meant...

Either Maisie had been pregnant when she'd slept with him, or had fallen pregnant immediately after. Or, he realised with a sickening rush, had become pregnant by him.

He hadn't used birth control. He'd been too drunk and emotional even to think of it at the time, and later he'd assumed Maisie must have been on the pill, since she hadn't seemed concerned. But now he remembered how she'd come to see him—how many weeks later? Two, three? She'd wanted to talk to him. She'd looked distraught. What if she'd been pregnant?

Why had he not considered such a possibility? Antonio retrained his shocked gaze on the man and baby, only to realise they'd already gone. Maisie had turned around and was walking back towards the ballroom, and presumably her waitressing duties. And his child might have just been hustled out of the door.

'Maisie.' His voice came out in a bark of command, and Maisie turned, her jade-green eyes widening as she caught sight of him. Then her face drained of colour, so quickly and dramatically that Antonio felt another rush of conviction. Why would she react like that if the child wasn't his?

'What are you doing here?' she asked in a low voice.

'I'm a guest at the dinner.'

'Yes, but…what do you want from me, Antonio?' She looked wretched, and more than once her gaze darted towards the doors and then back again.

'Let's talk in private.'

'You weren't so interested in doing that the last time we met,' Maisie snapped, summoning some spirit.

'Yes, I know, but things are different now.'

'They're different for me too.' She took a step backwards, her chin raised at a proud, determined angle. 'You didn't want to know me a year ago, Antonio, and now I don't want to know you. Doesn't feel very good, does it?' She gave a hollow laugh.

'This is not the time to be petty,' Antonio returned evenly. 'We need to talk.'

'No, we don't—'

'Maisie.' He cut her off, making her flinch. 'Is the baby mine?'

Continue reading
THE SECRET KEPT FROM THE ITALIAN
Kate Hewitt

Available next month
www.millsandboon.co.uk

LET'S TALK

Romance

For exclusive extracts, competitions
and special offers, find us online: